BLOOD
ON THE TRACKS

BLOOD
ON THE TRACKS

A NOVEL

TOM GRASTY

iUniverse, Inc.
New York Lincoln Shanghai

BLOOD ON THE TRACKS
A NOVEL

iUniverse books may be ordered through booksellers or by contacting:

iUniverse
2021 Pine Lake Road, Suite 100
Lincoln, NE 68512
www.iuniverse.com
1-800-Authors (1-800-288-4677)

Because of the dynamic nature of the Internet, any Web addresses
or links contained in this book may have changed
since publication and may no longer be valid.

This is a work of fiction. All of the characters, names, incidents, organizations,
and dialogue in this novel are either the products of the author's imagination
or are used fictitiously.

ISBN: 978-0-595-46180-6 (pbk)
ISBN: 978-0-595-69984-1 (cloth)
ISBN: 978-0-595-90481-5 (ebk)

Printed in the United States of America

"To reveal art and conceal the artist is art's aim."

—Oscar Wilde, 1891

"Never trust the artist. Trust the tale."

—D.H. Lawrence, not much later

TABLE OF CONTENTS

PART III
The Record Factory

Author's Note

It is a widely known fact that once someone takes up residence on Elysian Row they rarely leave. Every now and then, however, a few do find their way out. If you detect a similarity between a character depicted in this book and someone you may have come across earlier this morning, please be advised that the author has gone to great lengths to prevent this rather unsettling situation from happening. One such precaution was to rearrange the names of the characters, and make sure their newly assigned names are not their own. Mannerisms, speech patterns, annoying ticks and distinguishing physical attributes have also been amended and/or modified. Accordingly, any similarities to persons who currently reside or may have at one time resided on Elysian Row are purely coincidental, and quite unintentional.

Blood on the Tracks has been bundled with Special Features, including an interview with the author, insights into characters' motivations, recently discovered handwritten Bob Dorian lyrics and much more. To access these free bonus features, log on to: www. bloodonthetracksnovel.com and click on "Behind the Book."

Cast of Characters

(In order of appearance)

BOB DORIAN—He's been hailed a poet, a prophet, the voice of a generation. But Bob Dorian never wanted to be any of these things. Bob Dorian always hated the attention fame brought. Funny how turning up dead attracts the most attention of all.

COMMISSIONER TIRESIAS—He may turn a blind eye to fraud and corruption, but Elysian Row's top cop knows a good con when he sees it. And this one's shaping up to be the best he's seen in a long time.

JACK FROST—Dorian's manager for the last 20 years, Frost knew the rock deity better than anyone. Which, of course, raises the question: If the two were so close then why did Dorian leave Frost out in the cold?

DELA CROIX—Rumored to be the last to see Dorian alive, she'd make a credible witness—but first they have to find her. After all, this isn't the first time Dela's gotten tangled up with the men in blue.

DR. REICH—Transvestites, extortionists, tightrope walkers—the only thing shiftier than his clients just might be the good doctor himself.

MISTER JOHNS—When they were looking for someone to take the fall, this pitiful poser fit the profile perfectly. Johns was set up the minute he walked into the room—and he never had a clue.

SOPHIA—Dorian's first true love, for the last 40 years she's been known as the woman spurned by Bob Dorian. He gave her his heart, trouble is she wanted his soul. Perhaps he should have thought twice before crossing her.

MR. TREMOLO—Nobody goes back further with Bob Dorian than Tremolo. But what *really* happened on that cross-country trip in '64?

ELIJAH BLUE—A perennial favorite of the folk set, his influence on an impressionable young Bob Dorian was immeasurable. But after Fairport, it was all over for Elijah Blue.

PENNY—Everyone knows Penny was the brains behind Bob Dorian's early success. But when Dorian got tired of scrubbing the floor for dimes, it was Penny who had to pack up the farm.

LONESOME TOM—Produced the biggest hit of Bob Dorian's career, only to be dropped in favor of someone else who was willing to make a deal.

TINY BOBBITT—No one held Bob Dorian in higher regard than the man who ran his final recording session. But you put a man on a high enough pedestal, sooner or later he's bound to fall.

MINNESOTA SLIM—Minnesota Slim's big mouth may have made him everybody's favorite informant, but it's also the thing that probably got him killed.

MEMPHIS BLUES—Says he saw three men down by the tracks the night of the murder. But everyone knows you shouldn't get mixed up with railroad men—especially one who can't seem to tell the story the same way twice.

HUSK THE SIBERIAN—A cold-blooded killer who lives out among the lumberjacks, Husk will be the first to tell you all about the joint—just don't ask him what he was in for.

RHIANNON—An acrimonious breakup with Dorian years ago inspired some of the greatest tracks of his career, but in the process he bled her dry. Has the time come for the former Mrs. Bob Dorian to return the favor?

HANNAH—If Bob was the king of the '60s folk scene, Hannah was his queen. Some say Dorian rode her coattails all the way to the top. But what goes up must come down. And you know what they say about the fall—it's a killer.

TOMMIE THE MAKE & JULIUS THE SQUEEZE—Hired to promote Dorian's heralded return to Elysian Row, it's not their abilities that are suspect—it's their motives. After all, nothing sells better than death.

JUDAS—Once considered Bob Dorian's closest confident, the word on the street is the man who made Bob Dorian a star wants back in the game. But who will he betray this time?

PROLOGUE

▼

"Zeitzman's dead—"

Commissioner Tiresias' words rang out like two pistol shots in a barroom night.

"Robert Zeitzman?"

It was the first time Jack Frost had heard him called by that name in close to 40 years.

"Terry, Timmy, Bobby, Zimmy—take your pick. Turned up down at the rail yard this morning. Blood all over the tracks."

"Jesus—"

"Now that's one I ain't heard yet." Commissioner Tiresias stopped for a moment to consider the thought. "But I wouldn't put it past him." The Commissioner continued his ascent up the creaky old staircase.

"Any suspects?" Jack Frost called out.

"Suspects?" Commissioner Tiresias huffed as he reached the landing and turned to face Frost—

"Are you kidding me? This is Elysian Row, Jack. Everybody's a suspect."

Commissioner Tiresias reached the top of the stairs, turned and followed a well-worn Oriental runner that slithered like a snake down a dank, dimly lighted hallway. The rug was torn and frayed on the edges and the center was completely threadbare. It was evident the

1

carpet had not been replaced in a long time, that is if it had ever even been replaced at all.

The two men walked in darkness for a moment before stopping at a door, which had been left slightly ajar. The numbers '211' were engraved into a tarnished brass plate. The plate hung loosely on the door. Clearly, it had been screwed into the wooden door on more than one occasion.

The Commissioner took hold of a rusty chain dangling from the ceiling. He gently pulled the chain, causing the filament inside a dusty bulb to flicker and sputter.

"In here," Commissioner Tiresias said, pressing against the door. The hinges made a creaking sound as the door slowly swung open, and the two men stepped inside ...

PART I

▼

The Chelsea

CHAPTER 1

▼

DARKNESS AT THE
BREAK OF NOON

He wore a pair of loose-fitting jeans, a white collared shirt ripped at the sleeves, scuffed up Spanish boots of leather and a matching Bolero vest. His hair, once black and straight, was curled and kinky and graying slightly at the temples. A narrow, pencil thin mustache extended across his upper lip. The mustache was slim and precise, so much so that it looked like it had been drawn on that very morning.

In short, the man stretched across the red crushed velvet chaise looked exactly like what he had aspired to become: a vagabond, a vagrant, a drifter, a traveling troubadour for the ages. And while a few issues surrounding the cause of death still needed to be sorted out, one thing was certain: he had assumed the role perfectly.

"My God," Frost said, the realization finally sinking in. "How did this happen?"

"Well, I'm no doctor, but I'd say being hit head-on by a train probably did the trick."

"A train?"

"That's right."

"What the hell was he doing down by the railroad tracks?"

"You tell me, Frost. You're his manager. I didn't even know he was in town. Didn't know *you* were in town either, for that matter," Commissioner Tiresias said, arching his eyebrows slightly. Obviously, Jack Frost's presence on Elysian Row was a subject to which they would be returning.

"So who found the body?"

"Dela Croix."

"You get a statement?"

"A statement?" the Commissioner taunted.

"Yes, a statement," Jack Frost sniped. "Correct me if I'm wrong, but you *are* the Chief of Police. I would imagine a statement from the person who found the body would be well within your jurisdiction— even in a shit hole like this."

"A shit hole?" Commissioner Tiresias said, clearly savoring Jack Frost's ever-darkening mood. And Jack Frost wasn't sure which irked him more: that snide, condescending Cheshire grin stretched across the Commissioner's face or the fact that he was going to have to stand there and take it from this low-life louse. Or maybe the source of Jack Frost's ire wasn't ire at all. Maybe it was just the fact that it was finally sinking in that Bob Dorian wasn't going to leap up from that chaise lounge, slap him on the back and let out a loud, boisterous guffaw at the implausibility of the whole damn situation.

But when Dorian didn't budge, Jack Frost realized the implausible had become inescapable. Those unmistakable pale blue eyes staring up at some unfixed point on the ceiling removed all remaining uncertainty: Bob Dorian was dead.

"You okay, Frost," Commissioner Tiresias said, his gruff, granular voice jarring Jack Frost back to reality.

"I'm fine," Jack Frost said, doing his best to contain his contempt for Commissioner Tiresias.

"You want to throw a blanket over him or you just want to keep staring?" the Commissioner prodded. "I'm fine either way, but we got a little business we need to take care of. So make up your mind."

"And what kind of business could you and I possibly have?" Frost sneered.

"Just a few loose ends," Commissioner Tiresias said, flashing that Cheshire grin Jack Frost so abhorred.

"Well, if it's loose ends that need tying up," Jack Frost said matter-of-factly, "I redirect you to a loose end you seem determined to overlook."

"Are we talking about Dela Croix again?" Despite the Commissioner's attempt to feign affability, it did little to endear him to Frost. Jack Frost had long grown immune to the Commissioner's unwarranted charms.

"Anybody know where she is?" Frost inquired.

"Kind of hard to track someone down when they don't give out their address. But don't worry," the Commissioner said dismissively, "we're looking for her."

Jack Frost didn't buy it for a minute.

"So you actually expect me to believe that your entire investigation hinges on whether Dela Croix comes back to Elysian Row," he said incredulously. "I think we all know once someone leaves this place they tend not to come back."

"*You* came back—"

Commissioner Tiresias was trying to get a rise out of him, and Jack Frost knew it. But Jack Frost had been in this business a long time. He may not have liked Commissioner Tiresias, but he knew how to handle people like him. And rule number one was never let anyone *really* know what you thought—or how much you really knew. If he'd learned anything from his 20-plus years with the enigmatic Bob Dorian, it was that. Keep 'em guessing. Always keep 'em guessing.

"So are we just going to talk in circles all night or are you going to tell me what you know?" Jack Frost said evenly.

"Why don't you start by telling me what *you* know," Commissioner Tiresias countered. "And you can start by telling me what the two of you were doing in town."

Frost just stared at Commissioner Tiresias. *Just let him do the talking,* Frost thought to himself.

"Why don't I help you out a bit," the Commissioner said, filling the space between them. "Ran into Minnesota Slim this morning. Had to bloody him up a little bit, but he finally talked. You really *weren't* going to tell me, were you?" Commissioner Tiresias said with mock indignation.

Jack Frost continued to stare silently at the Commissioner.

"Listen, Jack, you and I been friends a long time."

Jack Frost remained stoic.

"Let me rephrase that. A long time ago we were friends—" Commissioner Tiresias clarified. "That better?"

"Not really."

"And when we were on a little friendlier terms, you'll recall I let your boy sing in those coffee houses over on MacDougal Street before he took off for the big city. We all knew he was underage, and I didn't say anything."

"Judas—" Jack Frost said derisively.

"There's no need for name-calling, Frost," Commissioner Tiresias said, placing his hand over his heart mockingly.

"That was Judas. Judas found him over on MacDougal Street. I was later."

"Oh, yes, that's right," Commissioner Tiresias snapped his fingers as if the memory had just come to him. "You entered the picture *after* Dorian was a star."

The Cheshire grin returned.

"Just so you know, Commissioner," Frost said, once again doing his best to suppress his scorn, "it was his idea to come back, not mine. But now that he's gone, I am too."

Of course, Jack Frost had no intention of leaving Elysian Row, and both men knew it. Commissioner Tiresias, however, wasn't taking any chances. He reached into his pocket and pulled out a silver .45 caliber pistol. He placed it on the table. The metal on wood made a hard 'clicking' sound that stopped Frost cold.

"Have a seat, Frost," the Commissioner said coolly. "You ain't goin' nowhere."

Jack Frost always said he would have laid down his life for Bob Dorian. He always believed it, too. But now that he was staring down the barrel of a .45 caliber pistol he wasn't so sure. Frost lowered himself into a matching red crushed velvet chair across from the chaise in which Dorian was lying, and turned his eyes in the direction of Commissioner Tiresias.

"Like I said," Commissioner Tiresias said, slowly picking up the gun as he ran his thumb across the ivory bone inlay, "I ran into Minnesota Slim earlier today."

"Slim?" Frost said dismissively. "You're holding me at gunpoint because of something Slim said? Minnesota Slim's nothing but a two-bit snitch! You know as well as I you can't trust him as far as you can throw him."

"Well, even if only a hint of what he told me this morning is true, he's thrown quite a monkey wrench into your plans," Commissioner Tiresias replied.

"My *plans?*" Jack Frost countered noncommittally. He knew Commissioner Tiresias had something on him, the problem was what and how much. And until he figured out the answers to those two critical questions, Jack Frost figured it was best not to commit to anything. "And what *plans* would that be?"

"Over the years your boy made a lot of friends—"

Commissioner Tiresias was playing with the pistol again.

"Fame and wealth will do that, I suppose," he continued. "But with friends come enemies, and when he left Elysian Row, he left a lot of enemies behind. He left you behind, if memory serves."

It was a cheap shot, but at least the shot the Commissioner had taken hadn't come out of the end of that .45.

"I don't have to take this shit."

"Aw, there's no need to blame yourself, Frost," Commissioner Tiresias said condescendingly. "It's not all your fault. Fame comes with a price. And eventually we all cash in—that's why you came back, isn't it? To cash in? Throw a party … put on a show … round up the usual suspects. Like I said, I know all about your 'Million Dollar Bash,'" the Commissioner said tauntingly.

"Well, I'm happy to see things haven't changed," Jack Frost replied. "One hand in your pants, the other drawn like a tight rope around the throats of the tenants of Elysian Row. And as for a concert? Hard to stage a show without a star, don't you think?"

"Oh, you've got a star. Biggest star in the world, a cultural icon, closest thing to a rock n' roll messiah since Elvis. Yes, sir. You got a star, all right. In fact, I'd say he's a bigger star now than ever. You see, some might see the pesky fact that Zeitzman's dead as a problem. I, on the other hand, see it as an opportunity. And I'd like you to see it that way as well."

"An opportunity?"

"Don't play dumb with me, Frost. You know as well as I that a dead rock star is worth more than one who's alive any day."

"He's hot, he's sexy, and he's dead—that what you're saying?"

"Jann always could write a hell of a headline," Commissioner Tiresias replied, immediately catching Jack Frost's cryptic reference to the 1981 *Rolling Stone* cover featuring Doors frontman, Jim Morrison. By all accounts the cover was a classic. Bare-chested and barely able to contain his smoldering sexuality, Morrison stares seductively into the camera looking like a cross between a caged animal and Christ on the crucifix.

When Jack Frost first saw that cover, he thought Morrison was going to leap right off that magazine. That, of course, would have been a difficult trick indeed. As Commissioner Tiresias had so aptly observed, by the time the magazine hit the newsstand the rock deity had been dead for close to a decade.

"Well, I don't know what your angle is, but I don't want any part of it."

"Too late, Frost—you already got a part of it. According to the boys out on Interstate 29, you got a rather sizeable part. Frankly, I'd like a little part of it, too," Commissioner Tiresias said, rubbing his thumb and forefinger together. The implication was clear—if money was going to be exchanging hands, some of it would need to pass through his.

"I don't know what you're talking about."

Frost was lying and both men knew it. Commissioner Tiresias knew it because he *had* talked to the boys out on Interstate 29; Jack Frost knew it because he *did* have a sizeable part of what the Commissioner had so sardonically referred to as 'The Million Dollar Bash.'

And while Slim's little conversation with the Commissioner earlier that day had tipped the Commissioner off to a show that was in the works, what Elysian Row's best-known snitch hadn't told the Commissioner was that the concert was going to generate a lot more money than a million dollars. A hell of a lot more. And therein lay the real problem for Jack Frost: Commissioner Tiresias probably knew that, too.

"Actually, I think you do know what I'm talking about," the Commissioner said, clearly savoring the moment. "You see, Minnesota Slim wasn't the only guy I talked with before you blew into town. Took a little trip out to the aforementioned Interstate 29. Ran into Tommie the Make and Julius the Squeeze. And they told me the three of you had been planning this show for months. You were going to make a real killing, pardon the expression."

"What are you suggesting?"

"I'm not suggesting anything. I'm simply stating the facts."

"Well, considering who's feeding you your information, I'd be very interested to know exactly what the 'facts' are."

"That you have quite a lot to gain from your loss—if you play your cards right, that is."

This son of a bitch is enjoying every minute of this, Jack Frost thought to himself. *A career spent trading on the misery of others. He's gonna milk this for all it's worth ... milk me, too, if I give him the chance.*

"I always knew you were a crooked cop," Frost said disdainfully.

Commissioner Tiresias smiled.

There was a moment when Jack Frost actually considered taking that bullet just to smack that smart-ass smile off Commissioner Tiresias' face.

"Frankly, I don't care much for your tone, Frost, but I love the alliteration. You've got quite a knack for turning a phrase." The Commissioner's smile broadened to a full shit-eatin' grin. And for the second time that evening, Frost rose from the red crushed velvet chair.

"Where do you think you're going?" Commissioner Tiresias demanded.

"Back to New York City—I've had enough of this crap."

"You're welcome to leave. Of course, if you do you won't be able to see firsthand who murdered your client." That stopped Frost cold. "Don't you want to be in the courtroom when the verdict comes down? I know I would."

"Now you think he was *murdered*?"

"Oh, that's right, I didn't mention the bullet hole in his chest yet, did I?"

That got Frost's attention.

"Dela found him down by the railroad tracks all right," Commissioner Tiresias continued. "But how he got in front of that train has yet to be determined."

Commissioner Tiresias didn't come right out and say it, but the implication was clear—"Now let's not jump to any conclusions," the Commissioner said coyly.

"It sounds like you already have."

"Listen, Jack, I'm not saying you off'd your client. You're capable of a lot of things. Frankly, I'm not convinced murder is one of them. Jury might see it differently though ..." The innuendo was not lost on either of them. "But as for me, no, I don't think you killed Bob Dorian." The smile returned to the Commissioner's face. "However, considering the fact he was your client—your *only* client, mind you— my advice to you is to capitalize on the hand that's been dealt. Hence the 'play your cards right' expression. Now as for this whole bit about *you* actually being the one who killed Bob, I'll be honest with you, Frost. I can't prove that. However …" Commissioner Tiresias picked up the .45 caliber pistol from the table. He dislodged the magazine from the body of the gun and slid a bullet into the magazine. "I *can* prove you had motive," he said, jamming the magazine back into the handle of the gun.

"Motive!?" Frost sputtered. "What motive would I possibly have to kill my client!?"

"Ah, yes, the old 'Why kill the golden calf conundrum?'" It seemed Jack Frost wasn't the only one with an affinity for alliteration. "The concert," Commissioner Tiresias said. "Tommie the Make … Julius the Squeeze? That thing we were just talking about. Is it true you were thinking about adding a few extra names to the bill? I like that idea. I'm assuming it's yours. That's one thing you and Zeitzman always had in common—both of you always had a head full of ideas. A 'Tribute Show'—has a nice ring to it. I can only imagine how fast those tickets are going to sell when word gets out Zeitzman won't be there to bask in the adulation."

"You can't prove any of this. The concert … that I brought him back … that I was talking with Tommie and Julius—you can't prove any of it."

"Actually, I can," Commissioner Tiresias said as he reached inside Zeitzman's leather jacket and retrieved a piece of white paper. "Well, what have we here?" he said, slowly unfolding the paper. "If it isn't a contract retaining the services of one Tommie the Make and one Julius the Squeeze, Esqs. I'm assuming they added the 'esquire' thing at the end to disguise the fact they're nothing more than moneygrubbing concert promoters. And wait a minute," Commissioner Tiresias said, feigning surprise. "Yes, it would seem that this other piece of paper is a set list." Commissioner Tiresias laid the list on the table. "And would you look at this …" he said, turning his attention to a small hole in the middle of a long list of songs. "A bullet hole. Like I said … blood all over the tracks."

"What is this?!" Frost exclaimed, yanking the paper off the table.

"That, my friend," Commissioner Tiresias replied calmly, "… is motive."

Frost stared intently at the bloodstained set list. But he wasn't staring at it to determine its authenticity. He knew it was real. Frost had picked the songs himself three days ago. Instead, Jack Frost was staring at the two letters scribbled across the bottom of the page in a thin cursive script, "O.K." The handwriting was unmistakable: it was Bob's.

Jesus, Jack Frost thought to himself, *that's probably the last thing he ever wrote.*

It only took a moment for the realization to set in, but once it did Jack Frost let out a long, exasperated sigh. But Commissioner Tiresias didn't hear the sound of a sigh: what Commissioner Tiresias heard was the sweet sound of defeat.

Jack Frost had been away from Elysian Row for a while. But he hadn't been away long enough to forget just how good Commissioner Tiresias really was. This was the Commissioner's town. Jack Frost was only visiting.

"So what do we do now?" Jack Frost inquired as he lifted his eyes from the crumpled set list. It seems the unfinished business the Commissioner had alluded to at the top of the conversation was about to be resolved.

"We do what any other partners do—we make a deal …"

Chapter 2

▼

The country
doctor rambles

Jack Frost and Commissioner Tiresias had put most of their cards on the table, but each man still had a few aces up his sleeve. Jack Frost's 'ace in the hole' was something that had yet to come up in his little tête-à-tête with Commissioner Tiresias. And frankly, he hoped it never would.

Despite Bob Dorian's relative low profile over the last few years, Jack Frost had managed to make a fortune for his client. A steady string of touring dates, a movie soundtrack every few years, maybe a lingerie ad here or a car commercial there. Jack Frost was good at what he did. He made millions for Bob Dorian and Bob Dorian didn't have to do a thing. But as good as he was, Jack Frost wasn't infallible. Jack Frost had made a bad decision or two. And his most recent decision had cost Bob Dorian more than his client would ever know.

Jack Frost was unsure exactly how much he had actually lost in the venture, but he was sure it was everything Bob Dorian had. It was everything he had, too. And the only way he was ever going to get even a fraction of it back was to stay on Elysian Row. And staying on Elysian Row meant getting into business with Commissioner Tiresias. The Commissioner was right: Frost wasn't going anywhere.

It pissed off Jack Frost to no end that the man who had made his life a living hell on more than one occasion was going to get a piece of Bob Dorian, but this was a cutthroat business and Jack Frost knew that sometimes you simply have no control over whom you cut in. So Jack Frost had made the deal with the Commissioner. Bob Dorian may have been dead, but in the truest sense of the old adage, 'the show would go on.' The only catch was that it would have to go on with Commissioner Tiresias.

And while Jack Frost had no way of knowing it at the time, Commissioner Tiresias wasn't the last person he was going to have to cut in on the deal. In fact, his newest partner had just stepped through the door.

"SO WHO MOVED the body?"

When neither man answered, Dr. Reich repeated his question. His words were as level and lifeless as the man he would soon be staring down on.

"Dela found him down by the railroad tracks this morning," Commissioner Tiresias stated matter-of-factly.

"Right—" Dr. Reich said slowly. "I saw that in the police report. But who *moved* him?"

"Couple of railroad hands," Commissioner Tiresias lied.

"And do these railroad hands have names?"

"With all due respect, Reich, why don't you let my men follow up on those kinds of details. The purpose of this evening's inquest is two-fold—to determine the time and to determine the cause of death," Commissioner Tiresias said, ticking off the reasons for bringing in Dr. Reich.

"Right," Dr. Reich said drolly. It was a typical Dr. Reich response: succinct, a tad reticent, but completely reliable. And there was no question that Dr. Reich was a man who could be relied on. 'Reliability,' after all, was the reason Dr. Reich had been called in in the first place.

"So," Frost said. "Any ideas when this happened?"

"Best guess? 12:07 a.m.—"

"12:07 ..." Frost repeated.

"Best guess."

"That's pretty specific. I mean, you haven't even seen the body."

"Don't need to see the body."

"You don't need to see the body?" Frost was still trying to figure that one out.

"No—I've just been told everything I need to know to determine the time of death."

"How's that?"

"When I asked the Commissioner who moved Mr. Zeitzman, he told me a couple of railroad hands. That is what you said isn't it? I have a copy of the police report. I am reading the report correctly, aren't I?"

Commissioner Tiresias hesitated. It was only for a moment, but he did hesitate. It turns out, he had good reason to pause. True, Dela had found Zeitzman. But she had nothing to do with his being transported to the Chelsea. The reason for Commissioner Tiresias' hesitation was that there was more to the story than he had let on. As it turns out, Commissioner Tiresias hadn't come completely clean with Jack Frost: he hadn't even come close.

"It seems the report was a tad premature," Commissioner Tiresias said.

"Premature?" Dr. Reich repeated.

"There seem to have been other factors at play. What those in my profession refer to as 'mitigating circumstances.'"

"Mitigating circumstances ..." Dr. Reich's sentence trailed off as he considered how carefully the Commissioner had chosen his words. Commissioner Tiresias switched between conman and cop so effortlessly that it was often hard, if not impossible, to tell exactly which 'profession' to which he was alluding.

"That's right," Commissioner Tiresias said. "A few things have come to our attention since the call was placed to you."

"And by 'our' you mean you and Mr. Frost's attention?" Dr. Reich observed wryly. His words were tainted with more than a tinge of suspicion.

It was the closest Commissioner Tiresias had come to being rattled all day. And while nothing would have made Jack Frost happier than to watch Dr. Reich get under Commissioner Tiresias' skin, Frost knew if that happened Dr. Reich could make this a lot more complicated than it needed to be. Reich had been brought in to provide them with an alibi, not become an albatross around their necks.

And as much as Jack Frost despised Commissioner Tiresias, Frost decided the time had come to do something he despised with equal fervor: back up his old adversary. That decision, however, was not entirely altruistic. After all, he too had a rather sizable stake in how this all shook out.

This is all Bob's fault, Frost thought to himself. *If only he hadn't trusted me. That son of a bitch didn't trust anyone, and then he trusts me with every goddamn penny he ever made. And then I went and fucked it all up.*

"By 'our,'" Frost said comfortingly, "I think Commissioner Tiresias means the attention of those of us who are now involved in this matter."

"Which I am assuming now includes me," Dr. Reich replied, realizing the mitigating circumstances to which the Commissioner had referred were going to involve a lot more than a simple pronouncement of the time and cause of death.

"I think that's a fair assessment," Frost replied.

"Very well," Dr. Reich said as he turned and motioned toward the stairwell. "Sounds like I'll need to see that body, after all ..."

THE SOUNDS OF AMBULANCES and calypso singers, which had filled the street below, were noticeably absent here. The fact that there was a man lying motionless in the corner only heightened the heaviness that hung over the room like a dirge. Dr. Reich's eyes swept across the room. It was a slow, methodical sweep. Partly because he wanted to take the whole scene in; partly because his eyes needed a little time to adjust to the darkness.

Dr. Reich pulled a leather cup from the left breast pocket of his overcoat. From his right pocket he withdrew a silver flask. He unscrewed the cap of the flask, then in a single, fluid motion he filled the cup with a thick, syrupy liquid. He took a swig from the cup. Then, as would be expected from a man who had fallen under the influence of absinthe, his eyes rolled back into the sockets of his head. A soft, carefree smile stretched across his face.

"Well, let's see what we have here—" he said, crossing the room with a newfound commitment to the verdict he was about to render.

Despite his renewed fortitude, Dr. Reich was operating at a disadvantage. Coroner's rule number one: Ensure the crime scene is preserved. By Commissioner Tiresias' own admission that rule had been violated. Whether it had been a premeditated violation or a simple attempt to avoid a barrage of unwarranted publicity, Dr. Reich couldn't be sure. But there was one thing Reich knew with steadfast certainty. He knew why he had been asked to come: he was going to set the time and cause of death. Commissioner Tiresias had been crystal clear on that point. What happened after that was out of Dr. Reich's control. Or so Commissioner Tiresias thought. But Commissioner Tiresias was in for quite a surprise, however. Commissioner Tiresias, it just so happens, wasn't the only one who knew how to turn an unfortunate situation to his advantage. And when Dr. Reich figured out exactly what the situation was that he had been called in to assess, Dr. Reich was going to turn the whole thing on its ear.

Having reached the dead man's side, Dr. Reich bent down and began to unbutton Zeitzman's Bolero vest. The vest was drawn around the rock star's midriff tight as a tourniquet. And as Dr. Reich loosened the vest, it looked as if Zeitzman was taking a short, little breath. But he was not breathing. He was quite dead, and with each button Dr. Reich unfastened, the stench of death, not the breath of life, filled the room. Dr. Reich inhaled deeply and the stench filled his lungs. It was evident this was a smell to which he had grown accustomed; it was evident the smell of death was one he had actually grown to like. Like an addict getting his fix, Dr. Reich let the sensation of death flow through him. And then, just like that, he was back. And when he returned, it was as if his senses had been heightened, for it only took him a few seconds to realize the number of buttons and buttonholes did not correspond. And at that moment, Dr. Reich realized the thing Commissioner Tiresias and Jack Frost already knew: there was an extra hole in the vest.

"That would be the 'mitigating circumstance,'" Commissioner Tiresias said.

The hole was no more than an eighth of an inch in diameter, and the bullet that had passed through it had lodged itself deep inside the dead rock star's chest. "What do you make of it?" Commissioner Tiresias continued.

"A very interesting shot, indeed," Dr. Reich said, his composure regained. The intoxicating, entrancing effects of death had apparently worn off.

"How so?"

"Well, the bullet went in here," Dr. Reich said, pointing to the red ring just below Zeitzman's heart. "However ..." Dr. Reich turned the body on its side, "the bullet did not come through the other side."

"And that's important?"

"It is if you want to rule out suicide."

Dr. Reich and Frost exchanged a furtive, knowing glance. Commissioner Tiresias, who was running his hand along Zeitzman's backside, looked up in time to catch the tail end of the exchange.

"And why would you want to rule out suicide?" Commissioner Tiresias inquired. Judging from his abrupt tone, Commissioner Tiresias hadn't liked the tail end of the exchange he had caught between Reich and Frost one bit.

"It would render a life insurance policy null and void," Dr. Reich replied, hoping Commissioner Tiresias wouldn't press the point.

Commissioner Tiresias took hold of Dr. Reich's wrist and squeezed tightly. Clearly, the point was being pressed. Dr. Reich laid the lifeless body back on the ground and let out a long sigh—

"It's not uncommon for life insurance companies to have a special rider that allows them to default on payout if they can prove the policyholder took his own life."

"So suicide's an 'out'?" Commissioner Tiresias said, cutting to the chase.

"That's correct. They're off the hook, so to speak."

"Just out of curiosity—in those cases, who might be the beneficiary?"

"Oh, I couldn't say for sure. It varies. Spouses, children, friends ..."

"Former managers?" Commissioner Tiresias said, the pitch of his voice rising as he turned in the direction of Jack Frost. Just because the two men were in business together apparently didn't rule out the possibility that one of those men would stab the other in the back the first chance he got.

"Screw you," Frost sputtered. "Bob was a rock star. A rock star who took full advantage of the trappings inherent in that particular lifestyle. It'd be awfully hard for me to benefit from a policy nobody would have given him in the first place."

"He's got a point, Commissioner. Mr. Zeitzman's numerous 'indiscretions' are legendary. His visits to Hazelden over the past few years are fairly well documented."

"So why'd you look at him?"

"I'm sorry?"

"When you said suicide could be ruled out, you looked at Frost like that piece of information might be of great interest to him."

"I'll admit. The thought crossed my mind," Dr. Reich confessed.

"Well, you can both go straight to hell," Frost said, rebuking the allegation. "And you can dispel whatever notions you have that we have stepped into some hard-boiled, film noir detective story. This is

Elysian Row, not *Double Indemnity*. Besides, it's a mute point," Frost said conclusively.

"Really?" Commissioner Tiresias said.

"Really," Frost said defiantly. "Like Dr. Reich said, those trips to Hazelden were pretty well documented. Bob couldn't have gotten a life insurance policy even if he'd wanted one."

"Mr. Frost is correct," Dr. Reich said, wishing he'd never shot Frost that look in the first place. "The point is mute. But it has nothing to do with Mr. Zeitzman's aforementioned 'indiscretions.' You see, in order for a man to commit suicide—in order for him to take his life by his own hand—he must have the gun in his hand to begin with. The size of the entrance wound indicates the gun used was powerful enough to go clean through the body. If, that is, it had been fired at close range—which, it was not."

"So you're saying—"

"I'm saying that your suspicions were correct, Commissioner. The gun used to kill Mr. Zeitzman was fired at a distance—a distance longer than from his hand to his chest. What I'm saying is that this is a case of cold-blooded murder."

His diagnosis complete, Dr. Reich began re-buttoning the Bolero vest.

"May I ask you gentlemen a question?" Dr. Reich inquired, a tinge of trepidation in his voice.

"Of course," Commissioner Tiresias said, answering for both of them.

"Was Mr. Zeitzman on medication? Prescribed, I mean," Dr. Reich quickly clarified to avoid self-incrimination should Jack Frost decide to answer the question.

"Well, he'd had a heart scare a few months back," Frost said.

"What kind of a heart scare?" Reich replied.

"He was riding his motorcycle up on his farm in North Dakota. Complained of chest pains a few days later."

"Histoplasmosis," Dr. Reich said matter-of-factly.

"Yeah—how did you ..."

"Common fungal infection, especially in that part of the country and other moist, low-lying areas. Causes swelling of the sac surrounding the heart," Dr. Reich said. He had added the last part for Commissioner Tiresias' benefit. "We get a few cases ourselves here on Elysian Row from time to time." Dr. Reich turned his attention back to Frost—

"So he was taking capsofungin?"

"That's right."

"And he was taking this medicine regularly?"

"I assume he was."

"Well ..." Dr. Reich reached into Zeitzman's Bolero vest and removed a vial of pills. "It would appear your assumption is correct." Dr. Reich shook the bottle, causing the contents to rattle. "Now may I ask you another question?"

"You may," Commissioner Tiresias interjected, giving his response just enough emphasis to suggest that if there were any more questions they should be addressed to him.

"Very well," Dr. Reich replied, turning his attention to Commissioner Tiresias. "Besides Dela and the rail hands—who else knows of Mr. Zeitzman's 'condition'?"

"The heart thing or the fact that he has a bullet buried in his chest?" Commissioner Tiresias replied rhetorically. He knew exactly what Dr. Reich was asking.

"The bullet," Dr. Reich replied without missing a beat.

"Just you—" Commissioner Tiresias replied.

"Dela Croix and the rail hands? They don't know he was shot?"

"I don't think so, and besides it really doesn't matter."

"And why's that?"

Dr. Reich was a coroner, not a cop, but in his experience something like that *did* matter. It mattered a hell of a lot.

"It doesn't matter because Dela Croix has skipped town."

"And the rail hands?"

"They haven't turned up either. For all I know they rode the rails right out of town—same way they got here." Commissioner Tiresias raised his chin slightly, and drew a deep, suspicious breath. "Why do you ask? Your job is to determine a time and mode of death, not figure out who killed him."

"That's right."

"So why all the questions?"

Dr. Reich did not reply. Not with words anyway. Instead he walked across the room to the window and pulled down the shades.

Shit, Commissioner Tiresias thought to himself. *Here it comes. We're about to get shaken down by the goddamn coroner. A guy I brought in no less.*

"Well, I know I'm just a country doctor," Dr. Reich said in a rambling, folksy manner. And while he never actually said the words, 'aw-shucks,' it was more than implied. "And I wouldn't purport to know all the 'ins' and 'outs' of the entertainment business, but my advice is not to let the boys in."

"The boys?" Frost said quizzically.

"He's talking about the press—" Commissioner Tiresias clarified.

Apparently this isn't his first time conning the cops, Commissioner Tiresias thought to himself. *The 'country doctor' shtick is a nice touch, though. Wonder when he started working that into the routine?*

"I'm assuming you want to find the man who killed Mr. Zeitzman?" Dr. Reich inquired.

"Of course we do," Commissioner Tiresias said, playing along.

"Well, if the press gets a hold of it, you'll never have a chance. If it gets out that the biggest rock star on the planet has turned up dead on Elysian Row it's going to be a pig-circus."

And though he didn't say anything, Commissioner Tiresias was giddy.

A pig-circus? Really? You think so? Well, well, well. The louder they come, the harder they crash, Commissioner Tiresias thought to himself. *Revise the estimate; make that a 'Two Million Dollar Bash.'*

After all, Commissioner Tiresias hadn't—what was the expression Jack Frost had used earlier—he hadn't drawn his hand 'like a tight rope around the throats of the tenants of Elysian Row' overnight.

That feat had taken years of carefully crafted deceit and deception. 'If the press gets a hold of this, you'll never have a chance—' Dr. Reich's words continued to rattle around in the Commissioner's head like some forgotten loose change he'd just found in his pants pocket. Clearly, Dr. Reich thought he had them over a barrel. Dr. Reich, however, didn't realize with whom he was dealing. Blackmail was the Commissioner's game, and no one knew how to play it better.

"You make a very good point, doctor, a very good point indeed. Your assessment of the situation is spot-on—keeping this on the QT is without a doubt in everyone's best interest," Commissioner Tiresias said earnestly.

"Oh, you don't need to worry about me," Dr. Reich said, picking up his leather cup. This time, however, Reich did not press the cup to his lips. "You don't need to worry about me at all." Dr. Reich glanced down at the empty cup, his eyes saying what he refrained from actually speaking aloud.

Commissioner Tiresias and Frost exchanged a knowing glance: Frost knew exactly what to do. He reached into his pocket and took out a roll of bills. He peeled off a few and stuffed them into the cup. In return, the Dr. Reich reached into his suit jacket pocket, took out a crème colored business card and placed the card in Jack Frost's palm.

"In case you need to reach me—" he said with a lupine smile as he sucked in the damp, dank air then turned and stepped into hallway. Jack Frost briefly glanced at the card. The only words were the doctor's name and title—*Arthur D. Reich III, Pathologist.* Frost slipped the card into his front pants pocket. And just like that, Dr. Reich was in on their dirty little secret.

THE COMMISSIONER AND JACK FROST WATCHED Dr. Reich take hold of the termite-infested guardrail and begin his descent down the stairs to the first floor of the Chelsea Hotel. With each step he took, the stairs creaked and cracked beneath his feet. And though the creaking was muffled slightly by the frayed Oriental runner, the sound of the stairs giving way to the weight of his short, portly body sounded like a ragtime rummy trying to pick out a very bad version of "Chopsticks" on an old, out of tune barroom piano.

When they were certain that Dr. Reich was out of sight, or perhaps more importantly out of earshot, Frost turned his unspoken, smoldering ire on Commissioner Tiresias.

"What the fuck was that?" Frost sputtered.

"That, my friend, was our alibi," Commissioner Tiresias replied coolly. He then turned and walked back into the room where the dead man lay.

"Our alibi?" Frost said, following Commissioner Tiresias into the room. "What the hell do I need an alibi for? I didn't kill Zeitzman!" Clearly, Frost was starting to get a little hot under the collar. "I need answers! I need to know who killed Bob!"

"In due time, Frost, in due time."

"What the hell does that mean?"

"You are aware that the good doctor was trying to blackmail us, aren't you?"

"*Trying* to blackmail us!" Frost sputtered. "He *was* blackmailing us. My wallet is a lot lighter because of the fact was blackmailing us!"

"How much money did you give him?" the Commissioner said, moving across the room toward the window. He reached up and removed a series of nails that had been driven through the muslin blinds and into the wall.

"Five hundred."

"Best money you ever spent."

"That's easy for you to say—it didn't come out of your pocket," Jack Frost replied in disgust.

"In my experience money doesn't talk, it swears," Commissioner Tiresias said as he continued to remove the nails from the wall. "Five hundred, you say?"

"That's right."

"Then I think it's safe to say you just told the good doctor to keep his fucking mouth shut."

Commissioner Tiresias employed a final, forceful tug on the curtains, causing them to collect in a pile at his feet. And for the first time in three days, light entered the room.

"Very dramatic," Frost said, raising his hand to shield his eyes from the light. "I always knew you had a knack for the flair."

"What's up with those curtains, anyway?" the Commissioner inquired. "He always nail them shut?" As far as Frost could tell, the question was genuine.

"Bob never liked the light. Liked to keep everyone in the dark. Speaking of 'keeping people in the dark'—I'm starting to think you might be keeping me in the dark on a few things."

"Such as?" Commissioner Tiresias replied.

"Such as that little comment about finding out who killed Bob in due time. That doesn't sound like a cop talking. Delaying a murder investigation. That doesn't sound like a cop talking at all."

"Oh, I'm not going to be conducting this investigation," Commissioner Tiresias said. That familiar Cheshire grin had returned—"You are."

"Excuse me?"

"That's right. *You're* going to find the man who killed Bob Zeitzman."

It took a lot to render Jack Frost speechless. But that last comment had done the trick.

"Don't worry," Commissioner Tiresias said feigning comfort. "You're going to have a little help."

Frost knew Commissioner Tiresias. He knew him well. As well, that is, as you can know anyone who never plays poker with a losing deck. And if Jack Frost knew anything about the way Commissioner Tiresias played his cards, he knew he wasn't about to turn over the biggest story to hit the Row in 20 years to someone else. And he *damn sure* wasn't going to turn it over to someone he couldn't keep under his thumb. But instead of forcing his hand, Frost decided to keep quiet just a little longer. Perhaps the Commissioner would answer the question himself. Frost's silence was about to pay off in spades—

"You see, Frost," the Commissioner said slowly. "Dr. Reich thought he had us over a barrel when he suggested that he might go to the press with this."

"He did have us over a barrel, Commissioner. Biggest rock star in the world turns up dead in a hotel room on Elysian Row, murdered no less, with no suspects to speak of. The press gets a hold of this and we are in a jam," Frost replied.

"Not if we go to the press first."

"I just put five Franklins in Dr. Reich's pocket to make sure he *didn't* go to the press. Now you're telling me we want them in on this?"

"Listen, Frost. This show, this tribute show you and I are now partners on. We need to protect our investment. We need insurance. Maybe we get the press to write our policy."

It burned Frost just to hear the words, 'you,' 'I,' and 'partners,' together in the same sentence, especially since the 'I' in that scenario was the one man he despised more than anyone. Jack Frost would rather swallow razor blades than partner up with Commissioner Tiresias. But Jack Frost was beginning to see where this was going. 'The boys,' as Dr. Reich had so dismissively referred to them, were nothing to dismiss. They could slice you to pieces just as easy as they could carve a place for you in the minds of the masses. They could relegate you to the ash heap of history, or they could bestow immortality. And, as Jack Frost was acutely aware, immortality cuts both ways.

Over the years, Robert Zeitzman had been on both sides of that sword. In his early days down in the Village when he was playing for nickels and dimes, the press hailed him 'the poet of a generation.' They had taken a scraggly street singer and turned him into the 'next big thing.' In fact, if it weren't for the press there wouldn't even have *been* a Bob Dorian. Sure, it was his idea to change his name and create a new image for himself, but the press bought into the image and, in the process, turned him into a legend.

In recent years, however, the press had crucified Bob Dorian. 'Live by the sword, die by the sword': For some, it was just a pithy expression, a toss-away line that meant nothing. But for Bob Dorian, the press had turned his life into a living hell. The institution that had put him on a pedestal had decided a few years back that it was done with him. And just as effortlessly as they had placed him on that elevated platform, they knocked him to his knees. Bob Dorian hadn't had a hit in close to 10 years. Live by the sword, die by the sword.

But just because he wasn't getting the support of the press didn't mean he wasn't making music. Bob Dorian never stopped making music. But that was the problem. The music he made, the music he *had* to make, was the very thing the press had used to shred his dignity and denigrate his place in the annals of rock history.

'A surprising disappointment,' one critic wrote about Dorian's 1974 reunion with the band that backed him on his biggest hits of the '60s. 'The vocals are shockingly bad, not to mention almost always off key. And the mid-70s synth-mania drowns what should be familiar tunes in a sea of electronic malaise.'

Even after releasing one of his most prolific and most well-received albums of his career later that year, the press pounced on his follow-up LP mercilessly: 'This album is worth listening to,' the press collectively chided, 'but I can't really say why. While there's a conscious attempt to return to the protest songs of his youth, what's Bob Dorian got to protest about now, anyway? It's hard to protest against the establishment when you have become the establishment.' Bob Dorian always said he never read his own press clippings. Maybe he did, maybe he didn't. But after that particular review came out, Bob Dorian didn't step in the studio for the next 10 years. The desire, it seemed, was gone.

So when Bob Dorian came to Jack Frost a few weeks earlier and told him that he was ready to embrace the thing he had spent his entire life running from, that he was ready to return to Elysian Row, Jack Frost didn't hesitate. His first call was to Tommie the Make; his second to Julius the Squeeze. Sure they were a pair of pitiless promoters who were out to make a fast buck. They didn't give a rat's ass about Bob Dorian, not like Jack Frost did. But they could get the job done, and that's what Jack Frost needed. Jack Frost needed this show just about as bad as Bob Dorian. Actually, Jack Frost needed it more. A lot more. His little 'indiscretion' with Bob's fortune had cost him everything. Talk about living with a mistake. Jack Frost was going to have to live with that one for the rest of his life. Of course, the irony was that Bob Dorian wasn't alive to see how badly Jack Frost had screwed the pooch. And the more Jack Frost thought about it, the more he thought Bob Dorian had gotten off easy.

So when Bob Dorian told Jack Frost he wanted to return to Elysian Row, Jack Frost leapt into action. Jack Frost knew a concert on Elysian Row—the one place Bob Dorian had vowed never to return—would go a long way toward helping refill the coffers Frost had so carelessly depleted. Not to mention the lengths to which a tribute show would go to reclaiming his client's rightful place in the pantheon of rock royalty.

And while Commissioner Tiresias wasn't completely on to Jack Frost, he was on to something. And it was now dawning on Jack Frost what that something was: the press was going to find out about Bob Dorian's untimely demise whether Dr. Reich told them or not. Dela Croix, the rail yard hands, Tommie, Julius, Slim … hell, even Commissioner Tiresias himself could go to the press any time and present the scenario any way they chose. What Commissioner Tiresias was suggesting was actually a stroke of brilliance.

The press is going to be a part of this story sooner or later, Frost thought to himself as he let the argument play itself out in his head. *Why not control the story? Why not use this to our advantage? Why not do exactly what Commissioner Tiresias is suggesting? And why not let him think it's his idea to boot?*

"Are you sure about this?" Frost said with mock caution. "Bringing someone else in, I mean."

"Of course I'm sure," Commissioner Tiresias said confidently. "Trust me, this guy doesn't have a clue. Been stuck on the obits desk at the *Elysian Plains-Dispatch* for years. I'm just throwing him a bone."

"And you think it will work?"

"My job, Frost, let me do my job."

"You've already called him, haven't you?" Clearly, it was a rhetorical question.

"Is that a problem?"

"It'd be nice if you'd told me."

"And why's that?"

"I know most of the people on the Row, but I've never heard of this guy. Makes me nervous hearing that there's a guy on this that I don't know anything about."

"Like I said, he's been on the obits desk for a couple years. Not an especially high-profile job. Apparently he wants to change that. Wants to be a reporter. Needs a break, a big story. Can't think of a bigger story than this."

"So he's a hack?"

"You could say that. But he's *our* hack," the Commissioner said, clearly pleased with himself.

"So how much does he know?"

"He knows there's been a murder. He knows I learned of this murder an hour and fifteen minutes ago. He knows you were on the scene shortly thereafter."

"What about Reich? Does he know about Dr. Reich?"

"For Christ's sake, Frost, of course he knows about Reich! I've already told you—Reich is our alibi. First rule of leading an investigation: Remove yourself as the primary suspect."

"Don't talk to me like I'm an idiot, Commissioner. I know why you got Reich involved. But this guy you want to bring in—he's going to be asking a lot of questions."

"The only question he's going to be asking—the only question he *should* be asking—is who killed Zeitzman. And I'll tell you exactly what I told him: 'This is an open-and-shut case. Dr. Reich set the time of death at 12:07. Your job is to find the guy who clocked him.' Now let me ask *you* a question—" Commissioner Tiresias said, turning his attention back to Jack Frost. "Where were you at 12:07?"

"I was downstairs in the parlor."

"Anybody with you?"

"Couple of seasick sailors having a couple of pops before heading home."

"Well, I was down at the station when I got the call. The whole damn riot squad can vouch for me."

"So we got alibis. That's all fine and well, but what makes you so sure this guy's going to keep his eyes in his pocket and nose to the ground? When word gets out about Bob, a lot of people are going to want to start running their mouths. There're going to be a lot of distractions."

"Which is why you're going to stick with him—make sure he doesn't start thinking *he's* the story. Make sure he doesn't start running *his* mouth."

"So I'm a glorified 'minder.'"

"Call it what you want, Frost, I don't give a damn two ways to Sunday. Just keep an eye on him."

"And you trust him?"

"He'll do what we tell him. Now," Commissioner Tiresias said, shifting tone and tenor in one fail swoop, "who were the last two people to see Zeitzman alive?"

"According to you, the rail hands who brought him back to the Chelsea."

"General rule of thumb—and even the most clueless poser like him will know this. And if he doesn't, be sure to remind him—the last person to see the victim alive is usually the one who killed him."

"Find the rail hands and we've found our killer—that what you're saying?"

"That's exactly what I'm saying. And we find our killer, that little concert you were planning on putting on isn't so little anymore. It's the biggest thing to hit this place in years. Now, we got our story straight?"

"I think so."

"Good."

Commissioner Tiresias returned to the window and stared across the alleyway and in the direction of the lights flickering in the opposite loft—

"Then let's bring him in ..."

CHAPTER 3

▼

SOMETHING'S
HAPPENING HERE

He walked into the room, a pencil in one hand and a pair of eye-glasses in the other. Silent and solemn, he slipped the glasses into the pocket of his dark, wool suit that was, like the man himself, painfully prosaic and nondescript. That lack of description, however, spoke volumes. The fact you couldn't say anything about him, well, that really said it all. Even his name was ordinary: Mister Johns.

And while Frost didn't care much for Commissioner Tiresias, he had to give him this much: Commissioner Tiresias had pegged this guy to a tee. If anything were to go wrong, Mister Johns would be the perfect patsy.

"How you doing, Johns?"

"Fine, Commissioner, thanks for asking."

"You sure? You look a little thin—" Commissioner Tiresias observed. "Ma Raney over at the Tombstone hasn't been letting you skimp out on meals now has she?"

The 'Ma Raney' to whom Commissioner Tiresias was referring was a fixture on Elysian Row. And the Tombstone, the old bed and breakfast she'd been running for as long as anyone could remember, was equally well renowned. But for all the notoriety surrounding the Tombstone, little was actually known about its proprietor. It was common knowledge that Ma Raney had been born Gertrude Pridgett in a shanty shack somewhere in the outskirts of Columbus, Georgia. Other than that one, single fact, however, everything else that was known about Ma Raney was pure speculation. A census had been taken in 1900, but there was always some debate over whether the men conducting it had actually traipsed all the way out to shantytown to count the 'black folk.' The actual year in which Ma Raney had made her entrance into the world, therefore, was anyone's guess. It seems Ma Raney used this imprudence on the part of the census takers to her advantage, and promptly backdated the year of her birth from 1886 to 1882. And while a woman doesn't typically confess to her age, much less make herself older, in the case of Ma Raney she did it willingly. Those extra four years let her work the ragtag juke joints and seedy bordellos which would have otherwise turned her away.

Her birthday wasn't the only thing the wily old blues singer changed. In 1902, she changed her name when she married a song and dance man who went by the name of "Pa" Rainey. She liked the idea of perpetuating the tradition of the old traveling minstrel show, and the pairing of a "Ma" and "Pa" seemed to fit the bill. And so, from that moment on she was always known as Ma Raney. As for the 'i,' it had been dropped by a promoter who, legend had it, simply misheard her name. To hear Ma tell it, it was even more innocuous than that: 'Lazy soma-bitch simply ran out of ledders for the marquet.' In addition to occasionally slurring her words—'ledders' was really 'letters,' for example—she also had a tendency to make up words altogether. 'Marquet,' for example, sounded like her favorite bird, 'parakeet.' The word she really meant to say was 'marquee.'

Only adding to the mystery and cachet surrounding Ma Raney was the fact that she had invented the Blues—or so she claimed. 'Didn't know what it was when I started out,' she'd tell anyone who'd listen. And once Ma Raney got started it was hard not to hear her out.

'All I knew is what I felt, and damn if I didn't feel bad.' 'Didn't' came out like, *did-jent*. 'Bessie felt bad, too.' The 'Bessie' to whom she was referring was none other than Bessie Smith, widely regarded as the most popular and successful blues singer of the 1920s and 1930s. And while some might say Bessie Smith was *the* most influential performer in blues history, those were not words you said in front of Ma Raney. 'I taught that little blackbird everything she knew,' she'd say, telling the story with a familiarity that comes from repeating the same story again and again. 'Yes sir, when she came to me she felt real bad. If anyone had the blues it was Bessie. But it ain't enough to *have* the blues,' she'd clarify in a low, seductive voice. 'You gotsta know how to get them out! And that's exactly what's I showed old Bessie how to do,' she'd say, indulging an old habit of rubbing a rabbit's foot between her forefinger and thumb. 'I showed her how to get them's blues outs and outs for good.' By this point in the story, Ma Raney had typically been indulging liberally in another old habit of pressing a sandy colored clay jug of moonshine to her lips. It was a good story, but then again there was never a question Ma Raney could tell some good stories. Her idiosyncrasies and eccentricities made her one of the most colorful characters on Elysian Row. Of course it didn't hurt that she'd share that bottle of shine she with anyone willing to listen to those stories.

"Yeah," Mister Johns replied to the Commissioner's inquiry, "Ma Raney's treating me just fine."

"Well, I'm glad to hear it," Commissioner Tiresias said flatly, making no attempt whatsoever to mask his indifference. "Oh, forgive me," Commissioner Tiresias continued, realizing that Jack Frost was waiting for an introduction. "Johns, this is Jack Frost. Frost was the manager."

Mister Johns acknowledged Frost with a slight tilt of the chin. Then without a moment's hesitation Mister Johns moved across the room. He knelt beside the slain rock star, rolled back the sleeve of the singer's well-worn leather jacket and wrapped his hand around Dorian's thin, agile wrist.

"Are you taking his pulse?" Commissioner Tiresias said incredulously.

"It's a formality," Mister Johns replied.

"I can assure you he's quite dead."

"Your assurances are not needed," Mister Johns said, letting go of the dead man's arm. "He's dead all right." But the arm did not fall to the side. Instead it remained upright, hard and rigid. And while Johns knew it usually took a few hours before rigidity set in, he kept his prognosis—for the moment anyway—to himself. Something else, it seems, had captured his attention—

"You sure you're okay, Johns?" Commissioner Tiresias goaded. "You look like you've seen a ghost."

"I'm fine," Johns replied. "It's just ... I can't put my finger on it, but there's something about seeing him in person that just ... well, frankly like it's not really him."

"He got that a lot," Frost chimed in, eager to engage the man with whom he had been unwittingly paired. "He once told me he felt like he was in an Edgar Allan Poe story. But he just wasn't the person everybody thought he was."

"Who'd they think he was?"

"Who *didn't* they think he was? A prophet, a savior ... hell, one woman thought he was an actor playing him. People would always come up to him and say: 'Is it you?' And he'd say: 'I don't know, who do you think I am?' Then they'd say: 'You're not *really* him.' And he'd say: 'If you say so.' Happened all the time. Just went on and on. That's the funny thing about fame I guess—nobody really believes it's you."

"But it *is* him?" Mister Johns said.

Of all the stupid fucking questions, Jack Frost thought to himself. *Of course it's him.*

"I have to ask," Mister Johns said, sensing Jack Frost's wariness. "Formality, really. I don't know if the Commissioner told you what I do for a living."

Jack Frost smiled, "Yes, Mister Johns, I know what you do."

But even if Commissioner Tiresias hadn't told him that Johns wrote obituaries for the *Dispatch*, it probably wouldn't have taken a lot for Frost to peg this guy as someone who worked with stiffs for a living.

Admittedly, Frost hadn't spent a lot of time with obits writers, but he knew Johns' kind. In his two decades in the music business, Jack Frost had seen a million guys like Mister Johns. Guys who wanted to be in the game, but didn't have the first clue how to get in on the action. They were paralegals, pariahs, lowlifes and lackeys. People who sucked the life out of the room the minute they walked through the door.

And as Mister Johns stood there in his dark, dour suit, he was beginning more and more to resemble the most disgusting lowlife of them all: a pestilent, parasitic pest some 354 million years in the making. Mister Johns was metamorphosing into a cockroach right before Frost's very eyes. Johns' jacket hardened into the insect's stiff black shell; his starched white shirt took on the appearance of the pest's pasty, pallid underbelly. *Jesus Christ, I've become Franz Kafka and this poor SOB has become Gregor Samsa.* But the more Frost thought about it, the more he realized that Gregor Samsa's alter ego wouldn't stand a chance back at the Tombstone. After all, what would a cockroach eat in a place where every crumb was swept up the moment it hit the floor? Not that he would want to, but Frost was confident if he were to accompany Mister Johns back to the Tombstone, he knew exactly what he'd find. The room would be spotless. There wouldn't be a hair out of place. It certainly didn't take much imagination to conjure up a picture of the contents of Mister Johns' closet. He probably had dozens of those black suits in there, each hung with precision and aligned perfectly. His dresser drawers were probably filled to capacity with neatly folded starched white shirts, pressed and preserved in individual cellophane wrappers. And what about his shoes? No doubt he had *at least* half a dozen pairs. And they were all the same: black, patent leather, polished to perfection. And though he probably took great care to ensure that each shoe was perfectly matched with its respective counterpart, the joke was lost on Johns. It didn't matter: they were all the same shoe.

Indeed, Frost knew Mister Johns' type well: straight-laced, ramrod-backed, completely unimaginative. And though Jack Frost didn't harbor any resentment toward the obits writer, he didn't have a lot of faith in him, either.

But he'll fit the bill, Frost thought to himself. *He'll play the part.*

"So it is him?" Mister Johns repeated.

Frost glanced down at Dorian's lifeless body. A gold chain with a crucifix and Star of David hung loosely around the dead rock star's neck. It was all Frost needed to know. The man was indeed Bob Dorian: a man of constant contradiction. A man, who even in death, was just as enigmatic as he had been in life.

"It's him," Frost said, lifting his eyes back up to Mister Johns. "I'm assuming that's what you want me to do—I.D. the body."

"It helps to be sure," Mister Johns said with the detachment that came from years of staring not into the face of death, but staring into the faces of those who were dead. And though Jack Frost couldn't bring himself to look into the eyes of the man he had known nearly all his life, Mister Johns, it seems, couldn't *stop* staring at him—

"Hand me your handkerchief," Johns said, unable to resist his macabre curiosity. It was like some powerful, unseen magnet drawing him to the dead man. It simply would not let him go. "In your left breast pocket—if you wouldn't mind."

Frost and Commissioner Tiresias exchanged a look.

"Trust me gentlemen," Mister Johns said, picking up on the exchange, "I've seen a lot of dead people. I guess you could say it's just one of the occupational hazards of beating the pavement down on Rue Morgue Avenue." The obits writer's joke fell on deaf ears. "Anyway, my point is this—dead people *never* look like they did when they were alive. But look at him! He looks *exactly* like he did when he was alive."

"I thought you'd never seen him before?"

"Pictures, Mr. Frost. And album covers. Back when they still made albums, that is." The man in the dark, dour suit was growing inpatient. "Now, if you don't mind, Mr. Frost, your handkerchief, please."

Commissioner Tiresias motioned for Frost to hand Mister Johns his handkerchief. Frost reached into his left breast pocket and removed a silk handkerchief. He handed the handkerchief to Mister Johns.

"How well did you know your client, Mr. Frost?"

There was a tinge of innuendo in Mister Johns' voice. It wasn't quite a rhetorical question, but it was getting close.

"About as well as anyone, I'd imagine," Jack Frost replied. "I was his manager for 20 years."

"His quirks, idiosyncrasies, peculiar habits …"

"I knew him well, 'yes,' why do you ask?"

It was the manager's turn to get a tad impatient.

Mister Johns drew the handkerchief across the dead man's skin. "So you were aware he wore makeup?" Mister Johns said, holding the handkerchief up for the two men to see. A brown, powdery, cakelike substance was smeared across the otherwise unsoiled handkerchief.

"It's called foundation and, 'yes,' he wore it from time to time. It's quite common among performers."

"I see—"

The derisiveness in Johns' voice was evident. Both men knew that there might be a good deal more to Bob Dorian's penchant for makeup than Frost was letting on.

Mister Johns folded the handkerchief into halves, then quarters, then placed the handkerchief on the wooden table.

"The Commissioner tells me you're a reporter," Jack Frost said, attempting to move the conversation forward.

"Obits desk at the *Dispatch*," Johns replied flatly before turning his attention to Commissioner Tiresias, "but thanks for the promotion, Commissioner. No, my job consists mostly of fact-checking."

"Well, as I'm sure the Commissioner has apprised you, the facts in this case are pretty straightforward."

"Actually," Mister Johns politely contradicted, "you'd be amazed how the facts start to change when the guy they're talking about isn't there to refute them. But don't worry, Mr. Frost, Commissioner Tiresias brought me in to help you find out who killed your client, not open a dossier on his personal life," Mister Johns said, putting to bed any escapades that might have been best left behind closed doors.

"If I may step in here for a moment, gentlemen," Commissioner Tiresias interjected. "Mister Johns is very good at what he does. And that's get the facts right. Which shouldn't be a problem," Commissioner Tiresias said, turning in the direction of Mister Johns, "since we are giving you the facts on a silver platter. Access, too. So if you want to get out from behind that obits desk, I suggest you and Mr. Frost learn to play nice."

Assured that he had quelled the animosity that had arisen between Mister Johns and Jack Frost, Commissioner Tiresias smiled and continued, "Now, I was telling Frost here before you arrived that you're just the man for the job. Your tenacity is just what this case needs. Elysian Row can be a difficult place to navigate. Our residents aren't—how shall I put it—the most forthcoming. Don't like answering a lot of questions, especially from the cops. They don't always trust us."

"I can't imagine why—" Frost said drolly.

"And as for Hollywood types like yourself," Commissioner Tiresias continued, clearly ignoring Frost's dig, "well, I don't have to tell you, Frost, they'd clam up faster than a virgin on prom night if you started poking around. You may have spent a little time on the Row when you were a kid, but you ain't been around for a while. I guess what I'm saying is now that the two of you are working this you're going to be spending a lot of time together. So like I said—let's play nice. Now can we get back to the matter at hand, please?"

"You'll forgive me for belaboring the point, gentlemen," Mister Johns said as he rolled the sleeve of Dorian's leather jacket back over his wrist, "but this *is* the matter at hand. I appreciate your vote of confidence, Commissioner, and I certainly mean no disrespect …"

"Get on with it, Johns—" Commissioner Tiresias' impatience was clearly on the verge of giving way to anger.

"I was brought in to cover the murder of the former Mr. Zeitzman under two assumptions. The first is that Mr. Zeitzman was, in fact, murdered. Well, judging from the size of that bullet hole, I would say that unless some monumental piece of evidence is uncovered to refute a .45 caliber pistol being fired into Mr. Zeitzman's chest at point-blank range, the first assumption is a sound one. The second assumption—that the murder of Mr. Zeitzman occurred within the last 24 hours—well, that assumption no longer stands."

"What are you talking about, Johns? This is an open-and-shut case," Commissioner Tiresias stated with a bluntness that all but made it so. "Dr. Reich set the time of death last night …"

"At 12:07. Yes, I've read Dr. Reich's report, Commissioner, and to his credit it's quite thorough."

Commissioner Tiresias smiled.

"Unfortunately, it's also inaccurate—"

That wiped the smile clean off the Commissioner's face.

"Let me ask you two a question—" Mister Johns knelt down next to the body. "Have either of you actually touched this body?"

"Of course not. Why would we?"

"You wouldn't have. Or should I clarify, you would have no reason to. But I'm assuming Dr. Reich did. His report said the bullet didn't pass through the entire body—that it stopped somewhere in the chest cavity. Well, he couldn't have known that unless he rolled the body over. And when he did, he would have immediately noticed the very thing that occurred to me the moment I walked into the room."

"And what's that?" Jack Frost inquired.

"You see, the Commissioner laughed at me when I checked for a pulse. And frankly, Commissioner, I don't blame you. You were right

Mr. Zeitzman is quite dead. In fact ..." Mister Johns hesitated, "... he's been dead for three days."

"Three days?" Frost said disbelievingly.

"The body has succumbed to rigor mortis."

"Rigor mortis?"

"It's when metabolic activity continues in the muscle after death, causing the body's extremities to harden," Mister Johns explained.

"I know what rigor mortis is, Mister Johns," Commissioner Tiresias replied tersely. "I've seen a few dead bodies in my day, too. And if this guy had rigor mortis, he'd be as blue as my left nut."

"Well, I can't speak to that, Commissioner ..." Mister Johns said dryly. Jack Frost suppressed a chuckle. Clearly, Jack Frost was beginning to appreciate to Johns' acerbic wit. "But you're right—" Mister Johns continued, "discoloration is common. And blue is typically the color."

"Well, does he look blue to you?"

"Actually, Mr. Zeitzman's complexion is very lifelike. Which brings me back to the makeup—"

Mister Johns retrieved Jack Frost's silk handkerchief from the table and drew it across Zeitzman's face a second time, revealing the true color of his skin was an odd mixture of blue and purple. As he had done before, he held up the handkerchief for the men to see.

"It would appear your open-and-shut case is now wide open, Commissioner."

Commissioner Tiresias and Frost exchanged a glance. Unsure what to say, neither man said a word. They didn't have to—their expression said it all: *shit.*

CHAPTER 4

▼

ON YOUR OWN ...

The fact Bob Dorian had been dead for three days was an unexpected development to be sure. And while neither man had seen it coming, the situation they found themselves in hardly set precedent. This wasn't, after all, the first time Bob Dorian had brought Commissioner Tiresias and Jack Frost together.

It was the winter of 1961, February to be exact. A scrappy young performer by the name of Robert Zeitzman had arrived the month before and taken up residence at a small walk-up over Nero's Neptune, a popular fish store at the far end of Elysian Row. Zeitzman didn't have much: a guitar, a harmonica, a couple of beat up old folk records and a half-empty brown gunnysack to keep his treasured possessions in. But what Zeitzman lacked in material wealth, he made up for in talent, ambition and what those familiar with the entertainment business refer to as 'fire in the belly.' One look in his eyes and you saw the smoldering intensity that would, one day, spark a cultural revolution. But Zeitzman hadn't come to Elysian Row to set the world on fire. Setting the world ablaze—that would come later. Zeitzman had come to this godforsaken place to meet his idol.

Forrest Guthridge, an old folkie who had almost single-handedly invented the folk genre, lay dying in a small, poorly lighted 10-by-10 foot room in a dingy sanitarium on the outskirts of town. Those who knew Guthridge's location also knew just how dire his condition was: they'd given him six months. When six months came and went, they gave him another six months. But like the people, places and things Guthridge sang about in his songs, Forrest Guthridge was resilient. And though he was in and out of hospitals, psychiatric wards and convalescent homes for the rest of his life, his final journey into darkness would last a little longer than the six months the doctors had initially given him: it would last another 12 years.

And while Bob Zeitzman was drawn to Guthridge's music from the first note he heard, it was Guthridge's resilience, his undeterred refusal to lay down his weary tune and fade away, that made Bob Zeitzman know he had to meet him. So Bob Zeitzman came to Elysian Row for the same reason everyone seemed to come to Elysian Row. Bob Zeitzman came in search of something he hadn't been able to find anywhere else. The problem that confronted him when he arrived, however, was that in the winter of 1961 Bob Zeitzman was not yet 'Bob Zeitzman, poet of a generation.' And he damn sure wasn't Bob Dorian. Instead, he was a snot-nosed kid from Pembina, a small township in rural North Dakota. He was a nobody. And even if he did know where his hero lay dying, slowly rotting to death under the watchful eyes of doctors, nurses and internists who didn't have a clue how to save him, Bob Zeitzman knew if he didn't take matters into his own hands he'd never get to see his idol.

It was right around this time that the paths of Jack Frost and Commissioner Tiresias crossed for the first time. And while the relationship between Commissioner Tiresias and Jack Frost could hardly be called 'adversarial' when they met in the winter of 1961, their relationship wasn't especially cozy, either. Perhaps the best way to describe the tenuous tethering that brought these two men together then was the same way to describe the thing that bound them together now: it was 'an arrangement.' And at the heart of that 'arrangement' was Robert Zeitzman.

Jack Frost wasn't much older than the passionate young performer when their own paths crossed that winter. In fact, later when Jack Frost and Bob Zeitzman got to know each other well enough that Bob finally began to let his guard down, the two men realized they were actually the same age, born on the same day, a mere three minutes apart. But in 1961, the men did not know each other. They did, however, know *about* each other. Jack Frost knew that Bob Zeitzman was an aspiring folksinger whose talent, though not fully developed, was clearly abundant. Bob Zeitzman knew that Jack Frost managed the Hoot, the hottest club on MacDougal Street. It seemed destined that the two would meet. And when they did, on that cold, snow-filled February day in 1961, Zeitzman told Frost he was tired of playing small "basket" clubs where the pay was lousy and the exposure limited to the 10- to 15-minutes it took to pass the small wicker basket around the club. And though Jack Frost couldn't help Bob Zeitzman meet Forrest Guthridge, he came up with a way to keep him on the Row long enough that someone who could might come along.

Jack Frost offered to pay Zeitzman a small stipend if he would agree to an exclusive arrangement at the Hoot. Zeitzman agreed immediately. But there was a catch. Later, Frost would realize there was *always* a catch with Bob. And as much as Jack Frost wanted to facilitate that introduction between Bob Zeitzman and his languishing hero, Jack Frost had no contacts inside the Greystone Park Psychiatric Hospital in which Guthridge was being housed. But the man who worked the door of the Hoot, a well-built, barrel-chested brute with a smile that could charm the skin off a snake, knew a guy who knew a guy. And while it wasn't like Jack Frost to enter into an agreement that was going to eat into his profits, Jack Frost desperately wanted the exclusive on this up-and-coming musician. And so he agreed to concede to the bouncer's seemingly innocuous request: a small cut from the door. It was a simple concession, but it ended up costing Jack Frost a small fortune, not to mention the extremely bad precedent it set.

So while this wasn't the first time Jack Frost and Commissioner Tiresias had been brought together by their mutual interest in the success of Bob Dorian, based on this latest development—the recently revealed fact that Dorian wasn't just dead but had been dead for the past three days—there was a good chance it might be the last. And to say that realization didn't sit well with Jack Frost was an understatement. There were no two ways around it: Jack Frost was apoplectic.

"You want to tell me exactly how is it that a cop and a doctor—a doctor, I might add who's on your dole—missed something that someone completely unfamiliar with the situation caught in less than fifteen seconds?"

"Like I said, he's good. Very observant," Commissioner Tiresias replied. "And he probably isn't deaf, either. So I would suggest you keep your voice down. These walls are paper thin."

"So's the ground you're standing on, Commissioner."

"What's that supposed to mean?"

"It means Johns is your man. You brought him in. He's your play."

"That's right."

"Well, if you ask me, he's getting ready to play us."

"Relax, Frost. Take a deep breath and just relax." It was sage advice. Commissioner Tiresias knew it; he suspected Jack Frost knew it, too. You lose your head, you lose control. You lose control, you lose the game. And though he knew Jack Frost would never concede it, the Commissioner had summed up the situation just as he had summed up Mister Johns—perfectly.

"Now?" Commissioner Tiresias said calmly. "How is Mister Johns going to play us?"

"Didn't you hear what he said? Bob's been dead for three days, maybe more."

"Yes," Commissioner Tiresias replied, a tinge of innuendo in his voice, "about that."

"About what?" Jack Frost snapped.

"The timing is all off on this." Commissioner Tiresias paused. "Three days, that's a long time, don't you think?" Again, the Commissioner paused. "I mean, considering your 'personal relationship' with Dorian and all ..."

"I didn't know," Jack Frost said, cutting to the chase. "Isn't that what you were going to ask me? How could Bob have been dead for three days and I not have known? How could I be his manager and not have spoken with him for three days? That *was* what you were going to ask me, wasn't it?"

"And to think, all these years I've prided myself on my skills as an interrogator," Commissioner Tiresias said, slightly stunned by Jack Frost's candor. "But you seem to be doing just fine grilling yourself without the least bit of heat from me. But since you brought it up, would you like to elaborate on your admission that you 'didn't know.' What exactly didn't you know?"

"I didn't know he'd come back to Elysian Row." It was Jack Frost's turn to move to the window. Pensiveness overcame his otherwise vociferous demeanor. "He had *agreed* to come back," Frost continued, alluding to the conversations he had had with Tommie the Make and Julius the Squeeze. "But I didn't know he was here. I didn't know he'd come back. Last thing Bob said to me before he left was, 'I need a little perspective.'"

"And that was three days ago?"

"That's right."

"So three days ago, Bob tells you he's heading out for a pack of smokes and when he doesn't come back you don't wonder where the hell he went?"

"I was his manager, Commissioner, not his nursemaid."

"'Was' being the operative word there," Commissioner Tiresias said, sticking the knife in. "But that's of no concern to either of us now," the Commissioner continued, waving his hand dismissively in the air as if he were swatting a fly. "We need to focus on the facts."

"And the 'facts' in this case being that Bob's been dead for three days," Jack Frost replied. "Assuming Mister Johns' diagnosis of the situation is even correct," Frost said, hoping to hell it wasn't.

"Again, doesn't matter," Commissioner Tiresias was waving his hand in the air again. This time it appears he *was* actually swatting a fly—the best evidence yet that Bob Dorian had been dead for some time. "Mister Johns' diagnosis can be refuted if it needs to be. Or …"

"Or what?"

"Or embraced to serve our needs."

"Don't you mean *your* needs, Commissioner?"

"I'm getting the distinct sense that you and I are not on the same page, Jack," Commissioner Tiresias said condescendingly. "My needs and your needs are one in the same. The facts may have changed slightly, but the situation hasn't."

"Let's talk about the situation for a moment," Frost said. "Specifically, Mister Johns' assessment of it."

"Very well," the Commissioner said calmly, knowing full well Jack Frost's assessment probably wasn't going to bode too well for him. After all, the Commissioner *had* been the one who'd brought Johns in. "Let's hear your take."

"Mister Johns asserts that Bob's been dead for some time—perhaps as long as three days. Do you believe that appraisal to be accurate?"

"I have no reason to doubt it," Commissioner Tiresias replied.

"So when he identified the murder weapon as a .45 caliber pistol, you trust that to be an accurate assessment?"

"I can only assess what Mister Johns has actually told us."

"Meaning?"

"He never identified the murder weapon as a .45 caliber."

"That's where you're wrong. He said a .45 caliber pistol had been fired into Bob's chest at point-blank range."

"What's your point?" Commissioner Tiresias didn't even try and mask his disdain. He knew exactly what Jack Frost's point was.

"You own a .45 caliber pistol, don't you, Commissioner? You don't need to answer that," Frost continued. "It's a rhetorical question. We both know you own a .45 caliber. In fact, you threatened me with it but an hour ago."

"And I have a right mind to use it this time," Commissioner Tiresias said snidely.

The gall of this guy, Commissioner Tiresias thought to himself. *If Frost doesn't cut the 'Matlock' routine, Bob Dorian isn't going to be the only one with flies buzzing around his head.*

"So he was shot with a .45 caliber pistol," the Commissioner said contemptuously. "Proves nothing. I'm a cop, cops carry guns—"

"So it's just a coincidence, that's what you're saying?" Frost replied, pointing out the faulty logic. "That the gun used to kill Bob is the exact same make and model as the one in your pocket?"

"Some might see it as a coincidence," Commissioner Tiresias said with tempered, even-keeled bravado. Despite his assuredness, however, there was only so much Commissioner Tiresias could protest before he found himself backed into a very tight corner. After all, Jack Frost did have a point. Indeed, Commissioner Tiresias packed a .45 caliber pistol. Right now it was nestled in a leather holster inside his suit jacket, but only an hour ago he *had* used it to threaten Jack Frost. But the Commissioner knew the old axiom that 'the best offense is a good defense' was more than just some pithy saying. That old axiom had gotten Commissioner Tiresias out of more than a jam or two in the past. And a jam was the last thing Commissioner Tiresias wanted right now. It was time to go on the defensive—

"Of course, others—and by that I mean those who aren't jumping to conclusions—those people would know that a .45 is standard issue down at the department. So if you're accusing me of something, Frost, you best come right out and say it. When I found Zeitzman, he was dead."

"I don't doubt that he was."

"Really? Because—and correct me if I misunderstood—didn't you just have me putting a bullet in his chest?"

"I was merely pointing out that you had the means to kill him. Because—and this is where *you* can correct me if I'm wrong—it takes three things to prove murder: means, motive and opportunity. Now, as we've already discussed, the .45 gave you a means. Motive, well, that's a little tougher. We both know you didn't have a reason to kill Bob. I mean, thanks to our little deal, the one where you get half the take at the door, you certainly benefit from his death—we both do— but that came after he was dead. Now as for opportunity ..."

"I already told you, Frost—"

"I'm not accusing you of killing Bob, Commissioner."

"Sure sounds like it to me."

"You *couldn't* have killed him. Like you said, when you found him he *was* dead. According to Mister Johns—and I'd like to have Dr. Reich confirm this—he'd been dead for three days."

"So what are you driving at, Frost?"

"Who found the body?"

"I told you, Dela Croix."

"You're positive?"

"Absolutely. She signed the register when she left the Chelsea."

"And that was this morning?" Frost replied.

"That was this morning," Commissioner Tiresias repeated.

"And who brought the body to the Chelsea?"

"Couple of rail hands—Frost, we've been through all this."

"Let me ask you a question, Commissioner. What are the chances those railroad men are still in town?"

"Slim to none—that was the whole point of bringing Johns in. Have him look for the killer, stir up a little publicity for our little bash, but make sure he doesn't stir up *too* much publicity."

"Control the story by controlling the source—"

"That was the plan, Frost. If you're not on board with the plan, I need to know."

Frost remained silent.

"Rhetorical question, Frost."

"We're never going to track down the railroad hands. You know it, and I know it," Frost said matter-of-factly.

"So you and Johns poke around for a few days, nothing turns up, except perhaps ticket sales, and then it goes in the 'cold case' file."

"The 'cold case' file?"

"Yeah, unsolved, unsettled, unanswered—take your pick. And Zeitzman's in pretty good company, if you ask me. Sam Cooke, Chet Baker, Brian Jones—all died under mysterious circumstances, all bigger in death than they ever were in life. Murder may be the best career move Bobby Zeitzman made since changing his name to Dorian," Commissioner Tiresias said, his malicious sarcasm bordering on the maniacal. "And besides, what makes you think the person who killed Zeitzman isn't halfway to Damascus by now, too?"

"Because whoever did kill Bob spent a lot of time trying to make it look like he'd been killed the night the body was found. That person had means, motive and opportunity—a perfect trifecta. Now I'm not a betting man, but if I had to wager, I'd put my money on the fact that whoever killed Bob is still on Elysian Row. Whoever killed Bob Dorian killed him for some reason *other* than simply wanting to see him dead."

"And what reason would that be?" Commissioner Tiresias said wearily. The Commissioner enjoyed a good little tête-à-tête as much as the next two-bit blackmailer, but clearly the back-and-forth banter with Jack Frost was growing tiresome.

"They wanted to see how we would react to his being dead," Jack Frost said emphatically.

"It's an interesting theory, Frost. But I'm not buying."

"Well, what do you 'buy,' Commissioner?"

"I believe Zeitzman was murdered—that bullet hole in his chest is all I need to buy into that angle—but I think it was a smash and grab. End of story."

"Smash and grab?"

"Zeitzman gets anxious one night," Commissioner Tiresias explained, "goes for a walk down by the railroad tracks. Somebody sees him, tries to rob him, not because they recognize him or anything—you saw the way he was dressed, the guy looked like he was homeless. Anyway, Zeitzman resists, the perp gets carried away, shoots him by accident, maybe on purpose—really doesn't matter—then takes off into the night with whatever he can lift off him. Smash and grab."

Commissioner Tiresias smiled. It was, after all, a pretty good theory. But as good as it was, it was evident from Jack Frost's stone-faced expression that the manager had another idea.

"Wait a minute," Commissioner Tiresias said, the realization dawning on him. "You're not suggesting what I think it is you're suggesting? You think someone he *knew* killed him?"

A moment passed between the two men. That was exactly what Frost was suggesting. "You'd be surprised what friends are capable of," Frost replied, "especially when you don't really know who your friends are."

"Even if Zeitzman has been dead for a few days, even if the person who killed him is still at large, even if it's exactly as you suspect it to be, you go down this road you're asking for nothing but trouble."

Frost remained stone-faced.

"Listen to yourself, Frost." Clearly, Commissioner Tiresias was growing concerned, "I mean it's one thing to look for a couple of rail hands you ain't never gonna find. It's entirely something else when you start stirring up the past."

"Is that so?" Jack Frost replied.

"Yes, that's so," the Commissioner said flatly. "You see, the problem with the past is that the past is never as far behind us as we think. Sometimes the past comes back to bite us in the ass."

"I thought the past was supposed to set us free," Frost said unflinchingly.

"You're thinking of 'truth,' Frost. The past and the truth got nothing to do with each other—not on Elysian Row anyway. But you want to unearth a bunch of stuff that's best left buried, that's your prerogative. You just need to know out of the gate that I ain't gonna be there to lend you a helping hand if things get out of control." Jack Frost expected nothing less from his old adversary.

"But look on the bright side," Commissioner Tiresias said, flashing that trademark Cheshire grin for the final time that evening, "if you do end up getting buried, you'll know just the guy to write your obituary. Cause he'll be right there with you."

PART II

▼

Elysian Row

CHAPTER 5

▼

SOPHIA

"Looks like we're going to be partners."

"Looks that way," Frost replied, brushing the fat raindrops off his overcoat as the two men stepped out into the slow, even drizzle.

"That's not going to be a problem is it?" Mister Johns inquired.

Frost didn't respond. Frankly, he didn't have to: Mister Johns could sense Jack Frost's uneasiness a mile away.

"So how long did the two of you know each other anyway?" Johns said, changing his tact. Clearly, Jack Frost wasn't planning on getting too friendly too quickly.

Despite his new partner's reticence, Johns wasn't worried. He knew it was just a matter of time: he'd get what he needed. You don't write close to two hundred obituaries and not learn a few things. And if there was one thing Mister Johns had picked up after a lifetime in the obits business, it was that people love to talk about themselves.

It never failed. Whenever Mister Johns asked the people left behind to say a few words about the dearly departed, those in a position to give the dead some lasting dignity always responded as if *they* were the ones who'd been done in. Grieving widows, spurned exes, and estranged acquaintances, it didn't matter. The conversation was always the same: 'What about me?' All Johns was looking for was a few innocuous details, something to add a little flavor to the facts. Yet whenever he asked, the conversation was always the same: 'Don't you want to know about me? Don't you want to know how *I* feel? After all, *I'm* the one who's alone now.'

It was ironic, really. There are probably three moments in a person's life when they are the sole, focal point of attention: the day they're born, the day they get married and the day they die. And even one's wedding day is suspect. After all, the groom isn't the only one standing at the altar.

So I'll just throw it out there, Mister Johns thought to himself. *Ask the question. See what he says. But I have a sneaking suspicion where the conversation will go. The first thing out of his mouth will be something about himself.*

"I was his manager for 20 years."

"Right," Mister Johns said without missing a beat, "I got that from the Commissioner, so let me rephrase—how *well* did you and Mr. Zeitzman know each other?"

"If I had to categorize our relationship, I'd say it was a professional one."

"Friendly, but not friends," Mister Johns said circumspectly.

"In my line of work, it's best to maintain a certain amount of distance," Frost replied tersely. "Keeps people from casting a suspicious eye."

"In my line of work they call that 'plausible deniability.'"

"Well, call it what you will, but as of this moment you and I are in the *same* line of work, Mister Johns," Jack Frost said, betraying his growing exasperation with both the situation he had found himself in and the partner with whom he had been paired.

"And what line of work would that be, Mr. Frost?"

"Finding out who murdered Bob Dorian," he replied curtly. "So why don't you knock off the Woodward and Bernstein shtick and just tell me what's on your mind."

What was on Mister Johns' mind was that load of bull Jack Frost was attempting to feed him. Frost had said that in his line of work it's best to maintain a certain amount of distance, but Mister Johns suspected the only distance Jack Frost had placed between himself and his former client was there to distract everyone from the real bond that had kept them together for all those years. After all, you don't spend 20 years with someone and not let a little emotion seep in. And Johns knew that whenever someone says 'it's just business' what they really mean is, 'it *was* just business until we let our emotions get in the way.'

One of these guys fucked up, Mister Johns thought to himself. *One of these guys trusted too much. The question is which one? The guy lying face-up on that chaise back at the Chelsea or the guy standing next to me?*

And while Mister Johns had a theory on the subject, it was too early to know for sure. But Mister Johns wasn't worried. Because at the end of the day he knew that all he needed to do was keep the man standing next to him talking. If he did that, Jack Frost would tell him everything he needed to know.

"You say you and Zeitzman weren't close. Maybe you *weren't* friends. But I assume you were friends with many of the people with whom we'll be talking."

"I haven't seen, much less spoken to anyone on Elysian Row in 20 years."

"But you did know them? At one time you were friendly with them?"

"What's your point, Johns—" Frost said, knowing perfectly well what Mister Johns' point was.

"My point, Mr. Frost, is that I shouldn't be—how shall I put this—concerned that you might be influenced by those former friendships?"

"The only issue concerning me right now, Mister Johns, is who killed my former client. And as far as I'm concerned, we're wasting time."

"Let's stop doing that, then."

"So where do we start?"

"We start with the girl."

"The girl?"

"I'm assuming there was a girl …"

"Open the phone book. He had a different girl in every town."

"Then let me narrow it down a bit—did he have one in *this* town?"

"That's your theory? That some broad is behind this whole thing? Surely you can do better than that."

"Mr. Frost, I write obituaries for a living. Trust me, there's always a girl. So humor me."

Jack Frost hadn't been exaggerating when he said Bob had a different girl in every town. And considering Bob Dorian had been to a lot of towns over the years, that added up to a lot of girls. But there's only one 'first true love.' And even though Bob Dorian had spent the last 40 years trying to forget her, Jack Frost suspected her memory was probably with him until the end.

"Yeah."

"Yeah, what?" Mister Johns pressed.

"There was a girl. She wasn't the first, and certainly she wasn't the last. But she was there at the beginning, and frankly I always thought he fell for her the hardest."

"And this girl … she have a name?"

"Sophia."

"All right," Mister Johns said, slapping his hands together with mock joviality, "now we're getting somewhere. This Sophia—she live nearby?"

"You're in luck, Mister Johns," Frost said drolly.

"And how's that?"

"Her house—"

"Yes—"

"You're standing in front of it."

MISTER JOHNS TURNED AND LOOKED in the direction of what appeared to be a tenement housing project. Clearly, there had been a time when this unassuming two-story brownstone had been a grand and glorious structure. That time, however, had come and gone, and the building in front of which they were standing had fallen into complete disrepair. The bricks were discolored, the color of burnt gingerbread. The wooden sashes were cracking at the corners and bubbling at the creases. And the windowpanes, once clear, clean and crisp, were now opaque, clouded with age.

But when Jack Frost looked at the building's edifice, frail and fading, he saw beyond all that. He saw what had at one time been a shining, glistening example of elegance, sophistication and style. But when Mister Johns peered up at the old, decrepit structure that scraped the gray, rain-soaked sky, he saw something else entirely. For Mister Johns, there was no difference between this two-story brownstone and every other tenement house on Elysian Row.

Of course, this particular brownstone *was* different. Because behind those heavy oak doors, somewhere inside that dark, seemingly deserted row house, was the one person who could help them understand the man who had been despised so much that someone had decided to put a bullet in his chest.

There was just enough light making its way through the seemingly impenetrable windowpane embedded in the thick, oak front door for the men to make out a figure standing behind the glass. The figure was a thin, lanky silhouetted profile that looked like it had been sculpted by Amedeo Modigliani himself. And the profile was of a woman; and the woman was clearly watching them.

"So how'd it end?" Mister Johns said as he pulled the heavy, wrought iron gate back and stepped onto a cobblestone path.

"An excellent question, Johns," Frost replied, "but I'd suggest you hold off on asking that one until the end."

They hadn't even taken their second step toward the landing that jettisoned out from the building's façade when a series of padlocks snapped and popped and unfastened. Then the front door flew open and a woman with jet-black hair and skin the color of Arabian sand burst through the doorway and walked quickly toward them. "Here," she said, handing a large, plastic trash bag to Mister Johns. "It'll save you the hassle of having to climb over the fence."

Mister Johns stared at the woman … then at Jack Frost … then back at the woman again. He looked like a guy who'd just been caught jaywalking by a cop hell-bent on meeting his daily ticket quota.

"I think there's some confusion," Mister Johns said, clearly a little confused himself.

"I doubt it," the dark-haired woman said assuredly. "You all come for the same thing. Why you think rummaging through my garbage is going to help you find it is beyond me, but I just planted some flowers in the garden and that fence won't support the two of you." And without another moment's hesitation, she turned and headed back up the stone path toward the open door.

"We just have a few questions," Mister Johns called out, still holding the garbage bag.

"I'm sure you do," she said over her shoulder without breaking stride. She had almost reached the door, when suddenly Frost said something, or more accurately quoted something he had heard Bob recite to her a long time ago—

"'And amongst them a lady, a willow-wand, a thirsty gazelle, perfect in beauty and grace and amorous languor.'"

The words stopped her cold.

"Wait a minute, how did you …" she slowly turned to face the man who had called out to her.

"He once told me meeting you was like stepping into the pages of *1001 Arabian Nights*—that you had a smile as bright as a streetlight."

"Frost? Jack Frost?"

"Hi, Sophia, it's been a long time."

"It has," she said, moving back down the pathway toward the two men. "It's been a long time, indeed."

He expected her to say more. After all, the two of them hadn't seen or spoken to each other in close to 20 years. But it hardly took Jack Frost by surprise that the dark-haired woman was a tad tongue-tied.

An apparition could have just as easily appeared on her porch and it would have elicited the same reaction. So when she continued to stare at him without saying a word, Jack Frost filled the 20-year space between them, "Sophia, this is Mister Johns. Johns this is Sophia."

"Jack Frost—well, I'll ... be ... damned ..." she replied as she allowed the image of her lover's former manager to register. "So what brings you back to Elysian Row?" Her voice was cautious and non-committal.

"Like Mister Johns said—we need to ask you a couple of questions."

Perhaps it was the tenor of Jack Frost's voice. Perhaps it was the sparseness of his words. Or maybe it was the fact that an old friend she hadn't seen in 20 years had just shown up on her doorstep accompanied by a man dressed as if he'd just fallen out of a 1940s film noir double feature. But the dark-haired woman knew. She may not have known exactly why Jack Frost had come back, but she knew who was behind it.

"This is about Bob, isn't it?" she asked knowingly. And when neither man said a word, she knew she was right. "Come on inside," she said shaking her head from one side to the next. "I'll fix us some tea." As instructed, Jack Frost and Mister Johns ascended the landing stairs and followed her into the brownstone.

Once inside, they stopped in the foyer long enough to allow her to refasten the arsenal of deadbolts, locks and door chains she had amassed over the years to keep the world out and herself in. "Like I said," she repeated, sliding the final lock in place, "we get a lot of kooks out here."

"We?" Frost inquired.

"I remarried."

The information was clearly news to Frost, though he did his best to hide it. "Congratulations," he covered. "When was this?"

"A few years ago. And don't act so surprised," she chuckled to herself as she continued to pad down the long, oak-paneled hallway. "We don't *all* live in the past here on Elysian Row. Some of us have managed to move on with our lives." She was halfway down the hall now. "Make yourself comfortable," she said, motioning toward a doorway opening into the room in which she wanted them to wait. "I'll be back in a minute with some tea and whatever else I can scrounge up."

The two men stepped out of the foyer and into a room—a library they now realized. It was like stepping into another world. The shelves were lined with thousands of books of all descriptions. Classic literature, contemporary novels, history books, art books, reference books: it was as if truly *every* book ever written was somewhere on these shelves.

Apparently, Jack Frost wasn't the only one impressed by the books she had amassed. Frost watched as Mister Johns gingerly ran his finger down the spine of a leather-bound collection of poems by Rimbaud.

"Tell me about her," Johns said in a hushed, almost reverential tone. And for a brief moment, Jack Frost wasn't sure if the reverence in Mister Johns' voice was for the artist whose words filled those pages, or for the woman who shared the affinity Johns also seemed to possess for the renowned 19th century French poet.

"She was an artist," Frost said. "Brecht, Byron, Baudelaire—all the writers Bob was compared to later in his career—she introduced him to every one of them." And judging from the thousands of books that filled this cavernous space, the introductions she had made were vast.

Jack Frost continued to eye the shelves enviously. Certainly, it was a library to be envied. *The Lonely Life*, the forlorn 1962 autobiography by Bette Davis in which she famously wrote, 'I do not regret one professional enemy I have made. Any actor who doesn't dare to make an enemy should get out of the business,' was a collector's item to be sure. Bette Davis may not have regretted making enemies. Apparently her adversaries didn't share the sentiment: the book was out of print the same year it was published.

The next book on the shelf that caught Frost's eye was Charles Perrault's *La Cenerentola*, nestled between two plays by a fairly well-known English playwright from the 16th century. The first play by the Bard with a penchant for iambic pentameter was about a couple kept apart by their rivaling families; the second play was about a Danish prince whose madness results in the suicide of his lover, who slowly submerges herself beside a babbling brook. Unlike his English contemporary, however, Perrault's classic retelling of unjust oppression concludes on a happier, more upbeat note when a downtrodden chambermaid is transformed into a princess. It was a fitting finale, a fairy-tale ending really. But then again if the shoe fits ...

Frost continued to move methodically around the edge of the library, and as he did it became increasingly evident that Sophia not only possessed an affinity for 16th century French literature, but she also exhibited a real empathy for those literary figures who had found themselves mistreated simply because they had been misunderstood. Victor Hugo's tale of a misshapen bell ringer whose back may be eternally bent but soul is far from broken, and Gaston Leoux's account of a physically deformed genius who haunts the Opéra Garnier so he can mentor a beautiful soprano were certainly two of the most enduring arguments for compassion ever written. But it was the book Frost came across next that truly caught his eye.

It was a simple paperback that could have been purchased—probably *had* been purchased—at the cut-out bin of some discount bookstore. It did not have ornate, faux gold lettering embossed on a rigid, upright leather-bound spine. In fact, the spine—if you could even call it a spine—was broken, and cracked and frayed at the edges. And though it seemed out of place—a store-bought book sitting next to some of the most pristine, well-preserved books Jack Frost had ever seen—this book was the most enduring classic of them all.

Every great library has, or should have, a Bible. And while most people will proudly tell you it sits up there on the shelves alongside the other "classics," most Bibles are rarely taken down, opened up and read. This Bible was different. It was dogged and earmarked. It hadn't just been read: it had been *consumed.*

It has been said that if all the existing copies of the Bible were destroyed, this 'great book' could still be reassembled word for word because literally every word found in the Bible has been quoted at one time or another somewhere else. But it isn't just the language of this book that has inspired generation after generation. It's the stories. These stories, like the moniker bestowed on the book itself, are great. The Bible isn't just 'the greatest story ever told,' the Bible contains enough anecdotes to inspire the imagination of even the greatest of writers.

There's the story of sibling rivalry that ends in murder in a desolate field east of Eden; the story about a good man who is attacked, robbed and left to die by the side of a road, only to be redeemed by another's saving grace; and, of course, there is the story of the man with whom God makes a covenant that will allow him to restore integrity not only to his family but goodness to the world after the deluge destroys it.

And as Jack Frost continued to canvass the vast, seemingly endless shelves, he noticed that in addition to the literature of a bygone era there were also some titles from contemporary authors as well: a complete three-volume set of Ezra Pound's, *The Cantos*, a signed copy of T.S. Eliot's, *The Wasteland*, Jack Kerouac's, *Desolation Angels*, a first edition of John Steinbeck's, *Cannery Row*. Of course, the inclusion of these books in her expansive collection hardly took Jack Frost by surprise. They were, after all, not only the works of writers of Sophia's generation; they were some of the most important cultural touchstones of the 20th century.

But as Jack Frost continued to peruse those same shelves, he didn't quite know what to make of "Does the Inertia of a Body Depend Upon Its Energy Content?" in which a 26-year-old German patent examiner explained the relative equivalence of matter and energy. Nor was he sure why the story of a swashbuckling robber baron from the 13th century, whose immensely popular mantra was 'to steal from the rich and give to the poor,' had been positioned next to a book chronicling the building of the Canguro Verde, aka 'The Calypso' as the massive ocean liner came to be known. The Calypso may have caught fire, but it was the Titanic that took over 1,500 people to an ice-watery grave. *If you were going to include a book that recounted a maritime disaster why the Canguro Verde?* Jack Frost thought to himself. *It just seems out of place.* So, too, did the placement of an account of 1st century Rome in which Nero famously fiddles next to a biography of Casanova. And what was up with that the thick tome telling the tales of the seafaring Neptune? Shouldn't that have been next to the book on the Calypso disaster? Instead it was next to an instructional manual offering advice on the oddest activity Jack Frost had ever heard: how to dissect and eat the guts of dead birds.

And as Jack Frost took a final moment to reflect on the thousands of tomes that encased the room, a nagging question persisted: 'Where did a healthy interest in accumulating knowledge end and insatiable self-indulgence begin?' And then Jack Frost realized he had been looking at this vast collection the wrong way. These books may have been assembled one by one, piece by piece, but now that they had been brought together, the parts comprised a whole. Taken apart, they didn't make sense; but together the collection told a story that made all the sense in the world. And if it is true what they say, that perusing a person's bookshelves is like peeking into their mind, then the books on these shelves were a window into the complexity of the woman who had collected them. And judging from the vast cultural acumen of the man with whom she had shared them, Bob Dorian had read them all.

"How does someone even *get* all these books in the first place?" Johns said, turning to face Jack Frost.

"It helps if you come from a family that instills the importance of the arts in you at a young age."

"And she came from a family like that?"

"You see that picture over there?" Frost said, pointing to an oil portrait hanging on the wall at the far end of the library. As instructed, Mr. Johns glanced in the direction of the painting. "Her uncle."

"And her parents? What's the story there?"

"Political activists. Perhaps a little *too* political some would say."

"Meaning?"

"Meaning they got friendly with a Soviet spy in the 1950s. Got them in a lot of hot water, but she inherited the political bug from them. Some attribute Dorian's penchant for politics to her."

"So what you're saying is that she had an impact on him?" Johns said, stating the obvious.

"Look around you, Mister Johns," Frost motioned. "How could you not be influenced by all this?"

"So what's she do now? Aside from locking herself away in this place, and accosting would-be fans of her former boyfriend? God knows how long it's going to take me to get this smell out," Mister Johns said, holding his hands up to his nose and taking a brief, albeit pungent whiff of that morning's garbage.

Suddenly, both men heard the sound of footsteps growing closer. Rather than risk the embarrassment of having to explain why they were talking behind her back, they opted to take a seat as they had been instructed.

"I really should apologize," she said sheepishly as she entered the room, and in a single, fluid motion placed the tray on the table, "about the way I behaved when I first saw you. Bob and I haven't been together for over 40 years, but like I said you'd be amazed at the nutjobs who still come around. Just last week I had a guy who said he actually saw Bob's face in some three-week-old coffee grinds."

"No apology necessary, Mrs.—"

"Sophia is fine, Mister Johns. Any friend of Jack's is a friend of mine."

She lifted the top of a cookie tin, and elevated the container at an angle. Both men took one of the sugary confections from the tin and placed it next to their teacups.

They were being polite. Neither of them actually intended to eat the cookies. Judging from the look of that beat up old tin from which she had ceremoniously plucked them, they couldn't help but think that perhaps those cookies might have been procured around the same time as many of the books they had just been admiring.

"So you got remarried …" Frost inquired, intentionally letting the sentence trail off.

"And I wish he were here. I'd love for you to meet him. But he's out of town on business."

"Maybe next time," Frost replied.

"Right, 20 years. I'll be sure to pencil you in. So …" She started to bring the cup to her lips, but stopped short. She placed the cup back on the table and took a deep, distinctly dramatic breath, "I know I'm going to probably regret asking this, but how is he?"

Frost and Johns exchanged a glance. "He's dead, Sophia."

In an odd way, Jack Frost suspected Sophia would be happy to hear that there was no chance Bob would ever be able to ingratiate himself back into her life. The reappearance of Bob Dorian on Elysian Row, strike that—the mere knowledge that he was back on Elysian Row—that knowledge alone could disrupt everything she had done to put his memory behind her. But therein lay the rub, to quote that English playwright from the 16th century.

Hell, Jack Frost thought to himself, *no need to quote Shakespeare. Commissioner Tiresias said it just was well as the old Bard himself, 'The problem with the past is that the past is never as far behind us as we think. Sometimes the past comes back to bite us in the ass.'*

And while Jack Frost hoped that Sophia would be relieved to hear that Bob Dorian was out of her life forever, he suspected the past had a stronger grip on her than that.

"What?" she sputtered disbelievingly.

It turns out Jack Frost was right. The realization that her former lover, a man who had caused her so much heartache and pain, was dead still impacted her profoundly.

"They found him last night down by the tracks. Mister Johns and I are trying to piece it together."

"Piece what together?" Sophia said, waiting for the other shoe to drop.

"We think he was murdered." *Plop.*

"But … but who would want to kill him?"

"That's what we wanted to talk to you about," Mister Johns interjected.

Sophia's eyes darted between the two men. She may have misread them as fans at the outset. She did not, however, misread the innuendo in Mister Johns' voice.

"Don't worry, you're not a suspect," Mister Johns said, perhaps a bit too quickly. "This is all just routine. We're just talking to the people who knew him and Mr. Frost here says that the two of you were close?"

"Close? Is that what you said, Jack, that we were 'close'?"

It was at that precise moment that Jack Frost realized how poorly he had prepared Mister Johns for this meeting. Sure, he had told Johns that Dorian and Sophia were lovers. That Sophia was, in fact, Bob Dorian's first real love. And he had been able to squeeze in a little back-story about the family. That impromptu walk through the library had helped him cover a lot of ground quickly. What he had not done, however, was explain the extent of the pain and suffering that Bob Dorian had inflicted not just on Sophia, but the mental anguish he had caused her entire family.

"I'm not sure of the exact phraseology, Sophia," Jack Frost said quickly, realizing that everything he had inadvertently held back from Mister Johns was about to be revealed in full detail.

"Well, I have news for you, Mister Johns, Bob and I were a little more than 'close.' Now I'm not sure what the correct phraseology is for giving up your dreams, your hopes, your aspirations so that someone else can realize theirs, but I'm pretty sure the word is a little stronger than 'close.'"

"Sophia, listen to me—" Frost pleaded.

"No, *you* listen to me, Jack. He may not know what I've been through," she said, dismissively waving her hand in the direction of Mister Johns, "but you do. Of all people, you would know! And to think, I was actually happy to see you."

She rose from the chair and started for the door. She didn't say anything. She didn't have to. The implication was clear: *Get the hell out.*

Jack Frost slowly rose from the chair, and clearly grasping the unspoken explicative moved toward the door. Taking Frost's lead, Mister Johns also rose from his chair. But instead of following Frost into the hallway, Mister Johns paused to brush a small piece of lint off his trouser leg. It was obvious he was stalling, but he hoped that his brief moment of hesitation would give Sophia enough time to reconsider and ask them to stay.

Sophia did not reconsider. Instead, she maneuvered around the two men, walked straight to the front door, unfastened the bolts and flung the door open. And just like that, the men they were back on out on the street.

"Do you think this has been easy on me?" Frost said, spinning around on the landing.

"Excuse me?" Sophia sputtered.

"I said, do you think this has been easy on me?" Jack Frost repeated.

It seems Jack Frost was doing a little stalling of his own. And while his tactic was different from that of Mister Johns', their objectives were identical: keep this woman engaged. *And if compassion won't work,* Frost thought to himself, *it looks like I might just have to run the risk of pissing her off completely.*

"You may have spent the last 40 years trying to erase the affection he felt for you. Well, I've spent the last 20 years trying to earn it. So you see, Sophia, we really aren't so different. We both fell under his spell." Frost eyed Sophia's fingers as they wrapped themselves back around the deadbolt lock like a vise. "Please, this will only take a few minutes." The fingers paused.

Frost held his breath and waited to see what she was going to do next. Judging from the fact she was no longer gripping the deadbolt between her fingers, it looked like his strategy might just have worked.

"Did you guys bring something to write with?"

"Of course," Mister Johns said, quickly retrieving a small, spiral notebook from the left breast pocket of his jacket.

"Well, I suggest you get it out. Because if you want to know what really happened, it's going to take a little longer than a few minutes."

And in that instant she made a decision. She decided to tell the tale of a dead man.

"APRIL 5, 1961 ..."

"You remember the date?"

Clearly Mister Johns was more than a little suspicious of the relative ease by which she was able to recall the exact date she and Bob had met, "I mean it was over 40 years ago?"

"One of the benefits of being associated with someone about whom close to five hundred books have been written—helps you to fill in the blanks. We met in April, but we didn't start dating for another three months or so. June, I think."

"So what attracted you to him?"

"Bobby was like a sponge," she said as she fingered through the tin, finally finding the cookie she was looking for. She popped the sugar-coated confection into her mouth. "All he had to do was experience something one time and he had it all figured out. He could listen to an old Bobby Goldsboro song and play it back note-for-note. Or read a book, close the cover, then quote the passage line-for-line."

"So you're saying he had a good memory," Mister Johns attempted to clarify.

"He had a lot more than that, Mister Johns." Sophia smiled. Whether she was remembering a time in general or a specific moment in particular there was no way of knowing for sure. But it was evident she was remembering not just a moment, but a man as well. And clearly, she had loved them both. "He had a talent, and his real talent was how he could take the essence of what he had just heard or seen and put his own spin on it so you thought you were experiencing it for the first time. He got started with books and records—but people, it was with people that he perfected the art of boiling something down to its pure essence. But to answer your question—what it was that attracted me to Bob? Frankly, I think I just wanted to clean him up."

Judging from the fact Mister Johns had neither written a word in his notebook, nor come up with some witty repartee, he was clearly unsure exactly what that meant.

"When I first met Bobby, he was so scraggly and disheveled," Sophia elaborated. "Later, I think I fell for him. But at first, all I wanted to do was take care of him. Truth is I probably wanted someone to take care of me, too."

"What do you mean?"

"My father died right around the time Bobby showed up on the scene. And after Dad died, there was just my mom, my sister and me. We were tight, the three of us."

"So I assume they approved of him?"

"My sister didn't like the fact he was borrowing more records than he was returning, but she never stood in the way. She knew how talented he was."

"And your mother—"

"Never a big fan," she said. The sarcasm was unmistakable. "Even in the beginning she had her suspicions. 'That boy tells nothing but lies,' she'd tell anyone who would listen."

"Well, did he—"

"Did he what?"

"Lie."

Sophia glanced over at Jack Frost. It was all she could do to maintain a straight face. "I'm assuming I'm the first person you've talked to."

And hopefully the last, Mister Johns thought to himself. But Johns knew that wasn't going to happen. Not unless Sophia just came out and confessed to murdering her former lover in a moment of uncontrollable, irrepressible rage. Of course that would be difficult since she hadn't seen him in 40 years. No, the purpose of this impromptu meeting wasn't to pin a murder on anyone. The objective of this little get-together, as Jack Frost had explained, was more to give Mister Johns a little background on Bob Dorian so they could find the person who *did* pull that trigger.

"I don't think he spoke one true sentence in his life, Mister Johns," Sophia said, completing her own thought. "Not in the way we define truth anyway. When most people want to get to the bottom of something, facts are important. They assemble them, pull them together, study them. But for Raz—"

"Raz?" Mister Johns interrupted.

"His initials—R. A. Z.—I used to call him by his initials."

"I see," Johns said. And while Mister Johns didn't let his reply betray his true feelings, the truth was that he had arrived at the same place as Jack Frost in terms of the direction this conversation was going. *All this cat-and-mouse shit. Half answers, partial disclosures, pieces of a puzzle trickling down like some Chinese water torture. Why doesn't this woman just give a straight answer and be done with it? 'I loved the guy once, he screwed me over. I'd have killed him if I'd had the chance. We all would have.'* But Mister Johns didn't say these things. Instead, he diligently wrote the letters, 'R-A-Z,' in his notebook.

"Anyway, for Raz," Sophia continued, "the truth wasn't a set of facts. He had no respect for facts—facts were only good to him if they helped to advance the 'truth' he was trying to put forth."

"And when they weren't?"

"He lied," Sophia replied. "Do you remember the WNYC interview in 1961?" she said, turning her attention to Frost.

"Oh yeah."

"What happened at WNYC?" Mister Johns said, raising his pencil like an insect raising his antennae. *At last some facts, something that can be verified and isn't contingent on speculation and supposition.*

"Raz is supposed to play a concert at the Town Hall in ... was it October?"

"November—" Frost corrected.

For Christ's sake, at least get the facts right, Johns mused to himself.

"That's right—it was right around Thanksgiving. So anyway," Sophia turned her attention back on Mister Johns, "Raz gets this interview on WNYC to promote the show. Now WNYC was a major station in the New York market. Getting that spot was a major coup. The Town Hall show was going to be his 'coming out' party so to speak. So the interviewer asks him where he's from, where he gets his ideas—your typical stock interview fare. And what does he do? He tells the guy he was raised in Dillon, Montana, raced motorcycles across the Utah salt flats, was a farmhand in Kansas, sung in carnivals from the age of 14 and—and this was the topper ..." she said, relishing the brashness of this last part, "Bob tells the guy he's an orphan."

"I'd forgotten about that," Frost said with a chuckle, clearly relishing it, too. "It took him years to shake that one about his parents being dead."

"So none of that was true?"

"Not one word."

"Well, I could see how your mother might have been wary about him. Guy sounds like a real schizo."

"It's to be expected, I imagine. Parents are always concerned about a young man's intentions. But what my mom and sister never quite got was that it was *because* of his lies—because he discarded the facts if they got in the way of the truth and not the other way around—*that* was what made him a great artist."

It got you to go to bed with him at least, Mister Johns thought to himself.

"You said your sister instantly knew how talented he was," Mister Johns said aloud. "When did you realize?"

"Probably after the article. There was this guy over at The *Times*— *New York Times,*" she clarified. "He was a reporter—art critic, I think—anyway, he had written this story about Raz not too long after he got to the city. Really was in his corner. Rumor had it that Columbia was on the fence. Then this article comes out—Bob's in the studio in less than a month."

"Must have been some article."

"Did everything but anoint him as the Second Coming."

"Sounds like heady stuff."

"Oh, it definitely went to his head. Later he always managed to portray himself as being above the media fray, not influenced by the press, insolated from the critics."

"Not giving a damn," Johns summed up.

"Well, he gave a damn back then. He cared. It mattered. Now, I don't want to suggest he coddled the press—even the critic at The *Times*, who was his biggest advocate—he handled him with kid gloves. But he knew how to use the press. First shot out of the gun and he knew how to harness the press. Turned it into a weapon in his favor. That review was his magic bullet and he knew it, and he made everyone else know it, too. I think he bought 20 pounds of newspapers the day that article came out. Then he cut out the headline and proceeded to show it to anyone who would look at it. If he could have, he probably would have stapled them to his chest."

"So it was this flattering article, not so much the album that started to change things?"

"I suppose. But something did change after the first album. You see, when I first met Raz, he was so young, so innocent. Like I said earlier, I just wanted to take him in and clean him up. I don't know how to explain it. He just had this incorruptibility about him. It was like ... like ..."

"Like an aura?" Mister Johns said, filling in the blank. *For Pete's sake, let's move this along. The guy had you and everyone else 'hook, line and sinker.' The word you are looking for is 'aura.'*

"Exactly. In those early days, that's exactly what it was—an aura. But after the first album, things started to change. He started to change. It was as if he had traded that aura of innocence in for some sort of protective armor. And that powerful force that had once attracted me to him became the very thing that pushed me away."

"I had no idea the change took place so early," Frost said.

"Well, by the time you started managing him, he was completely walled off. But there was a time when he wasn't so guarded. You see, most people live with the hope that tomorrow will bring a better day, you know. In '61, '62, Raz had that hope. He embodied that hope, that dream, if you will. I think that's why the folkies were drawn to him, why I was drawn to him. But as his fame began to grow, a darkness started creeping in. By '64, whatever hope had once burned bright inside him had been completely snuffed out."

"It's ironic, don't you think?" Mister Johns said, giving voice to some of the inner monologue that was starting to distract him from the job at hand.

"What's that?"

"He was heralded as a 'voice of the youth generation' and yet from what you're telling me, he cut himself off from everyone when he was just a kid himself."

"I was the closest person to him, and even I couldn't get in."

"So what happened?"

"I left. I moved out in June. Went to Italy."

"So you broke up with him?"

"Why is it that men always think when a woman leaves she's breaking up? It's not always that black and white. Relationships, Mister Johns, especially a relationship as complicated as ours had become, are often best defined in the gray areas. I needed time."

"So the parting was amicable?"

"There wouldn't have been a second album if it had been amicable. No, Mister Johns, it most definitely was *not* amicable."

"So he was upset?"

"You could say that," Sophia said, her staccato reply dripping with sarcasm. "I hadn't even been in Umbria a week when I got a letter from my sister telling me how Bob was moping around the Village, carrying his guitar over sloped shoulders, complaining about how he'd been abandoned at the most important point in his life."

"Certainly your sister saw through that."

"Oh, I'm certain she did. And don't think he didn't start to turn on her, too, when he realized she wasn't falling for his 'man of constant sorrow' shtick."

"So did he write you letters?"

"Did he write me letters?" she asked rhetorically. "He wrote some of the most beautiful letters you've ever read. I've never read anything quite like them before or since. He once told me all he wanted to do was to live like a poet and die like a poet. I'm not one prone to hyperbole, but those letters were on par with the best Shakespearean sonnet."

"Sounds like he was still in love with you."

"You got it half right, Mister Johns. He was in love—in love with the concept of love. Me? He detested me. He really did think I'd abandoned him."

"How can you be so sure?"

"Because from the first day he set foot in Times Square he'd been the 'darling of the Left.' The Left had a lot riding on him, and they weren't about to let him fall. So when they saw how hurt he was after I left, they rallied around him."

"But *you* eventually rallied around him, did you not?"

"That album cover is one of the biggest regrets of my life," she said, anticipating what was coming next. Those who knew the history between Sophia and Bob knew that Sophia had always been reticent to accept her place in that history. Frost wasn't, however, about to let her brush the past aside so easily—

"Sophia, how can you say that?" Frost asked incredulously. "That photo of you and Bob walking hand in hand wrapped in each other's arms is one of the most iconoclastic pictures of the '60s. Certainly it's one of the most memorable album covers of the last four decades," Frost asserted.

"Which is exactly how many years of unwanted attention it's brought me. Our entire relationship. It's all there. For Christ's sake, all you had to do was look at the cover to know who the songs were about."

"Sophia, I know the subject matter of those songs was difficult," Frost pressed. He wasn't about to let Sophia get away with that old 'I was just a blimp on the screen' defense that was so popular with Bob's former acquaintances after they'd been burned by him. And while Jack Frost wasn't going to go as far as to hold Sophia's feet to the fire, clearly he wasn't going to let her off scot-free, either. "But they were necessary—the songs, that is. And your relationship with him, as pained as it was, it was necessary, too. He was changing, you helped him change."

"And how many songs did he write about *you?*"

"Sophia—" Frost had only been trying to pay her a complement. He now realized he'd gone too far.

"How many?" she seethed.

"None," Frost said solemnly, sounding like a kid who'd just gotten his hand caught in the cookie jar. Frost reached down, picked up the putrid confection from the lip of the coffee saucer and shoved it in his mouth.

Good idea, Mister Johns thought to himself. *Maybe that will take away the taste of the foot you just firmly lodged in there.*

"None that you are aware of," she replied. "And here I was trying to help you, Jack. I welcome you in my home, open my heart to you, and this is the shit I have to take! You think Bob just wrote songs about *me?* Well, he didn't. He took notes. He took notes on us all. And whether you're willing to admit it, he probably wrote a few songs about you."

"I doubt that, Sophia," Frost said dismissively.

"None that were as transparent as the ones he wrote about me. But I suspect as you snoop around, as you talk to people over the next few days, you mark my words—you are going to find out he used you. He used you the same way he used everyone he ever met. In fact, he's probably using you now, and by the time you figure out how he's doing it, it will be too late. Just like it was too late for me."

Mister Johns reached into his pocket and took out a red handkerchief. He handed the handkerchief to Sophia.

"And here I thought I was so special," she said as she brought the handkerchief to her eyes. "I guess in the end, I was no different from the rest of them. I gave him my heart, all I wanted in return was a little part of his soul."

And just like that, she took the dark out of the nighttime, and in that moment the thing that had been welling up inside her all those years—everything she had spent a lifetime vowing not to look back on—was illuminated for all to see.

"SHE'S STILL IN LOVE with him," Mister Johns said as they retraced their footsteps back along the Row toward the Chelsea Hotel.

"She may have loved him once." Jack Frost wasn't convinced. "But that was 40 years ago."

"Did you see the way she broke down? She cried like a little girl."

"That's just like a woman, Johns. Women are emotional. Women cry."

"There was a lot a pain in those tears."

"Of course, there was a lot of pain. He broke her heart."

"Judging from the way she talked about him at the end, he did more than that."

"Johns, she's married now, has a kid, a life. I'm not saying their relationship wasn't tempestuous, perhaps even torrid. But I can assure you she's moved on."

"Then explain the ring."

"What ring?"

"The Egyptian ring she wears on her right index finger."

"I didn't see any ring."

"That's because she wasn't wearing it."

"I thought you said ..."

"I said she *wears* it. I didn't say she *was* wearing it."

"I'm not following you, Johns."

"It was on the coffee table, next to the sofa. She had taken it off just before she sat down to talk to us. That's how I know she wears it on her right index finger. The indention on the finger was fresh."

"And the fact that it was an Egyptian ring?"

"I don't know if it's important yet or not. And frankly, I'm not sure the ring is from Egypt at all. But I do know it's from a Middle Eastern country."

Okay, he's observant, Jack Frost thought to himself, *very observant. I'll give him that. Even before she spoke, he saw that ring. But the make and model?*

"How do you know that?" Frost asked. "Where the ring came from?"

"Something *you* said, actually. When we first arrived you quoted a passage from *1001 Arabian Nights.* 'The Sweep and the Noble Lady,' I believe."

"You've read 'Sweep and the Noble Lady'?" Frost inquired dubiously.

"I work in a morgue, Frost. Lots of time on my hands. Got a guy over at the library who sends me stuff to help while it away." Mister Johns shrugged his shoulders noncommittally. "Some of it's pretty obscure—what can I say?"

And though *1001Arabian Nights* was a rather obscure piece of literature to come across, much less take enough interest in that you would actually read it, Mister Johns was nothing if not interested in the obscure. And 18th century literature seemed to be his bailiwick. His curiosity in the collection of Rimbaud poetry in Sophia's library was testament to that.

"Well, Bob always described her beauty as being akin to an Arabian princess," Frost said, explaining the significance of the line and why he'd cited it. "I thought quoting her favorite story might be the fastest way to cut through the clutter. Clearly, she wasn't going to let us in."

"Considering the fact that she thought we were deranged fans, you're probably right. I imagine inviting us into her home wasn't at the top of her list," Mister Johns concurred in a dry, monotone voice.

This wasn't the first time Mister Johns had demonstrated his proclivity for sarcasm. Frost had noticed an occasional, unassuming cynicism in Mister Johns' delivery that sometimes made it difficult to tell whether he was being serious or facetious. This was one of those occasions. Though given a choice between the two, Frost assumed the latter. Johns' comment about them not being on the top of her list of people to see was very tongue in cheek. But as for his power of observation, the guy had a gift. A ring, a gold ring no less, sitting on a table right there in front of him and he didn't see it.

That's pretty good, Frost thought to himself. *Talk about obsessive-compulsive. No wonder the guy's wound like a top.*

"Okay, so she was wearing a ring and takes it off when we get there," Frost said, assembling the pieces of a puzzle he felt certain Mister Johns had already started to put together. "But how does this ring give us something to go on? A ring's a ring, right?"

"Well, there was an inscription on the inside of the ring. Now, I don't know what it said since it was written in Arabic. These three things I do know, however. One, I know he gave the ring to her. His initials R-A-Z are just after the inscription. Two, I know the date he gave it to her. March 12, 1964. That, too, is engraved on the inside of the ring. And finally, because of the crease on her right index finger, I know she still wears it after 40 years. Now, I ask you, Frost—does that sound like a woman who's completely moved on with her life?"

Frost didn't answer. He knew it wasn't a question.

"It sounds to me like a woman who is still in love with, or at the very least still thinks about the man who broke her heart 40 years ago."

"Well, Sophia didn't kill him, if that's what you're implying."

"It's too early to rule anyone out just yet. But chances are you're correct. But I wouldn't rule out her animosity toward him."

"You might have a point there," Frost conceded. "That little tirade at the end—I don't think I've ever seen her so beside herself."

"Love and hate often run hand in hand. And as we've just established, she still cares for him deeply."

"It's a shame. They really were a beautiful couple."

"Don't get all weepy, Frost, it would never have worked out."

"Why do you say that?"

"Something she said. When she was talking about how he started to change after she met him."

"What was that?"

"She said when she first met him he was filled with hope. But that as his fame began to grow, things began to change." Mister Johns pulled out his notebook and read from the pages, "'But by 1964, whatever hope had once burned bright inside him had been completely snuffed out.'" Mister Johns closed the notebook, then slid it back into his pocket. "So my question to you," he continued, "is what happened in 1964? Maybe he met someone who might have had a big influence on him—another woman perhaps?"

"Like I told you, there were lots of women. But—" Frost let the conjunction dangle a moment before continuing, "there was a guy. One of his early 'handlers' if you will. He and Bob were close. Bob hired him to be his road manager on a trip they took together in February of '64. Ended up staying with him for close to 35 years."

"You know how to get in touch with this guy?"

"Sure. He lives just a few blocks away. Used to anyway—"

"Sounds like someone we ought to talk to—"

"Setting it up isn't a problem. Getting him to talk might be a bit more difficult. Mr. Tremolo isn't much of a conversationalist."

"You let me handle this 'Tremolo.'"

"You care to clue me in on what you're planning to do?"

"Just going to rattle him a little bit—see if he'll play us a tune."

CHAPTER 6

▼

MR. TREMOLO

The man known around the Row as 'Tremolo' knew Robert Zeitzman better than just about anyone. He had been his friend, his confident, his companion. He had been the gatekeeper to the rock star's private, paranoid world for longer than anyone, including himself, cared to remember. And now, if things went the way Mister Johns hoped, he was going to give them a glimpse into that motorpsycho nightmare world of the man to whom he had dedicated the better part of his life.

"Gentlemen—" he said, lifting a long, lumbering arm as he motioned for them to enter the foyer. The man stepped back. The door swung open.

What's with all this cloak-and-dagger crap? Can't anyone just open a door and answer a few questions? Mister Johns thought to himself as they passed underneath the arched transom, and walked down the hall toward the parlor. The tall, slender man with stern, saturnine features followed closely behind, his six foot, six inch frame towering over them.

The three men turned the corner and passed a bronze statue of Chiron, the haunted, haggard boatman forever destined to ferry lost souls across the River Styx. And though the analogy did not occur to them at the time, it was an apt description, for that is precisely the role Tremolo had played in the life of Bob Dorian for close to 40 years. *How had Frost explained it?* Mister Johns' mind continued to churn, *'Like an Edgar Allan Poe story.' That's it. That's it exactly. No wonder Dorian thought he was in some macabre murder mystery. This place is a dead ringer for Roderick and Madeline's place in "The Fall of the House of Usher."* And then, as if on cue, he saw it. The punch line to a joke Mister Johns didn't know he was making. Hanging on the wall was a daguerreotype of the fabled author himself. Poe's eyelids, heavy under the influence of years of alcoholic abuse, stared down on them. *Unless that comes up naturally in conversation, I'm going to let that one slide.*

They took their seats in a pair of Tudor style armchairs. Their haunting, hovering host sat on a chaise lounge, which despite the fact it was a full six inches shorter than the man, fit him perfectly. He leaned forward, elbows perched precariously upon his two knees—

"So somebody finally got to him?" he said evenly. His voice was disheveled and gravelly.

"You say that as if you don't seemed surprised," Mister Johns said.

"Well, I don't know how much Frost here told you about what I did for Bob, Mister Johns, but I can assure you if I was still working for him this would never have happened."

Jack Frost had told Mister Johns little about Tremolo and his relationship with Bob Dorian. Other than saying the two of them had met and become friends when Bob Dorian was still Bobby Zeitzman and playing the coffeehouses down on MacDougal, Jack Frost had been rather tight-lipped about the 'particulars' of the relationship between the two men. After all, a lot can happen in 40 years. And while Jack Frost knew a man's mind can play tricks on him, memories are not entirely arbitrary. Often what he chooses to remember is as important as what he chooses to forget. Tremolo would tell Johns what he chose to tell him; what he didn't, Jack Frost could fill in later.

"Mr. Frost told me you and Mr. Zeitzman met in 1963, and you worked with him until a few months ago. As to what you actually did, Mr. Frost didn't go into specifics."

"Well, my job description was largely unspecified."

"So—" Mister Johns said, removing his notepad from his pocket. "You mind giving me a few of the specifics?"

"I made sure nobody got too close to him … among other things," he added somewhat elusively.

"Too close to him?" Johns pressed, picking up on the evasiveness of his response.

"I put up barriers, Mister Johns—" Tremolo clarified, "made sure Bob didn't see people he didn't want to see, and vice versa."

"What kind of people?" Mister Johns pressed.

"People who might want to put a bullet in his chest."

Talk about a 180-degree shift, Mister Johns thought to himself. *The first person we talk to does everything in her power to distance herself from Dorian. This guy's practically admitting to murder.*

"And were there a lot of people like that? People who wanted to kill him, I mean?" Mister Johns clarified, hoping that Mr. Tremolo would do the same.

"I'd say one a week. Of course that was at the height of his fame—'65, '66—Jesus, on the '66 tour we used to get three, four a night. But that was when he actually meant something to people," Tremolo said wistfully. "I doubt he got them much in the last few years, but you'd have to talk to this guy—" he said, motioning to Frost. "Frost you still get them?"

It turns out Jack Frost had received a rather alarming call just a few nights ago. But that was one of the 'peculiars' Frost had conveniently left out when he'd briefed Mister Johns on this little meeting.

"A few," Frost replied quickly, moving the conversation forward.

"Well from everything Mr. Frost tells me about him," Mister Johns said, turning the page in his notebook, "Dorian was tough to read, hard to get to know." He hoped his question would result in Tremolo's telling him something to fill that page.

"I'd say that's a fair assessment." The page remained blank.

"But you know him. Or should I say, you knew him?"

"For a while, yeah." The pencil did not move. An uncomfortable silence fell across the room.

But the silence that resulted from Tremolo's sitting there pensively was not intended to create apprehension or angst. Rather, it was filled with a pained, heartfelt hesitation, like someone taking a long, deep breath before revealing something they had spent their entire lives trying to keep to themselves.

"How did he die?" Tremolo said. The question was asked in the same way a child might ask why the sky is blue or the grass is green. There was a meekness, a timidity to his demeanor that instantly transformed him from a man who, only moments ago, dominated the room and everything in it into a docile, unassuming giant. "How did it happen?"

"Commissioner Tiresias discovered the body at the Chelsea," Frost said tentatively. He wanted to paint a picture of the scene for Tremolo, give him enough to get him to start talking. What he did *not* want to do is give him too much. "As far as we can determine, a single shot to the chest."

"The Chelsea's not a big place," Tremolo said. "Walls may be thick, but the rooms are right on top of one another. You say he was shot, but nobody heard anything?" And while Tremolo's questions were genuine, the timidity that had been present in his voice a few moments ago was gone. Sure, Tremolo was asking valid questions. Nobody could fault him for that. The problem was the *way* he was asking them. It almost seemed as if he wanted to know if the person had gotten away with it.

Jack Frost wasn't the only one who noticed the specificity of Tremolo's rapid-fire inquiry. Johns had picked up on it, too, and his suspicion of this recently transformed gentle giant was growing.

"As far as we know nobody heard a thing," Mister Johns said reassuringly, hoping to coax Tremolo into getting comfortable, getting careless. "In fact, we're not entirely positive he was even shot at the

Chelsea. They found his body down by the rail yard tracks. He was brought to the Chelsea. He could have been shot there for all we know."

Another protracted silence settled across the room. This was the turning point, and all three men knew it. Either Tremolo was going to talk, tell his side of the story, or Jack Frost was going to tell it for him. Tremolo pursed his lips pensively and exhaled. Whatever he had needed to hear to get him to talk, he'd heard it—

"I don't know her name, but she was Norwegian." *Talk about a non sequitur,* Mister Johns thought. "The reporter over at *Life*—" Tremolo continued. "That is what you want to know isn't it? How I met Bob? I mean that's why you're here, isn't it? You want to know how the two of us met. You want to know about our relationship, how I could stay with a guy like that for 40 years?"

"I think that's a fair assessment." Mister Johns readied his pencil.

"It was a reporter over at *Life*. She was the connection between me and Bob."

"You were introduced to him by a reporter?"

"No, no. I introduced the reporter to Bob. Then Bob turned around and hired me to keep her away. I think my job description was 'human restraining order.'"

"What did she come after him with—a bad review?"

"Oh, no, it wasn't a review she wrote. Reviews never bothered Bob too much. He got a lot of scathing reviews. With the exception of The *Times* piece, his first album was pretty much panned by the critics. Sure a bad review was a thorn in his side, but it never made him bleed. One thing Bob never did was accept anybody's point of view about him. 'The minute somebody defines you, it's over,' he used to tell me."

"So what did this reporter at *Life* say that got him so upset?"

"It wasn't what she said. It was what those around him said."

"'What those around him said'—"Johns repeated. "I'm not quite following you."

"First The *Times* writes a story about him, then *Life*—it was heady stuff for a 21-year-old kid."

"He got cocky—" Johns understood now.

"Worse—he opened his rolodex to her. Said she could talk to anyone she wanted to ... friends, family, old flames."

"I take it he got burned."

"Listen, from the first day Bob arrived on the scene he had an agenda. But by late '63, '64, his drive for success had begun to consume him. Most people think Bob was out for himself from the beginning. I disagree. I think he truly cared for his fellow 'folkies' when he started out, but once fame entered the picture things began to change. He didn't care what happened to those who fell by the wayside."

"I take it that caused some problems?"

"Let's cut to the chase, Mister Johns," Tremolo said. The gruffness had returned. "I mean that's why you're here, isn't it? You and Jack are looking for the guy who put that bullet in Bob's chest, and in all likelihood the person who did was someone who knew him. So, 'yes,' Mister Johns," Tremolo said defiantly, "I would say that those who fell by the wayside definitely were causing some problems. If your theory is correct, they still might be."

"We have no theory on who shot Zeitzman," Mister Johns lied. "Too early in the investigation to construct a theory—one that holds up, anyway. But you're right about one thing. Why we're here, that is. We need to find out a little bit about those people Mr. Zeitzman tossed to the wayside over the years. And judging from what you're telling me, the road is littered with them."

"Let's just say, Bob's so-called 'friends' were more than happy to talk to that reporter at *Life*. They took full advantage of the situation. Knocked him down and stood there grinning. The next day I got the call—'Hey man,' he says to me, 'I'm putting together a game of 'Go,' just a couple of guys, you interested?' I show up at 8:00 the following morning. With the exception of a brief stint in '86, I've been working for Bob ever since. Probably the longest game of 'Go' in history—lasted 40 years."

"So that's how he hired you? He asked you to play a game?"

"I'd never thought about it that way, but 'yeah,' I guess he did. In hindsight it makes a lot of sense."

"How so?"

"Bob loved games—checkers, chess, 'Go'—anything that involved strategy, patience and persistence. But, yeah, that's how he hired me. The guys at that first game were the ones who stayed with him for the duration."

"So what exactly did you do for him?"

"Well, it goes back to this reporter at *Life*. So the story comes out—I think it was on a Tuesday. Wednesday morning anyone whose name appeared in the article was history. Anyone Bob even *thought* had talked to that reporter was frozen out."

"Frozen out?"

"Barred, blackballed, couldn't sit at the table—if you know what I mean." It was evident that Mister Johns didn't. "You married, Mister Johns?"

"Once."

"I'm assuming that the two of you had arguments from time to time?"

"Like I said, I'm not married anymore," Mister Johns replied dryly.

"Well, I don't know how it was with you, but when most couples fight and the wife really wants to stick it to her old man she gives him the 'cold shoulder.' Doesn't tell you why she's pissed off, what she's pissed off at. Hell, she might not even tell you she's pissed off at all." Mister Johns turned the page in his notebook. Despite the fact the story seemed to be nothing more than a meaningless allegory he continued to scribble furiously, writing down every word that was spoken. "My point, Mister Johns," Tremolo continued, "is that even in '63, everyone wanted to sit at the table with Bob. Which meant that if

Bob wanted to screw with someone, he'd give them the cold shoulder. 'Freezing 'em out'—that's what he called it."

"Sounds rather vindictive."

"Like I said, he loved games. And trust me, the silence game—that was one game you did *not* want to play with Bob. Nobody ever won that one. And when you lost, you were never invited back to the table."

"So what you did for him. Your role—'... putting up barriers, making sure Bob didn't see people he didn't want to see,' is I think the way you described it."

"Right."

"That must have afforded you a rather unique role."

"A lot of people didn't care for me, if that's what you're suggesting."

"It sounds to me as if you didn't care for a lot of the people who were coming into Bob's life, either."

"You know, I was working for Bob for close to a year before I even knew I was on the payroll. I mean, I never thought of what I was doing as a job. I did what I did because I liked Bob. I liked spending time with him. I didn't do it because I thought he was going to be a star and I wanted a piece of the action. I mean, we all knew Bob was going to be a star. Shit, don't take my word for it," Tremolo said, turning in the direction of Jack Frost, "Frost, you were at the Hoot in '61. You knew didn't you? You knew the guy was going to take off?"

"I wasn't sure the guy was even going to show up for work in '61," Jack Frost said disarmingly, trying to keep the story moving, keep Tremolo talking.

"Bob always did march to his own drummer," Tremolo chuckled. Frost's strategy seemed to have worked. Tremolo continued, "But by '62, '63 most people knew Bob was on his way up. And what those of us didn't know in '63, we damn sure figured out by '64."

"What happened in '64?" Mister Johns interjected.

"We went on the road, that's what happened. Twenty days, New York to California. Just me, Bob, a red Chevy station wagon and end-less bottles of Beaujolais. Best month of my life."

"So you don't mind if we talk a little bit about the '64 road trip?"

"Shit," Tremolo lit up. "Where do you want me to start?"

"Why not east and move west?"

"Well, the first album hadn't really reached a mainstream audi-ence, but the second one—that was the one that really solidified him as the standard-bearer of the folk set. And it was a lot of pressure on him, you know? The whole 'voice of a generation' thing was starting to drive him nuts."

"You're the second person to tell us that. What was the problem? Did he not like the attention? The praise? Did he think he wasn't worthy of it? That he was a phony?"

"Oh, he thought he was worthy. He knew he was the real thing—that wasn't the problem. The problem was they wanted him to be a prophet, a savior. And not just any savior, but *their* savior."

"Well, I can see how he might not want to be tagged as a 'savior,'" Mister Johns said, defending the dead rock star, "that's a pretty heavy burden to carry. No matter whom you're carrying it for."

"Oh, don't get me wrong—it wasn't that Bob didn't like the atten-tion. All performers crave attention to some extent or they wouldn't get on the stage in the first place. But Bob never wanted to be a prophet or savior. Elvis maybe. We all wanted to be Elvis. But a prophet? No. That was never his bag. But that's the rap he was get-ting. So when I told him I'd booked him at this festival in Northern California—Berkeley, I think it was—we scraped together some cash, bought a car and headed west."

"So how important was the Kerouac book in all this?" Mister Johns said, jotting down a few notes in his notebook.

"What are you talking about?"

"You mentioned 'on the road' earlier," Johns said, looking up from his notebook, "I assume you were referencing Jack Kerouac's *On the Road*?"

"I mentioned *On the Road?*"

Tremolo wasn't a man to be careless with his words, so naturally he was taken aback by a reference to a book he hadn't recalled making. But it wouldn't have been that surprising that he would have mentioned the 320-page sophomore novel by Jack Kerouac. After all, Kerouac's nascent novel of reckless abandonment had become an instant classic when it was published in the spring of 1957. Only adding to its lore was the fact that Kerouac had allegedly scrawled his sprawling tale across a single, 30-foot piece of parchment during the seven years he traversed America. And while both Bob Dorian and Mr. Tremolo had definitely read Kerouac's *On the Road*—dozens of times, in fact—Tremolo simply had no recollection whatsoever of mentioning it. Of course, Tremolo didn't need to remember referencing *On the Road*. Mister Johns had a record of it—

"Right here," Mister Johns said, flipping the page back to the place he had written it down. He read the notes aloud, "'We went on the road, that's what happened. Twenty days, New York to California. Just me, Bob, a red Chevy station wagon and endless bottles of Beaujolais. Best month of my life.'"

"Impressive. Word-for-word."

"Words are important, Mr. Tremolo. I've often found what people say isn't as interesting as the way they choose to say it."

"Well, you and Bob would have had something in common, then. He was a big fan of words, too. Anyway, back to *On the Road*—"

Mister Johns turned the page. Tremolo continued the tale of Bob, a red Chevy station wagon and endless bottles of Beaujolais—

"Yeah, Jack Kerouac was an influence. A huge influence. Bob didn't just read Kerouac, he devoured him. Bob loved Jack Kerouac. Loved every thing about him. The way he wrote, the way he lived ... and as macabre as this may sound, Bob even loved the way Kerouac died. Yeah, he'd read *On the Road*, all right. Carrying around a copy of *On the Road* was sort of a badge of honor for the beat generation. I think that's what made the idea of driving across the country so appealing to him. Later in his career, Bob ended up becoming many things to many people, but in those early days he was always a romantic. He never came right out and said it, but I think he always thought of our trip as his own personal 'on the road' as it were."

"North or south?"

"I'm sorry?"

"Did you take the Northern or Southern route?"

"Southern—" Tremolo replied fondly. "Bob wouldn't have had it any other way."

"And why's that?"

"Bob had already seen plenty of the North. In fact, he'd had a job working up north as a cook for a spell back in '58. Bussed tables during the day and sang at night."

"Really? I never knew that?" Frost was genuinely surprised by this new piece of Dorian's past.

"Oh, yeah. Only 'real' job he ever had. And the reason you probably never heard about it was that he only had it for a week."

"What happened?" Mister Johns inquired.

"Asked for a raise. Next morning when he shows up for work he finds out he's been fired. So, yeah, we took the Southern route— North Carolina, Virginia, Georgia, eventually drifting down to New Orleans. Bob didn't want anything to do with going back up North. Said he'd seen enough snow storms, frozen rivers and howlin' winds to last him a lifetime."

"So how did you guys spend your time? Twenty days in a car seems like a long while."

"The fact that we hit New Orleans right smack dab in the middle of Mardi Gras accounted for a large chuck of the trip—and brain cells, I might add. Not to mention the money was running a little low."

"How *did* you support yourself then?"

"You know, you ask a lot of questions, Mister Johns," Tremolo said.

"Comes with the territory," Johns said in his best 'aw-shucks' tone, lifting the pencil and waving it back and forth.

"Right," Tremolo said slowly. Mister Johns' best 'aw-shucks' tone needed a little work. "But even for a reporter you ask a lot of questions," Tremolo said suspiciously.

"I've been down on Rue Morgue a long time. The Commissioner's giving me a break. I don't want to screw it up. I want to get it right. And getting it right means asking questions. So if I seem a little rusty, you have to remember I don't get a whole lot of practice with a roomful of stiffs." Johns' 'aw-shucks' shtick might have needed a little work, but his disarming charm was dead-on.

Problem was Tremolo wasn't much for charm. After nearly four decades on the road with one of the biggest acts in show business, he had met a lot of people who had spent a lot of time honing their charm on him. Distributing backstage passes, authorizing interviews, procuring autographs, letting people sit in on recording sessions: these were but a few of the tasks Tremolo had rendered over the years on Bob Dorian's behalf. So charm, especially the transparent, self-effacing charm Mister Johns was employing on him right now didn't fool Tremolo for one minute. He knew Johns wanted something, and he knew exactly what it was. It was the same thing they *all* wanted: Johns wanted to know more about Bob Dorian.

And while Mister Johns' charm hadn't fooled Tremolo, his suspicion of the acerbic obits writer had been placated to the point where he didn't believe Mister Johns was out to betray him. And so Tremolo decided to cut Johns a break. Tremolo continued to talk about the 21-year-old folk musician who, in the winter of 1964, stood on the cusp of fame.

"Bob had just signed with a new manager who persuaded him to license his songs to other acts. It happened just before we headed out West."

"You sound surprised," Mister Johns said, picking up on the shift in Tremolo's tone.

"I couldn't believe it."

"What do you mean?"

"Bob loved his songs. They were like his children. But you have to remember—he had three albums out at this point and none of them was tearing up the charts. Furthermore, his deal with the label was for shit in terms of royalties. So he did the deal. But I think he always regretted it."

"Regretted what?"

"I think he always thought he was prostituting himself hawking his songs on other acts. Certainly he didn't get rich off it, but he didn't have to play every night to earn his keep either."

"Publishing is a lucrative business. I'm surprised he had to play at all," Mister Johns countered.

"It *can* be—lucrative, that is—it all depends on who owns the publishing. Like I said, someone else set it up for him. But back to your question about playing shows. We played three."

"Three? You traveled three thousand miles across the country and you only played three shows?"

"Bob always liked to tell this story about how we played every hall that would have us. That we'd talked to people in bars, talked to people in mineshafts. That whole Forrest Guthridge, 'salt of the earth' angle really appealed to Bob. But the truth of the matter is that we played a grand total of three shows. And the only 'people' we talked to were some kids in some college town in Virginia. And that lasted all of five minutes before Bob wanted to split because there were too many."

"What do you mean, 'too many'?"

"Too many people. It turned into a fucking mob scene. I mean, I would have understood it up north. The Liberals would come out in droves just to hear him read the damn phone book. But here we were in the South. And these were white, middle-class kids. With trust funds, and fancy cars and not a care in the world except which fraternity party they were going to get shitfaced at and what sorority girl they were going to bang that night. And then it hit me—hit him, too. We had to accept that he was now a famous figure, and that talking to people in bars—that old Guthridge, folksy manner—was a thing of the past. So, no, we didn't play a lot of shows on that trip out west. We couldn't, really. He was just getting too big."

"And how about songs? Was he writing?"

"Bob was always writing. If he wasn't banging something out on a typewriter, he was scribbling something on a matchbook or napkin—anything he could get his hands on. I remember one night when we had pulled together enough scratch to pay for a hotel room, Bob reaches into his pants and starts emptying his pockets. I mean his pockets were just bulging with all these shreds of paper he'd been stuffing in his trousers, in his shirt pockets, in his jacket sleeves. And I reached down to take a look, and he snatches them all up and stuffs them back into his pants before I can see them."

"Sounds like he was protective of his work," Mister Johns dead-panned.

"I think the word you're looking for is 'paranoid,' and Bob was like that from the moment I met him. And frankly, he had every right to be paranoid," Tremolo said, his voice infused with what seemed to be a newfound admiration. "In fact, it was his responsibility. He had to be careful what he said. You have to remember, the things he was singing about—social oppression, racial equality, corrupt politicians—these were explosive topics. And the songs weren't written in a vacuum. He named names. That pissed a lot of people off. But his most dangerous songs were the ones that raised questions he didn't dare answer."

"What do you mean?"

"Well, it's one thing to say the answer is out there blowin' in the wind. It's something else entirely to say even the president of the United States must sometimes stand naked. You go into the temple and ask a few pointed questions, you might raise a few eyebrows. You start turning over the tables of the moneychangers, they come looking for you."

"Don't you think that's a bit dramatic? I know a lot of people put him on a pedestal, but at the end of the day they were just songs."

"That's what he always said, 'It's just a song, man. What you get-tin' so worked up about?' Of course, he knew what he was writing was more than that. He knew what his words meant to people."

"Did he talk about his songs with you?"

"Nope."

"But you were his friend—"

"Yep."

"And that didn't bother you?"

"Not really."

"Care to elaborate?"

"See, part of the reason Bob took that cross-country trip—aside from wanting to see the places where his heroes had lived and worked—was that he wanted to break free of the folk-rock scene. He wanted to look inside himself. Find inspiration, set a new direction. So even if he had talked about the songs he was writing, I wouldn't have known what he was talking about anyway. Because when it came to setting a direction, Bob was eight miles ahead of the rest of us. But here's the ironic part. The song he wrote—the one that took him off in that new direction, the one he banged out in the back of that old red station wagon—that song was about me."

"Really?"

"Remember how I told you we spent a few days more than we'd planned in New Orleans?"

"Mardi Gras."

"Well, the reason is that Bob loved the place. Who'd have thought?" Judging from his tone, Tremolo certainly didn't. "Here's Bob, the most claustrophobic, paranoid guy in the world stuck smack dab in the middle of the world's biggest carnival—clowns to the left, jokers to the right. And you'd think—I did anyway—that he'd be totally flipping out. Instead, he's just standing there in the middle of the street taking it all in. Me, of course, I'm the one totally wigging out—completely out of my mind, blowing on this old Tremolo har-monica I'd found in the street. So anyway, the next morning, we're heading out. I'm driving and Bob, he's all cramped up in the back seat working something out on this old typewriter he'd brought with him. And I said, 'Bob, can you please do that later. The sound is driving me crazy. What the hell are you doing anyway?' And he says, 'I'm writing a song about you and that funky Tremolo you were trying to suck off last night.'"

"And that's how you got your nickname?"

"I like to look at it as that's how Bob got his new direction," he said with a chuckle. "Turns out the reason Bob got such a kick out of it was that the harmonica was electric. The thought never even occurred to me to plug the damn thing in. But, yeah, that's why they call me 'Mr. Tremolo.'" He leaned back in his chaise lounge, and for the first time allowed himself to laugh. Then, just as quickly as he succumbed to the memory, he stopped. "The biographers—the guys who write about him—they always try and pin a moment on him when he became the artist we all know today. Like there is one, single moment. An artist, a true artist anyway, is always changing, defining himself. Anyway, a lot of people point to that cross-country trip as the moment he 'became' Bobby D."

"Bobby D?"

"Bob Dorian."

"What do you think?"

"Listen, the truth is—and I'm not sure I've ever told anyone this— I don't think he ever was Bob Dorian."

"What do you mean?" Mister Johns inquired.

Frankly, Tremolo wasn't sure exactly *what* he meant. Sure, he had a vague notion of what he was getting at. But as insightful as it may have sounded, the God's honest truth was that he didn't have a clue what he meant when he'd said that Bob Dorian wasn't really Bob Dorian. It had just come to him. But, Tremolo thought to himself, perhaps it was a notion worth exploring. "He wanted us to believe—" Tremolo continued, letting some sort of instinctive intuition that had lay dormant inside him for 40 years take over, "You, me, his fans, the critics: he wanted us all to believe that he was 'Bob Dorian.'"

"Whoever that was?" Frost chimed in. It seems the persona that Bob Dorian had so carefully crafted had resonated with Frost much in the same way it had with Tremolo.

"Exactly—whoever that was," Tremolo said knowingly before continuing. "Bob spent close to 40 years keeping everybody guessing. But in the end he was in the same boat as the rest of us. Spent his entire life trying to find out who the real Bob Dorian was."

Tremolo was only the second person with whom Jack Frost and Mister Johns had spoken, but one thing was becoming increasingly evident: those in a position to know Bob Dorian best didn't really know him at all. And based on their conversation with Sophia and now with Tremolo, it seemed the best way for those people to learn more about the mysterious figure who, at one time, had stood at the center of the web that connected them all was to talk about him.

"You probably knew him better than anyone—" Frost said respectfully. "Do you think he ever found who he was looking for?"

Tremolo hesitated for a moment then leaned forward, his gangly, six foot, six inch frame balancing precariously on the edge of the chaise lounge. He pressed the palms of his hands together and laced his fingers. There was a brief moment when Jack Frost and Mister Johns both thought Tremolo was about to lead them in prayer.

"I'm not sure he did. I'm not sure any of us ever really figured him out. I'm not sure he ever figured himself out." And with that, Tremolo rose up from the chaise and extended a large paw of a hand, "Listen, I hope I was helpful, gentlemen."

"Yes, thank you for your time," Mister Johns said, sliding his notepad back into the breast pocket of his suit. "You've been very helpful. Very helpful indeed."

"SO WHEN EXACTLY were you planning on telling me?"

Mister Johns reached into his pocket and pulled out a small plastic case. He casually offered the open container to Frost.

"No, thank you," Frost replied, waving his hand back-and-forth in the air to indicate that he didn't want whatever it was Mister Johns was offering. Mister Johns shrugged, popped what appeared to be a breath mint into his mouth, and slid the case back into his pocket.

"Plan on telling you what?" Frost inquired dismissively.

"The death threat," Mister Johns replied with equal indifference. "When were you planning on telling me you'd received a threat on Zeitzman's life?"

The exchange that had taken place in the parlor under the daguerreotype of the 18th century English mystery writer had been quick and, Jack Frost thought, relatively inconspicuous. Clearly, however, it had not gone unnoticed. And while it had never been Jack Frost's intention to hide the fact that he did, on occasion, receive a threat on Bob Dorian's life, frankly Frost had hoped that it wouldn't come up. Now, of course, it had. But rather than play into Mister Johns' acidic paranoia, Frost decided to play dumb.

"If I took every threat made by every kook seriously, I'd never get my job done," Frost said casually. "I wanted to see what we turned up."

"And you were planning on telling me before or after someone made good on his threat. Because if it was before, you're a little late." Paranoia, it seems, had given way to anger. There were no two ways about it: Mister Johns was pissed. And Jack Frost knew if Mister Johns' mixture of anger and paranoia was to be placated, he better cut Johns off before he really got going.

"Perhaps I should remind you," Frost said, stopping cold in his tracks to emphasize his point, "it wasn't just the Commissioner who brought you in to assist in this investigation. I brought you in, too. And when we find the guy who killed Bob you're going to have one hell of a story. Now I have been very accommodating putting you in touch with the people who knew him. *More* than accommodating— so don't treat me like *I'm* the goddamned suspect!"

"I'm simply doing my job, Mr. Frost. And I think you would agree following up on a death threat that appears to have been made good on is well within the parameters of my job."

If you only knew, Frost thought to himself as he fingered the piece of paper that had been in his pocket for the last three days. *I've got the number of the guy who just might have killed Bob Dorian in my pocket as we speak. Talk about suppressing evidence. Talk about derailing an investigation.*

But since Jack Frost did not share this information with Mister Johns, since he did not tell him he had the only direct link to the person who, in all likelihood, had put a bullet into Bob Dorian's chest, Jack Frost was able to avoid a bullet of his own.

It turns out the reason Mister Johns hadn't pressed Jack Frost on his little 'oversight' was that there were a few other pressing matters Mister Johns wanted to review with Jack Frost. Mister Johns removed his notepad from the left breast pocket of his suit. He flipped back a few pages and made reference to his notes as he spoke—

"Since it appears we are laying our cards on the table," Mister Johns continued, "perhaps we can take a moment to talk about the people with whom you have so accommodatingly put me in touch. First there was Sophia, whom you were hesitant to have me speak with from the beginning."

"That's ridiculous," Frost huffed.

"Is it? Because when I asked you if there was a girl, you danced all around that like grease on a hot skillet. That girl gave him his start. She inspired him. There may have been 'a woman in every town' as you said, but there was only one who broke his heart. But you didn't want me to talk to her—why?"

"The press hounded her for years when he was alive. I hardly see why she needs to continue to be harassed now that he's dead. That woman has been through hell and back because of her association with him. And for the record—he didn't just break Sophia's heart, he tore it out and held it up for the whole world to see."

"I couldn't have said it better myself. Except I might have used the word 'spurned'—it's a bit more direct, more to the point, more frequently used in situations where a woman who feels betrayed ends up taking matters into her own hands. We figure out what the inscription on that ring I mentioned earlier says, we find out how spurned she truly was. Maybe it was enough to pull a trigger, maybe it wasn't. Until then, she stays on the list." Mister Johns turned the page, "Now as for Tremolo—"

"Wait a minute," Jack Frost interjected. "I'll be the first to admit that that ring is suspicious, but Tremolo? Tremolo had no reason to kill Bob. The two of them have been together for 40 years. Those guys were fused at the hip."

"Not entirely," Mister Johns said, reaching into his pocket and popping another breath mint into his mouth. "What happened between Tremolo and Zeitzman back in '86?"

"What makes you think something happened in '86?"

"Something he said," Mister Johns replied, casually peeling back the cover of his notebook. "'With the exception of a brief stint in '86, I've been working for Bob my entire life,'" he said, reading from the page. "'Probably the longest game of 'Go' in history—lasted 40 years.'"

Frost considered the man in the dark, dour suit. He may have been a poser, a patsy brought in to take the fall, but he was nothing if not persistent. And Frost knew the best way to counter a pestering persistence is the path of least resistance. And since the fallout between Tremolo and Bob Dorian was not a path Jack Frost wanted to go down, Frost gave Mister Johns what he was looking for—or enough of it to keep Johns' nagging cynicism in check before it got everyone into a hell of a fix.

"I really don't think this has a thing to do with anything," Frost said noncommittally, "but since you seem adamant in pursuing it, fine. When Bob started to get famous, started to realize he was going to need to be more closemouthed about his personal life, he built a team of people around him to look after him, to ensure his privacy. Well, over the years that team has had a revolving roster—except for one guy."

"Tremolo—"

"As Bob's de facto tour manager, his job entailed making sure there was a certain amount of buffer between those people Bob did and did not want to see."

"I *have* been taking notes," Mister Johns said snidely as he held up his spiral notebook.

Ignoring Johns' derisive comment, Frost smiled briefly before pressing on—

"Well, the '80s were a tough time for Bob."

"Tough? In what way?"

"Suffice to say, Bob was running around with people he shouldn't have been."

"Finding comfort in the arms of strangers?" Mister Johns said suggestively.

"And one of Tremolo's jobs," Frost said, acknowledging Mister Johns' astute assessment, "was to find Bob those arms in which he could find comfort."

"Something tells me arms weren't the determining appendage on which the women were being evaluated."

"So the tour hits some small town down South and this girl decides the best way to get to Bob is through Tremolo."

"Not the first time, I assume."

"Not the first, but the last—for Tremolo anyway. Things go fine that night. Tremolo gets his rocks off, the tour rolls on. The problem is when they get to the next town, which happens to be in the same county, the sheriff is waiting. He takes Tremolo downtown, throws him in jail and charges him with sodomy."

"That's illegal in the South now, huh?" Mister Johns said with a slight chuckle.

"It is with a 17-year-old who also happens to be an African American. And trust me, it was no joking matter. Bob himself had to go down there and bail Tremolo out."

"Really, I'm surprised that ..."

"That little story didn't make it into the books you've been reading?"

"Well, yeah," Mister Johns replied. "It's pretty scandalous, especially considering Zeitzman himself was involved."

"The reason it never made it into the books is that Tremolo was never charged."

"So the cops never asked him any questions?"

"And neither did Bob," Jack Frost elaborated. "Instead, Tremolo was relieved of his road manager duties and stuck in an office off Elysian Row until everything blew over."

"So Tremolo got 'frozen out,' to use his words," Mister Johns said matter-of-factly.

"He and Bob eventually worked it out, but, 'yes,' he was out of the picture for a while."

"This is '86?"

"This is '86," Frost confirmed.

"You joined the organization in '86 didn't you?" Mister Johns inquired.

There was a moment of hesitation, a moment akin to that brief, albeit painful silence that passes between two people who know that what hasn't been said doesn't need to be said: it's already out there.

"Yes, I started managing Bob in '86," Frost replied curtly. "But what's that got to do with anything?"

"Don't be coy, Frost. Tremolo worked for Zeitzman for 40 years. It doesn't take Picasso to paint the picture. Dorian was a son of a bitch to work for, I get it. But Tremolo had a good thing going. Like you said, he and Zeitzman were fused at the hip. He was his best friend. To hear him tell it, those two were like brothers."

"What's your point?" Jack Frost said impatiently.

"That *is* my point, Frost. Friends, good friends anyway, are hard to come by. Especially in your line of work. And especially if your name is Bob Zeitzman. Friends just don't walk away from one another, not after sticking it out for 40 years. A rough patch comes along, you weather the storm."

"It was a pretty rough storm, Johns. That little stunt Tremolo pulled down in Jackson put Bob in a hell of a bad position."

"Is that why you fired him?"

"Fired him!" Frost shot back. "What the hell are you talking about, Johns! I just told you what happened in '86. Tremolo got in some hot water, Bob didn't like the heat he thought it might bring, Tremolo left for a while, they patched things up, and then he came back."

"That may have been what happened, Frost, but I don't think that's the way it went down," Mister Johns said undeterred.

"Then why don't you tell me the way *you* think it went down?" Frost replied, hoping that Mister Johns was grasping at straws.

"Zeitzman wasn't the one who was afraid of the heat that little sodomy charge might have brought—it was you." The tone of Mister Johns' voice was not accusatory. It was to the point. Quite factual, actually. And the facts he was laying down were dead-on. "You'd just joined the organization," he continued, "and your first order of business as Bob's new manager was to get rid of the guy who was turning up the heat. That's what I meant by 'the way it went down.'"

Straws might have been what Johns was going for, Frost thought to himself, *but I'll be damned if he didn't just come up with a handful of short and curlies.*

"Bob had hit bottom," Frost conceded. "He'd started drinking and drugging again. A stint at Betty Ford, a month at Hazelden. Then his best friend gets into a jam, and Bob has to do the one thing he hates more than anything—"

"Put his neck on the line," Mister Johns said, completing the sentence.

"And I wasn't going to let him get it cut off."

"And he never knew it was you who was behind it, did he?" Mister Johns said.

"It was a tough decision," Jack Frost acquiesced. "But the toughest part was letting Tremolo think Bob was the one who had frozen him out."

"Well, at least he had *your* shoulder to cry on."

If there had been any compassion in Mister Johns' demeanor before, it was gone now. There was no mistaking Mister Johns' words for anything other than what they were: an attack on Frost and the sincerity of his 20-year allegiance to Bob Dorian.

"Fuck you, Johns," Frost sputtered. "I've been nothing but a friend to Bob. In good times and in bad."

"And from what I've read, the last few years haven't been all roses for Mr. Zeitzman, so I'm sure he could have used a friend like you."

The fact that Mister Johns had done a little background reading on Bob Dorian hadn't been particularly troubling to Jack Frost. In fact, up until now Johns' due diligence when it came to digging up the dirt on Bob Dorian had been a good thing. It meant that Jack Frost didn't have to get in the mix if he didn't want to. But now, Jack Frost was very curious just *exactly* what Mister Johns had read about what had happened over the last few years. He imagined that some of the books out there had alluded to Jackson and what had gone on down there, but Jack Frost had read most of those books, too, and he knew for sure that nowhere in any of them did it talk about how he had canned Tremolo. Mister Johns had figured that out himself. And the way Jack Frost figured it, that type of spot-on deduction was going to cause a lot of problems if it went unchecked. But instead of responding to the innuendo that he had taken advantage of Bob Dorian, Jack Frost decided to borrow a page from Commissioner Tiresias' playbook: Jack Frost went on the offensive.

"You know—and of course you *wouldn't* know this, Johns, because you didn't know him—but having a relationship with Bob was a two-way street. It went both ways. It's not like the only thing Tremolo did was stay Mississippi a day too long. He screwed up. He was a wanted man down there. He and Bob may have had a unique relationship, but he took advantage of that relationship. And to answer your question, 'no,' Tremolo didn't have a clue I was the guy behind his being frozen out in '86."

"And you're sure about that?"

"Of course I'm sure, Johns. In case you didn't notice, Tremolo isn't the most levelheaded guy. Spooks easily, scares the shit out of most people. He scared the shit out of me sometimes. No, Tremolo didn't know I was the one who came between him and Bob. Trust me, if he did *I* would have been the one with the bullet in my back," Frost replied with bravado.

"So who'd he think fired him, then?" Mister Johns inquired. And just like that, the page Jack Frost had borrowed from the Commissioner's playbook had been tossed back in his face. By going on the offensive, Frost had just played into Mister Johns' hands.

"Bob," Jack Frost said. *Jesus Christ,* the realization hit Frost like a ton of bricks. *All those years, Tremolo had thought Bob Dorian had fired him and now Bob Dorian was dead, a bullet in his back.* "So are you telling me that you actually think Tremolo killed Bob over something that happened 20 years ago?"

"It damn sure doesn't take an accountant to add it up," Mister Johns replied.

"Maybe not," Frost conceded. "But to think that Tremolo somehow discovers the truth about Jackson and finally acts on it 20 years later—that's a hell of a stretch. He and Bob patched up what happened down in Jackson a long time ago. And even if Tremolo did harbor any animosity, as I said, he had the last 20 years to act on it. Why act now?"

"I don't know," Johns said. "Maybe he didn't want to end up like Elijah Blue."

Shit, I never told him about Elijah Blue. "How do *you* know about Elijah Blue?" Jack Frost inquired uneasily.

"Like Sophia said, they've written a lot of books on Mr. Zeitzman. And all the books seem to be consistent on this. There were three people on that cross-country trip: Zeitzman, Tremolo and a man by the name of Elijah Blue."

"You're grasping at straws again, Johns."

"Am I?"

"Straw men, too, for that matter."

"Really? Because I find it very curious that we just spent the better part of our morning listening to a guy talk about the 20 days he spent driving from New York to California—'best month of my life' was how he described it—and not once did he mention there was some-one else in that station wagon. But you know what's even more curi-ous?"

"What's that?"

"You didn't mention him either."

"Whether I mentioned him or whether Tremolo mentioned him, Elijah Blue has no bearing on this case."

"And why's that?"

"Because Blue's out of the picture. Nobody's heard from Elijah Blue in close to 40 years. In fact, the last I heard, he was living out in a little farming community on the outskirts of Elysian Row—place called Massey's Grove. Yes, he was on that cross-country trip. And when it was over, he hung around for a while. But by '64, '65, he and Bob went their separate ways."

Unlike the little 'incident' down in Jackson—an incident which he had conveniently kept to himself—Frost wasn't trying to be duplici-tous on the topic of Elijah Blue. Frost really didn't think that Elijah Blue had anything to do with what had happened 40 years, much less three days ago.

And while Frost had offered up a perfectly plausible explanation as to why he had kept Elijah Blue's name to himself, the problem was that Mister Johns wasn't a big fan of 'explanations,' especially expla-nations that could be rendered with such ease and speed.

"Well, you must have some thoughts on the subject as to what went down," Mister Johns said doggedly. "And since Tremolo didn't offer his, I'd like to hear yours."

"I have no idea," Jack Frost said succinctly. It was the easiest ques-tion he'd answered all day. "None whatsoever. Whatever happened with Elijah Blue happened long before I was involved. The only thing I can tell you is that the word at the time was that he got 'attached' to Bob, a bit too devoted for Bob's tastes."

"What does that mean?"

"Like I said, I don't have a clue. And frankly, I don't care."

"Not even a little?" Mister Johns goaded. "A guy gets as close as anyone has ever gotten to the most elusive rock star in the world, then suddenly he's gone—no one hears from him for 40 years—and you're not even a *little* curious what happened?"

"Whatever happened between Elijah Blue and Bob is between them. And like I said, it happened forty years ago. It has no bearing whatsoever on the events of the last few days. They can both take it to their graves for all I care."

"It appears one of them already has," Mister Johns said sarcastically. "So if it's all right with you, Mr. Frost—and this goes back to me doing the job I was asked to do—I'd like to see if the other guy would like to get something off his chest while he still has a chance."

CHAPTER 7

▼

ELIJAH BLUE

The road leading to Massey's Grove was a typical country road. It rose and fell, and rose again, until it disappeared altogether. Looking over their shoulders, they saw a string of decrepit old buildings interspersed with a few deserted steel and glass towers rising up from the earth like a row of rotten teeth poised to devour the distant horizon. And for a brief, fleeting moment, Elysian Row seemed a million miles away. But try as you might—and at some point everyone tried—you simply couldn't escape Elysian Row. Commissioner Tiresias had been right when he said that 'every one comes back to Elysian Row.' It was a lot like that scene in *Chinatown* when John Huston utters that final, prophetic line to Jack Nicholson: "Forget it, Jake. It's Chinatown." Tragic and touching, but in the end the place was nothing but a trap. Chinatown *was* Elysian Row. It was as if this place wasn't real, like it was some sort of dark, distorted dream. But even that description was too kind. It was closer to a living, breathing nightmare populated with all the people you had spent your entire life trying to put behind you.

A lot of people had written about Elysian Row. Poets, priests, politicians—they had all tried to put in words an apt description of this place. But in the end, they all got it wrong. It would be like trying to explain a Salvador Dali painting to a blind man. Hell, Jack Frost was standing on the outskirts of town, a good mile away. Plenty of perspective from this vantage point, and even he couldn't find the right words to capture it.

The only guy who ever got it right was Bob, Frost thought to himself. *Bob captured this place perfectly. It was a Bosch triptych, a three-ring circus, a* Howl *heard over moans and cries, a carnival of the grotesque, an apocalyptic vision through Laertes' sister's eyes. Bob nailed this place and everything in it. No wonder he didn't want to come back. He hung a lot of people out to dry. Nailed a lot of people to the cross. It only makes sense they'd want to return the favor.*

Jack Frost remembered how back in the 1920s, at the height of the unbridled hatred between the blacks and whites, they had routinely hung those 'uppity niggers' when they got out of line. Judging from the number of broken branches still visible nearly a century later, there had been quite a few incidents of 'uppitiness' back then. The story Jack Frost heard when he was a kid was that they actually sold postcards of the hangings. Bob must have heard those stories, too. But the moment he put the line into one of his songs, it was no longer a story: it was fact. Bob had a way of doing that—turning folklore into fact.

Of course, the pendulum swung both ways. After 40 years in the spotlight, Bob's life was nothing *but* folklore. There wasn't a single fact left in the wreckage. And Jack Frost couldn't stop his mind from wandering back to that final, climactic scene in *Chinatown*. John Huston has just removed a small .38 caliber pistol from his coat pocket, then without a moment's hesitation pulls the trigger, lodging a bullet into the chest of an unsuspecting Faye Dunaway as a horrified Jack Nicholson watches in paralyzed disbelief.

According to the folklore surrounding the film, Bob Towne, from whose twisted mind this tale of deceit, corruption and familial incest had sprung forth, wrote a second ending. In this alternative version, Dunaway lives and John Huston doesn't get away with murder. It was an 'up' ending as they say in Hollywood. It had the kind of closure that audiences like to see so that they leave the theater feeling good about themselves, feeling good about the story and feeling good about the world. It was bullshit, of course. Life doesn't always come up roses. In fact, Frost knew just as well as anyone that you were damn lucky if you could even get someone to toss a couple of flowers on your grave after you're dead and buried. Roman Polanski, the director of the film, knew that, too. Life doesn't always end happily. And not wanting to suggest that it did, Polanski nixed Towne's alternate ending the minute the pages came over the fax machine. And just like that, *Chinatown* had the iconoclastic ending that made it a classic.

That's just what Bob would have done, Frost thought to himself. *Bob wouldn't have put up with that Hollywood crap ending for a minute. Because people do get away with murder. Happens all the time. It might just happen here.*

And the two men continued down the well-worn dirt path that would take them to their destination; and neither man said a word.

THEY HAD BEEN WALKING for close to 20 minutes now. Up at the bend where the dirt road turned east, the shadowed silhouette of a woman came into view. She was standing on the top of a grassy knoll in front of an old, decrepit shack. Her back was to the sun, so they could not see her face. But even at a distance, they could hear her whistling a tune to herself.

"May I help you gentlemen?" she said, lifting her head.

"Perhaps," Frost said pleasantly. "I'm looking for someone—an old friend actually—I haven't seen him in a while."

"Does he live out here? Cause if he lives out here, chances are I know him."

"Like I said, I haven't seen him in a while. But last I heard he was living out in Massey's Grove."

"Well, that limits it a bit. But it don't altogether narrow it down—couple folks live out that way. What's his name?"

"Well, when I knew him he went by the name of Elijah Blue."

The woman didn't even bristle.

"He don't go by that name anymore."

"Well, is he around? We'd really like to talk to him."

"I'm sorry, what'd you boys say your names were?"

"My name is Jack Frost and this is Mister Johns."

"Are you an old friend, too, Mister Johns?" the woman said suspiciously.

"No," Mister Johns replied, almost as if he were disgusted by the notion of being lumped in with the poor sots who'd gotten tangled up with Bob Dorian.

"So I'm assuming you were going to do the talking then, Mr. Frost. Since you were the one who knew him."

"Actually, we both have a few questions for ..." Mister Johns pulled his spiral notebook out of his breast coat pocket.

"Pablo, Mister Johns," she said filling in the blank, "he went by Pablo."

And then she just went right back to doing whatever it was she had been doing before they had interrupted her, which apparently was seeding a small patch of a hopelessly barren herb garden. Obviously, they had expected her to elaborate on this new name, 'Pablo,' she had tossed ever so nonchalantly into the conversation. But, it seems, the name was the end of the discussion, not the beginning.

She lifted the hoe and drove it into the embittered earth with amazing tenacity for a woman her age. She gave a few, taut pulls on the hoe, prying the ground apart where the incision had been made. She reached into the pocket of her apron, removed a few seeds and dropped them into the broken ground. Jack Frost and Mister Johns watched as the woman struck the earth with the hoe a second time. The ground blew apart in a dozen directions. As she had done moments before, she dropped the seeds to the ground.

"I'm sorry, ma'am," Frost said, attempting to capture the woman's attention before she repeated the three-step process a third time, "but

one of our mutual friends—someone we both used to work with—
has passed and ..."

"... And you can cut the country bumpkin' act, Frost," Mister
Johns said abruptly. Clearly, irritation had gotten the best of Mister
Johns. One person was pecking at the ground like an idiot savant; the
other was doing his best impression of Gomer Pyle. It was simply too
much for the impatient Mister Johns to take. "Lady—" Johns said,
taking hold of the hoe, "you can go back to tilling the fields in a
minute. We came a long way out here looking for this guy, and we'd
appreciate it if you'd help us out. Now," Mister Johns said in a
remarkably civil tone considering the fact he had just physically
threatened a woman old enough to be his grandmother, "if you know
this guy we're looking for then you know he used to be friendly with
Bob Dorian. You do know who Bob Dorian is, don't you?"

"I know the name," the woman said noncommittally.

"Well, Dorian's dead. And he didn't 'pass.' He was murdered.
Shot in the chest. So if you know where this Elijah Blue or Pablo or
whatever name it is he goes by is, we'd like it if you'd go 'fetch 'em'
for us."

The woman smiled, set the hoe against the wooden banister and
turned her full attention to her two visitors. Judging from the look of
the run-down shack to which that banister was attached, the men
were probably the first visitors she'd had in a very long time.

"I appreciate your directness, Mister Johns," she said coolly. "So
let me be equally direct. I'd be more than happy to take you out to
Massey's Grove, Mr. Frost. But it sounds like you're in a hurry. So if
that's indeed the case, then I'd suggest you ask me your questions. I
knew Elijah Blue as well as anyone—knew Dorian, too—and I'm
assuming this has something to do with their falling out. So if your
friend here wants to make his deadline," she said, noting the notepad
in Mister Johns' hand, "you got 10 minutes, and the clock's ticking."

"Don't you want to know how he died?" Mister Johns inquired.

"Unless something's changed in the last 30 seconds, he was shot in
the chest. I may be old, but my hearing's fine, Mister Johns." The

woman leaned against the banister and knocked her heavy, patent leather boots against the edge of the rotten, wooden porch. A few pieces of red clay fell to the ground. They were thick and matted together and were the color of dried blood. "I believe what you meant to ask me was who it was that killed him. You're putting together a list of suspects, I imagine. And since you're looking for Pablo my guess is that he's made that list."

Yeah, he's made the list, Mister Johns thought to himself. *But there's always room for another. You keep jerking us around, lady, and your name's going to be on that list.*

"So when exactly was it that you said you knew Pablo?" the woman said, turning to Frost. It was clear to her she wasn't going to get anywhere with Mister Johns.

"'63, '64."

"Before the falling out?"

"That's right."

"And you knew Bobby then, too—that what you said?"

"That's right."

"What'd you say your name was again?"

"Frost, Jack Frost."

"The manager," she said slowly. Clearly she had been trying to place the name. Now, it seems, he'd placed it for her.

"That's right."

"You were with him a long time."

"Twenty years."

"You came in after ..."

"Right," Frost interjected, perhaps a bit too quickly. A thin, uneven smile crept across her face. She loved the fact Frost couldn't even bring himself to say his name.

"So I don't need to tell you Bobby was a complicated person," she said still focused on Jack Frost. "So I'll tell you, Mister Johns. Because in order to understand what happened to Pablo, you need to know a little about Bobby. Even before he got rich and famous, he hated people getting hung up on him."

"Hung up on him?" The lilt in Mister Johns' voice invited elaboration.

"Fixated … obsessed …" she said, accepting the invitation. "I mean here's a guy who only needed to point his finger and the temples trembled. To his devotees he was sacred, his every word scripture. People flocked to see him, touch him, sit at his feet."

"And you're telling me he didn't like that?"

"Oh, I'm sure he did at first. But it grew old for him. Things grew old very quickly for Bobby."

"Including his friends?"

"*Especially* his friends. He discarded his friends about as frequently as he'd toss a lyric that wasn't working. Twenty years—" she said, turning to address Jack Frost. "That's got to be a record. Only guy who lasted longer than that was Tremolo."

As much as Mister Johns would have loved to hear Jack Frost's response to that little gem, Johns had a job to do and that meant getting this cranky old broad to tell them where the illusive Elijah Blue had disappeared. So rather than watch Jack Frost explain Jackson a second time, Mister Johns asked the question that had brought them out here in the first place—

"So why'd he toss Elijah Blue?"

"Bobby tossed most of the 'folkies' after Fairport, Mister Johns. But Elijah Blue, he stuck around. Tried to anyway. 'Til Bobby finally got rid of him. The end …" she hesitated, "… the end was messy. But then again, ending things with Bobby was always messy. I don't know anyone who ever made a clean break. You were always haunted by Bobby, even when he was gone. Listen, I can see the two of you are pretty determined to get to the bottom of this little mystery, but frankly I don't think I can help you," she said, brushing her thick, cumbersome fingers across her overalls. "Long walk out here I know," she said as she turned and began to ascend the rickety old stairs. "Sorry it turned out to be a dead end."

"I'm not so sure it was …" Mister Johns called out.

The woman stopped, turned and cocked her head slightly. "And how's that?" she said in a tone that suggested that she was genuinely interested.

"Well, it brought us to you, didn't it?" Mister Johns replied.

"I don't really see how I factor into a murder investigation, Mister Johns?" The interest was fading.

"You knew Bob Dorian, didn't you?"

"I already *told* you I knew him, Mister Johns. Everyone 'round here knew him. Doesn't mean any of us killed him. Truth is, with the exception of the characters over on Elysian Row, Bob's outlived most of the people he ran with back in the day. Bob was a lot of things. And one thing he always was was a survivor."

"So how about telling us a little bit about this Elijah Blue?"

"You're nothing if you ain't persistent, Mister Johns,"

"Just filling in the blanks. Trust me, we got a lot of blanks here."

She glanced up at the sky. A few dark clouds had appeared on the horizon. It looked like rain. Whatever work she'd been planning to complete before the end of the day had just been dashed. She knew she had a good 10 to 15 minutes before the clouds reached them. And considering the rather abrupt manner in which things had ended between Bob and Elijah Blue, she figured 10 to 15 minutes was more than enough time to tell them how it had gone down.

"Perhaps the best way to understand what came between Pablo and Bobby is to understand what brought them together in the first place," she said, reaching into her top left pocket of her blue overalls. She took out a shiny tin container the size of a matchbook. She pinched a small amount of finely ground tobacco between her fingertips. "Pablo got his start in 1952 when he was with the Dixie Mountain Boys," she continued, packing the tobacco between her gums and her thin, crimson lips.

"Dixie Mountain Boys?" Mister Johns said. "Never heard of them."

"Most folks haven't. But Bobby had," she said, pausing for a moment to savor the cool, numbing sensation of the tobacco as it slowly dissolved in her mouth.

"So you would say he was an early influence?"

"That's putting it mildly. Bobby idolized Pablo, Mister Johns. He was in awe of him. Yeah, Bobby thought Pablo hung the moon. Everyone always talks about how much Bobby wanted to become Forrest Guthridge. But if you ask me Pablo was his real mentor, especially in the early days. Guthridge may have embodied the lifestyle of the 'traveling troubadour,' but Pablo was always a stronger songwriter … in terms of melody anyway."

"Melody?"

"Well, Bobby never had trouble with words—words came easy to him. But Bobby was always looking for a melody to stick his words onto."

"So you're saying that the great Bob Dorian—prophet and poet for a generation—that he stole his songs?"

"The word, I believe he used was, 'appropriated.'"

"And how often did this happen?"

"A couple of times. Frankly, I don't think Pablo thought twice about it."

"So he was all right with the fact Zeitzman was essentially ripping him off?"

"If Pablo hadn't been so enamored with Bobby, I suspect he might have seen it that way. But I think he just saw it as the price of being Bob's friend."

"Hell of a price to pay," Mister Johns replied.

"Listen, I don't know what exactly Mr. Tremolo told you," she continued. "I'm assuming the two of you talked to Tremolo—"

"We had a conversation," Mister Johns confirmed.

"Well, it doesn't sound like Tremolo told you a whole lot. But the truth is that trip he, Bob and Elijah Blue took across the country in '64—it had nothing to do with some romantic vision of America. That trip was about getting juiced, pure and simple."

"Juiced?"

"Stoned … wasted … fucked up. The whole trip was planned around what they could score and where they could score it. And guess who was in charge of setting up the deals?"

"Score one for Elijah Blue—"

"Now don't get me wrong, pills had been a part of the scene from the beginning. And Bobby was the biggest hophead of them all. Or so everyone thought. According to the stories Tremolo told when he got back, Pablo's suitcase was like an apothecary shop."

"So if they're all popping pills why would the fact that Elijah Blue was popping more than the others make any difference?"

"It didn't. The fact he was using wasn't the issue. I think what bothered Bobby was that Pablo had let himself fall so far. You have to remember he'd been a hero of Bobby's when he'd started out. To see him reduced to a mascot really destroyed whatever relationship had formed between them. You see, by '64 no one questioned Bobby. He was infallible. And as much as he might have enjoyed being told he was right all the time, I don't think he ever really trusted the people who fed him that bunk. No sir, that 'let me wash your feet, it would be an honor' shit never worked on Bobby. The best way to win over Bobby—in the long run anyway—was to challenge, not compliment him."

Mister Johns hadn't written anything down for a good 10 to 15 seconds. And frankly he didn't need to. None of what the woman in the blue, mud-encrusted overalls was telling him was new. He'd heard it all before. "You know all this talk about 'messiah complexes' and 'star trips' is all fine and well," Mister Johns said, an irritated edginess creeping into his voice, "but the fact of the matter is that two men go on a trip. Both presumably start out as friends. One stays with him for 40 years; the other hasn't been heard from since. Now something happened, and I still don't know what it was."

"Join the club, Mister Johns," the woman replied flatly. "Nobody knows for sure what happened on that trip. Certainly, I don't. I wasn't there. But I know this—at one time Bobby looked up to

Pablo. But the moment the tables turned, the moment Pablo started looking up to Bobby, it was all over for Elijah Blue."

"What do you mean 'all over'?"

"You said it yourself, Mister Johns. Two men go on a trip across the country. One challenges him, keeps him on his toes, makes sure fame doesn't go to his head. The other kowtows to him, tells him what he thinks he wants to hear, gets caught up in the scene. One becomes a true friend; the other nothing more than a fan, no better than the rest of them."

"But to just pull the carpet out from underneath him like that ..."

"Like I said, he was like a messiah to those who surrounded him. But once you were excommunicated from the 'Church of Bob' nobody would have anything to do with you."

"So he never saw him again? Never felt any remorse?"

"Well, I can't speak to remorse. I suspect the answer is, 'no.' As for seeing him again, once you were out of Bob's life, there was no sense rapping at the door. The only person he ever let back in was Tremolo. Truth is nobody could ever figure out why Tremolo was tossed out in the first place."

It was just the sort of throwaway line that Mister Johns would have ordinarily pounced on. Instead, he let it go. After all, Johns knew *exactly* why the plate had passed Tremolo. It was why Elijah Blue had lost his place at the table that Mister Johns was interested in getting to the bottom of.

"So let me get this straight—" Mister Johns inquired. "Zeitzman steals this guy's songs, takes him on a cross-country tour, let's him get strung out on pills, then when he doesn't like the way he looks at him, cuts him off from all his friends—basically ruins his life."

"I suppose that's one way of looking at it, 'yes.'"

"I'm not sure how else *to* look at it. The facts seem to speak for themselves."

"And what are the facts telling you, Mister Johns?"

"That we might just have ourselves a murder suspect."

"Except for one small fact ..." she said, clearly relishing what she was going to say next—

"And what's that?"

"Your suspect's been dead for 40 years."

Considering the gathering storm on the horizon, not to mention the bombshell the old woman had just dropped, it wouldn't have been totally unexpected for the sound of rolling thunder to be heard in the distance. Instead, the only sound was the long, lingering sound of silence as Mister Johns stared blankly at the old woman. Jack Frost was staring at her, too.

"Suicide," she said with an odd aplomb that indicated just how much she had enjoyed watching the condescending Mister Johns recoil when he learned the only person his suspect had killed had been himself. "Electrocuted himself in his bathtub," she continued. "But considering it happened over 40 years ago, that's one death you won't have to follow up on."

It was all Mister Johns could do not to pick up that hoe leaning against the wooden banister and whack her across the head with it. The fact she was grinning ear to ear, exposing that smug smile in all its rotten, decayed glory, didn't help matters either.

Hell, Mister Johns thought to himself, *I'd actually be doing you a favor knocking out a couple of those teeth.*

As the man whose job was to sum up the lives of the recently deceased in 100 words or less, Mister Johns knew better than anyone Elysian Row was filled with a cagey cast of Cretans, misanthropes and malcontents. Apparently, that assessment also applied to the people populating the outskirts of town.

There was no question this crotchety old farmhand had certainly knocked the wind out of Mister Johns' sails. It might have been different if they'd just lost out on the big lead that was going to break this whole murder investigation wide open. But the fact that Elijah Blue had been dead for 40 years wasn't as major a setback as Johns had originally suspected. Truth be told, Elijah Blue was nothing more than a pesky loose end that needed to be tied up in the off chance that it came back later and threatened to unravel their case. Once again, Johns was just doing his due diligence. But nowhere in his agreement with Commissioner Tiresias did it say he had to have his hat handed to him. And if Johns was going to get his cage rattled by this feisty old broad he was going to make damn sure he shook a few answers out of her in the process.

"Listen, lady, this is a murder investigation," Mister Johns snapped. "You want to play games, you can play them downtown. Now I suggest you come clean. And you can start by telling us just who the hell you are."

"Name's Penny—" she said, "and this here's my land. And while you may be looking into a murder, as far as I know I'm not a suspect. So unless you plan on naming me as one, you and Mr. Frost best leave before I have *you* taken downtown for trespassing."

"Like I said," Johns continued, punching the air with his index finger, "you want to play games we can play games. Because if I have to come back up here, it won't be a subpoena I'll be carrying. It'll be a warrant for your arrest signed by Commissioner Tiresias himself. Withholding information—" Mister Johns said with a grin, "it trumps trespassing every time." Mister Johns turned and started back down the old dirt road that led back to Elysian Row.

"Frost, you coming?" Mister Johns called out impatiently.

Frost, however, did not move. "We're not going anywhere," Frost said flatly.

"And why's that?" Mister Johns demanded.

"Because we'd only have to come back."

CHAPTER 8

▼

PENNY

It was as if Jack Frost had seen a ghost. And while the woman standing in front of him clearly wasn't a figment of his imagination, she *was* a figure from his past. And Jack Frost couldn't believe he'd almost let her disappear into thin air.

"You're Penny?" Frost said disbelievingly.

"That's right," she said, her thin, crimson lips curling upward into a smile. Clearly, she was relishing this moment.

"And this ..." Frost said, motioning to the vast open space that surrounded them, "... this is your farm?"

"That's right."

"Wait a minute," Johns said abruptly. "You *know* this woman?" His finger was drawn on her like a loaded gun.

"Well, we've never met. But I know who she is. Everyone knew Penny back in the '60s. Everyone in the Folk Movement, that is."

"An enlightened conscience might get you to heaven," Penny said, reciting what had clearly been a mantra for her back when she thought she could actually make a difference, "but it makes paying the bills a living hell."

"What the hell is she talking about, Frost?" Mister Johns balked.

"I used to organize rallies, Mister Johns. Hired Bobby and other up-and-comers from the folk scene to play."

"Wait a minute," Mister Johns was still trying to wrap his head around that one. "Zeitzman worked for *you?*"

"Phil, Joan, Tom, even the legendary Bobby Zeitzman, they all worked for me at one time or another back in the '60s. There was a lot of injustice in this country in the '60s, Mister Johns. Still is. Problem is that there are so many grey areas these days. Back then it was a bit more 'black and white,' if you get my drift."

"And you *knew* this, Frost?" Mister Johns demanded.

"I know Bob worked Penny's Farm a couple of times," he confessed. "But I had no idea we were talking to *the* Penny Bently, though."

"And how many of these rallies did Zeitzman play?" Mister Johns asked.

"About half a dozen. Trust me, the ACLU paid a lot better than the people dropping dimes into Bob's guitar case on the corner of Fourth and MacDougal. Went well for a while, too. 'Til he said he was tired of being labeled as a protest singer, that is. Tired of playing songs he didn't want to play, singing words he didn't want to sing. He even went as far as to announce he was going to quit singing altogether. And this was '64, when he was at the height of his popularity."

"So what happened?"

"He left," she said emphatically. "That's what happened. 'I ain't working this farm no more,'" she said in the tinny, nasal-affected Bob Dorian drawl that was almost as famous as the man himself. "Said he was tired of 'scrubbing the floors'—whatever the hell that meant. Frankly, I never saw Bobby lift a hand in my life. But he was done with the Movement. He wanted to move on from being a singer of songs that spoke for others to a writer of songs that spoke for himself."

"So he left?" Mister Johns said. "Just like that?" The skepticism in his voice was unmistakable.

"Just like that," Penny replied. There wasn't an ounce of reticence in her response. "Like I said, there was even talk of him walking away from the business altogether."

Mister Johns wasn't a big fan of unforeseen twists, but this one was definitely turning in his favor. *Maybe this isn't such a dead end after all,* he thought to himself.

"But you know, as much as I wished he *had* quit—" Penny continued, "I mean, to be on the receiving end of that pen was never enviable. But the truth is if he had walked away, if he had gone off and written that novel like he was threatening to do, it would have been a great loss for all of us."

"He might still be alive, though," Mister Johns morbidly observed. "Rock stars have a better track record getting knocked off than novelists."

"Perhaps, but a part of all of us would have died if he'd stopped."

Mister Johns considered the thought.

"So let me get this straight," Mister Johns said, raising his hand in the air like a traffic cop in the middle of a four-way intersection. Clearly, he wasn't buying it. "After everything you did for him—give him a job, fill his dwindling financial coffers, raise his profile with all the people who could help him. After all that, Zeitzman just waltzes in one day and tells you he's walking away from everything he believes in, walking away from everyone who believes in him?"

"Why is that so hard to believe, Mister Johns?"

"Because people don't change overnight like that," Mister Johns said succinctly. "Something happened. And whatever it was, from what you're telling me, it happened right here," Mister Johns said, pointing emphatically at the ground with his index finger.

"Not 'something,' Mister Johns," she said forebodingly. "'Someone' ..."

Mister Johns was about to ask the inevitable question, 'And who is this someone?' but he didn't need to waste his breath. She was planning on telling him that name from the start.

"He had a manager—" she continued, "big fat guy. Real pit bull. Didn't talk a whole lot—mostly hung out in the background, kept to himself. But when he thought his boy—and by '64, Bob was clearly his 'boy'—when he thought he was getting a raw deal, he wasn't afraid to push people around. Like I said, he didn't do a whole lot of talking, but when he did, man, it sounded like a Somali war dance."

"This the same guy who got mixed up with Zeitzman around '63?" Mister Johns said, turning to Jack Frost. "The guy Tremolo told us about?"

"That's the one," Frost confirmed. Frost's stoic, stone-faced expression gave nothing away. But beneath that calm, cool exterior Jack Frost was sweating bullets.

"Guy have a name?" Mister Johns said, pen poised.

"Judas," Penny replied, slyly looking out of the corner of her eye. She hoped to catch Jack Frost's reaction to the name he had tried to gloss over when it had come up earlier in the conversation. She was woefully disappointed, however.

Tremolo was right when he'd told them Bob had loved games. And one of Bob's favorite games was Texas Hold 'Em. Over the years, Jack Frost had played a lot of cards with Bob Dorian. And if he'd picked up anything from Bob, it was how to put on a poker face. Jack Frost was wearing that face right now. So when Penny peered out of the corner of her eye in the direction of Jack Frost she might not have known exactly what it was he was thinking, but she did know one thing for sure: Jack Frost wasn't about to fold.

"Seriously, what was the guy's name?" Mister Johns said, looking up. He had had his head buried in his notebook so he had missed the exchange between Penny and Jack Frost.

"That *was* his name," Penny replied. "And it fit him like a glove. He was always whispering in Bobby's ear, kissing up to him. Telling him how great he was."

"From what you told us earlier, that sycophant shit didn't work too well for Elijah Blue."

"Elijah Blue wasn't making him rich."

"And this Judas," Mister Johns said, pressing Penny for clarification, "he was making Zeitzman rich?"

"Let's just put it this way—Judas knew how to 'recognize' a situation, knew how to turn it in his favor."

"What does that mean?" Mister Johns said, a tinge of annoyance creeping into his voice. "He 'knew how to recognize a situation,'" he chided. "What the hell does that even mean?"

Penny was fully capable of answering the question. And considering her checkered past with Bob Dorian, she would have loved nothing more than to take a whack at it. But when it came to dredging up Bob's past with Judas, she figured it was only right to defer to the man standing next her. But when it became clear to her Jack Frost wasn't going to tell the story, she decided to tell it herself—

"Judas saw Bob was being exploited, taken advantage of by people who wanted to ride his coattails. But that's why they made such a perfect pair. You see, Judas wasn't the only one who could take advantage of a situation. Bob had been doing it for years. Of course, we just didn't think he do it to us. In all fairness, though," she continued, "we did give him the fodder." The noxious tone present earlier was now replaced by a poignant, almost painful sadness. "We gave him everything he needed, and we gave it to him on a silver platter."

"What are you talking about?" Mister Johns said. Clearly, his patience for recollections of days bygone, not to mention all this heady hyperbole, was wearing thin. "Gave what to him on a silver platter?"

"Look around, Mister Johns. What do you see?" Penny said, her voice filled with more heartbreak than hate.

"Land," he replied.

"That's right, and this land's been in my family for over 150 years. Beans, tobacco and cotton—that's what this land was used for."

"It's beautiful," Mister Johns observed. And he meant it.

"And profitable ... was for a while anyway," Penny said wistfully. She reached into her silver tin and pinched a little more tobacco between her thumb and index finger. It was only then Mister Johns realized that there was writing on the top of the tin, a single word: '*Bently's.*' The tobacco may have been fresh. The tin holding it, however, was not. It was dented and dinged. The logo was old, and flaked and faded. Clearly, this tin had not held tobacco harvested from this farm for a very long time.

"And who do you think worked this land back then?" Penny continued, placing the tobacco between her cheek and gum. There was another one of those pesky rhetorical questions, Mister Johns so abhorred. "It's okay, Mister Johns, you can call a spade a spade. They don't work here anymore." Johns hesitated—

"African-Americans," Penny said, uttering the word Mister Johns couldn't, or perhaps wouldn't, bring himself to say. "Of course, my great-grandfather had another word for them. But, 'yes,' the land you're standing on was at one time one of the largest plantations in the country. There was therefore some symbolism to the rallies we held here in the '60s—a former slave plantation now the bastion of forward-thinking liberalism and equality," she said, spelling it out in case the symbolism had been lost on Mister Johns. Judging from the contemptuous look on his face, it hadn't. "But Mr. Frost here is right," she said, turning in Jack Frost's direction, "the Left defined him. He'd become our 'boy' so to speak. And he turned it around on us the way he turned everything around. All those needling images of a southern plantation family he conjured up—it was nothing more than a cruel reversal of the symbolism of this place. And we handed it to him on a silver platter."

"So in the end he was right," Mister Johns said haughtily.

"Right about what?" Penny replied. She had clearly picked up on the smugness in Mister Johns' voice.

"Being a sloganeer? A hawker for the Left?"

"Listen, Mister Johns, I'm not going to lie to you. Nobody likes to admit this—certainly nobody would have copped to it at the time—but in the end there really is no 'Left' or 'Right.'"

"I think there are a lot of people in Washington who would beg to differ," Mister Johns countered.

"What I mean to say is there are extremes in our political system, you *can* pick sides. But the dirty little secret—and the politicians in Washington know this better than anyone—is that in the end it doesn't matter. Whichever side you pick you end up in the same place."

"And where is that?"

"The middle. Corporate America, the financial establishment and organized religion," she said, ticking them off one by one. "That, Mister Johns, is the Holy Trinity of politics. And where do they meet?" she asked rhetorically. "Right smack dab in the middle of America."

"I think you might just be oversimplifying things a bit, Penny," Frost interjected. "You may be upset by what Bob did—turning his back on the Left, taking what he needed and moving on. But don't tell me after 40 years of fighting for causes you believe in, now you've bought into that cynical point of view."

"You're damn right I was upset with what Bobby did. We all were, especially after he had the gall to say: 'I've never written a political song. Half a million people marching on Washington couldn't change the world—what makes you think one of my songs can? I've gone through all that.' He went through it all right," she sneered, dropping the faux Bob Dorian impression, "and he left this place and everything it stood for in his wake."

And though she hadn't come right out and said it, it was evident that Penny and her beloved farm weren't the only things Bob Dorian had left in ruin: Bob Dorian had destroyed her entire family.

It turns out, when Penny had been talking about how she had turned her plantation into the focal point of the Civil Rights Movement in the '60s, she had left out a few details. A few *very* important details. Like telling Mister Johns who paid for those rallies in the first place. Penny's brother made more money on Wall Street by the time he was 30 years old than any of the folkies who played Penny's farm would see in their collective lifetimes. Funny how whenever they started running a little low on cash, checks always seemed to arrive at just the right time. And of course Penny couldn't have had a rally without people. And Penny's father had sat on the board of GM for close to a quarter-century. Awfully convenient, especially when they had trouble with the local 'color.' One call and "Pa" would have a field of union men ready to get those uppity agitators back in line. And if you want to control the hearts and minds of young America what do you do? Control their soul. And Penny's mother, "Ma" as she liked to be called, she was the real brains behind the operation, not to mention an elder in the local Baptist church. No question, "Ma" attended more church bake sales than anyone in Smith County. Corporate America, the financial establishment, organized religion. Penny's family wasn't just involved in American politics in the 1960s: they *were* American politics. And when Bob Dorian got wind of that incestuous little secret, he picked over that family like a vulture picks over a carcass on the side of the road.

In many ways what Bob Dorian did to Penny's family was justified. After all, they did represent the very things he was railing against in his songs: deceit, deception and institutionalize corruption. Not to mention the fact that none of the members of Penny's family had been especially forthright about how they had gotten that farm where Bob was staging those protests. A lack of full disclosure, it seems, was a trait Penny had inherited. Clearly, she had no intention mentioning the duplicitous role her family had played in manipulating the American political system, either.

"Contrary to what we said and sang about in the '60s," Penny continued, "God was never on our side. He may have been on Bobby's, but he was never on ours. If you ask me, he'd be better off if he'd just been taken down by the railroad tracks and left for dead." She kicked at the dry, barren ground one final time as if she were kicking a dog that was down on his luck.

"So anyway—" she said quickly, having purged the last vestiges of vitriol and venom left in her, "where *did* they find Bobby?"

"A COINCIDENCE," Frost replied, the hard-packed dirt crunching under his feet as he led the way back to Elysian Row.

"How long have you been in the music business?" Mister Johns let the question hang like a noose. It was more of an accusation than an inquiry.

"All my life."

"And how many years did you work for him?"

"What's your point, Johns?"

"My point is that nothing that guy did was a coincidence. It was all planned."

"That may be," Frost concurred. "But the fact that she said he'd be better if he'd just been taken down by the railroad tracks and left for dead is an expression. It's a colloquialism, Johns."

"But he *was* taken down by the railroad tracks and left for dead. What she said may be a colloquialism—the fact she said it is no coincidence."

"I'll admit it's a bit odd that of all the words she could have chosen to express her disdain for Bob, she'd choose those."

"It's the second time it's happened. She's the second person to allude to someone dying by the railroad tracks."

"You're hearing things, Johns."

"Not hearing things, Frost. Just filling in the blanks. Remember how Tremolo described the cross-country trip as their version of *On the Road*?"

"That doesn't prove anything," Frost said, rebutting whatever charge Mister Johns was on the verge of making. "Tremolo's not the only one who's described the trip in that way, Johns. Like Tremolo said, Zeitzman was a fan of Kerouac's."

"But not just a fan, Frost. Tremolo said Zeitzman loved Kerouac. Loved the way he wrote, the way he lived."

"It's hardly a secret Bob was enamored with Kerouac."

"It seems Mr. Tremolo was, too," Mister Johns said, opening his notepad, "'… and as macabre as this may sound, Bob even loved the way Kerouac died.'" Johns closed the notepad, "Do you happen to know how Kerouac died, Frost?"

"No."

"He disappeared—nobody knew where he was," Mister Johns explained. "Out on a bender. Turns out he took plenty of booze, but forgot to take a coat. When they finally found him a few days later, he'd frozen to death."

"What's this got to do with Bob? What's this got to do with Tremolo? Hell ..." Frost was getting worked up, "what's this got to do with *anything*?!"

"They found him by the railroad tracks," Mister Johns said. Johns paused, allowing what he clearly considered an all-too-convenient fact to sink in. "You may not have known how Kerouac died, but Tremolo did. We've told three people about Zeitzman's murder. Two of them alluded to the railroad tracks. It's almost as if they already knew he was dead." There was a suspicious tone in Mister Johns' voice, and Jack Frost was nobody's fool. He knew exactly upon whom the suspicion was being cast.

"Bob Dorian was my friend!" Frost sputtered, defending himself against the unspoken allegation. "What motive would I possibly have to sabotage this investigation by leaking facts about it? I want to catch the bastard who put that bullet in his chest so badly it hurts."

"Then why'd you give them the opportunity to kill him?"

"The opportunity to kill him? What the hell are you talking about!" Frost exploded.

"You let him come back to Elysian Row, didn't you?"

"I didn't make that decision but, 'yes,' I did support it once it had been made. Bob was my ..."

"Cut the 'client' crap, Frost," Mister Johns snapped. "He may have been your client, but you don't spend 20 years with someone and not begin to see them as a friend. And as far as I'm concerned, you betrayed that friendship."

"And how do you figure that?"

"This town is filled with people who knew Zeitzman—people, I might add—who were not on as friendly terms with him as you. And you knew that. You knew they hated him. You knew they all had axes to grind. But you still let him return."

"So what are you saying? That I set him up? That I *wanted* him to be killed?"

Frost was furious, damn near foaming at the mouth. And though Mister Johns was off base in his thinking that Jack Frost had wanted Bob Dorian to turn up dead, Mister Johns was spot-on when it came to the fact Jack Frost had been extremely pleased that his client had decided to return to Elysian Row.

Actually, 'pleased' was an understatement. Jack Frost was ecstatic. Dorian's decision to play Elysian Row was going to solve all Jack Frost's problems. It was going to solve Dorian's problems, too. Only difference is that Dorian didn't know the extent of those problems. Jack Frost hadn't found it in him to tell his client he'd misappropriated his fortune in some harebrained 'get rich' scheme that had gone decidedly off course.

So had Jack Frost been happy when he learned that Bob Dorian had agreed to return to Elysian Row and play that concert? The answer was decidedly, 'yes.' It was big news, or it *was* going to be big news once the show was announced. A lot of people were going to want to see that show. But Johns was dead wrong to think that Jack Frost would have ever wanted to see Dorian die. That was one thing he would never have wished for in a million years, no matter how many millions it might have brought in.

Jack Frost suspected there might come a time when he was going to have to explain why Bob's decision to come back to Elysian Row wasn't just something he 'supported'; it was actually something he had been encouraging Bob to do for months. But now wasn't the time to have that discussion. Now was the time to defend himself against an allegation that had done more than cast suspicion on him: it had cast him as a suspect.

"There's no need to get worked up," Mister Johns replied calmly.

"You haven't even begun to see me get worked up," Frost said, matching Mister Johns' aloofness with cool detachment.

"Is that a threat, Mr. Frost?"

"You're good, Mister Johns. Very good. I'm beginning to see why Commissioner Tiresias wanted you on this case. But if we're going to continue working together, I need to know that we're on the same team. I need to know that we're looking for the same man. And I need to be certain you don't suspect that *I* am the person we're looking for."

"Kill him?" Mister Johns said in disbelief. "Is that what you think I'm saying? That *you* killed Zeitzman?" It was all Mister Johns could do but explode with laughter. "For God's sake, Frost, I don't think you killed him. I think it's unfortunate you let him return to Elysian Row. For as we are finding out, there are a lot of people who would like to see Zeitzman dead. But, 'no,' I don't think you're one of them."

"Then why are we having this conversation?" Jack Frost said, wondering if he had really misread Johns as badly as he was being led to believe, or if Johns was just covering for an accusation that had cut a bit too close to the bone.

"Because things just aren't adding up, Frost," Mister Johns said. There was a deadly precision to his words. "The fact that two of the three people we've spoken to said they didn't know Zeitzman was dead, yet both just happen to mention the place where the body was found; the fact that Sophia didn't want us to know she had that ring Zeitzman gave her all those years ago, yet she places it out in plain view; the fact that while we're out on a stretch of deserted Interstate, we don't see anyone for miles, then just *happen* to run into another one of Zeitzman's so-called 'friends' who proceeds to tell us the guy we're looking for has been dead for 40 years. You may believe in coincidences, Mr. Frost, but I don't. The fact Zeitzman even wanted to return to Elysian Row is, in and of itself, too coincidental for my liking."

"So what are you saying, Johns?"

"I'm saying that something is happening here. Something is definitely happening. And what bothers me ..." Mister Johns looked up from his notebook toward the ramshackle houses that dotted the distant horizon, "... is that I don't know what it is."

And while Frost was not a big proponent of conspiracy theories, there was no question something was definitely going on. Jack Frost may have convinced Bob Dorian to return to this place, but from the moment Bob stepped back on the Row things had started to get very strange indeed. And Jack Frost couldn't help but think Mister Johns might be on to something.

It was, after all, Elysian Row ...

CHAPTER 9

▼

LONESOME TOM

They walked for several blocks along Rue Morgue Avenue, past the carnival barkers, past the tightrope walkers, past the insurance men, past the fishermen selling flowers. On the corner, some local loser was handing out placards that read: 'Have mercy on his soul.' The woman defiantly thrust one of the placards in Jack Frost's face. Frost took the card, glanced at it long enough to read the inscription, then slid the card into his pocket. And as he wondered to himself exactly whose soul he should be having mercy on, he couldn't help but think that it might just be his own.

Jesus, Frost thought to himself, *he got out, left this cyanide hole behind. Why would he ever have agreed to come back?*

And though Jack Frost accepted the fact that he would never know with complete certainty the answer to that question, he was beginning to think that maybe Mister Johns had gotten it right: maybe Jack Frost had killed Bob Dorian. After all, you don't take an alcoholic on the mend back to the bar where he used to drink. You don't take a junkie who's kicked the habit back to the fiend who used to sell him his fix. And you damn sure don't let a man who spent his entire life trying to put his past behind him come back to the one place where his past would be staring him right in the face. But that's exactly what Jack Frost had done. Jack Frost had coaxed and cajoled; he had pleaded and persuaded; he had spent the last year and a half trying to get Bob Dorian to consider the thought of coming back. And while Jack Frost didn't pull the trigger, he knew he'd have to live with the inescapable fact that he was the man who had convinced Bob Dorian to return. And as Jack Frost passed the people and places who comprised this vast wasteland filled with foul and populated with freaks, Frost knew he should never have let Dorian come back to Elysian Row.

"This is the place?" Mister Johns said, the stark, staccato phrasing of his question jarring Jack Frost out of his guilt-ridden jaunt down memory lane.

"Yeah, this is the place," Frost confirmed.

They were standing in front of a large plate glass window. A brightly colored neon thumb was pressing down on a saxophone. When the thumb moved, an array of multi-colored musical notes flew out of the instrument in every direction. In the right-hand corner of the window the words, "Tom Thumb's Blues," were flashing over and over in time with the muted rhythms coming from inside.

"Yeah, this is it," Frost repeated.

"You sure?" Mister Johns asked.

Jack Frost eyed Mister Johns with a mixture of contempt and outright irritation.

Do you really think I would have brought us all the way down here if I weren't? Look at this place—it's a cesspool. Talk about a hole in the wall, this place is a portal to Hell.

And while Jack Frost may have been racked with guilt over his role in Bob Dorian's untimely demise, his decision to bring Mister Johns here was one decision with which he hadn't had to wrestle. 'I'm tired of talking with friends, tired of talking with people who are only too happy to talk about Bob Dorian until the conversation hits a rough spot,' Johns had griped with childlike insolence as they'd slogged their way from Penny's farm back to Elysian Row. 'I'm tired of misplaced loyalty and bruised egos. I want to talk to someone who's got a *real* axe to grind.' That talk suited Jack Frost fine. The sooner this whole sordid affair was behind him, the better. If Mister Johns wanted to talk with someone who had a score to settle, well, Jack Frost was more than happy to oblige.

"Yeah, I'm sure," Frost replied, confirming this was the place where they would find the man who hated Bob Dorian more than any other person on the planet.

"So what's this guy's name?"

"Lonesome Tom," Frost replied.

"Please tell me that's not his real name."

Frost gave it some thought. The thought didn't come.

"To tell you the truth, I don't know," Frost said, continuing to rack his brain. "Never did know his real name. None of us did. 'Lonesome' was Bob's nickname for him, so that's what we all called him. Bob was big on nicknames."

"Well, that one's a keeper."

"I suppose," Jack Frost replied equivocally.

As the man attributed with producing Bob Dorian's biggest hit, Lonesome's successful, albeit brief run with Bob yielded some of the most influential music of the rock era. And while their time together was short-lived, the fruits of their precipitous partnership were hardly a fluke. Lonesome ran his recording studio like a football coach runs a sideline. He knew every nuance of every player who wanted in on the game. In their three and a half years together, only one player slipped past Lonesome; and even that misstep had been turned in Bob's favor by the fastidious producer.

There was no question Lonesome had the Midas touch. And while Lonesome hadn't been the first producer to work with Bob Dorian, Lonesome had been the first producer to encourage Bob to embrace change. And though Lonesome was out of the picture by the time Bob's fame and notoriety had come to full fruition, he had been there when the change had taken place. Mr. Tremolo may have witnessed Robert Zeitzman shed his skin and 'become' Bob Dorian, but Lonesome was in the studio when Bob's newly assumed personality struck out at the world like a snake devouring its prey. And while Lonesome had been able to charm the snake for a while, even Lonesome wasn't immune to Bob's venomous attacks. Eventually even he, too, was devoured. And as much as Jack Frost would have liked to explain to Johns how Lonesome got his nickname, it was hard to tell a story that he himself didn't know.

But as Jack Frost watched the neon thumb move up and down in solitary, muted silence, it occurred to Jack Frost the name with which Bob Dorian had saddled the prodigious producer all those years ago made all the sense in the world. Despite Bob Dorian's musings to the contrary, Dorian had *always* known Lonesome's fate. He had known the moment he met Lonesome that one day he would cast him aside, banish him to a small, out-of-the-way club at the end of Elysian Row just as he had cast out everyone he had allowed to get too close. 'Friendless' and 'forlorn' are, after all, both found in the dictionary under the moniker Bob bequeathed on his one-time trusted friend and confidant.

"Yeah, nickname's a real keeper, all right," Jack Frost said. "But like I said, the chances of his talking are slim to none, the emphasis being on the none."

"You know, you've said that about every person we've met," Mister Johns said contemptuously. "Funny how you've been wrong every time."

"Well, this guy's different."

"Zeitzman fucked him, didn't he?" Mister Johns shot back.

"Big time. I'd say of all the people in this town, Bob fucked him over the most."

"Which is exactly why he's going to talk."

"And how do you figure that?"

"Because everybody loves to tell their side of the story," Johns said, pulling at the door handle. "After you—"

A waft of dingy, dirty cigarette smoke slithered out as the heavy, wooden door slowly opened. Inside, the smell of cigarette smoke intertwined with stale beer. A long slab of green and yellow speckled linoleum ran the length of the room. At the bar, a sordid collection of panderers, politicians, hypocrites and hucksters were drowning their sorrows in drink and asking the bartender for absolution.

On stage, a large black man was playing a more than passable version of John Coltrane's, 'Equinox.' The man's face was obscured in smoke and darkness, and as they watched him play they were amazed at how little effort it took for him to conjure up the notes. First an 'E,' then a 'C,' then back to an 'E.' The notes seemed to seep from every crevice of his horn. They danced across the stage, effortlessly carried across the room as if they were being lifted up to heaven on perpetual clouds of smoke. And then, just like that—"poof"—the smoke was gone, and so, too, was the note. Watching the man play that baritone sax was like watching a magician perform a perfectly executed slight of hand trick. It was, in a word, effortless.

"How can I help you?" a voice said, slicing through the smoky haze.

"I'm looking for a guy," Frost responded.

"'Noah's Rainbow'—next door," the bartender said without looking up.

"Not that kind of guy," Mister Johns replied quickly, wishing he could smack that smile off the bartender's face. "We're looking for a guy named 'Lonesome,'" Johns clarified.

"And who's 'we'?" the bartender replied protectively.

"Name's Johns. And this here is Jack Frost. We just need a few minutes."

"A few minutes can turn into a long time." The bartender was looking at them now. "You guys cops?"

"Listen, pal, it's nothing like that."

"Nothing like that, huh?" the bartender repeated, lifting a dirty glass out of the washbasin.

"I used to know Lonesome a while back," Frost interjected. "Just tell him it's Jack Frost."

The bartender wiped the glass clean with a damp towel, then filled it with a healthy dose of Scotch. He placed the glass on the counter.

"Why don't you tell him yourself—" the bartender said, lifting his chin to acknowledge the man who had seemingly appeared out of nowhere.

The man took the Scotch and downed it quickly. "Evening, gentlemen—" he said unenthusiastically.

The man standing in the shadows was the same man they had been watching play the saxophone on stage moments before. Frost and Johns had both attributed the fact that his face had been obscured to the lighting on the stage. The lighting, it turns out, had nothing to do with it. There he was, standing just a few feet away from them, just as dark as night. If it wasn't for the light flickering from the candle in the middle of the bar they might not have seen him at all.

"You told the bartender you weren't a cop?" the dark man said, his eyes fixed on Mister Johns as he lowered himself into a faux leather chair. "That is what you said, wasn't it?" His voice was smooth and soothing, and sounded a lot like the baritone sax he carefully placed on the ground beside him.

"I'm not," Mister Johns replied.

"You sure were asking a lot of questions for a guy who said all he wanted was a beer."

"I'm a reporter," Mister Johns replied.

"Reporter, cop, same damn thing. You're a real joker, man. Hey— here's one you might not have heard—a reporter and a manager walk into a bar …"

"Bob's dead," Frost said, cutting to the punch line. "Found him in the Chelsea this morning."

"You came all the way down here to tell me *that.*"

"You don't sound very upset," Johns said.

"That's because I don't get upset, Mister Johns. Oh, no, wait a minute—I take that back. I got upset about 40 years ago when that cunt bastard fucked me over. Or didn't Frost tell you about that?" Lonesome turned and acknowledged Jack Frost for the first time since the conversation had begun. "Good to see you again, Jack," he said, not meaning a word of it.

"Good to see you, too, Lonesome," Frost replied with equal enthusiasm.

"But as I was saying," Lonesome turned his attention back to Mister Johns, "that was a long time ago. Thirty-eight years to be precise. I'm over it by now. Though I must confess, I do like the sound of those words."

"And what words would those be?" Mister Johns knew the words—he just wanted to hear him say them.

"'Bob's dead'—has a nice ring to it. Serves him right coming back here."

"What do you mean, 'serves him right coming back'?"

"Johns, is it?"

"That's right," Mister Johns replied reticently.

It was apparent that Mister Johns hadn't taken much of a shine to the guy Bob Dorian had dubbed 'Lonesome' so many years ago. And a large part of that mistrust was derived from the fact that in all the time they had been talking, not once had the dark man looked either of them in the eye. In fact, Lonesome seemed to be more concerned with what was happening everywhere else *other* than at that table. And while Lonesome's annoying habit of avoiding eye contact hadn't raised an eyebrow with Jack Frost, it was bugging the hell out of Mister Johns.

"So you're a reporter, huh?" Lonesome said, addressing the bottom of his Scotch glass.

"That's right," Mister Johns replied coolly. *Look me in the eyes, you shit. That glass ain't asking the questions, I am.*

Lonesome lifted and lowered the empty drink over a watermark on the table as if he was peering through a magnifying glass. Evidently, something had caught his attention, and whatever it was told him a lot more than either of these men had cared to reveal.

"So who you working for?" Lonesome asked, still looking at the floor. "I know most of the names of the flatfoots down at the *Dispatch,* and I ain't never heard yours."

"Consider yourself fortunate—" Mister Johns replied.

"And how's that?"

"I work the morgue—obits desk."

"Get a load of this guy—" It was clear Lonesome was hoping to elicit a chuckle. "That's good. Really, that's good. Now—" suddenly Lonesome's voice grew low and threatening, "you want to tell me who you're *really* working for?" His eyes rose up, and for the first time his penetrating gaze was squarely affixed on Mister Johns.

"Commissioner Tiresias brought me in if you must know," Johns said undeterred.

"Everybody's gotta serve somebody," Lonesome replied, finally getting that chuckle out. "Course the Commissioner's nothing but a thief, but like I said—you gotta serve somebody." He took a sip of his drink. "So, what'd Penny say?" He placed the glass back on the table.

Jack Frost and Mister Johns exchanged a glance. *How did he …*

"Your shoes," Lonesome said, pointing toward the floor. "There's mud all over them." The two men looked down at their shoes. Indeed, there was mud all over them. "I know you're new to this, Johns," he continued, clearly relishing the fact that he had turned the tables on his interrogator, "but I think you're supposed to be following a trail, not leaving one." Lonesome picked up a cloth napkin and slid it across the table. "Now, do me a favor, and wipe your feet. Both of you. I don't want you tracking that shit around my bar." The two men wiped the mud off their shoes and placed the soiled napkins back on the table.

So that's what he was looking at, Johns realized. *He was looking for clues.*

And though Mister Johns didn't want to admit it, the truth was staring him smack in the face. Despite Mister Johns' earlier assessment, Lonesome was probably the most attentive guy in the room.

"So what's the thinking here?" Lonesome inquired. "Someone from the Row got wind that Bob was back in town and popped him. Someone who hated him, someone with a past ..." the dark man brought the glass to his lips. He took a sip of whiskey, then placed the glass back on the table, "... someone like me."

"Listen, we're not accusing you of anything," Mister Johns said defensively.

"Of course you're not." The sarcasm wasn't lost on either of them. "You just show up unannounced in my bar asking a lot of questions, want to talk to the guy who had every reason in the world to kill the man who's just turned up dead. Oh, and I almost forgot—the guy who's poking around just happens to be a reporter placed on personal retainer by the chief of police. Now, why in the world would I think you were accusing me of anything?"

"We'd just like to ask you a few questions," Frost said.

"Well, I know the one that's foremost on your mind, so I'll cut straight to the chase—I didn't kill him. There, I just saved us both a whole bunch of needless conversation. But at least you and I got to see each other, Frost." The Scotch had taken a little of the edge off the roughness of his voice. It had not, however, washed away any of the sarcasm. "I never really understood why you wanted to get mixed up with that asshole, but then again he ended up fucking you in the end, too, didn't he?"

"And how's that?" Frost asked.

"Kind of tough being a manager without any clients, isn't it?" he said, firing a final salvo.

"All right, Lonesome, let *me* cut straight to the chase," Johns said. "I'm a reporter—not a cop—a reporter working on an unsolved murder. And Frost here is, as you so astutely put it, a manager without a client. So you don't need to worry about wasting our time. Because the two of us—" Mister Johns motioned between himself and Frost with his forefinger, "we ain't got nothin' but time."

The dark man could have walked away. He could just as easily have slipped back into the shadows. But he didn't slip away. Instead, he remained in the warm, uneven flicker of the candle as it desperately gasped for air.

But Johns knew he would have to talk fast. He didn't want to give this guy enough time to start selling him a handful of alibis.

"You said you didn't kill him," Mister Johns continued. "Fair enough. Then perhaps you wouldn't mind answering a few questions. Who knows—you might tell us something that helps us find the person who did."

"Fine," Lonesome said, lowering himself back into the faux leather chair.

On stage the three members of the quartet were fidgeting nervously. With a slight lift of his chin, Lonesome instructed them to go ahead and start the next set without him. And in that instant it was clear: the man who had been almost invisible to them when they first entered the bar was now the most commanding presence in the room.

"Fine," Lonesome repeated, motioning for the bartender to bring him another drink. "I got no secrets to conceal ..."

"SO LET ME GUESS," Lonesome said, draining the contents of the glass, "Penny said she didn't even know he was in town." Neither of the men replied. "Obviously—" Lonesome said, answering his own question. "Or you wouldn't be here. Hell, you can't throw a stone in this town without hitting someone who didn't hate that bastard."

"Does that go for you?"

"Does that go for me?" Lonesome asked contemptuously, repeating Johns' question. "You're damn straight that goes for me," Lonesome said without missing a beat. "Shit, I told you how I felt about him the minute you walked through the door. Listen, Mister Johns," Lonesome continued, "Bob made a few enemies on the way up. Probably figured he wouldn't be coming down. Of course, things do change—" he said, clearly taking pleasure in the fact that they had. "Just the nature of the beast, I suppose. But if you plan to get to the bottom of this, you're going to need to distinguish legitimate gripes from sour grapes."

"Sour grapes?"

"Like I said, you can't throw a stone in this town without finding someone who didn't harbor a grudge against Bob. But Penny, she harbored one of the biggest."

"Well, he did cost her her farm," Johns rationalized.

"Is that what she said?" Lonesome said incredulously. "That Bob's the reason she lost her farm?"

"Well, I could certainly check my notes, but 'yes' that's pretty much the gist of it."

"Shit, I don't need the 'gist.' I can hear it now," Lonesome said, his voice taking on a slight Southern drawl reminiscent of Penny's. 'Bob was the most self-serving, opportunistic bastard I ever met. If it hadn't been for him,' blah, blah, blah ..." Clearly, when it came to Lonesome's relationship with Penny, that relationship had soured a long time ago.

"And he *wasn't* self-serving, opportunistic?"

"Penny is nothing but a bleeding heart, a believer in causes that, like Penny herself, are past their prime. Whatever problem she attributes to Bob is an excuse for her own failures. If there's one thing I learned from Bob it's that those folkies were a fucking nest of vipers."

"I take it you weren't a fan?"

"Are you kidding me!" Lonesome exclaimed. "I didn't give a rat's ass about folk music. I was a jazz guy ... Sun Ra, Coltrane ... those were the guys I dug. Those were the cats I was recording—on my own label, no less. That's right," Lonesome said, anticipating Johns' thought, "a black man with a business."

"I didn't—" Mister Johns sputtered.

"You didn't have to," Lonesome continued. "And besides, I thought folk music was for the dumb guys. That whole 'aw-shucks, let's ride the rails' crap was just dumb. And when I first heard Bob, he sounded liked the rest of them. Real clumsy, chord changes were all off, just ... well ... dumb."

"So why'd you record him?"

"Oh, I didn't record him for the music he was playing. I recorded him because of the things he was saying. The words. Jesus, when he opened his mouth and the words came out, I was floored. You have to remember, I was once a believer, too."

"You don't strike me as someone who wears his heart on his sleeve," Johns said drolly.

"Maybe I wasn't as gregarious as the others, but I always believed in Bob. In fact, I'd say there was a time when I was his biggest believer."

"Obviously that's not the case anymore."

"No."

"So what happened?"

"Six words—'That guy ain't an organ player.' Those six words ended my relationship with Bob Dorian." Lonesome took another sip of his drink.

"'That guy ain't an organ player'—" Mister Johns repeated the six words. "He fired you over that? There's got to be more to the story than that."

Oh there's more to it than that, Jack Frost thought to himself. *There's a hell of a lot more to it than that.*

"Listen, I'm not much for living in the past," Lonesome said with a tinge of irony. Everyone at the table knew he was planning on telling the story about the organ player the minute he uttered those six words, "you know, telling stories of the 'good old days' as it were. But this is a story worth telling."

"Do tell," Mister Johns said, turning over a fresh page in his notebook.

Yes, do tell, Jack Frost silently concurred.

"It was June of '65, Bob was at the height of his power—" Lonesome raised his hand slightly, signaling the bartender. Without further provocation, the bartender reached under the slab of linoleum and retrieved a fresh bottle of Scotch. He crossed the room and set the bottle on the table. "Black jacket, black shirt buttoned up at the top, black leather boots with high Cuban heels. Bob wasn't a very tall guy—5'9" maybe 5'10"—but man if he didn't look like he was 10 feet tall when he marched into that control room. We used to joke the heels gave him two inches, his afro four, and his bad-ass attitude made up the difference." Lonesome unscrewed the top of the bottle and refilled his glass. "Anyway, I'd brought this guitarist with me to the session—young kid who was hoping he might get a few licks in with Bob. So, Bob's been working on this one particular song all morning. He's already been through like three takes. And Bob was not the kind of guy who liked to do a song more than once. So anyway, my point is that he's stuck: He wants to bring it all home, but he's just not sure what direction to take it. And the last thing he wants to do is be a babysitter. So he tells the kid to sit over in the corner. Well, there's an organ over in the corner. Like I said, I was producing a lot of jazz artists then and the B3 was big at the time. So this guy starts noodling around on it during the fourth take. Well, Bob hears what this guy's doing and yells out for me to turn up the organ. And I yell back, 'Hey man, that guy ain't an organ player.'" Lonesome paused, allowing a moment for the words to sink in. "That was my last song with Bob. He laid the track down and when we were done, he had someone in his 'inner circle'—I think it was Tremolo—inform me that my future services would no longer be required."

"He got rid of you because you wouldn't turn up an organ track?"

"Like I said, he got rid of most of us—the bass player, the drummer—those guys were gone the next day. But here's the best part—" Lonesome said, playing the moment for all it was worth, "he kept the organ player."

"You must have been pissed."

"I wanted to kill him." There was a long silence. "I said I *wanted* to kill him—stop salivating. Wanting to do something and actually doing it are two different things. And besides, that was almost 40 years ago. Truth be told, I made more money because he fired me than I ever would have if I'd stuck around. After Fairport, they were lining up to get in the studio with me."

"Because you'd produced the song that broke it all wide open? The guy who took him electric?"

"I think it's because they were hoping I'd tell 'em stories," Lonesome said with remarkable modesty for a man who really *had* broken it all open. The song that came out of that session with the organ player hadn't just cracked it all wide open … it had changed everything. "The first thing Andy Warhol asked me when he showed up with the Underground was, 'What's Bob like? I hear he's a genius?'" Lonesome said with an affected tone. It wasn't a half bad Warhol. "Trust me," Lonesome continued, "when the king of the freaks is calling you a genius, you have officially arrived."

"May I ask you a question, Lonesome?"

"Sure, Jack," Lonesome replied, turning in Frost's direction. "Hell, I'd almost forgotten you were there."

"I've heard the organ story before."

"Sorry to have wasted your time, Jack," Lonesome snapped.

"What I mean is that I know the story. But as often as I've heard it, I've never actually figured out why Bob got rid of you? I mean arguing over an organ part is hardly enough to end a three-year relationship."

"He's ended longer relationships over a lot less," Lonesome replied tersely. It was clear the 'organ story' comment, as Jack Frost had rather glibly referred to it, hadn't sat too well with Lonesome. "But Bob's also kept a few people around for a lot longer than he should have." Lonesome didn't come right out and say it, and he didn't have to. Because the 'people' to whom he was referring to was actually a single person—and that person was sitting right across from him. "But to answer your question, Jack," Lonesome continued, "he never gave me a reason. Frankly, I never expected one. That would have been very out of character for Bob."

"How so?" Mister Johns pressed, hoping that perhaps Lonesome might offer up some explanation.

"Listen, the guy was a slime when it came to stuff like that. He hated confronting people. Ideas, concepts—he loved challenging preconceptions—but people? He didn't want to have a thing to do with people."

"So there was never a face-to-face?"

"Nope."

"Do you think he regretted that?"

"He never looked back." Lonesome brought the glass to his lips and drank the entire contents in a single gulp. "You know the old saying: 'A rolling stone gathers no moss'?"

"Sure," Mister Johns replied.

"Well, Bob was like that. Always moving forward—learning, absorbing, taking what he needed, what he thought would last. But as soon as he got what he wanted he moved on. I gave that guy three and a half albums, two years of my life, the biggest hit of his career."

"Despite whatever came between the two of you, it sounds like you admired him," Mister Johns said, hoping to draw Lonesome out a little further.

"We all admired him," Lonesome said, inching the conversation forward. "Warhol was right, too. Bob *was* a genius. Nobody could believe how brilliant the guy was. And that was the problem. Everyone thought, 'He can't be doing this by himself. He *has* to have someone helping him. He has to have someone feeding him ideas.' But those of us who saw the way Bob worked, we knew the truth. It was all him. But the critics, the press, they just didn't buy it. So they said I was responsible for changing his sound, that I was the one who pushed him to go electric—that I was the 'man behind the curtain.' I wasn't saying these things, other people were. The last thing I would have ever wanted to do is steal Bob's thunder."

"Considering the way it shook out, I take it Dorian didn't see it that way."

"I think he thought I was enjoying the stories they were planting in the press."

"Who was planting in the press?"

"Hell, I have no idea—could have been Bob for all I know."

"So he *was* self-serving?"

"What's that old expression, 'There's no 'I' in 'team.' Well, Bob's gone by two names in his life—the name his family gave him and the name he gave himself. And there's an 'i' in them both. Just because he was a genius, doesn't mean he wasn't the most self-centered, arrogant bastard you've ever met." Lonesome turned the Scotch bottle on its side and drained its contents. The brown, caramel-colored liquid dripped into the glass. "Listen, I know I probably came off a bit strident at first saying I was happy to hear he was dead and all. But anyone who ever knew Bob had a love-hate relationship with him. The more you loved him, the more you ended up hating him. Believe it or not, even after he took everything from me he could steal, I still loved Bob." Lonesome brought the glass to his lips a final time. It was evident the booze had started to kick in. "Anyway, I always thought it was a real shame the way it went down between me and Bob. There was a real bond between us at one point—something I've never had with another artist—before or since. You know, everyone thinks a musician just walks in, plays a song, walks out. Bob could record like that if he wanted, but he wasn't recording like that when he was with me. There was a lot of 'downtime' between takes, and Bob and I used to spend hours talking. I really got to know him. Well, as well as you could get to know anybody who doesn't tell you a damn thing about themselves. Still we saw eye to eye on a lot of stuff."

"You say that like it surprises you?"

"Mister Johns, the fact that Bob and I saw eye to eye on anything isn't surprising—it's amazing. Let's face it, we were worlds apart, the two of us."

"And how's that?"

"I was everything Bob wasn't. I dressed well, went to the finest schools, never lived out on the streets. Everything about me was antithetical to what Bob was railing against in his songs. I should have been a complete unknown to Bob. But I swear at times I think he knew me better than I knew myself."

"So what'd the two of you talk about?" Mister Johns inquired.

"Hell, what *didn't* we talk about—" Lonesome said brightly. "Cars, girls, music, civil rights—what was going on with the Movement and what our responsibilities to it were."

"Your 'responsibilities'?"

"Bob's role as a spokesman of sorts, my role as a black man living in America. In the end, however, I think we were both let down."

"How so?"

"After the initial successes of the '50s, then the major strides made in the '60s, Bob started to feel the Left should have stopped complaining and gotten on with it. By '65, Bob was adamant that the Left caused many of their own problems by carrying such a large chip on their shoulder. 'I'm tired of riding around on their chrome horse like some diplomat—' Bob opined whenever anyone asked him why he'd allegedly abandoned the 'cause.'"

"Well, did he abandon the cause?"

"Let's just put it this way … it was time for a new direction," Lonesome replied cryptically. "But like I said, for a while there it worked. Something about it worked."

"And then it stopped working," Mister Johns said, completing Lonesome's sentence.

"And then it stopped working," Lonesome repeated forlornly.

It wasn't just the booze that was kicking in, it was the memories. And judging from his melancholy tone, when it came to memories Bob Dorian and Lonesome shared a trunkful. And while the booze may have loosened Lonesome's memories, it hadn't loosened his lips: Lonesome was planning on keeping those memories to himself. But it was in that instant that Jack Frost understood what had come between Bob and Lonesome.

The Movement, Jack Frost now realized, *the Movement was the key to their whole relationship.*

Bob Dorian and Lonesome may have discussed an array of topics, by Lonesome's own admission, however, it was their discussion about civil rights that brought them closest together. But Bob's pronouncement that he was 'tired of riding around on a chrome horse like some diplomat' was, like so many of Bob's pronouncements, made in a song. Ironically, it was a song he was working on with Lonesome at the time. Bob may have told Penny he wasn't going to 'play for dimes' anymore, but that conversation had been held in private. It wasn't until Fairport that he was ready to announce to the world that he was breaking ranks with the Movement. But in the months leading up to Fairport, Bob was transforming, he was changing. And Lonesome was right there when the transformation was taking place. Lonesome saw Bob wrestle with the decision to change his musical direction; change his allegiances; change everything about himself that could be used to pin the mercurial musician down. But rather than try and change Bob's mind, rather than try and keep Bob in the fold, Lonesome hadn't said a word. Instead, he sat silently and watched Bob lay down the tracks that would sever his ties to the Left. What Lonesome had no idea of knowing, however, was that that song would sever Bob's ties with him as well.

And now it all made sense ... the realization hitting Jack Frost like a ton of bricks.

Contrary to what everyone thought, what everyone wrote, what everyone said, it was never about a disagreement over an organ part. This is why Jack Frost had heard the 'organ story' so many times and had never figured it out. And it wasn't about a change in 'musical direction,' either. That was part of it, but it wasn't that simple. It was about something else. *It wasn't the threads on their backs that came between them; it was the color of their skin.*

And so, Frost realized, in the end the thing that had bound these two men together like brothers was the very thing that tore them apart. The moment Bob saw himself as part of the problem rather than part of the solution it was over. Bob walked away from the Movement and everything—and everyone—associated with it. And just like that, one of the most promising collaborations of the rock era was no more. And Lonesome was—like everyone else who at one time or another had gotten close to Bob—on his own.

"Like I said," Lonesome said wistfully as he turned the bottle on its side a final time, draining the last few drops into his glass, "at some point it always stopped working with Bob. Now, if you gentlemen will excuse me, I really need to get back up on stage. I come in on four bars." Lonesome pushed his chair back from the table. He started to turn, but before he did he stopped, "Just out of curiosity, besides Penny who else have you talked to?"

"Sophia, Mr. Tremolo," Frost replied.

"They tell you want you wanted to hear?" Lonesome asked.

"Yeah," Johns replied. "That's the problem."

"Well, as long as you're talking to people who knew him, you ought to talk to this guy—" Lonesome said, scribbling a name and number on a napkin. He handed the napkin to Mister Johns. Johns took a cursory glance at the name, then passed the napkin to Frost.

Lonesome reached down and picked up his baritone sax. He blew a few times quickly through the instrument to clear out the saliva, then stepped over the lip of the stage and walked toward the microphone. The drummer hit the snare with a 'pop,' signaling the fourth bar had ended and it was time for a solo. Lonesome took a deep breath and started the magic act up once again: he had timed his exit perfectly.

Back in the darkness, Frost was still staring at the napkin. But it wasn't the name Lonesome had scrawled across the napkin that shook him to his core. It was the phone number, a number Lonesome had written almost as an afterthought. Seven digits. And it was those seven digits Jack Frost realized that were the combination that would unlock the mystery ... and lead them to the man who had killed Bob Dorian.

CHAPTER 10

▼

TINY BOBBITT

Lonesome Tom's nickname may have been an enigma to Jack Frost, but the name by which the man sitting before them had been known for the last 40 years was pitch-perfect—'Tiny' Bobbitt. The name fit him like a top. In addition to being diminutive in stature, Tiny was a complete and total pariah. Over the years, the little runt had run up tabs and welshed on debts all over town. The only reason anyone even did business with him was that Tiny brought a lot of business to Elysian Row.

It was common knowledge that Tiny Bobbitt had been the brains behind Bob Dorian's biggest albums, and there were still enough rock and roll outfits out there willing to risk a few days on Elysian Row hoping that some of 'Bobbitt's magic' might rub off on them. And for that reason and that reason alone, people were willing to forget a few 'indiscretions' on the part of the reclusive, reptilian record producer. Money's money. And over the years, Tiny Bobbitt had brought a lot of money to Elysian Row.

But despite the unique status conferred on Tiny, the truth was that he really wasn't any different from the rest of the residents of Elysian Row. He was a scum, a bottom feeder, a total leech. And during the years he'd worked with Elysian Row's biggest act, Tiny Bobbitt was undoubtedly Bob Dorian's biggest lackey. With the exception of that last trait, Jack Frost might have been able to stomach Tiny Bobbitt. But Frost never could warm up to Tiny the way his old boss had. The way Jack Frost saw it, Tiny was nothing more than a fraud and a phony. Suffice to say, there was no love lost between Jack Frost and the man known around the Row as Tiny Bobbitt.

"Well, I'll be—as I live and breathe—Jack Frost," Tiny said, spinning around in his chair.

Considering all the bad blood that had passed between them over the years, it was a surprisingly amiable welcome: Tiny Bobbitt could have cared less for Jack Frost.

"Interesting choice of words, Tiny," Frost fired back. "But we'll get to that in a minute."

Jack Frost tossed a damp rain jacket on the leather sofa. Tiny Bobbitt cringed. Tiny's reaction was almost imperceptible, but Jack Frost picked up on it instantly. In fact, it had been Jack Frost's intention to elicit that very reaction. Jack Frost knew Tiny Bobbitt hadn't garnered a reputation as the best-known producer in the business without a careful cultivation of two things: a great ear and a meticulous attention to detail. But those qualities—the second one anyway—didn't come without a price. And as is often the case with people who are in the business of details, Tiny Bobbitt was afflicted with a severe case of obsessive-compulsive disorder. *He's going to be thinking about that jacket and the damage it's doing to that freshly conditioned leather sofa for as long as I stand here.* And for Jack Frost, the thought was simply sublime.

"I'd like to introduce you to someone—" Frost said, motioning to the door as if he were a late night talk show host bringing on the next guest. "This is Mister Johns," Frost said with breezy effortlessness. Mister Johns stepped into the control room and acknowledged the introduction with a slight tilt of his chin.

"I know you and I didn't end it on the best of terms, Frost," Tiny said underplaying a topic to which they would return, "but you didn't have to bring a bodyguard." Tiny was struggling to get his words out. It had not been as evident when Tiny had initially greeted them, but now it was inescapable … that voice. Simply put, it was one of the most wretched sounds either man had ever heard. It sounded like he was gargling razor blades.

Jack Frost had warned Mister Johns about Tiny's tinny, high-pitched voice, but no warning could have ever adequately prepared him for what he had just heard. As Jack Frost had explained to Mister Johns en route to the studio, Tiny's physical features weren't the only thing that had been stunted as a result of a debilitating bought with polio he had fought, and clearly lost, as a child. In addition to his abnormally minute appendages, Tiny's voice box had also failed to develop beyond the size of a six-year-old's. But in a cruel twist of fate, his lungs had grown to full capacity. As a result, when Tiny spoke it sounded like Dizzy Gillespie blowing through a penny whistle. There was too much air trying to get through a space that was just too narrow. Worse still, every time Tiny attempted to speak his larynx suffered further damage, causing the words that came out to be more garbled, more grotesque than the time before. And though some said hearing the sound of Tiny's voice 'took a little getting used to,' in the end they were just being polite. There was no getting used to the horrendous sounds that emitted from Tiny every time he opened his mouth.

"Nice to see you still have your sense of humor after all these years, Tiny," Jack Frost said, tossing Mister Johns' raincoat on the sofa. "Actually, Lonesome gave me your number."

And while Jack Frost suspected Tiny was probably wondering why he had shown up at Tiny's studio unannounced in the middle of the night, that last comment about Lonesome giving him Tiny's number would have certainly let Tiny rule out 'a social visit' as a possible explanation.

"And how is Lonesome?" Tiny said with causal indifference as he nonchalantly got out of his chair, removed the raincoats from the sofa and hung them up on a hook next to the end table.

"Don't play games with me, Tiny. You know exactly what he's up to considering the two of you talked this morning. The better question is what are *you* up?"

"Since when is it a crime to come back to Elysian Row?" Tiny said unapologetically.

"Like I said, we'll be getting to that in a minute."

"With all due respect, Jack, I really don't have a minute," Tiny said, climbing back into his chair with the aid of a small upholstered footstool that had been strategically placed under the console, "I've got two dozen tracks to mix down." It was an odd, somewhat peculiar sight, this diminutive little man sitting in a chair that was clearly too large for him, his legs dangling a few inches off the floor like a marionette's. The image was only compounded by the fact that he was speaking in a voice that could scrape paint off the walls. "And since it would appear you and I are not going to be able to get beyond our past differences," Tiny angled the chair in the direction of Mister Johns, "perhaps there's something I can do for you, Mister Johns?"

"Over here, Tiny—" Frost said, repositioning the chair so that Tiny was facing him, "I'm the one with the questions."

"Questions," Tiny said, twisting a few knobs on the soundboard in front of him. "You got questions, let's hear them. Cause all I'm hearing is a bunch of accusations."

"Got a call the other day," Jack Frost said, taking his time. "A threat on Bob's life."

"I'll alert the media," Tiny said dismissively. "We used to get those all the time. Price of fame. You of all people ought to know that."

"Well, this time someone made good on it."

And in that brief moment, it was as if the light had gone out of the day. There was a long, poignant pause.

Finally, Tiny found the courage to speak. "So he's not here?" Tiny said, his bravado all but evaporated. "He's ..." there was a lengthy pause as he searched for the word, "... gone? They actually killed him?"

It was hardly the reaction either of the men had anticipated. Either Tiny really *was* learning of Bob Dorian's death for the first time, or it had just dawned on him that he had been pegged as the man who'd popped the prolific rock star. Whichever it was, one thing was certain: Tiny's world had just imploded.

"How …" Tiny hesitated, stumbling for the words that did not come. "How did it happen?"

"Shot in the chest. Three days ago."

"He's been dead three days."

"That's right," Frost replied curtly.

"And no one's seen him? Nobody's heard from him?"

"What part of 'dead' don't you get," Mister Johns bristled, interjecting himself back into the conversation. Tiny continued to process the news. It was beginning to seem as if he really *was* hearing of Bob's death for the first time. Mister Johns walked across the room and reached into the pocket of his raincoat. He removed the napkin that Lonesome had given them, and waited for the appropriate moment when he could ceremoniously slap it down on the console in front of their newly minted suspect.

"Did you at least get a number," Tiny said, staring blankly into the empty studio. "We always got a number—" Tiny continued, his mind rewinding.

"As a matter of fact, we did—" Johns said, taking full advantage of the opening Tiny had afforded him. Johns laid the napkin on the console. Then, just like that, Tiny Bobbitt's demeanor changed. Whatever grief and sorrow he had experienced only moments ago quickly dissipated.

"Wait a minute, is this a set-up? Am I being set up?" Tiny sputtered, the realization finally dawning on him.

"All we're saying Mr. Bobbitt is that a call was made from this studio the night Robert Zeitzman was murdered," Mister Johns said.

Tiny reached down, picked up a phone receiver, and started dialing a new set of digits in rapid succession. "I'm calling my lawyer," Tiny said, the high-pitched, tinny tone returning to his voice. "You can't come in here and try to pin some murder on me just because someone made a call from my studio. Are you a cop, Johns? Cause if you are, you better go back from wherever it is you came. I got rights, you know. I gotta lawyer."

Frost reached over, took the receiver out of Tiny's small, clawlike hand, and placed it back on its cradle. "Relax, Tiny—" Frost said in a calm, even tone, "no one's trying to pin anything on you. We just want to talk."

"So we're just talking here, right?"

"That's right," Frost replied reassuringly.

"Cause if you're a cop, you gotta read me my Miranda rights," Tiny said, turning to Mister Johns. "I know my rights, and you gotta read me Miranda."

"He's not a cop, Tiny. He's a reporter."

"A reporter!" Tiny exploded. "You brought a reporter into the studio!"

It was unclear which upset him more: being named as a suspect in a murder case or the fact that a reporter had been brought into in his inner sanctum. But before Jack Frost could determine exactly how Tiny had prioritized his paranoia, Tiny broke back in—

"Reporters are not allowed in the studio! How could you, Frost!" Tiny sputtered, his feet swinging back and forth wildly as his voice shot up an entire octave. "You know the rules! No hacks in the studio! I can't believe you brought a reporter into the studio!"

"Are you finished, Tiny," Frost said calmly. The fact that Tiny didn't respond suggested he was. There was, of course, also a very good chance that his silence could be attributed to the distinct possibility that he had finally blown out his voice box for good. "Mister Johns here is not a cop and he's not a reporter trying to break a story."

"Then who the hell is he!" Tiny demanded.

"As of 7:00 this morning, I *am* part of the story," Mister Johns said, taking it upon himself to clarify his reason for being there in the first place. "Insomuch as anyone investigating a murder is part of the case, that is."

"He's telling the truth?" Tiny said, turning to Jack Frost for confirmation.

"He's telling the truth, Tiny," Frost said reassuringly.

"So we're just talking here?"

"And you can stop talking anytime you want, Mr. Bobbitt," Johns interjected.

"Okay, that's fine, I can talk," Tiny was still certain that talking was *not* the only thing Jack Frost and this Mister Johns had come to do. "So what do you want to know?"

"Why don't you start by telling us who was here that night," Mister Johns said, removing his ever-present pad and pencil. "Might help us figure out who made the call."

"It's a recording studio, Mister Johns," Tiny replied condescendingly. "Anybody could have made a call from here that night. Hell, for all I know Bob coulda made the call himself."

"Zeitzman was here?" Johns said without missing a beat. "What was Zeitzman doing here?"

"It's a recording studio, Mister Johns," Tiny replied. "What do you *think* he was doing? He was recording." It was all Frost could do not to fall on the floor. Clearly this was news to him. "It would seem without the consent of his manager," Tiny said, a sly smile crossing his face.

"I was his manager, Tiny, not his babysitter," Frost said still trying to recover from the shock that a dead man was recording songs in the very room from which a hit on his life had been called in. "Now cut that crap and let's get back on track here."

"I agree with Mr. Frost." Mister Johns sounded like a mother trying to broker the peace between two rival siblings. "Now can you tell us who exactly was here that night."

"Well, let's see—there was Dulcimer Don, Middle-Eighth Ed, Virgil, Van, Baritone Bill."

"Anyone else?"

Tiny snapped his fingers, "There was another guy named Bello, I think, moving around mysteriously."

"Alfred Bello?" Johns pressed.

"You know this guy?" Frost inquired.

"Yeah, Bello's a bad seed. Cops used him to frame that fighter a few years back," Mister Johns said, responding to Frost's inquiry. "You sure it was Bello?" Mister Johns said, turning his attention back to Tiny with a newfound sense of urgency.

"I think so, but I can't say for sure. I was trying to produce an album, Mister Johns. I wasn't taking attendance. You can check the logs if you want. I run a tight ship. If anyone comes to my sessions, they sign in."

"This doesn't make any sense," Frost said, the wheels of his mind still turning.

"What's that?"

"Bob and I had talked about going back into the studio maybe cut a few tracks—but an album? He didn't have enough material to record an entire album."

Tiny arched his eyebrows as if to say: '*Really? Care to take a listen to this you schmuck, cause this sure sounds like an album to me.*' But instead of saying that, Tiny pressed a button on the console. The voice that filled the room was haunting, foreboding, frightening, ferocious. And while the voice belonged to Zeitzman, it was a voice Frost hadn't heard in close to 20 years. Tiny pressed the button again. The music stopped, but the voice lingered—

"And I got 16 more just like that that say you're wrong," Tiny said proudly.

"He recorded 16 songs in a single session?"

"Just like the old days. Like those tapes he recorded in the basement of that house he holed himself up in in '67. One track after the next—bam, bam, bam. All I did was kept the tape rolling."

"You're sort of known for that, aren't you?" Frost needled.

"Why are we still having this conversation after 20 years, Frost? You know as well as I Bob never did anything the same way twice." The animosity between the two men, which up to now had been successfully suppressed, was clearly about to rise to the surface.

Mister Johns sensed the animosity. He wanted to avoid the distraction, however. "And how about the other musicians—" he said, glancing down at his notes. "Dulcimer Don, Middle-Eighth Ed, Virgil, Van, Baritone Bill—any of those guys engage Zeitzman in any idle banter between takes? Make a suggestion? Something you might have gotten on that tape you kept rolling?"

"Suggestions? Are you kidding me? They were session players, Mister Johns. Session players do not make suggestions. Not if they want to work another session with Bob, that is. They didn't tell Bob what to do and he didn't tell them. He just showed up, sat down and started playing. Didn't say a word to nobody. And nobody said a word to him. And when he was done, he was gone. Just disappeared."

"So nobody left with him?" Mister Johns pressed.

"Hell, nobody knew he was gone until the band finished."

"Now wait a minute. I get that everyone was in awe of this guy—hell, that's all I've heard for the last 24 hours. But do you really expect me to believe half a dozen people were in a room the size of a phone booth for seven hours and no one says a word? Then Zeitzman—the guy who everyone's eyes are on—gets up and leaves and no one realizes he's gone? Is that what you're telling me? Is that what you expect me to believe?"

"That's exactly what I'm telling you," Tiny replied matter-of-factly. "Whether you believe it or not is not my concern." There was a finality to Tiny's tone that suggested the conversation was over.

"So I'm assuming you're done talking," Mister Johns said.

"Actually, there is one last thing—"

"Yes—"

"This is for Mr. Frost's benefit," Tiny turned his eyes toward Jack Frost. "Aren't you going to ask me about Nashville?" he goaded. Judging from Jack Frost's reaction, whatever acrimony had accumulated over the last 40 years between these two men was summed up in that single word.

"What about Nashville?" Frost bristled.

"Don't you want to know why Bob agreed to come down there? Let's face it, we both know Music Row wasn't the center of 'hip' in the mid- to late-60s."

"You and I both know why Bob went to Nashville. You fed him some bunk about how special he was, how talented he was. What was the word you used—"

"It wasn't 'bunk,' Jack," Tiny said, clearly taking offense of Jack Frost's word selection. "It was the God's truth. And *I* wasn't the one feeding it to him."

"You weren't—" Frost didn't believe it for a minute.

"You really *don't* know do you?"

"Know what, Tiny?" Like his new partner, Jack Frost was starting to regard rhetorical questions as nothing more than a pesky nuisance.

"Judas. It was Judas who convinced him to go."

"Judas?" Frost said incredulously. "Is that the best you can do? You got 40 years to cook up a story explaining Nashville, and that's the best you got?" It was evident, however, that Tiny's best had gotten under Jack Frost's skin.

"Frankly, I'm surprised Bob never told you himself," Tiny said. "I may have been the reason Bob came to Nashville. But I didn't have anything to do with what happened once he got there. Other than the albums we made, of course. Couple of good ones, too. And 'touched'—" Tiny continued, his confidence and bravado fully restored, "the word you were looking for earlier. The one that describes the 'bunk' I was allegedly feeding Bob. The word is 'touched.' As in touched by the hand of God. Bob really was filled with the Holy Spirit. I believed it then, and I believe it now."

"That's not the only thing you were filling Bob with in Nashville," Frost said coolly.

"Bob was very special," Tiny continued, ignoring the jab, "he was a special person. And not just to me, but to everyone whose lives he touched. I always said his full impact wouldn't be felt until he was gone. And now he is. So why don't you let me worry about keeping my side of the street clean, and you worry about yours. And judging from the fact that you no longer have a client, and you—" Tiny turned in the direction of Mister Johns, "don't have a suspect, I'd say your side of the street is a little messier than mine."

Johns had heard enough. "Listen you little shit! I may not have had a suspect before I walked into this two-bit rathole of a studio, but I think I might have one by the time I leave. Or have you forgotten about that little piece of paper in your hand? The one with your phone number on it?"

"Are you sure I don't need my lawyer?" It was more of a threat than a question.

"We just want to know what went down that night, that's all," Mister Johns said, doing his best to assure Tiny that legal representation would not be required.

"Look, Mister Johns. It's exactly like I told you, I get a phone call from Bobby. He tells me to put a band together, says he's got some tracks he wants to lay down. So that's what I do—I put a band together."

"Right," Johns said, tapping his pencil on the opened notebook. "I got it."

"Obviously I'm not giving you the answers you're looking for," Tiny said, fully imbued with his newfound resolve, "so why don't you go ahead, poke around. Do what I suggested—call the guys who were here that night."

Tiny reached into the drawer and removed a thick, leather-bound ledger. He placed the ledger on the console.

"What's this?" Mister Johns said, staring at the ledger.

"Recording logs. The names and numbers of every person here that night—they're all in there." Tiny Bobbitt slid the ledger across the console.

"You're just going to give us this?" Mister Johns inquired incredulously. "The recording logs? You're just going to give them to us?"

"I'm not giving you anything, Mister Johns. That's a copy. You got yours, I got mine. You know ... in case something happens to that one. Now, if we're done here, I'd really like to get back to work. Like I said, I got a lot of tracks to mix."

Mister Johns opened the ledger and removed a slender silver disc that had been wedged between the pages.

"Thought you might be interested in hearing what a genius can do when left to his own devices," Tiny said, referring to the CD Mister Johns was holding up. It was evident that last sentence had been for the benefit of Jack Frost. The sentence didn't get a rise out of Frost. Jack Frost was done with Tiny Bobbitt.

"All right," Mister Johns said, as he slid the CD back into the log and tucked it tightly underneath his arm. "We'll follow up on these names—let you know if anything turns up."

"You know how to find me," Tiny said, picking up the napkin and waving it in the air tauntingly.

THE RECORDING STUDIO DOOR had hardly closed behind them—

"Why'd you lie to me?" Mister Johns said.

"Lie to you? What are you talking about?"

"You told me you hadn't talked to Tiny Bobbitt in 20 years."

"That's not a lie."

"But it's only half the truth. You and Bobbitt might not have been talking, but he and Zeitzman were. And you knew it."

"With all due respect, Mister Johns, Bob was his own person, marched to his own drummer. Bob and I were close, but we weren't joined at the hip. There were a lot of things he did I didn't know about."

"But you knew he was shopping producers."

"And how would I have known that?" Frost said defensively.

Mister Johns pulled out his trusty notepad from his jacket pocket, "'Bob and I had talked about going back into the studio maybe cut a few tracks—' Sound familiar?" Johns closed the notepad and slid it into his breast pocket. "Because if you ask me, that sounds a lot like someone who knew his client was thinking about recording again.

And judging from that little exchange as we were walking out the door, I'd say Tiny wouldn't have been your top choice."

"Let's just say, Tiny and I didn't always see eye to eye."

"Yeah, toe to toe is more the way I'd describe the exchange back there."

"Listen, I'll be the first to admit I don't care much for Tiny. Never have."

"Sounds like you and the manager—" Mister Johns looked down at his notes. "Judas—" he looked back up, "sounds like the two of you didn't see eye to eye either."

"No one saw eye to eye with Judas," Frost said succinctly, hoping the conversation would move on to another, less volatile topic.

"Right," Mister Johns replied. "So what happened in Nashville?"

"What about Nashville?" Frost bristled.

"Seems like an awfully sore subject between you and Tiny," Mister Johns said nonchalantly. "But something tells me this Judas was the fly in the ointment." But when Jack Frost didn't respond, Mister Johns pressed the point—"His name keeps coming up, Frost," Mister Johns said in that simple, off-putting way he phrased a statement when what he was really doing was issuing an ultimatum.

"Judas gets a bad rap," Jack Frost said breezily, hoping his candor would assuage the challenge Mister Johns was issuing. But the moment the words came out, he knew they would need to be clarified. Judas had been saddled with a lot of baggage over the years, a 'bad rap' was not one of them. By all accounts, Judas had earned every condemnation he'd been collared with. Realizing that he needed to put his statement into some sort of context lest he be accused of being an apologist for the most detested person on Elysian Row, Jack Frost continued, "A lot of people think Bob just latched onto the Folk Movement because he thought that was his ticket to stardom. Not true. Penny hit the nail on the head. The minute Bob realized he'd been turned into a spokesman, some sort of sloganeer for the Left, he packed up and left the plantation for good."

"Nashville," Mister Johns said tersely. "We're talking about Nashville." Clearly, Jack Frost's attempt to mollify Mister Johns had not been as successful as he had hoped. In fact, it had been an outright failure.

"You want to know what happened in Nashville?" Frost conceded. Judging from the fact Mister Johns had removed his pencil from his breast pocket, he did.

"Fine," Jack Frost said, resolved to the fact that it was probably best to paint the whole picture for Mister Johns. After all, this was not your typical 'paint-by-numbers' story. This was a story in which the nuances were important. The success of this story was in the details. And there were a few key details Jack Frost wanted to make sure got left out—"But do me a favor and put the pencil away. What I'm about to tell you, I'd like it to stay between us." Mister Johns slid the pencil and pad into his overcoat pocket.

"There's been a lot of revisionist history with Bob," Jack Frost said, beginning what he knew was going to be a hell of a story.

"So set the record straight," Mister Johns said flatly. And while Frost didn't own up to the fact that he knew exactly what was implied by Mister Johns' snide comment, Jack Frost did recognize that if he told the story the right way it'd make things a lot easier when news of the tribute concert broke, which by Jack Frost's estimate would probably be in tomorrow's morning edition of the *Elysian Plains-Dispatch*.

"I plan to set the record straight," Frost hedged. "But in order to get to Nashville, we need to start in Fairport."

"Okay," Mister Johns conceded.

"This hot new outfit out of Chicago had been asked to open the festival," Frost began. "Sort of open the whole thing with a 'bang.'"

"What kind of 'bang'?" Mister Johns asked.

"Electric blues," Frost replied.

"This was a folk festival, right?"

"Biggest festival of the year," Frost confirmed.

"And that didn't bother the promoters—the fact that they were plugging in at a folk festival?"

"Not really—it was Chicago blues," Frost clarified, "Chicago blues is electric, so nobody was breaking rank, nobody was making a statement." Frost hesitated, "But it bothered the hell out of Judas. He actually took out one of the promoters over it."

"What do you mean 'took him out'?"

"Got into a fist fight. Knocked the promoter to the ground. Caused a huge ruckus. That night, the organizers held a meeting, wanted to ban him."

"Hell—if you ask me, banning him from the festival sounds like a slap on the wrist. He should have been happy they didn't press charges."

"Well, the whole reason Judas started the fight in the first place was he had just signed the act, the one that had played the day before Bob arrived. And he wanted to let everyone know—the guys in the band, the festival people, Bob—he wanted to let them know that he wasn't going to be pushed around. 'These guys want to play loud,'" Frost said, doing his best to replicate the low, tempestuous booming of one of Judas' famous war-drum diatribes, "'You let them do it or you deal with me'—that kind of shit. Anyway, they didn't do it—toss Judas, I mean. And the reason is because Judas didn't just have Bob, he had a couple of other acts on the bill. Big acts, too. And they knew if they pulled Judas, he'd pull his people."

"So it was a power play."

"And the way Judas played it was to goad Bob on—'Look what these uptight assholes are doing, telling people what they can play, how to play it. Pretty soon they'll be telling *you* what to do. You're the biggest star in the world. You gotta stand up for yourself. Let me help you.'"

"And Zeitzman bought it?"

"Hook, line and sinker. Put together a band as fast as he could. Mostly guys who had played on the album he'd just cut—"

"The one with Lonesome," Mister Johns interjected.

"Right," Frost confirmed. "Anyway, they all show up wearing these puff-sleeve dueling shirts, tight black trousers, pointed boots and the darkest shades you've ever seen. Everybody else is wearing a work shirt and jeans. In hindsight, they should have known something was going on behind the shades. I mean, Bob didn't have to play a note—he'd already made his statement."

"Which was?"

"Robert Zeitzman had left the building, and Bob Dorian had arrived," Jack Frost said matter-of-factly.

Mister Johns wasn't completely convinced, "Don't you think you're giving him a bit too much credit? I get that he was important to the Folk Movement, but the idea that one person could kill it all by himself by simply strapping on an electric guitar? I mean, what'd he play? Three songs."

"For a total of 16 minutes. But in those 16 minutes he pulled off a trick rarely achieved in popular culture. He abandoned his fan base while actually increasing his appeal in the process. He was bigger than the festival. The part was bigger than the whole. It was completely against everything the movement stood for. But you're right," Jack Frost said circumspectly, "Bob didn't kill the Folk Movement."

"Well, that's certainly the rap he's gotten," Mister Johns replied. "Certainly the rap all these people we've talked to are trying to pin on him, anyway."

"Which is why I said no one's really gotten it right. You want to know who killed the Folk Movement?" Frost asked rhetorically. "The festival committee. The members of the committee should never have made Bob a hero. If they hadn't anointed him their king, Bob would have never chosen the place they were planning to coronate him to break free."

"So you actually think he thought it that far through? You really think he planned on wreaking so much havoc?" It was a genuine question. One of the few genuine questions Mister Johns had asked since the investigation had begun. "I mean it's 40 years later, Frost, and people are still talking about Bob 'going electric' at Fairport."

"Who knows what was going on in Bob's head—" Frost said undeterred. "But he was certainly leaning in that direction. And if he was the least bit on the fence, I know exactly who pushed him to strap on that guitar." Frost paused for a moment to let Mister Johns fill in the blank. "Exactly," Frost confirmed. "But that was Judas—always whispering in Bob's ear while shouting in everyone else's." There was something about the way Jack Frost said the name of the man he had replaced as Bob Dorian's manager all those years ago that made it very clear that there was no love lost between the two men. "Judas and Bob were thick as thieves after Fairport. Judas had been on the scene for a while, but after Fairport he had a firm grip on Bob."

"And where were you when all this was going down?"

"I was in Nashville," Jack Frost replied, offering up a rather seamless segue to Mister Johns' initial inquiry. "I'd gone down there in '65 to work with a couple of acts I'd signed."

"Anybody I've heard of?"

"Probably not—couple of country and western bands, a rockabilly outfit. No one who ever really made it. But you *do* know the guy I was working with."

"Let me guess," Mister Johns said.

"That's right," Frost confirmed. "Tiny was the hottest producer in town. At the time I considered myself lucky to be in the same building, much less working side by side with him."

"So much for the old adage 'time heals all wounds,'" Johns wryly observed.

"You ever heard the expression, 'we'll fix it in the mix'?" Jack Frost was trying to tell his side of the story, and that meant sticking to his version. "It's what a producer says when he doesn't get what he needs on the first take—it means he'll go back and find it later."

"'Fix it in the mix,' I get it—sure," Mister Johns said.

"Well, the 'mix' wasn't the only thing Tiny was 'fixing' in that studio. Three albums in 18 months, four if you count the double album Bob released in '66. I was in the adjacent studio. It wasn't uncommon for Bob to go three, four days without sleeping."

"And you think Tiny was helping to keep him up?"

"I'm not saying that Tiny was *dealing*, but he knew damn well what was going on."

"And he let it happen ..." Mister Johns said, citing the source of the 40 years of animosity that had built up between Tiny Bobbitt and Jack Frost.

"Like I said, he knew what was going on."

"But you said you were in the other studio," Mister Johns pressed.

"I was his friend, why didn't I step in? Is that what you were going to ask me?"

"Maybe he would have listened to you," Mister Johns said.

"Hard to get a guy to listen when you can't get to him," Frost replied, his voice filled with ire. "And after their little triumph at Fairport, Bob didn't listen to anyone but Judas."

"So Judas knew—"

"Like I said, nobody got to Bob unless they went through Judas."

"But why would his manager want to turn his client into a junkie?" Mister Johns was having a hard time buying into Frost's side of the story. "That doesn't make any sense. I mean, what good is a dead rock star to a manager?"

A lot more than you'd think, Jack Frost thought to himself. *In fact, I'm doing everything I can to get my cut from a certain recently deceased rock star.*

"Let me ask you a question," Jack Frost continued, keeping that last thought to himself. "Do you know what the average career span of a rock star is?" Mister Johns did not reply. He figured he didn't have to. Frost was going to tell him either way. "Four, five years tops. After that it's over. Bob had hit the scene in 1961. Nashville is 1965. That's four right there. Most people figured Bob had another year, two tops, left in him."

"That hardly explains why his manager would let Bob turn into a dope fiend?"

"Coffee and cigarettes are one thing," Jack Frost explained. "But a steady diet of amphetamines is entirely another. You can get a lot of work done on amphetamines, especially if you have as many ideas running around in your head as Bob did."

The two men turned the corner and started to walk east along Rue Morgue Avenue. On the next corner, a red awning with the words, 'Chelsea Hotel,' written in tight cursive came into view. Jack Frost realized he had a block to bring the story full circle.

"Listen, I can't blame Bob for wanting to work with Tiny," Jack Frost conceded. "My real beef has always been with Judas. Shit, I hated the guy. Hated the way he looked at Bob with those fucking dollar signs in his eyes. Like Bob was a product, something to sell. Like I said, there's no secret there was no love lost between Judas and me. The day I got Bob out from underneath Judas' grip is one of the happiest days in my life. And while I don't agree with the way Tiny ran his studio, he got something out of Bob no one had been able to get before and no one has been able to get since. I've always respected Tiny for his talent. Tiny was a genius in his own way. But I hated what he let Judas do to Bob."

"You sure you're pissed at the right guy?"

"What do you mean?"

"Well, according to you, Judas is the guy who plied Dorian with enough pills to pop the heart valves on a rhino. Tiny, by your own admission, was someone you actually respected. Yet as near as I can see it's the producer you've been holding a grudge against for 40 years." Mister Johns was not trying to be argumentative. If anything, he was trying to clarify the situation.

Apparently, Jack Frost didn't see it that way—

"'Pop the heart valves on a rhino,'" Jack Frost mimicked, "that's a new one. But as long as we're going with animal analogies, Johns, here's one for you. There are people in this world who are born a certain way. No matter what they do they won't ever be able to change their stripes. Judas was one of those people. Judas was destined to betray Bob from the beginning. Tiny, on the other hand, could have changed. He could have intervened. Tiny could have stood up for Bob. Hell, I could have stood up for him. If I could have gotten to him, that is. No, Johns," Frost said, his voice resonating, "I'm pissed at the right guy."

"Well, like him or not—Tiny clearly respected Zeitzman."

"Listen," Frost said, "we all put Bob up on a pedestal. You had to if you wanted to work for him. But what Tiny did was different."

Jack Frost felt something land on the nape of his neck, something wet, something cool. He slapped at the spot with the same careless intensity an unwanted mosquito might warrant. Then, looking up to the sky, he realized where the wetness had come from. The rain that had threatened to come down earlier was about to make good on its promise.

"Are you a religious man, Johns?" Frost said as he lowered his eyes from the dark, encroaching sky.

"I know my way around the Bible," Mister Johns replied.

"Well, Tiny knew his way around the Bible, too. Too well, if you ask me."

"What do you mean?"

"You know how everyone keeps referring to Bob as a prophet, a sage, a messiah?"

"Right."

"Well, Tiny actually thought Bob *was* the messiah." Not sure how he was supposed to react to the statement, Mister Johns didn't react at all. "Look at your notes, Johns—" Frost instructed, "look at what Tiny said just before we left. He always thought Bob's full impact wouldn't be felt until he was gone."

"He also said he cared for him," Mister Johns said, now starting to get the gist of what Jack Frost was implying. "I think you're reading more between the lines than there really is."

It isn't like I'm reading tea leaves here. Clearly Jack Frost didn't agree with Mister Johns' assessment. *Jesus, for a guy who writes down every damn word people say, you really should try listening for a minute.*

"Tiny was interviewed once," Frost said. There was an ominous tone in Frost's tenor, "and this reporter asked him, 'What's it like working with Bob Dorian?' He said he thought Bob was the only prophet we've had since Jesus. He said he didn't think people were going to realize it for another two, maybe three hundred years but one day they'd realize how truly insightful Bob really was. One day they'd wake up and realize what it was they had." Frost hesitated. He glanced over at Mister Johns. Mister Johns shot Frost a look like maybe *he* was the one drinking too much wine at Mass. "You were there, Johns," Frost implored, "you saw the way he talked about him, going on and on about how special he was."

"Tiny's slavish devotion to Zeitzman is evident. It doesn't mean he murdered him. That is what you're getting at isn't it—that he killed him?"

"Maybe he didn't look at it as murder." Mister Johns waited for the punch line. The punch line didn't come. Jack Frost was serious. "Up until now," Frost continued, "I've kept my thoughts to myself on who might have killed Zeitzman. Suspicion and paranoia, that's been your department."

"You actually got a theory, Frost, or are you just busting my balls?" Johns bristled.

"You said you know your way around the Bible?"

"Right."

"Then you know there are four written accounts of Christ's resurrection. One in each of the four Gospels. And each begins, 'He is not here.'"

"So?"

"So that's what Tiny said when we told him Bob was dead. He said, 'He's not here.'"

"A coincidence," Mister Johns said dismissively.

"Correct me if I'm wrong, but aren't you the guy who said there are no coincidences?"

"I also don't think people go around whacking their friends just because they think they're talented."

"Motive and opportunity—isn't that what they tell you to look for in a suspect?"

"They generally go hand in hand, sure—what's your point?"

"My point is that everyone we've talked to has had a motive. Tiny Bobbitt's the first person we've talked to who also had the opportunity. You're holding it in your hands. The logs—" Frost said, motioning to the leather-bound ledger tucked underneath Mister Johns' protective arm. "He was with Bob the night he was murdered."

Mister Johns stopped dead in his tracks. "You really *do* think he killed him?"

"Tiny was a zealot," Frost said matter-of-factly, "and zealots believe that sometimes you have to die in order to live. Sometimes your physical death is the very thing that gives you spiritual life, gives you everlasting immortality. And what better way to achieve immorality than to be silenced in your prime. You heard Tiny—he said those songs were the best batch he'd ever heard Bob pull together. Yeah, I think there's a very good possibility he killed him."

A moment passed between the two men. And as the silent chasm grew between them, it was if the only sound in the entire world was that of the hotel's tattered awning flapping back and forth in the breeze. It sounded like water lapping on a distant, faraway shore.

"And the pendulum swings ..." Johns said suggestively.

"What the hell does that mean, 'And the pendulum swings ...'" Frost demanded.

"It means we've talked to half a dozen people. All knew Zeitzman, all had plausible motives for wishing ill will on him, yet you defend every one of them. Then we get to the one guy *you* don't particularly care for and you're convinced he did him in. With all due respect, Frost, it's a very convenient theory—considering the way you feel about Tiny."

Jack Frost had gotten used to listening to Mister Johns' pedantic, patronizing patter. He'd heard Johns hymn about this and haw about that with such regularity that he was certain he'd grown immune to Johns' condescending, demeaning demeanor. Apparently, he hadn't. That last comment had struck a nerve. But rather than lash out, Jack Frost decided to go another way.

"Listen, it's been a long day," Frost replied coolly. "And I'm tired. I'm sure you are, too. So I'm not going to dignify that last comment with a response because we have a lot of work to do tomorrow, and if I did, there's a very good chance you wouldn't come back in the morning. So—" Frost said, opening the lobby door to the Chelsea, "if you'll excuse me, I'm going to get a few hours of shut-eye. I suggest you do the same." Frost passed through the doors and into the hotel lobby, leaving Mister Johns alone in the dark, damp night.

Mister Johns reached into his pocket and pulled out a small plastic case. He popped a mint into his mouth, then slid the case back into his pocket. A light mist was starting to come down. And as it passed the electric streetlights, the mist instantly illuminated the city, causing the streets to glisten in the early evening moonlight. Mister Johns pulled the collar of his coat tightly around his neck, turned and began to walk east toward the Tombstone.

Through the window on the second floor landing, Frost stopped to peer out over Elysian Row. The neon sign above the awning over the front door blinked on and off intermittently, the light drizzle was beginning to pick up. And though Jack Frost had no way of knowing it at the time, a hard rain was about to fall …

CHAPTER 11

▼

MINNESOTA SLIM

Jack Frost reached the top of the landing, planted his hand firmly on the banister and pivoted himself in the direction of his room, located at the end of the long, dark corridor. Exhausted, Frost expertly maneuvered around empty trays of food and half-empty bottles of beer and booze that had yet to be collected by room service. *Does this dump even have room service?* he thought to himself. *I haven't seen a bellhop or chambermaid since I've been here.* Before he could answer that question, he realized that he was standing in front of the last barrier between himself and a good night's sleep.

He turned the doorknob, but the doorknob was stuck. The trick, the concierge had said was just to lean against the door with the weight of his body. 'Sorry for the imposition,' the concierge had told him. Frost was tired. He was beyond tired; he was completely depleted. Leaning against the door was hardly an imposition. In fact, it was a relief. Jack Frost pressed his beleaguered body against the door, and slowly turned the doorknob. The door popped open, and the light from the hall sliced across the floor of the dark, cavernous room.

It took a few moments for his eyes to adjust to the darkness, but when they did, Jack Frost realized the man sitting on the chaise lounge waiting for him was the man who had ratted him out. Were it not for the large, white gauze bandage pasted across his nose, he might have missed him altogether.

"Well, if it isn't Minnesota Slim—" Jack Frost said, almost as if he had half-expected to find the little runt sitting there in the shadows. "And to what do I owe the pleasure?"

"Knock it off, Frost. I know you're pissed as all hell at me."

"And why would I be pissed at you, Slim?" Frost said, inching closer. "Though I do have a right mind to finish what Commissioner Tiresias started," Frost said, alluding to the bandage pasted across Slim's pasty face.

"Stay away from me," Slim said, brandishing a small, gold-plated pistol. "I'll use it if I have to."

"Give me a break, Slim," Jack Frost said dismissively. "Why don't you save the theatrics and tell me why you're here."

"There're some things we need to talk about."

"You're damn straight there're some things we need to talk about. And you can start by telling me why you sold me out."

"I didn't sell you out, Frost. Commissioner Tiresias was squeezing me. He got wind you were in town. What'd you expect me to do?"

"I expected you to keep your mouth shut, Slim. That little conversation you had with Commissioner Tiresias cost me a shitload of change. Cost Bob a hell of a lot more. Your little indiscretion might just have cost him his life." Minnesota Slim didn't even flinch. Apparently, the word was out that Dorian was dead. It probably hadn't made its way back to the hacks at the *Dispatch* yet, but the word was clearly making its way around town and it had to have started somewhere. It seems it had started at the bottom. And of all the people on Elysian Row, Minnesota Slim was about as deep in the muck as you could get. He was a real bottom dweller—right down there with Tiny Bobbitt and the rest of the lowlifes who trolled the depths of Elysian Row looking for scraps, scavenging for whatever they could find. And as Jack Frost stared at Minnesota Slim all he could think about was another type of bottom feeder: a suckfish.

When Jack Frost was a kid living on the Row, the carnival used to come to town every year like clockwork. The faint strains of the organ grinder's familiar barroom tune, the deep baritone calls of the barker, the words, 'Brother Joiachim's Traveling Minstrel Show,' etched into the side of the boxcar in bright, psychedelic script. It was like a James Ensor painting, like *Christ's Entry Into Brussels* watching this bizarre cast of characters parade down the street and into the heart of Elysian Row: midgets, bearded ladies, strongmen, 'the world's largest this …,' 'the world's smallest that….' And when they got there, they didn't waste a moment. They would spill out into the streets and begin entertaining the crowd without a moment's hesitation.

For years, Brother Joiachim's star attraction, the jewel in his creepy cavalcade of curiosities, was an oddity called, 'The Amphibiman.' Half caiman, half man, the 'Amphibiman' was a full-on freak of nature. And while the 'Amphibiman' was one of the most bizarre sights Jack Frost had ever seen, it wasn't the 'Amphibiman' that captivated an impressionable Jack Frost; it was the tiny minnow-sized fish that seemed to be perpetually paired with this reptilian repulsion of nature. They were called 'suckfish'; and they were the ugliest, most disgusting creatures Jack Frost had ever laid eyes on. Big, bulging eyes that were disproportionately too large in relation to the rest of their body. A small, tightly drawn mouth that was good for nothing except affixing itself to some other, larger fish and hanging on for the ride. But what was even more disgusting than the way those fish looked was the reason the suckfish had been placed in the 'Amphibiman's' dingy glass tank in the first place. The suckfish's sole reason for living, its only purpose for existence, was literally to suck up the dark, dank excrement this oddity of nature would leave behind. And though Slim was a little further up the evolutionary ladder—exactly how far was certainly debatable—he reminded Jack Frost of those strange, scaly scavengers all the same.

"Listen, you have every right to be mad at me," Slim said, cutting straight to the chase. "You *are* mad at me, right?"

Jack Frost was furious. It was a clear as the bloody nose on Slim's face, but for a moment, Minnesota Slim wasn't sure.

"I'm not happy, Slim," Frost replied. "And I'm pretty sure when Tommie the Make and Julius the Squeeze find out you've been running your mouth they aren't going to be too pleased, either."

"You've talked with Tommie and Julius?" Slim sputtered.

"No, Slim, I haven't had a chance," Jack Frost replied, doing his best to suppress the indignation that was welling up inside him. "I've been sort of preoccupied. Now what the fuck do you want?" Then, almost as an afterthought, "And please put that gun away before someone gets hurt." Minnesota Slim did not put the gun away. But considering the safety was on, Jack Frost was sure Minnesota Slim probably hadn't planned on using it in the first place.

"I need to know what Commissioner Tiresias told you," Minnesota Slim inquired.

"What he told me about what?"

"The word down on Rue Morgue is that you're looking for a couple of railroad hands."

So the word had gotten out, Frost thought to himself, not the least bit pleased with the realization. *Looks like it's time to toss this little scavenger a few more scraps.*

"How do you know about the railroad hands?" Frost conceded.

"I just know, okay."

"No, it's not 'okay,' Slim. Nobody knows about that but me and Commissioner Tiresias." There was a brief hesitation on Minnesota Slim's part, but even that was too long—"How do you know about the railroad hands?" Frost demanded, grabbing Slim by the lapels of his overcoat and lifting him from the chair.

"I know …! I just know …!" Slim pleaded.

"Not good enough, Slim!" Frost exclaimed, tossing Slim across the room. Minnesota Slim collapsed in the corner, landing on the floor with a 'thud.' Frost picked up the gun from the table and started moving toward Slim.

"I know about the railroad hands," Slim said, putting his hands in front of his face, "because there are no railroad hands." Frost stopped cold.

"What do you mean? Commissioner Tiresias took a sworn statement from Dela saying that she found the body by the railroad tracks this morning, and two men helped her carry the body back to the Chelsea."

"Well, have you talked with Dela?" Slim said, lowering his hands as Frost lowered the pistol.

"Been looking but we can't seen to find her, either," Frost replied. "Sounds like you know more than you're telling me. A lot more. More than you told the Commissioner, too."

"Here's what I know," Slim said, slowly inching his way back up the wall. "Two men did carry the body back to the hotel. Dela's right about that. There were two men," Slim said, catching his breath, "but they weren't railroad men. At least *I* wasn't working the rails last time I checked." The two men stared at each other stone-faced. "That's right," Slim said, his bravado returning. "Two men carried the body back to the hotel that night. I was one of them—care to guess who the other was?"

"Commissioner Tiresias?"

"That's right."

"You and Commissioner Tiresias carried Bob's body back to the Chelsea?" Frost said, not believing it for a moment. "Is that what you're telling me?"

"That's exactly what I'm telling you."

"That's quite an accusation, Slim."

"It's the truth, Frost."

"And you expect me to believe you—someone who can't even hold down a job—over the chief of police? I mean, I'll be the first to admit that Commissioner Tiresias may be a liar and a cheat, but you've been known to have your hands in a few pockets as well."

"This isn't a shakedown, Frost. You've got to believe me."

"Actually, I don't," Jack Frost said defiantly. "Now crawl back under that rock you came from. As far as I'm concerned, you and I are finished."

"I'm telling you the truth, Frost. I don't know why the Commissioner told you two railroad hands carried the body to the Chelsea, but he's lying."

"Maybe he didn't want to go to jail."

"What?"

"Maybe he didn't want to go to jail, Slim," Jack Frost repeated. "If what you're telling me is true then you've just implicated yourself as an accomplice to murder, implicated Commissioner Tiresias, too. *You* don't want to go to jail now do you, Slim?"

"It's better than the alternative," Slim said without a moment's hesitation.

"The alternative must be pretty bad."

"They're going to kill me," Slim said, closing his eyes. There was an instant when Jack Frost thought those bulging, disproportionate eyes were literally going to pop right out of Slim's head and that the only reason this little snitch had even shut his eyelids in the first place was to keep his eyeballs in those oversized, hollow sockets.

"You always were a paranoid little shit."

"I'm not paranoid!" Slim screeched.

"Yeah, I don't know what would have ever given me that idea."

"You've got to believe me, Frost. Someone is *really* trying to kill me."

"All right, I'll bite. Who's going to kill you?"

"I don't know. That's the problem—someone's after me, and I don't know who it is. At first I thought it was you—I thought you'd gotten wind that I'd ratted you out. That I'd told the Commissioner about the concert. At first I figured it was you who wanted to 'off me."

"I wouldn't rule that one out just yet, Slim."

"But I've been following you, Frost," Slim said, eyeing Jack Frost up and down as if he were sizing up a Saturday night streetwalker. "I've been following you all day. And you're not the one."

"That makes me feel so much better, Slim."

"You gotta believe me!" Minnesota Slim pleaded. "I'm just coming clean."

"Wish the same could be said about your face. Here—" Frost said, dropping a handkerchief on the table. "Clean yourself up." Puzzled, Minnesota Slim looked at the handkerchief. "It's bleeding again—" Frost tapped his hand against his nose.

Tossing Slim the handkerchief may have been an instinctive gesture on the part of Jack Frost, but the moment he tossed that handkerchief on the table he knew he was going to regret it. But Frost couldn't help himself. He'd always been a sucker for the guy left to clean up the messes others left behind. Why else when he was a kid would he have saved up for months on end to buy a ticket to the carnival? Goddamned suckfish. It was never the 'Amphibiman' he was paying to see. It was the suckfish. He couldn't help himself. The curtain was only drawn back for a minute, but all that time all Jack Frost did was watch those dingy, besmirched bottom dwellers suck the shit out of that tank. There was just something about going around and cleaning up after everyone that Jack Frost inexplicably understood.

After all, he thought to himself, *I've been cleaning up after Bob for the last 20 years. How is that any different than what this little shit does every minute of every day of his miserable, misanthropic life?*

Jack Frost hated the realization. He hated that he had anything in common with Minnesota Slim, a man whose opportunistic existence he truly despised. But what he hated even more than the man cowering in the corner before him was the fact that his realization connected them at all.

"I'm telling you that's what happened," Slim said, pressing the handkerchief against his nose. Frost was right. Indeed Slim's nose was starting to bleed again.

"Why don't you tell it to me again."

"Dela found the body around midnight. She called the Commissioner. He called me."

"And he called you because …?"

"He was cashing in a chit."

"A chit?"

"I owe him a few favors," Slim explained.

"I know what a chit is, Slim," Frost said impatiently. "And it must have been some favor for him to agree to be an accomplice to murder."

"I didn't kill anyone!"

"That's where the 'accomplice' part comes in. You helped, you didn't do it all by yourself. But I'm sorry, I interrupted you. So the two of you brought the body to the Chelsea—"

"That's right."

"And that took you how long?"

"Twenty, thirty minutes." Frost started to do the math in his head. Twenty minutes, two people, two miles. Those were the numbers. Problem was the numbers weren't adding up. Transporting a dead body nearly two miles was a tall order, even for two men as determined as Commissioner Tiresias and Minnesota Slim. "And it was just the two of you?" Frost said, his suspicion seeping through. "No one else knew about it. No one else was involved?"

"Except for Dela."

"Right, except for Dela—who's conveniently gone missing."

"Frost, I'm telling you this is how it went down."

"Well, it doesn't make any sense. If you and Commissioner Tiresias brought the body to the Chelsea, why wouldn't the Commissioner just have told me the truth? He didn't need to come up with some story about a pair of railroad men carrying the body?"

"That all depends, doesn't it?"

"Depends on what?"

"Has it ever occurred to you that maybe he was trying to throw you off track? Set you in the wrong direction while he set a few things in motion for himself?" Frankly, that thought had been with Jack

Frost ever since the Commissioner had paired him up with Mister Johns. "Listen, you already told me you cut a deal with the Commissioner for a take at the door. I'm assuming that was the 'shitload of change' you mentioned earlier." Frost's silence confirmed Slim's assumption. "Well, can you imagine the kind of deal he'd have gotten if he'd had some time to squeeze Tommie and Julius? He might have cut you out altogether. Still might ... So you see, Frost," Slim continued. "I'm not here to shake you down."

"You're just here to set the record straight? Is that it?"

"I'm here to tell you that you are in danger."

"Danger from what?"

"Not what—whom. Think about it, Frost. It all makes sense."

Actually, it didn't make any sense at all. Ever since this whole sordid affair had started, from the very moment Bob had been discovered faceup, staring blankly at the ceiling, Jack Frost had felt like something wasn't right. Dorian's decision to come back to Elysian Row; Commissioner Tiresias' willingness to make a deal; the peculiar manner in which Mister Johns could coax people into talking about a man they'd spent a lifetime trying to forget. From the start, something wasn't right about the whole thing. And though Jack Frost wasn't especially keen on getting an impromptu lesson in the proper use of pronouns from this low-life loser, that wasn't what was bothering Jack Frost. What bothered Jack Frost was that Minnesota Slim was starting to make sense, *too* much sense for Jack Frost's liking.

"And from 'whom' am I in danger?" Frost inquired.

"How much do you know about this Mister Johns?"

"Johns ..." Frost guffawed. "Johns is the person I should be worried about?"

And here I thought Slim might offer up a clue, Frost thought to himself. *Clueless is more like it.*

"You break into my room, wait for me in the dark for God knows how long—almost get yourself shot—to tell me that?"

"I'm just asking a question. How much do you know about him?"

"Listen, Slim, the last person I need to answer to is you. Commissioner Tiresias trusts him, and that's good enough for me." The problem, of course, was that Jack Frost didn't trust Commissioner Tiresias. But then again, Jack Frost would rather have been in cahoots with the Commissioner than climb in bed with Minnesota Slim any day.

"But Commissioner Tiresias' a crooked cop, an accessory to murder. You yourself just said so," Slim said, exposing Frost's faulty logic.

"And we're going to finish up that conversation in a minute—" Frost said, correcting Minnesota Slim. "As for Johns, he was brought in to help me find the man who killed Bob."

"And how's that going?"

Frost ignored the sarcasm.

"Turns out Johns is doing a pretty damn good job. He has a way of getting people to talk. People who haven't said a word about Bob in close to 40 years are telling him things even I didn't know." Of course, this was exactly what made Jack Frost suspicious of Mister Johns, but he didn't cop to that.

"But what do you know about *him*?"

"You know, we really haven't had too many heart-to-hearts. We've been kind of preoccupied. Besides, Johns isn't much of a talker. Of course, nobody would make that mistake with you, Slim. You're *quite* a talker, and it sounds like you got something you're just dying to tell me. So go ahead—I'm listening."

"Well, you and Johns aren't the only ones asking questions," Slim said, his voice filled with a newfound bravado.

"Is that so?" Frost replied as he watched this little suckfish turn into a puffer right before his eyes.

"I've been asking a few questions myself," Slim replied. "I've been talking to a few people, too. And this Johns—nobody knows who he is."

"What do you mean nobody knows who he is?"

"I mean they know him, they know what he does, they know where he lives. You ask around town and everyone says they know

Mister Johns. They just don't know *who* he is. He's kind of like that character from that book. That F. Scott Fitzgerald book—" Slim said, searching his memory, "you know the one with the guy everybody is friends with, but nobody knows anything about?"

"*The Great Gatsby*?"

"That's the one. Gatsby—he's like that. He just blends in."

"He's investigating a murder, he's supposed to blend in. And besides, Gatsby ended up killing someone. He didn't blend in so well after that."

"All I'm saying is that no one knows the first thing about him. A lot of people's fortunes are riding on this. When this thing breaks it's going to be the biggest news to hit the Row in years. Yet the Commissioner sends in a complete unknown? Just doesn't add up—that's all I'm saying." Slim had a point—a very good point, in fact—and Jack Frost hated him for it.

"I appreciate your concern, Slim," Frost covered.

"Just answer me this—" Slim pressed, "do you trust him?"

"He does his job."

"That's not an answer."

"Sure it is, Slim."

"But not to the question I asked."

"You want an answer, here's an answer for you. I don't need to trust him. The only thing I need to do is keep my eye on him."

"Oh, I get it—'Keep your friends close, your enemies closer?'"

"Something like that," Frost said. "Now if we're done here, I'd really like you to leave."

"So that's it? I come all the way down here, tell you you're being set up and you tell me to get out?"

"That's about the long and short of it, Slim," Frost said succinctly. "Oh, and if you take my handkerchief, do me a favor and have it cleaned before you send it back."

"Man, you and the Commissioner—you must be in deep."

"On second thought—" Frost reconsidered. "Keep the handkerchief. My gift to you. Now get the hell out of here."

"Fine, Frost. You want to go alone on this, fine by me. But don't say I didn't warn you. You're getting played." Minnesota Slim got out of the chair, and walked across the room. He had almost passed through the doorsill—

"Oh, and one last thing. For what its worth, Tiny didn't do it." That brought Frost back into the conversation. "Outside the studio you told Johns you thought Tiny might have killed Bob," Slim continued. "He didn't."

"How do you know what I told Johns outside the studio?"

"Oh, I'm sorry," Slim said, feigning surprise. "I can stay now?"

"Cut the shit and tell me how you know what I said to Johns outside the studio."

"I told you, Frost, I've been following you. And you're right about one thing. Tiny had motive. There's no question he was crazy—emphasis on 'crazy'—about Bob. He had the opportunity, too. I mean, he was one of the last people to see him alive that night. But he wasn't the only one."

"I hardly think a few fly-by-night musicians who'd met Bob once, maybe twice in their lives would have any reason to kill him," Frost rationalized.

"They wouldn't. But perhaps an old girlfriend would. Someone like, say, I don't know … Sophia."

"And here I thought you were actually going to give me something I could use," Frost replied, remembering why he had such disdain for Slim in the first place. "Sophia was nowhere near the studio that night."

"Really?"

"Yes, really."

"And how can you be so sure?"

"Because Tiny gave me the logs. Every track, every musician, every person who was there," Frost said, wishing he had that log right now. He'd have slammed it on the desk at that precise moment. Point made. Case closed.

"Is my name in it?"

"And why would your name be in it?"

"Because I was there. And so was Sophia, as well as a few others you'd be interested in. They all had motive, and, as you've already noted, they had the opportunity, too."

"I don't know what your game is, Slim, but I'm not playing."

"I can assure you, Frost, this isn't a game. Bob's dead. The word is obviously out I have the second set of books. Whoever killed Bob is in all likelihood the person coming after me."

"What are you talking about—'the second set of books'?"

"You don't watch many mobster movies, do you Frost?" Slim said, slowly slithering back into the room. "There are always two sets of books—the 'good' set and the 'bad' set."

Jack Frost had seen plenty of mobster movies. He figured Slim had seen his fair share, too. And judging from this last comment about a 'second set of books,' there was a good chance Slim actually was beginning to think he *was* in a movie. Slim might have been a lousy lowlife, but he always did have a vivid imagination. Jack Frost figured it probably helped Slim rationalize his pitiful existence, helped him cast himself as a hero in a life that was hardly worth living. But whatever fantasy world Minnesota Slim may have been living in, it was starting to come very close to reality. Because as much as it sounded like something right out of an old 1940s Carol Reed film, Slim was telling the truth. There really *was* a second set of books. 'That's a copy,' Tiny had said as Mister Johns took receipt of the leather-bound ledger. 'You got yours, I got mine,' Tiny had been all too vigilant to point out.

And while Jack Frost couldn't prove the veracity of Minnesota Slim's claim that he had gone back to the studio and swiped Tiny's set, by Tiny's own admission a second set did indeed exist. How Slim had even known about that second set of books was as enigmatic as the spineless little urchin who was making the claim, but then again what did it matter? Minnesota Slim somehow knew, and he was trying to use that knowledge against Jack Frost. So instead of tossing Minnesota Slim out on his ass, an instinct that Jack Frost was fighting very hard right now, he decided to see where Slim's little subplot involving a second set of books was headed—

"And do you care to tell me how you came into possession of this second set of books?"

"I took them. Listen, you said it yourself. All the Commissioner needed to do was tell the truth. But he didn't. Instead, he makes up this elaborate story. And when he started doing that, I knew something was up. Didn't know what, but I knew it was something. So I went back to the studio, found the log and took it."

Slim was starting to make sense again. Fantasy was intersecting with reality, and the reality was that Jack Frost's world was getting smaller every minute. And while Jack Frost couldn't prove whether Minnesota Slim had Tiny's copy or not, he knew it wouldn't be that hard to check out Slim's story that there were other people in the studio that night. Actually, he already had—

"You are aware I talked with Sophia today."

"And Tremolo, and Penny and Lonesome," Slim said, listing the names in quick succession as if he were flipping through a set of index cards. "Yeah, I'm aware. Like I said, I've been following you."

"So Sophia just conveniently failed to mention the fact she was with Bob the night of his death? Is that what you're saying?"

"I know it sounds crazy."

"Maybe because it *is* crazy, Slim."

"How long have you known Tiny?"

"Get to the point, Slim."

"Hell, you think I'm wound tight, try sitting in a room with that guy for seven straight hours. He's wrapped tighter than a top."

"The point, Slim—" Jack Frost pressed.

"My point is that Tiny Bobbitt is probably the most paranoid person either of us has ever met. Hell, he gave old Bob a run for his money in that department. Maybe that's why the two of them got along so well. Yet he just offers up his logs, just like that? I mean, does that sound like something a paranoid person would do?" Slim paused, then finally made the point he'd been taking his sweet time getting around to—"He gave you those logs because he wanted to throw you off track."

"Like Commissioner Tiresias, right?" Frost said dubiously.

"I'm dead serious, Frost."

"And how do I know you're not trying to throw *me* off track?"

"What would it take for you to believe me?"

"You say there's a second set of logs—I want to see them."

"You don't think I brought them *with* me, do you? I mean that's all I got. That log is my insurance policy. I give you the log, I got nothin'."

"As far as I'm concerned, Slim, you got nothing now. The log or I walk."

"Sorry, Frost. I can't do it. Who's gonna protect me?"

"You give me the log, *then* we talk about protection."

The good news for Minnesota Slim was that Jack Frost was finally taking him seriously. The flip side of that reassuring revelation was that unless Jack Frost took him under his wing, Minnesota Slim was for all intents and purposes a dead man.

"That's not good enough, Frost," Slim demanded. "I told you already—someone's got it in for me. They already killed Zeitzman. And now they're coming for me."

"Well, I just hope they find you before Tommie the Make and Julius the Squeeze. And you better hang on to this," Frost said, placing the gold-plated pistol in Minnesota Slim's palm. "When they find out you told Commissioner Tiresias about the tribute show, that gun's going to become your best friend."

"You're making a big mistake, Frost."

"The only mistake made tonight was you showing your face here. Now get out."

Minnesota Slim slid the pistol into the breast pocket of his raincoat, walked slowly to the end of the hall and turned, "Remember how I told you someone was following me, Frost …" One of the benefits of being a guy who talked as much as Minnesota Slim was that he typically got the last word, "Well, they're following you, too." Minnesota Slim's voice was dead calm. The frenetic, frantic quality was gone. Minnesota Slim believed what he was saying. And for that split second, Jack Frost believed him, too. The two men exchanged a final glance before Slim descended down the stairs and into the darkness.

Frost walked over to the window and pulled back the curtains. He watched as Slim shot out from underneath the frayed, red awning and scurried down the street. The rain was coming down even harder than before. Suddenly, there was an explosion of light as a bolt of lightening cracked the sky in two. And though the storm was far off in the distance, it was the silence in the room that was like thunder. And for the first time since he had learned of the death of Bob Dorian, Jack Frost was starting to worry. Because he knew if there was even an ounce of truth to what Minnesota Slim had told him—that the Commissioner had brought the body to the Chelsea; that there were other people in that studio the night of Bob's death; that Mister Johns was working both sides against the middle—if any of these things were true then time was running out. And Jack Frost knew the only way to turn time back was to talk to the one man he hated more than anyone.

Frost reached into his pocket and took out his cell phone. He dialed a number, and waited for the person on the other end to answer. The time had come to pay the piper …

CHAPTER 12

▼

THE MAN IN THE LONG BLACK COAT

"You came alone, I see," the man said, peeling the door back slowly.

"You seemed surprised," Frost replied.

"It's just nice to see someone holding up their end of the bargain, that's all. So ..." he said, cocking his head to the left, then to the right, "where is your partner in crime anyway?"

"Back at the Tombstone."

"I wonder if Commissioner Tiresias left a mint on his pillow?"

"He's got him on a pretty tight leash," Frost concurred.

"But not you, right? Nobody's gonna put you on a leash, are they, Jack?"

"I'm my own man," Frost said flatly.

"Yeah, I used to work for a guy like that once. Oh, wait a minute," he said feigning surprise, "so did you."

Suddenly, the night sky lit up again, causing the shadows from the uprooted trees strewn across the front yard to clamber across the man's pale, ashen face. He always had managed to evoke an ominous, looming presence, but in that instant he looked like a figure straight out of the Bible. His coat, long and black, added a certain gravitas to his already daunting appearance.

"Sorry about all the mess out there," he continued as the sound of muffled thunder settled in the distance. "Bad hurricane came through here few weeks ago—didn't leave nothing standing but a few Paperback thorns and a couple Large-leaved Rock Figs." The man glanced up at the sky, "Speaking of storms—this one looks like it might get nasty. Care to come inside?"

"This isn't going to take long," Frost said, standing his ground. "Your name's been coming up a lot lately."

"Is that so? I'm flattered."

"Don't be. The portrayals aren't that flattering."

"So who've you been talking to?"

"Don't give me that crap. You know exactly who I've been talking to."

"Tiny?" he said with mock enthusiasm. "Have you talked to Tiny yet?"

"Yes, I have. It turns out the call came from Tiny's studio."

"Tiny doesn't like me very much," he said without missing a beat.

"Nobody likes you very much."

"You like me though don't you, Jack? I mean I got you off the Chitlin' Circuit, out of those old dance halls on the outskirts of town. How long had you been trying to get into the big leagues? Ten, fifteen years? I did it with a phone call."

"I appreciate what you've done for me," Frost said cordially. But judging from the way the words seemed to stick in the back of his throat, that conviviality hadn't come easily. "And just so you know, this isn't going quite the way you'd hoped,"

"And how had *you* hoped it would go?"

"Johns has been asking a lot of questions. Turning up a lot of dirt."

"And does Johns know you're here with me?"

"Of course he doesn't know I'm here. If he did, my ass would be in stirs. Yours, too, for that matter."

"What are stirs, anyway?"

"I think it would be best if you took this seriously. We're running in some rather shallow waters here. Minnesota Slim just paid me a visit."

"What the hell did he want?" the man said disdainfully.

"Protection."

"I can't protect you *and* Minnesota Slim—that would be a conflict of interest."

"Well, maybe this will help you choose sides."

Frost reached into his pocket and retrieved the CD Tiny had given him. He placed the CD in the man's hands. The man looked down at the disc, then turned and disappeared into the house.

It looked like Frost would be coming in after all …

THEY ENTERED a modest, albeit well-appointed library. The man crossed the room, stopping in front of an ornate oak cabinet containing a dozen pieces of electronic equipment. It was one hell of a sound system.

He opened the cabinet door and placed the disc in the stereo. He pressed the 'play' button and stepped back. A familiar, haunting voice filled the room—

"Is that Bob?"

"Yep."

"*Our* Bob?"

"The one and only."

"I've never heard that song before."

"That's because he just recorded it."

"Play it again."

Jack Frost pressed the 'play' button again. The song was as evocative the second time as it was the first, maybe even more so.

"Tiny recorded that?"

It wasn't like the man in the long black coat to be surprised. But he was. Because what he was hearing was unlike anything he'd ever heard before. Or rather it wasn't like anything he had heard from Bob

Dorian in a long time. Bob had been out of the picture for years. Booze, women, writer's block, simple lack of inspiration—take your pick. They all had contributed to Bob Dorian's steady decline as an artist of relevance. But this, this was different. This was genius—pure, unadulterated genius. This was the Bob he had found busking for dimes down on MacDougal Street; the Bob he had picked up by his lapels, brushed off and turned into the brightest star in the universe. And while it wasn't like the man in the long black coat to be surprised, he was floored.

"You're telling me this is Bob?" he said.

"Recorded three nights ago. The night he was murdered. Along with another 16 or so."

"And who else knows about this?" he said guardedly. He wasn't in the business of giving anything away, and he wasn't going to start now.

"Besides Tiny?"

"Yes, besides Tiny, Frost—who else knows?"

"That's where our friend Minnesota Slim comes in. A few days ago I put him in touch with Tommie and Julius."

"Why in the world would you do that?"

"I figured he could help. It was a mistake."

"Some people say there are no mistakes in life, Frost. I, however, beg to differ. And that one's a colossal mistake if you ask me."

"Not my finest moment, I'll be the first to admit. Anyway, the Commissioner got wind of the show, and figured of the three people who knew about the gig, Slim would be the easiest to shakedown. Apparently, that's just what he did—he shook him down, got him to confirm we were going to be staging a show here on the Row."

"You mean *you* were going to be staging a show."

"Right."

"Important distinction, Jack. You said my name's been coming up a lot. I just want to make sure it's not coming up in the same breath as yours."

"It hasn't. And it won't."

"Good. So back to Commissioner Tiresias—he squeezed Slim, and Slim squealed."

"Like a pig."

"Not good. Not good at all, Jack."

"Now just wait a minute—I did a little squeezing of my own. You see, Slim was sitting in my room at the Chelsea when I got back to the hotel tonight. It seems Slim had a few things he wanted to get off his chest."

"Such as?"

"Such as the fact that he can link Commissioner Tiresias to the crime scene."

"Really? And how does he make that connection?"

"He says he was with him."

"Well, as much as I can't stand the Commissioner, we can't let that get out. We still need Commissioner Tiresias if we want this to play out the way we planned."

"Slim's scared. Says someone's after him. For all I know he's making the whole thing up. It might not even be true."

"Can't take that risk, Jack. Commissioner Tiresias' name starts getting mentioned in the same sentence as the word 'murder,' he might shut this whole thing down. We've already lost the golden goose. I'd hate to miss out on the trimmings."

"Jesus, they were right about you. You'd sell your own brother down the river for a buck."

"My brother wouldn't fetch the same price as Bob, but your point's well taken."

"You know, for all your sermonizing over the years about what's 'good' for Bob, it's nice to finally know what really guides you. Clearly, it isn't your conscience."

"Well, I should hope not, Jack. We both know that every man's conscience is vile and depraved. And besides, in the end it's only ourselves we have to satisfy. Now back to Minnesota Slim—"

"What about Minnesota Slim?"

"Don't worry about him."

"What does that mean?"

"Stop beating a dead horse. It means I'll take care of Slim. Now as for this Mister Johns ... how much does he know about me?"

"Like I told you, nothing. But it's only a matter of time before any questions Johns has—well, he's going to be asking them personally. That would be the kiss of death for both of us."

"So you want to know how I should be ... how shall I say this ... 'represented.'"

"Why do you think I'm here?"

"Well, that all depends now doesn't it, Jack?"

"On what?"

"On how much *you* really know about me."

And just like that, the conversation was over. It had taken no more than three minutes, four tops. But in the brief span of those few minutes, everything had changed. Jack Frost had hoped he wasn't going to have to see him. Striking the initial deal was hard enough. A personal meeting was never in the plan. But desperate times call for desperate measures. And after Minnesota Slim showed up in his hotel room ranting like a lunatic about someone trying to kill him, Jack Frost knew things were starting to get desperate indeed.

And as he hurried along Rue Morgue Avenue back toward the Chelsea, his legs pumping like pistons beneath him, Jack Frost kept thinking about what the man had said to him just before they'd parted ways. He wasn't exactly sure what the man in the long black coat had meant when he said he'd 'take care of Minnesota Slim,' but he had a good idea. Jack Frost enjoyed a little tête-à-tête as much as the next guy. He also knew he needed to find Minnesota Slim before it was too late. And if he was going to do that, he was going to need to bring Mister Johns back into the fold. This was a whole new game: people's lives were on the line. If that second ledger fell into the wrong hands, Minnesota Slim wasn't the only guy who was going to need to start brandishing a pistol.

THE DOOR TO JACK FROST'S ROOM SWUNG OPEN to reveal Mister Johns standing in the transom.

"Got the message you called," Johns said, brushing the water off his lapels. "Came as fast as I could. What's up?" he said, stepping into Jack Frost's room.

"New development—"

"A break in the case?" Johns said, slowly unbuttoning his raincoat before dropping it on the chair in the corner.

"Not sure yet. All depends. You know a guy named Minnesota Slim?"

"Can't say I do," Johns lied.

"Well, he's a real lowlife," Frost continued. "Been on the dole for as long as I've known him, and that's been my entire life. Frankly, Slim's nothing but a two-bit hustler, but I sometimes helped him out from time to time when I could."

It was evident from the subtle shift in the tone of his voice that Jack Frost's disdain for Minnesota Slim was tinged with a bit of empathy. And though he didn't come right out and say it, the truth was that there had always been a soft spot in Jack Frost's heart for Minnesota Slim. That's, after all, why he told Slim about the concert in the first place. He had hoped Slim would see it as his chance to make an honest buck. After all, an honest buck was hard to make on Elysian Row. All Slim had to do was help pull the show together, take his one percent at the door, walk away and keep on walking. But Minnesota Slim did what everyone in this place ended up doing—he screwed it up. Clearly, Slim had never fully grasped the popular turn of phrase, 'a bird in the hand is worth two in the bush.' Real shame since that expression applied perfectly here. Jack Frost had given Slim a good deal. But Slim wanted to go out and shake the bushes, see if someone would give him a better one. The only problem was that the bushes were filled with vultures. And those vultures were now circling Minnesota Slim.

And as Jack Frost thought back on his longstanding relationship with Elysian Row's most infamous bottom feeder, he recalled the words of a writer he had read back in grade school when he and Slim were assigned the same desk in Mrs. Morrow's homeroom: 'You can't go home again.' Nearly three-quarters of Jack Frost's life had passed since he had encountered those words. And though he couldn't quite place the author whose prophetic prose he now recalled with new-found admiration, he knew one thing for certain: at some point in his life, the writer must have passed through Elysian Row. *Shame he didn't take Slim with him,* Frost thought to himself. *Of all the people in this place, Slim had wanted out the worst.* And Jack Frost had given Minnesota Slim a way out. But dammit if Slim hadn't gone and made a total mess of it. And now someone wanted to kill him to make sure Slim didn't make a mess out of their life, too. *You really can't go home again,* Jack Frost thought to himself, *not if you want to live to tell the tale.*

"Anyway, Slim's not the most likable guy you'd ever meet," Frost continued, doing his best not to wear his heart on his sleeve. "But like I said, I helped him out from time to time."

"Sure, sure. This place is filled with people like that—" Mister Johns said. "Low-life losers with a lousy sense of judgment. Need all the help you can dish out."

"Yeah, well Slim's starting to dish it back."

"How so?" Mister Johns replied.

"Remember how Commissioner Tiresias said two guys brought Zeitzman back to the Chelsea the night he was murdered?"

"Yeah—" Mister Johns confirmed.

"Well, according to Slim, *he* was one of those guys," Frost said, conveniently omitting the fact there was a very good chance Commissioner Tiresias was the other guy.

"So if Slim's telling the truth, then Commissioner Tiresias lied," Mister Johns said, grasping the situation. "That's a problem," he continued, adding the obvious.

"That's just the start of the problem. According to Slim, Tiny Bobbitt is also playing loose and free with the facts. That log he gave us—the one with the names of the people supposedly at the studio that night?"

"Right—"

"According to Slim, it's missing a few."

"Another problem I take it."

"It is when one of them is Sophia," Frost said matter-of-factly.

"So this Minnesota Slim—he tell you anything else?"

"Says the log Tiny gave us was a dupe," Frost replied. "Says he has the real one—which, of course, leads us to the next problem."

"He's not handing over the log."

"He's not handing over the log," Frost repeated.

Mister Johns reached into the breast coat pocket of his suit and took out a small, silver container. He unscrewed the top of the container and shook a breath mint into his hand. He brought his cupped hand to his mouth and swallowed the mint in a single, dry gulp.

"So where's this Minnesota Slim now?" Mister Johns inquired.

"Lord only knows. But he's a wildcard—I can tell you that. He'll do whatever it takes to save his ass."

"And you really think there's a second log—something that can put Sophia there that night?"

"He was pretty adamant about not handing it over. Said it's all he's got, his insurance policy. Said if he gave it to me, he'd have nothing."

"And your thinking is that if the logs were bogus he'd have handed them over."

"Like I said, Slim will do whatever it takes to save his ass. But he wasn't interested in saving his ass. He was interested in saving his own life. He really thinks someone is trying to kill him."

"He said that?" Mister Johns replied, perhaps a bit too quickly. "That someone was trying to kill him?"

For a guy who claims not to know Minnesota Slim, Frost thought to himself, *Johns seems awfully concerned about Slim's well-being.*

But just as quickly as the thought flashed through his head, Frost dismissed it. Sure Johns was a little cagey at times, but wasn't that why he'd been brought in the first place? Wasn't Mister Johns *sup-*

posed to be evasive and off-putting? Wasn't he supposed to make people feel uncomfortable? Isn't that precisely the thing that got them to talk? And while Johns had 'evasive' down pat, he'd never been evasive with Jack Frost. With Jack Frost he had been nothing but direct. Maybe a little *too* direct at times. There was no question Mister Johns' directness could be a little chafing. But from the outset, Mister Johns had been a straight shooter with Jack Frost.

There was something, however, something about the way Mister Johns had reacted to that last comment that made Jack Frost take notice. And while Mister Johns hadn't exhibited any of the common telltale signs that suggested he was hiding something, clearly he had grown uneasy when he learned that someone was out to get Minnesota Slim.

"Judging from all the trouble that guy seems to have caused you over the years, I'm surprised *you* didn't whack him yourself," Johns said dryly.

And though Mister Johns' wry observation didn't completely assuage Jack Frost's suspicion that Johns wasn't being perfectly forthright, it went a long way to allay his apprehension. There was just something about Mister Johns' self-effacing manner that could disarm a nuclear bomb.

"Just one question though," Mister Johns inquired. "If you thought Minnesota Slim was telling the truth about the log why'd you let him go? He starts talking to our suspects, we'll never find out who killed Zeitzman." Whatever brief flash of humor Mister Johns had just exhibited had clearly been usurped with a healthy dose of doubtful hesitation. Out with the new and in with the old: Mister Johns' paranoia had returned.

"I let him go, Johns, because he didn't have the log with him. But you're wrong about him talking to our suspects. He's too scared for that. He might not have had the log with him when he paid me a visit, but the minute he gets that log he's going to skip town."

"And how can you be sure he hasn't already?"

"Because I know a guy—and he's gonna make sure that doesn't happen."

CHAPTER 13

▼

MEMPHIS BLUES

He wore a pair of oil-stained overalls and a pair of heavy workman boots. His face was long and boney, his cheeks sunken, his eyes recessed into his head. He didn't smile too often, but when he did it was evident dental hygiene wasn't a priority. He had teeth like a horse: big, brown, cavity-corroded choppers that looked like they'd been picked up from the cut-out bin at a costume shop. There were a few tufts of hair protruding like wild weeds from the back of his head, but he was for all intents and purposes bald. The top of his head was like a fleshy, pallid skullcap, kept smooth and shiny as a result of a 40-year habit of caressing his cranium like a fortuneteller caressing a crystal ball. To see him in profile you would think you had just stumbled upon the Grim Reaper himself. He was a sight to be sure: a gaunt, world-weary figure of imposing size and stature. But it would be a mistake to refer to him as skeletal. To do so would imply that he was languorous and without life, and nothing could be further from the truth. As the man who literally 'made the trains run on time,' this tall, imposing figure was the Row's lifeline to the outside world. Nobody came or left Elysian Row without passing through Memphis Blues' rail yard. Memphis Blues knew where everybody came from, how they got here, where they were going, and when they had left. And that knowledge gave him power, and that power made Memphis Blues the de facto gatekeeper to Elysian Row.

"So what you're saying is no trains have come or gone tonight?"

"Something wrong with your hearing, Frost? I've been through all this twice." The man in the oil-stained overalls clearly didn't like to repeat himself. And judging from the tone of his voice, he didn't take too kindly to impromptu visits in the middle of the night, either. "This guy you're looking for must have really screwed you over."

"Not yet."

"But given a chance, right?"

"Right," Frost said with a smile. Memphis Blues reciprocated with a toothy grin of his own. "It's good to see you back on the Row, Frost," Memphis Blues said, picking up a dirty rag from a crowded workbench. He wrung his hands in the rag, then methodically folded the towel neatly first in half, then in quarters. "Sorry to hear about Bob," he said, placing the rag on the bench.

"No you're not."

"Actually, I am," Memphis Blues replied. "Unlike most everyone else in this town, I didn't have a beef with Bob. To tell you the truth, I kind of liked him."

"You didn't even know him," Frost said matter-of-factly.

"Probably why I didn't have a beef," Memphis Blues chuckled.

As it turns out, Memphis Blues did know Bob Dorian. But the Bob Dorian Memphis Blues knew wasn't the belligerent, bad-tempered bastard everyone remembered. The Bob that Memphis Blues knew was a snot-nosed, wide-eyed folksinger who'd showed up in the winter of 1961 with nothing but a guitar strapped to his back and a desire to write songs about things that were 'real.' And for Bob, the rails were the real thing. Anyone who'd ever picked up a book or read an article on Bob Dorian knew that if there were anything that rivaled Bob's love for music, it was his affinity for the rails. Bob didn't talk to the press too often, but when he did he always found a way to work trains into the conversation. There was just something about trains that captivated him. For Bob, trains represented a sense of autonomy and independence, an escape from the ties that bound. He loved the way the pipes and pistons glistened in the evening sun. He loved the way the slow, methodical churning of those pistons filled you with the promise of a new beginning. He loved the way the sound of the whistle split the night in two, dividing it into past and future. He loved the way the smell from the burning coal filled your nostrils as it rose up the smokestack and poured out into the night. And as for the people who rode the trains, Bob had nothing but admiration for them. He loved their sense of adventure; embraced their sense of longing; coveted the freedom they effortlessly embodied.

Over the years, Bob had written a lot of songs about trains. And while his songs about riding the rails would appear periodically throughout his career—a few peppered here, a few popping up there—every one of them had been written in a short, six week span when the aspiring folksinger and acerbic brakeman had formed a friendship that would endure long after Bob had moved on. It was only in later years—after Bob had become both heralded and hated for his skewering portrayals of the inhabitants of Elysian Row—that Memphis Blues was asked to comment on Bob's 'formidable years.' It was a short conversation. Memphis Blues simply couldn't comment on a man he didn't know.

So when Memphis Blues told Jack Frost he didn't know Bob Dorian, Frost knew Memphis Blues wasn't trying to be duplicitous. What Memphis Blues meant was that he didn't know *that* Bob Dorian. He knew another side of Bob Dorian. He knew a Bob that was kind, thoughtful, insightful and perfectly unassuming. Memphis Blues may have known a young, wide-eyed kid named Bobby Zeitzman; he definitely did *not* know Bob Dorian.

"So back to this guy you're looking for—"

"Minnesota Slim," Frost interjected, offering up the name for the first time.

"*That's* the guy that's got you so worked up?" It took a lot to surprise Memphis Blues. That last admission, however, had done it.

"I didn't know I was worked up, Memphis."

"Well, something's got your knickers in a twist to bring you out on a night like this. Weatherman said to expect rain. But, hell, none of us expected anything like this. It's coming down in buckets."

"I just need to make sure Slim stays in town until a few things are worked out," Frost said, glancing nervously at his watch.

"What makes you think he's going to skip town?" Memphis Blues said, noticing Frost's nervousness.

"Let's just say he's gotten in a little over his head."

"And this has something to do with Bob?"

"Not sure yet—" Frost glanced at his watch a second time.

"I already told you the '909' was stuck in Mobile," Memphis Blues said curtly.

"Right, I heard you."

"Then why do you keep looking at your watch?"

"What?"

"Your watch," Memphis Blues said, tapping his wrist. "You keep looking at it."

"Just waiting on someone, that's all. Guy I'm working with on this. He's staying over at the Tombstone. Went to get his pad and pencil. Very meticulous, likes to take notes."

As if on cue, Mister Johns entered.

"And there he is—" Jack Frost said, extending his arm in a sweeping motion to welcome the belated Mister Johns. "Mister Johns, Memphis Blues. Memphis Blues, Mister Johns." The two men shook hands. "Memphis runs the rail line," Jack Frost continued. "Like I said, Mister Johns here is helping me sort this whole thing out."

"Sorry I'm late," Mister Johns said, acknowledging Memphis Blues with a nod. "It's not exactly smooth sailing out there." Johns removed a black rimmed fedora and shook the rain off it. "So how much did you get into?" It was evident Mister Johns was ready to get down to brass tacks. Mister Johns placed his hat on the workbench.

"Told him we're looking for Slim. Says he hasn't seen him."

"Actually, I didn't say that. Tonight ..." Memphis clarified, "I said I haven't seen him *tonight*. He was here a few nights ago milling around by the tracks."

Frost and Johns exchanged a glance.

"Any idea what he was doing out there?" Mister Johns asked without giving anything away.

"Who the hell knows?" Memphis Blues may have had an affinity for Bob Zeitzman, but clearly the same could not be said for his feelings toward Minnesota Slim. "Slim's nothing but a bum. Everybody knows that. Welfare department won't even give him any clothes."

"And this was when?" Johns said. "When you saw him, I mean."

"A few days ago."

"How many?" Johns pressed. 'A few days' wasn't going to help them. If Memphis Blues were to amend his response to 'three days,' however, that would be another matter altogether.

"Well, let's see, today's Saturday," Memphis Blues said, juggling the dates around in his head. "This was Thursday, so what's that?"

"Three days," Johns said, turning a knowing eye to Frost.

"And you're sure it was Slim?" Frost pressed.

"It was Slim, all right. I'd know that high-pitched paranoid voice anywhere."

"But you didn't actually see him?"

"Like I said, I heard him," Memphis Blues replied. "But he was definitely talking to someone."

"Did you get a look?" Mister Johns interjected. "At the person he was talking to. Did you get a look at him?"

"Can't say that I did."

"You sure you weren't just hearing voices?" Johns said, glancing over at a bottle of railroad gin. The bottle was empty. Memphis Blues reached down and picked up a Styrofoam cup. He defiantly brought the cup to his lips and drained its contents.

"I'm sure," Memphis said tersely, placing the cup back on the workbench.

"And was there anybody else?" Jack Frost asked.

"Looked like there was a third guy. But he wasn't talking. So what's this got to do with Bob?" Clearly, Memphis Blues was losing interest in the conversation.

"We think one of the guys might have been Zeitzman," Johns said matter-of-factly.

"Wait a minute—are you saying Slim's mixed up in all this?" Memphis Blues wasn't absolving anyone of culpability, but it sure as hell didn't sound like he thought Minnesota Slim was remotely capable of getting mixed up in something as nefarious as murder. There were too many mitigating factors surrounding murder, and anyone who knew Slim knew he would have had a very hard time keeping all the facts straight.

"Maybe," Mister Johns replied noncommittally. "We don't know for sure yet."

"Hold the phone," Memphis Blues said, a second revelation dawning on him. "Are you telling me that Bob was killed in my rail yard?"

"Commissioner Tiresias said he got a call just after midnight from someone saying they saw a body over by the tracks."

"That call wouldn't have been made by Dela, would it?"

Again, Frost and Mister Johns exchanged a glance.

"There's only one train that leaves here that time of night—the '524' for New Orleans. Departs at 12:02. Dela was the only one on it. Jeez Marie, such a sweet girl," he said, pausing for a moment to reflect. "Sorry to hear she had to get mixed up in all this."

"Speaking of," Johns said. "You haven't heard from her lately have you?"

"Who? Dela?" Memphis Blues replied.

No, Mother Theresa, Mister Johns thought to himself. *Of course I'm talking about Dela.*

"Yes," Mister Johns said pleasantly. "We'd like to ask her a few questions."

"Can't say I have."

"Well, if you do ..."

"Right … right … give you a call. I know the drill. Now back to the body—if the dead guy was Bob, and Slim was the second guy, then who was the third man?"

"It would appear that's the sixty-four-thousand-dollar question," Johns said smugly.

"The word going around town is that there were two railroad men who carried Bob's body to the Chelsea that night you say you heard voices," Frost chimed back in.

"Oh, I get it. And you thought I was one of those railroad men? You thought maybe *I* was involved. This isn't just about checking on a train schedule is it?" Memphis Blues said, the realization now sinking in. "You wanted to check my alibi."

"Don't worry, Memphis, your alibi checks out fine," Frost said reassuringly.

"But you're still not going to tell me who the third man was?"

"Sorry, can't do it," Frost replied. "But you'll tell us if Slim shows up?"

"You'll be the first call I make."

Just then, Jack Frost's cell phone rang. Frost reached into his coat, removed his phone and brought it to his ear. An uncomfortable silence fell across the room.

"We'll be there in 10 minutes," Frost said, sliding the phone back into his pocket.

"Something wrong?" Memphis Blues said, asking the obvious.

"Let's just say you don't have to worry about Slim showing up anymore—" Frost turned to Mister Johns, "Grab your hat, Johns, we're taking a little walk."

"Where are we going?" Johns replied.

"Interstate 29," Jack Frost said, opening the door as he stepped out into the pouring rain.

"What's out on Interstate 29?"

"Minnesota Slim—" Jack Frost said without turning around, "what's left of him, anyway."

INTERSTATE 29 RUNS LIKE A DARK NIGHTMARE
through the heartland of America: a broken, beaten down dreamscape
where hucksters and hustlers prowl on the innocent and unassuming.
Out here nothing is above suspicion. And though it may seem like it
goes on forever, all roads end somewhere; and if what Commissioner
Tiresias had just told Jack Frost was true, the biggest lead in the case
was about to turn out to be a dead end.

He looked about the same as he had an hour ago with one minor
exception: Minnesota Slim's nose wasn't the only thing bloodied
now. "Ear to ear," Commissioner Tiresias said, drawing his finger
across his throat. "The three of us have got to stop getting together
like this. It seems every time we do someone turns up dead."

"What the hell happened?" Frost said, eyeing the nearly decapi-
tated Minnesota Slim.

"Somebody killed him."

"I can see that, but ..." Jack Frost searched for the word that
would describe the thing that had been done to Minnesota Slim.
"Jesus ..." was the best he could come up with. His best fit the bill
perfectly. Because whoever was behind this hadn't just killed Slim,
they had crucified him. Literally. With the exception of a pair of
white Jockey briefs that strategically covered his groin, Slim's squat,
bloated torso had been stripped completely bare. His short, stublike
arms were stretched tautly in either direction, each wrist bound in a
black leather clasp nailed into the wall. His legs, pale and emaciated,
dangled beneath him.

"I always suspected Slim was into some freaky shit," Commissioner Tiresias said smugly as he picked up a black leather bullwhip
and examined it circumspectly. "Guess in all the excitement of getting
his head whacked off, he forgot the 'release word.'" Commissioner
Tiresias cracked the whip for emphasis then dropped it back on the
bed.

Mister Johns walked into the room. The moment he saw the
naked Minnesota Slim, he shot Commissioner Tiresias a look, as if to
say: 'Who is that?'

Commissioner Tiresias picked up on the look immediately.

"Oh, that's right. The two of you haven't met." Commissioner Tiresias feigned an introduction, "Mister Johns, Minnesota Slim. Lowlife, louse, scum and scoundrel—in other words, a model citizen of our fair Elysian Row. And now thanks to that very large gash across his throat, the subject of your next obit."

"Who found the body?" Mister Johns inquired, staring vacantly at Minnesota Slim's lifeless body.

"The maid service. I guess whoever tried to cut Slim's head off forgot to leave the 'Do Not Disturb' sign when they left—poor girl walked right in."

"Any ideas?" Johns said, slowly moving to the left, then to the right, continuing to examine the body like a museum patron examining the intricate brush strokes of a painting.

"Shit, when it comes to this one, my head's filled with nothing but images and distorted facts," Commissioner Tiresias said with complete candor. "As to who killed him—haven't got a clue." Commissioner Tiresias smiled, exposing that old Cheshire grin that let Jack Frost know the Commissioner really didn't give two tits to Sunday who had killed Minnesota Slim.

"Well, that's not like you, Commissioner," Jack Frost interjected. "You're usually the first to jump to conclusions."

It was clear from the tone of his voice that Jack Frost had jumped to a few conclusions of his own. And Commissioner Tiresias wasn't known to be a big fan of conjecture, especially when he was the guy about to get collared.

"Would you excuse us for a moment," Commissioner Tiresias said coolly. "I need a moment in private with Mr. Frost."

"Take all the time you need," Johns said, clicking his heels as he turned and obediently backed out of the room.

"Very funny, Frost," Commissioner Tiresias simmered once Mister Johns was out of earshot. "That bit about jumping to conclusions, very funny. Speaking of conclusions, you and Johns any closer to figuring this thing out? Concert's just a few days away."

"We got a few leads," Frost replied.

"Well, let's hope so. We wouldn't want a killer on the loose. Be bad for business, if you get my drift. Though it would appear business is better than ever."

"What's that supposed to mean?"

"One less guy with his finger in the pie," Commissioner Tiresias said, motioning to Minnesota Slim. "You did give him a little taste of the action, didn't you? A little hush money to keep the concert quiet. After all, I had to rough him up pretty good to get him to talk. And nothing keeps a man tight-lipped better than a tight roll of bills." Commissioner Tiresias cocked his head, "Just trying to beat you to the punch, Frost."

"Beat me to the punch? What the hell are you talking about?"

"Don't tell me you didn't come down here thinking I didn't play a hand in Slim's untimely demise?"

"And why would I think that?" He didn't even attempt to mask the sarcasm.

"Well, for starters, I know you and Slim had a little talk earlier tonight. And if I know Slim—which I do—he probably had a whale of a story. The problem with our dearly departed friend Slim," Commissioner Tiresias started to pace back and forth in front of Minnesota Slim's lifeless body, "is that Slim was a great storyteller. Unfortunately, the facts didn't always check out." The Commissioner's movements, like the tenor of his voice, were slow and methodical. They reminded Jack Frost of the scene from *Hamlet* in which the deranged Danish prince speaks to the hollowed-out head of Yorick. "But of course you knowing Slim, you went and checked on the facts." Commissioner Tiresias spun around on his heels. It was an effective piece of staging, done more for dramatic effect than anything else. He obviously knew the answer to the question he was about to pose, "You did check the facts, didn't you, Frost?"

It took every ounce of restraint Frost possessed to prevent him from giving something away. Not that there would have been that much to give away in the first place: Commissioner Tiresias pretty much had the situation pegged.

"Does this little soliloquy have a point, Commissioner?" Frost replied, tactfully avoiding the question. "Because this whole line of questioning assumes Slim and I actually spoke to each other."

"I'm not assuming anything, Frost. You and Slim *did* talk earlier tonight." Commissioner Tiresias leaned down and pulled a handkerchief from Minnesota Slim's coat pocket. He handed the handkerchief to Frost. "That *is* your handkerchief, isn't it?"

It would have been hard for Frost to deny it. The embroidered initials, '*JF*,' pretty much gave it away.

"Now back to Memphis Blues and the night of the murder," Commissioner Tiresias said, continuing to pace back and forth in front of Slim. "I wasn't there. That is what Slim told you, isn't it? That he and I brought the body back to the Chelsea. It's okay, Frost. You and I are partners, and partners should be straight with each other."

"Slim told me quite a few things," Frost said, dropping the handkerchief into the trashcan.

"He did, did he?" Commissioner Tiresias taunted. "What kinds of things? Anything you might want to make your partner privy to?"

While Jack Frost wasn't ready to come right out and accuse Commissioner Tiresias of murder, clearly the Commissioner's caginess was doing very little to solidify their 'partnership.'

"Said someone was following him. I guess we know who that someone was—"

"Ironic isn't it?" Commissioner Tiresias conceded. "Maybe if Slim hadn't given me the slip, he might still be alive. But I digress—you were going to tell me about the progress on the Zeitzman case."

The Zeitzman case?

The words stopped Frost cold. There was just something about the way Commissioner Tiresias was able to refer to Bob's murder in that condescending, non-committal tone that rubbed Jack Frost the wrong way.

"Johns has been doing most of the questioning," Frost said, masking his growing contempt for Commissioner Tiresias. "Why don't I let him apprise you?"

"Wonderful idea," Commissioner Tiresias said, the condescension still in full force, "I just wanted to clear up any misunderstandings we might have."

'The Zeitzman case?'

Jack Frost just couldn't shake the words loose. Was that all this was to Commissioner Tiresias? A 'case'? Open as long as the killer was roaming the streets, closed the minute the man who put the bullet in Bob's chest was brought to justice? And what about justice? Justice wasn't even in Commissioner Tiresias' vernacular. Justice didn't have a damn thing to do with this. This was about the money. Hell, the money was what had put this whole squalid scenario in motion in the first place.

First, there was Tommie the Make and Julius the Squeeze. Frost had brought them in to promote the show like some back alley cockfight. But promoting a gig like this was tricky. Getting the word out too soon would have sunk the whole thing. So Minnesota Slim was given a little bit of the action to keep the lowlifes on the QT. Then when the guy who was going to make them all rich turned up dead, Commissioner Tiresias brought in Johns to make the whole thing go away. And what was the common denominator? What was the pin that had held this lynch mob together? It was the money. From the very beginning it had been the money. And now that the going was starting to get tough, it was probably going to be the money that blew the whole damn thing apart.

But who was Jack Frost kidding anyway? He was hardly immune to the lure of money. Never pretended to be. Sure, there had been a time when this had been about the money for him, too. It wasn't that simple anymore. Things had changed. Or more precisely, things *were* changing. Now it was about loyalty. Loyalty to a dead man, a man who would never know the way he really felt about him. Talk about a sick twist of fate. It was providence's personal 'fuck you' to Jack Frost, compliments of Commissioner Tiresias.

"We *are* clear, aren't we?" Commissioner Tiresias intoned ominously, jerking Jack Frost back to reality.

"Crystal clear," Frost replied coolly. And indeed they were. Seeing Slim hung up on the wall like a modern-day, S&M messiah had brought everything into focus. Because in that instant it became evident to Jack Frost that perhaps Slim's murder—a sight that had undoubtedly shaken him to the core—had actually been the thing that had liberated him.

"Good," Commissioner Tiresias said, unaware of the fact Jack Frost was seeing their relationship with a newfound clarity that, in the end, would bode very badly for Commissioner Tiresias. "Now why don't you go ahead and bring Johns back in," the Commissioner continued. "Turns out, I've got something for him."

Frost walked across the room, turned the doorknob and opened the door. He stepped into the hallway and motioned to Johns: they were ready to bring him back into the mix. Mister Johns arched his eyebrows in acknowledgement and followed Jack Frost back into the room.

Commissioner Tiresias was standing in the door, ready to greet him. "Mister Johns," the Commissioner said as he took hold of Johns' shoulder and directed him across the room. "Frost here says you've been making some real progress in the case?"

Judging from the way Mister Johns recoiled when the Commissioner laid his hand on his shoulder, Mister Johns was not especially comfortable with this newfound intimacy.

"We have some leads," Johns replied noncommittally.

"Yes, he mentioned that," Commissioner Tiresias said affably. "But he didn't get into specifics. Said you'd be better suited to shed some light on it."

"Well, we've talked to a couple people who knew Zeitzman."

"Everyone in this town knew Zeitzman. Specifics—" Commissioner Tiresias bristled. Whatever geniality the Commissioner had exhibited a moment ago was gone now.

"Sophia, Mr. Tremolo, Penny, Lonesome, Tiny Bobbitt," Mister Johns replied, rambling off the names of the people with whom they had spoken.

"Don't forget Memphis Blues," Commissioner Tiresias said abruptly. Mister Johns' eyes darted in the direction of Jack Frost. Frost nodded his head as if to say; '*It's okay.*'

"Yes, and Memphis Blues," Mister Johns added breezily as if the omission were inadvertent. "We just spoke with him."

"Which is odd because I would have suspected if he was the last person you'd talked to, then he'd be the first person you'd have mentioned—considering the conversation would be fresh in your mind."

"Memphis Blues isn't a suspect," Mister Johns said with his trademark evenness.

"Oh, that's right. You were just talking to him to see if I was at the rail yard the night of the murder." Commissioner Tiresias brushed his hand across the top of Johns' suit coat, smoothing out the shoulder line like a tailor. "You don't have to respond to that, Mister Johns," Commissioner Tiresias said, stepping back to size up Mister Johns. "Mr. Frost and I have already discussed your little visit with Memphis Blues. And since you didn't have the benefit of hearing that conversation, allow me to apprise you. You see, I think it's important that you know the kind of man you're working for, Mister Johns. It's important for you to know I'm someone you can trust. You do trust me, don't you, Johns?"

"I have no reason not to," Mister Johns replied, knowing full well he had every reason in the world not to trust the Commissioner.

"*Very* nice answer, Johns," Commissioner Tiresias said, suddenly coming to life. "Evasive, yet affirmative at the same time. You could learn a few tricks from this guy, Frost," Commissioner Tiresias said, turning in the direction of Jack Frost. "Now, another issue that came up while you were outside was the question of trust—as in 'could Mr.

Frost and I trust each other?' We came to the conclusion—albeit tenuous—that we could. Isn't that right, Frost?"

"That's right." *As in I can trust that you are up to something. What it is exactly, I don't know,* Frost thought to himself, *but you are definitely up to something.*

"I hope you and I can come to that same conclusion," Commissioner Tiresias said, refocusing his attention on Mister Johns.

"I'm not a very trusting person, Commissioner," Mister Johns replied with surprising candor. "I don't think you would have asked me to look into this matter if I was. But I don't think you played a part in Zeitzman's murder, if that's what you're asking." Mister Johns' candor clearly ignited a spark in Commissioner Tiresias.

"And the answers just keep getting better!" Commissioner Tiresias was ecstatic, damn near euphoric. "No, you're right—in your line of work suspicion is a virtue, not a vice, which by all accounts would make you the most virtuous person on Elysian Row. So back to the people you've talked to—the ones who *are* suspects—what's the verdict? Are we any closer to finding a killer?"

"While it seems just about everyone we've talked to had motive, finding someone who had the chance to murder him—well, we haven't been able to put those two pieces together yet."

"Pretty important pieces, wouldn't you say?" Commissioner Tiresias' reply was playful, and came across exactly as intended: a good-natured ribbing, more like a repartee than a reprimand.

"We'll put it together," Mister Johns assured him.

"I'm sure you will, Johns. I have every faith in you. It would appear, however, not everyone has the same appraisal of your abilities."

Once again demonstrating his flair for the dramatic, Commissioner Tiresias reached into his breast coat pocket and removed what appeared to be a piece of paper wrapped in a sandwich bag. Taking the edge of the paper between his forefinger and thumb, the Commissioner pulled the paper out with the careful precision of a surgeon.

Commissioner Tiresias handed the piece of paper, which they now realized was a note, to Mister Johns.

"Found it in Slim's mouth—where his tongue used to be."

Mister Johns tentatively took the note from Commissioner Tiresias. He read it through silently once to himself—

*'This ain't no run through,
it's the real thing'*

"I wouldn't worry about this," Mister Johns said to no one in particular as he slipped the note into his pocket. "Nothing but intimidation, pure and simple."

"I'm not the one who's worried," Commissioner Tiresias said. "But then again, the guy who carved Minnesota Slim up like a Christmas turkey didn't leave me a memento to remember the evening by. 'This ain't a run through, it's the real thing,'" Commissioner Tiresias said, repeating the words that had been inscribed on the note, in Slim's own blood no less. "Any idea what that means?"

"Not a clue. But like I said, Commissioner, we'll put the pieces together. It's just a matter of time."

"I certainly hope so," Commissioner Tiresias said, assessing the gravity of the situation. "Because, Mister Johns, it would appear time is rapidly becoming a valuable commodity."

THE WALK BACK TO TOWN should have taken about 20 minutes. It felt a lot longer.

"I know why I was brought in—"

Johns' words hung in the air like a noose. And the longer they remained out there, the tighter they became around the neck of Jack Frost.

"What?"

"Into the investigation—I know why I was brought in."

Frost waited to hear what Johns was going to say next. It was like waiting for a train wreck. Because Frost knew if Johns got it right—if he really *did* know why he'd been brought in—everything Frost had worked for over the last 20 years was going to go off the tracks.

"You thought this would be an open-and-shut case," Johns said matter-of-factly. "Zeitzman's been murdered, let's bring someone in, find the killer. And if anything goes wrong, blame the guy who screwed the pooch, got the facts wrong, defamed the image of the late, great 'Bob Dorian.'"

"What are you insinuating?"

"I'm not insinuating anything, Frost. I'm stating the obvious."

"Which is?"

"You and Commissioner Tiresias were setting me up. You brought me in to take the fall."

"That's ridiculous," Frost countered. "Commissioner Tiresias and I wanted another set of eyes on this, that's all."

Jesus Christ, Jack Frost thought to himself. *I'm actually doing the Commissioner's bidding. No wonder this guy's untouchable. He gets everyone around him to take the heat for him.*

"Another set of eyes—right," Mister Johns replied, clearly unconvinced. "Listen, Frost, I don't blame you. Frankly, I'd have done the same thing. You were covering your ass. You didn't know who to trust, so you trusted the guy who could screw you over most. You hoped that by playing ball with Commissioner Tiresias that he wouldn't call you out. Well, the game has changed, Frost. Commissioner Tiresias may think that note was for me, but the reality is that that little Chinese fortune he pulled out of Minnesota Slim's mouth was intended for both of us. I don't need to tell you—something is definitely 'foul' on Elysian Row."

"So now you're some back alley Shakespeare?" Frost said defiantly.

"I'm just telling you what I think you already know. Commissioner Tiresias may have brought me in to play the patsy, but it's the two of us he's playing now."

And while Frost couldn't dismiss Johns' assessment of the situation, Jack Frost took comfort in the fact that the walls were thick at the Fifth Daughter. That's probably why Slim had taken such a liking to that flea-infested roach motel in the first place. Based on that bull-whip and those leather clasps strapped across his wrists, Minnesota Slim's penchant for pain and pleasure were well served by thick walls. So, too, was the exchange between Frost and the Commissioner. Because if Mister Johns had heard the conversation that had taken place behind those walls, Johns wouldn't need his powers of perception to figure out Commissioner Tiresias was up to something: he would *know* it. Commissioner Tiresias *was* out to screw them both.

"Is that what you think? That the two of us are being set up by the Commissioner?" Jack Frost snapped, hoping his curtness would cause Johns to question his impeccable powers of perception.

"That's what I know. And you know it, too."

"So I should just trust you blindly?" Frost continued unfazed. "Is that what you're saying? Because you haven't been the most forthright person either, Johns. You're not exactly a model of candor and openness."

"My job is to help you find the man who murdered your former client," Mister Johns rationalized. "I hardly see how those things have anything to do with my ability to do that job. Certainly the man who killed Zeitzman isn't being candid and open."

"Fair enough," Frost conceded. "But tell me this—if you thought you were being set up then why did you agree to take the job in the first place?"

Mister Johns hesitated. His hesitation, however, was all Frost needed to know the answer to his question. And he didn't like that answer one bit.

"It's a puzzle isn't it?" Frost said. "That's the reason you're doing this, looking for the man who killed Bob. It's just a fucking puzzle for you to piece together."

"I look at it more as a conundrum."

Jack Frost could hardly contain his contempt for what appeared to be nothing more than a cavalier curiosity in the case. "Don't be glib with me, Johns! Bob Dorian was my friend! Mysterious, elusive, eva-

sive—sure. But whatever smokescreen he put up, he put it up to protect himself against people like you."

"And what kind of *people* might that be?"

"People who saw only what they wanted to see in him. Bob Dorian
was many things to many people, but I will not let you reduce his life
to a single word. You're a real son of a bitch, you know that!"

"You got a lot of nerve to say you were his friend," Johns said,
ignoring the swipe. "Few years back when he was down on his luck—
couldn't catch a break for tryin'—you just stood by and watched. You
were no better than the rest of that 4th Street crowd and you know it."

"That 4th Street crowd!" Frost sputtered. "You don't know the first
thing about what was going on back then. You don't know the first
thing about my relationship with Bob!"

Clearly, Mister Johns' nonchalance had struck a nerve with Jack
Frost. A very raw nerve, it seemed. And now that Mister Johns had
Jack Frost's attention, Frost could sense that Johns was planning to
get to the bottom of something that had been bothering him for some
time.

"I've never proclaimed to be an expert on your relationship with
Mr. Zeitzman," Johns conceded, "but I think I have a pretty good
indication of what went down. What forged your relationship with
Bob, I'm talking about. And you're right, it wasn't that 4th Street
crowd. It wasn't a crowd at all. Crowds are hard to rally people
against. Crowds are faceless. Nameless, too, for that matter. People,
on the other hand, are different. You create a villain—give him a
name, give him a face—and you got yourself something that brings
people together. You and I have talked to everyone in this town trying
to get to the bottom of this. And everyone we've talked to has mentioned the same guy."

"Judas," Frost said succinctly. He knew the nerve Johns was going
to hit next.

It was true. Every person they had talked to referred to Judas in a
way that left no doubt they had great disdain for the power Judas had
over Bob Dorian. And with the exception of Frost's short, rather

tepid defense of the man who had recognized Bob Dorian's talent and in the process given the world his genius, Jack Frost suspected that Mister Johns had surmised Frost despised Judas, too. Mister Johns was right about something else: Judas *was* the perfect villain.

"Yes, Judas. If there's one guy in this town they hate more than Bob it's him. By your own admission you hated him, too. Yet you were in business with him, for a while anyway. But something happened, didn't it?"

"I told you how it went down," Frost replied firmly, hoping Mister Johns wouldn't press the issue.

"I'm not talking about Fairport," Mister Johns replied. "I know how Judas wrestled Bob away from the Left. Penny gave us a pretty good account of that already. Yours wasn't half bad, either. What I'm curious about is how Bob was wrestled away from Judas. Something came between those guys, and frankly I'm curious what it was."

Or 'who,' Jack Frost thought to himself. *I think we both know where this is headed.*

Mister Johns opened his notebook and read from one of the loose-leaf pages, "'There's no secret there was no love lost between Judas and me. The day I got Bob out from underneath Judas' grip is one of the happiest days in my life.'" Mister Johns closed the notebook. "Tell me about *that* day."

Turns out it went right where Jack Frost had suspected.

"What I did in Jackson in '86, I did for Bob. It was a bad situation and I stepped in. I'd like to believe anyone who found themselves in a similar situation would have done the same thing. Bob needed a friend."

"And he got a friend—got a manager, too."

It was a sucker punch and Mister Johns knew it, but Frost had left himself so exposed Johns would have been a fool not to have taken it. And besides, Frost knew this was the punch Mister Johns had wanted to throw from the start.

"What are you saying?"

"I'm just saying that from what I've read you did more than step into a bad situation. From what I'd read you *created* the situation. Trumped up some charges that Judas had his hand in the till."

"Now you can stop right there!" Frost sputtered. "That's an allegation that's never been proven!" Frost's ire was irrepressible. "And who are you to judge me? Judge my friendship with Bob! You don't know for a minute what it was like to stand in Bob's shoes. To have been hailed as 'the voice of a generation,' to have been put on a pedestal, placed in a glass house, only to be repeatedly let down by those closest to you."

"Save the helpless rock star bit for someone who cares, Frost, because I ain't buying." Their little tussle had turned into quite a little sparring match. "But you're right, that charge was never proven. I got to admit though—" clearly Mister Johns wasn't ready to throw in the towel just yet, "all this talk that Bob shouldn't shoulder all the blame for what he turned into, that everyone bore responsibility for pushing him to the forefront, that people like you, his so-called 'friends' always had his best interest at heart—boy to hear you tell it, it sure sounds like you had him figured out."

"Of course, I didn't have him figured out," Jack Frost snapped. "That's why the two of us got along. I never tried to figure him out. Trust me, the first person who tells us he had Bob's number—that's the guy who did him in, because that's the guy who's lying through his teeth."

"I'll keep that in mind," Mister Johns replied coolly.

Frost was unsure if Johns' retort was intended to be ironic or a simple statement of fact. Either way, it didn't matter. Because that last little exchange, as heated as it had become, wasn't really about one man trusting the other. It was about two men testing each other's mettle. It was about seeing if these men had it in them to see this thing through. And though Jack Frost didn't like the fact he'd had to go toe-to-toe with Mister Johns, he accepted the fact it needed to be done. Because now both men knew they could rely on each other. But Jack Frost now knew something else. He knew why Johns had taken the case: Johns was just as interested in unraveling that enigma known to the world as Bob Dorian as Frost. In other words, they were in this together.

"So how's he setting us up?" It was an odd non sequitur to be sure, but the way Frost figured it if he and Mister Johns were indeed in this together, then it might be best if they were working out of the same playbook. "You said Commissioner Tiresias is setting us up," Frost continued. "So how's he setting us up?"

"I think the Commissioner knew about the recording session."

"He couldn't have known about the recording session," Jack Frost said dismissively.

"And how can you be so sure?"

"Well, for starters because *I* didn't know about it."

"But you said yourself that you didn't know everything Zeitzman was doing. Was that just a line?"

"No, that's true. But how would the Commissioner have known?"

"Listen, Frost," Mister Johns said, spelling it out, "it's no secret the Commissioner has his hands in everyone's pockets. Nothing happens on the Row without him not knowing about it. He knew about the concert before you even got to town. What makes you think the same guy who told him about the show didn't tell him about the session."

"And the only person who knew about both of those was Minnesota Slim," Frost said, catching on.

"By his own admission, Slim said he told the Commissioner about the tribute show. So why is it such a stretch that Slim wouldn't have told him about the recording session as well?"

Frost pondered the thought. It wasn't much of a stretch at all. In fact, it made perfect sense. "It would explain why he had someone following Slim," Frost said.

"Sure it would. Slim thought the Commissioner was setting *him* up. The Commissioner claims not to have been involved in moving Zeitzman's body. Slim claims he was. Only three people know for sure: Minnesota Slim, Memphis Blues and Commissioner Tiresias. Problem is the first guy's dead; the second was strangled up on Texas medicine and railroad gin the night it went down; and the third guy's credibility is shot full of holes. Now what's the first thing Memphis Blues said when we asked him why Slim was milling around out there in the rail yard that night?"

"You're the one with the notebook, Johns, you tell me."

Mister Johns opened his notebook, "He said, 'Who the hell knows? Slim's nothing but a bum. Welfare department won't even give him any clothes.'" Mister Johns closed his notebook and looked up at Jack Frost, "A guy who likes to talk and needs some cash."

"Blackmail …"

"Whether the Commissioner moved that body or not, I don't know. But Slim did. Slim moved the body, and he figured Commissioner Tiresias would blackmail him when the going got tough. The way I'm figuring it, Slim just wanted to make sure there was enough to go around. Now, I'm not that experienced in the blackmail game—"

On this point, Jack Frost wasn't so sure. Frost was beginning to think Mister Johns might have a little more experience in the extortion trade than he was letting on. That little tidbit about Jackson and what really went down there definitely could have gone the way of blackmail. "But I know enough to know half a dozen names are better than one," Mister Johns continued. "Especially when those half dozen names were all with Zeitzman four hours before he turned up dead."

"So you really do think a second log exists?"

"Oh, I know it does."

"So where are we going?" Jack Frost said, now realizing that they were no longer standing outside the Fifth Daughter. They were walking south along Interstate 29, *away* from town, rather than toward it.

Suddenly, up around the bend, the vestiges of what appeared to be an abandoned lumberjack camp came into view—

"We're going to talk to the guy who has it."

CHAPTER 14

▼

HUSK THE SIBERIAN

"You are aware that this guy is a cold-blooded killer?"

It was really more of a statement than a question. After all, *everyone* on Elysian Row knew what Husk had done in that Italian restaurant over in Red Hook a few years back.

"He's gotten a bad rap for that," Mister Johns said dismissively.

"A bad rap? For Christ's sake, Johns, he killed a man!"

"Three actually—" Johns replied as if he were adding a few flap-jacks to his breakfast order.

"And that's supposed to make me feel better?"

"He *did* his time."

"And how is it that he got this log again?" Frost said with uneasy trepidation.

"I haven't told you that yet."

"So I'm asking—how did he get the second log? *You* just found out about it."

"Yeah, about that," Mister Johns said off-handedly. "You remem-ber when you asked me if I knew Minnesota Slim?" Jack Frost's suspi-cion that Mister Johns might be playing both sides against the middle was about to take on a new twist—"Well, I kind of 'misspoke,'" Johns continued with unabashed bluntness. "You see, before Slim was turning evidence for the Commissioner he was turning up leads for me."

It took a few moments for Johns' words to register, but when they did it was evident Jack Frost was none too pleased by what he'd just heard.

"'Misspoke!'" he sputtered. "I asked you flat out if you knew Slim. You didn't 'misspeak,' Johns—you flat out lied."

"And you mean to tell me you've never told a little 'white lie,' Frost?"

"I'm in the music business, Johns, white lies are a steady part of my daily diet. But I don't lie to the people I want to trust me."

"And you want me to trust you?"

Frankly, it wasn't so much that Jack Frost *wanted* Mister Johns to trust him; he *needed* Mister Johns to trust him. It was a quid pro quo, plain and simple. But just because Jack Frost had cast his lot with Mister Johns, it didn't mean he had to give him carte blanche.

"That little argument you made a few minutes ago about Commissioner Tiresias setting us up," Frost said warily, "that he knew about the recording session—that was pretty convincing. Problem is I'm beginning to wonder exactly who's zooming who."

"Listen, you were right about Slim," Johns said, backpedaling slightly now that he realized his 'little white lie' had cast a shadow on his credibility. "He's a lowlife, bottom of the barrel, a hustler and a thief."

"Was—" Frost corrected. "He *was* a hustler and a thief."

"Right, and like I said he used to hustle for me. But I'm no fool. This is Elysian Row, allegiances change, I know that. But you were right about Minnesota Slim—guy was a human corkscrew. He'd turn on his mother if he thought it'd save his ass."

"Sounds like he's not the only one."

"Been doing this a long time, Frost," Mister Johns replied, a tinge of indignation in his voice. "You come to me, tell me Slim's in bed with the Commissioner, tell me there's a piece of evidence out there that may rip the lid right off this story—well, I'm not going to take any chances."

"Even if it means selling me out?"

"I didn't sell you out, Frost," Johns said, brushing off the accusation.

"You lied to me, though."

"I've never made apologies for my actions, and I'm not going to start now." Judging from the curt change in his tone, Mister Johns had finished backpedaling. "Yeah, I lied to you earlier about knowing Slim, but my cards are on the table now. I'm dealing straight up with you, Frost. You asked me earlier if I trusted you. Well, I do. The question is whether you trust me."

Frost stared at Mister Johns for what seemed a very long time. Time teetered back and forth between them like two schoolboys on opposite ends of a seesaw. If the last 24 hours were any indication, Jack Frost knew that Mister Johns had a tendency to distort the truth from time to time. But Jack Frost also knew that someone who had grown as comfortable distorting the facts as Mister Johns would eventually get caught. And now that he had, it was actually a relief to Jack Frost. Truth is a malleable thing. Trust is not. Once your trust in someone is broken, it cannot be mended. And though Mister Johns had distorted the truth, there was a part of Jack Frost that actually found it hard to blame Jones for his duplicity. After all, deception *was* the currency of Elysian Row. Sure, Johns had bent the truth a little. It could always be bent back.

"So how'd you meet this guy anyway?" Frost said, straightening out any unresolved resentment that might have surfaced between the two men as a result of Johns' 'little white lie.' "This Husk the Siberian—" Frost clarified, "how'd you meet him anyway."

"Interesting story actually—" Mister Johns brightened.

"As if the fact I'm trouncing out to a lumberjack camp to meet a contract killer isn't interesting enough."

"*Former* contract killer," Mister Johns corrected. "And do us both a favor—don't call him 'Husk the Siberian.' He doesn't like it."

"I'll keep that in mind," Frost said.

Contract-killer-turned-lumberjack—that one took the cake, Frost thought to himself.

"And how exactly does a former contract killer become a lumberjack, anyway?" Frost inquired.

"It was part of his rehabilitation—chopping down trees to build houses for the poor," Mister Johns replied. "Guess he liked the work and stuck with it."

The fact that Husk was a shining example of all that was right with the State Correctional Facility was very nice, but Frost really didn't give a damn about that. What he wanted to know was what Husk had done that had put him in that correctional facility in the first place. Frost waited for the rest of the story. The rest of the story didn't come.

"You going to tell me what he was in for, or am I going to have to ask him myself?" Frost said impatiently.

"Probably best you and I go over it first," Mister Johns said, underplaying the fact that if Jack Frost got into that rather sore subject with Husk that conversation would, in all likelihood, be his last.

"All right then."

"You remember 'Crazy' Joe? The guy over in Red Hook?"

"Sure," Frost replied. "Ran numbers, had a couple of brothers, got mixed up with the mob. Then Joe and his brothers got tired of working for those goons over on President Street, decided to rub them out. Course it didn't play out quite like they'd planned. The cops show up, and they end up having to take some hostages."

"You really *do* know the case," Mister Johns said, genuinely impressed.

"It was a big story, made all the papers," Frost said matter-of-factly.

"Well, it was nothing like that," Johns replied.

"What do you mean?"

"Wasn't that cut-and-dry."

"Maybe it isn't that 'cut-and-dry' to you, Johns," Frost retorted, "but Judge Magney certainly didn't see it that way. According to the reports I read, the day Joe was to be sentenced he approaches the bench. Judge asks him what time it is. Joe looks at his watch and replies, 'five to ten'—to which Magney says, 'that's exactly what you get.' Joe spends five years in the pen. Then, when he gets out, some guy blows him away in a clam bar. It's messy, but it sounds pretty 'cut-and-dry' if you ask me."

"The bit about 'what time is it' is somewhat of an embellishment, but you're right about it being messy," Johns concurred. "Took close to six hours to separate the pieces of linguine from what was left of his head." Frost stared blankly at Mister Johns.

And how in the world would you know that? Frost thought to himself.

"Hey, you never forget your first obit," Mister Johns replied, shrugging his shoulders. "Anyway, I'll take it from here because this part didn't make the papers. Joe's cellmate—the guy who'd bunked with him while he was on the inside—gets out a few weeks after the clam bar incident. And he is none too pleased Joe's been whacked. I guess they'd gotten close in the can. So this cellmate, he decides to take matters in his own hands."

"Kill the guy who killed Joe?" Frost replied. The logic made sense.

"Right," Johns corroborated. "Except the guy who killed Joe beats Joe's cellmate to the punch—literally. Beat him to death with his bare hands. Made mincemeat out of him."

"No shit."

"Nobody had seen nothing like 'The Mighty' Husk. Guess revenge can make you do some pretty irrational things."

"Revenge?" Frost had lost the logic.

"The family Joe and his brothers took hostage, the ones who were caught in the crossfire when the cops blew through the doors … that was Husk's family. Wife, kids, brother—all gone."

"That never came out in the press," Jack Frost said, realizing Johns' penchant for full-blown conspiracies might not be so half-baked after all.

"Like I said," Johns said, feeling fully vindicated.

"So how do you know about it?"

"In addition to running the obits desk down at the *Dispatch* I also typed transcripts for the court."

"I bet that was good for a few stories."

"You have no idea."

THE TWO MEN TURNED LEFT off Interstate 29 and entered a dense forest. They passed through the thick collection of oak trees that formed a protective wall around an enormous clearing. At the far side of the clearing was a sloping hill. Nestled into the side of the hill was a small, two-story cottage. A slender, crooked chimney rose out of a perfectly stitched thatched roof that resembled an unkempt tuff of sandy blonde hair. Upon closer examination, however, it became evident that what had originally looked like a thatched roof wasn't a thatched roof at all. It was actually corrugated cardboard painted to *look* like a thatched roof. A series of small windows resembling ship portholes dotted the first and second stories of the cottage. Each window was adorned with a hooded awning that hung out just far enough to keep the light out. The cottage itself was made out of a deep red wood-fired brick, but in the reflection of the evening light, it looked like gingerbread. Idyllic, isolated and tranquil, the scene looked like an Edvard Munch woodcut from *Hansel and Gretel,* one of the many Brothers Grimm fairy tales Jack Frost's mother read to him when he was a child. And for the first time since he had come back to Elysian Row, Jack Frost actually felt safe. The sensation passed quickly however.

Wait a minute, Jack Frost suddenly realized, *weren't those kids led out into the forest and left for dead?*

"Well, if it isn't 'Husk, the Eskimo.'" Mister Johns called out.

Jack Frost's face went ashen. *I thought you said ...*

The man turned to face them. Based on what Mister Johns had told him, Jack Frost expected Husk to drop them both right then and there. Instead, he smiled and dropped a few breadcrumbs on the ground for the pigeons that had come to him. He then brushed his hands together quickly and extended a big, hairy fist to Mister Johns.

"Sorry about the mess," he said. "Feeding the birds was about all the warden let us do on the inside."

For someone who had amassed a reputation as infamous and far-reaching as 'The Mighty' Husk, he hardly looked the part. He was small, some might even say slight, and he walked with a hunch, which made him seem shorter than he really was. But even when he stood up straight, he wasn't very tall. Five foot four, five foot five at the most. The fact the word 'mighty' was ever even uttered in the same sentence as his name was itself a contradiction. Despite the paradox, however, the name somehow seemed to fit him perfectly.

"Don't give it a second thought," Johns said courteously, then motioned in the direction of Jack Frost, "Husk, this is Mr. Frost."

"The manager?" Husk said, giving Frost the once-over.

"That's right," Frost said as he shook Husk's hand.

"Let's do this inside if you don't mind." And with that, Jack Frost willingly followed a three-time convicted cold-blooded killer across the garden and into the dark cottage.

Once inside, Husk closed the door behind them then pulled down the blinds. A few hints of Husk's new life—a black and red checkered shirt, freshly polished work boots, and a wool skullcap—were neatly arranged in a chair in the corner. Husk walked across the room, wedged his fingers between two faux wood panels and removed a small piece of paneling. His hands disappeared into the dark space then reappeared with a large, leather binder.

"*The Savage Innocents*," he said as he walked back across the room, binder gripped tightly in his abnormally large hands.

"I'm sorry—"

"The picture you were just looking at, Mr. Frost—" Husk said as he placed the ledger on the table. He reached up and removed the photo, then handed the black and white publicity still to Frost. "It's from an old Anthony Quinn-Peter O'Toole film shot in 1959. Anthony Quinn plays an Eskimo who accidentally kills a missionary and finds himself being pursued for murder," he explained. "Cellmate gave it to me."

Frost examined the still. The picture was of a young, broad-shouldered Anthony Quinn standing atop a dog sled, wearing a large winter coat with fur trim around the hood that hid most of his face. Snow was blowing all around him. It looked like a ticker tape parade thrown for a soldier returning home to claim the spoils of war.

"I umm ..." Frost stumbled for the words that did not come.

"Don't see much of a resemblance, I know," Husk interjected. "It was more a wordplay than anything else. See the guys in the joint used to call me 'Huskie' cause of the fact I ran the numbers over at Bridgeport—"

"The dog track?" Frost clarified.

"That's right—" Husk confirmed. "Place called Shoreline Star. So when word gets out I'm a big fan of the film, I guess the boys thought it would be clever to shorten my name to Husk and add the Eskimo part to the end since I'd gotten the rap of being a 'cold-blooded killer.'"

"So why not 'Husk the Eskimo,'" Frost inquired.

"Guess they wanted to keep the dog motif," Husk added, almost as an afterthought.

"So you don't mind that people call you that?" Frost said tentatively.

"Shit, I love it," Husk said jubilantly. Frost shot Mister Johns a look. In return, Mister Johns shot Jack Frost a wink.

"Well, it sounds like it stuck," Jack Frost said, clearly appreciating the fact that Mister Johns had pulled one over on him.

"No thanks to Bob," Husk replied, hesitating for a moment. It was evident he had something else to add. But Husk took his time. He was in no rush. And considering the fact he had once killed three grown men with his bare hands, he was pretty sure no one was going to rush him. "As you can imagine, at first I wasn't too high on being tagged with a name that reminded everyone of what I'd done. Sort of hard to start a new life being collared as a cold-blooded killer. But Bob, he heard the name, loved it and started calling me by it. Like you said, name stuck."

"And now you're stuck out here spending your days feeding the pigeons?"

"Something like that."

"So did you like him? Bob, I mean?" Frost inquired.

Husk thought for a moment before responding. And when he did, it was evident he was choosing his words carefully, "For me, Bob was one of those guys I could take him or leave him. Never my cup of meat. But boy that guy kept everybody on their toes, that's for damn sure."

"What do you mean?"

"Always jotting down notes—inside of gum wrappers, on the back of matchbook covers, whatever he could get his hands on. You had to be careful what you said around him, I guess that's what I'm saying."

"And why's that?"

"Cause he'd turn it on you in a New York minute. Doesn't surprise me in the least someone killed him. What does surprise me is that he came back to this place. Anyway," Husk said, taking the movie still from Frost, "you didn't come here to here me gab. You came for that ledger. And before you leave with it, there're a few things we need to be clear on. A few conditions, if you will. Because you see, one of the conditions placed on me as part of my parole is that I don't break any laws. Now, I know I've been out of circulation a couple of years, but I'm pretty sure breaking and entering is still breaking the law. So I'd like to just make sure we're clear—"

Husk shot a cool, steely stare at the two men. The fact he divided his gaze evenly was more of a formality than anything else. The person he was really eyeing was Jack Frost. The fact that neither man said a word, Husk took as confirmation that everything was clear and he could lay out the terms of their agreement.

"All right then," Husk continued, "condition number one: This little get-together never happened. It comes up that you were out here, I deny it. Johns, what you did a few years back is appreciated but that goes for you, too, my friend."

"Understood—" Mister Johns acknowledged.

"Condition number two: If you choose to look inside that ledger, you take it. What you do with it after that is your business, but I don't ever want to see it, or you, again. Clear?"

Husk's eyes darted between the two men. Then assured that everything was in fact clear, he stood up and placed the movie still on the hook where he'd found it. "Listen, I know it's none of my business—what's in that ledger," Husk said as he adjusted the frame. "Johns told me there were some names in there that could help you find the man who killed Bob. Frankly, that's more than I needed to know right there. But a word of advice: Be careful."

"Careful?" Jack Frost perked up.

"Watch your back. Don't do anything rash. Don't jump to any conclusions."

"Even if the facts suggest we're on the right track," Frost countered.

"*Especially* if the facts suggest you're on the right track. Trust me, Mr. Frost, if the names you think are in that ledger really are in there, that log's going to make Pandora's Box look like a keepsake chest." And just like that, it was over.

Jack Frost took comfort in the fact that he had just successfully completed his first business transaction with a cold-blooded contract killer and lived to tell the tale. For the time being anyway ...

A FORLORN LOVER, a languished lackey, a forgotten friend, a broken-down brakeman, a low-life louse, a cold-blooded-killer-turned-lumberjack: that was only a partial list of the people they had encountered since Bob Dorian had been discovered lying faceup Thursday morning in the Chelsea Hotel. And if the last 48 hours were any indication, the list of suspects was only going to get longer. It seemed that everyone had a motive, many had the means, and a few even had the opportunity. But finding the person who had all three was like finding the proverbial needle in a haystack.

For a while, Frost was convinced that Tiny Bobbitt was his man. After all, Tiny seemed to have the closest thing to a perfect trifecta: means, motive, opportunity. And as for his alibi—a ledger that allegedly proved he was never alone with Bob long enough to do the deed—in light of the recent discovery of a second ledger and the discrepancies it contained, Tiny's alibi was beginning to resemble his rather unorthodox recording technique: throw it out there and see what sticks. And while nothing would have made Jack Frost happier than to pin the murder on that two-faced turncoat Tiny Bobbitt, in the end it would have been nothing but a trumped-up charge and Frost knew it. Because whoever killed Bob had, in all likelihood, killed Minnesota Slim, too. That little crucifixion number was a nice twist, very in keeping with the Bobbitt mentality. But unless Tiny had grown three feet, bulked up 40 pounds and sprouted balls of steel it was highly unlikely he was the guy who silenced Slim. And so Jack Frost was right back where he'd started: anyone could have killed Bob Dorian.

And while there were moments when Jack Frost was convinced everyone was in on the gig, he knew the chances of that were about as unlikely as figuring out why Bob had really come back to Elysian Row. And though finding that needle in that haystack was proving to be more and more difficult with each passing moment, the prickly little fact was that after all this work, he still wasn't any closer to finding the man who had put the bullet into Bob Dorian. In fact, the killer was proving to be just about as evasive as the elusive rock star himself.

"So what did you do for him?" Frost asked as they passed through the doors of the Chelsea and began to ascend the creaky old stairwell.

"Do for whom?"

"For Husk. When he was reading us the riot act, he said he appreciated what you'd done for him. So what'd you do for him?"

When they reached the landing, Mister Johns stopped and turned. "Remember how I told you I found out that the family killed in the clam bar was Husk's?"

"Right—that's the stuff that didn't appear in the papers."

"Well, Husk and I had an 'agreement,'" Mister Johns continued, "I scratch his back, he scratches mine."

"What kind of agreement?" Frost asked.

"I wouldn't bring in his family and in exchange, he said he'd help me if I needed it when he got out. Figured we could use his help getting that ledger."

They reached the second floor, turned and walked down the hallway, stopping in front of Jack Frost's room. "Give me a minute," Frost said, motioning to the door. "The doorknob's busted." Frost finessed the doorknob. Indeed, it was still broken. Remembering the concierge's instructions, Frost pressed against the door. The door opened, and a wedge of light sliced across the floor.

Frost walked across the room, pulled the blinds and placed the leather-bound log on the table. He glanced up at Johns as if to say, 'Well, this is it. This is the moment of truth.' Both men took a deep, dramatic breath, then Frost peeled back the ledger's cover. Frost took a moment to scrutinized Sophia's tight, taut signature. He seemed almost relieved to be able to render the verdict ... "Slim was right," Frost confirmed, "there it is just like he said." He turned the page, expecting the next name to be one of the musicians there that night: Dulcimer Don, Middle-Eighth Ed, Lester.

It wasn't.

Suddenly, Frost's relief turned to panic.

"Something the matter?" Johns inquired.

Frost slid the ledger across the table. Frost figured Mister Johns was going to need to see this for himself. They had encountered a lot of bizarre twists over the course of this investigation, but this one was the biggest curveball yet. Mister Johns looked down at the ledger.

And there it was. Just as clear as day. The one name neither man would have expected to see in a million years ...

CHAPTER 15

▼

RHIANNON

She was his muse, his inspiration, the cause of his misery. They had met during the height of his career, at a time when he was beyond famous; he was infamous, one of the most written about and photographed men in the world. Yet there were few, if any, pictures of the two of them together. She bore him three children and brought a fourth from a previous marriage. Yet despite the circus atmosphere that swirled around them like a swarm of flies buzzing in a ditch, she had done her best to shelter her children from the storm. But in the end, the veil of secrecy she wrapped around the family was always cloaked tightest around her. And when they finally did go their separate ways, no one knew which direction she went. She changed her name, changed her address, changed everything about her life with him. But even then she couldn't truly escape. Because even in exile, they were the perfect pair. If he was an enigma wrapped in a riddle, she was the missing piece to the puzzle no one could ever put together. And though little was known about her, this much was on the record: when it came to Robert Zeitzman she talked to no one.

"But she's talking to us?" Frost said in disbelief.

"That's right."

"But how?" The fact her name had appeared in that ledger was one thing. The fact that Mister Johns had persuaded her to comment on it: Frost was still having trouble wrapping his head around this latest development. "How in the world did you get her to agree to talk? Wait a minute—" Frost stopped. "How did you even *find* her?"

"Apparently she goes by Kazinsky now."

"Kazinsky?"

"It's her maiden name."

"And you knew her maiden name," Frost said skeptically.

"I told you, Frost. There are lots of books written on this guy. Ten minutes with an appendix can save you a hell of a lot of time pounding the pavement."

"I'm impressed," Frost said dutifully. "Blown away, actually. I've known Rhiannon for 40 years and even *I* didn't know her maiden name."

"Ann Isadora Kazinsky. Born 1938 in Wilmington, Delaware. Father was in sheet metal. Married a fashion photographer twice her age, had a kid, marriage didn't work out—"

"… Moved to Manhattan to be an actress. Worked in a topless place for a while," Frost droned unenthusiastically. "Why don't you tell me something I don't know, Johns. Like maybe the story behind why she changed her name?"

"Changed it shortly after her father was murdered."

That was something Frost didn't know.

"Wait a minute—her father was murdered?"

"That's right. Before she changed her name."

"Yeah, I got the name-changing part. It's the murdered father that's news to me."

"Figured it would be," Johns deadpanned. "Have to dig a little deeper if you want to find the truth."

"Well, that one's a nugget all right. In all the time I knew Bob, he never mentioned his former father-in-law had been murdered."

"Maybe she never told him."

"So she just kept it a secret?"

"As we are coming to realize, Zeitzman isn't the only one with secrets."

"Pretty tough secret to keep, don't you think?" Frost replied flatly.

"Agreed, but judging from the fact she didn't tell anyone she was at that recording session the night he was murdered, I imagine she can keep her mouth shut if she has to."

"I'm impressed—" Frost said. Though he was also a little suspicious that Mister Johns had been able to dig up so much dirt on such short notice. "But I still don't understand how you got her to agree to talk," he continued. "She's only talked to the press twice in her life, and both times she refused to speak about him."

"Let's just say I emphasized my association with Commissioner Tiresias."

"So you told her you were a cop?"

"All I told her was that we're investigating a murder—"

"A murder in which the former Ann Kazinsky is now a suspect, I presume," Frost said, the content of Mister Johns' earlier conversation with Ann Kazinsky starting to come together. "She fails to cooperate, she spends a little time behind bars."

"Something like that," Mister Johns confirmed.

The two men turned the corner. A small, two-story town house came into view. Mister Johns removed his notebook from his jacket. He flipped through the pages quickly until he reached the one he was looking for. He read the address aloud, "29400 Methodist Lane. This is the place."

"No wonder nobody found her," Frost said, pushing on an old chain-link fence. "Who in the world would live here?"

The 'here' to which Frost was referring was Housing Project Hill, a notoriously run-down housing development located in the most desolate part of Elysian Row.

Methodist Lane my ass, Frost thought to himself. *Sure you can dress up a sow's ear and call it a silk purse, but this place is still the projects.*

Fortune and fame—she could have had them both. Instead, she chose obscurity. But then again, Frost considered, it made sense. After all she'd been through she didn't *want* to be found.

They passed through the wire mesh fence, walked up the cracked cement pathway and ascended the stone stairs. They stood together on the landing in silence, each waiting for the other to press the plastic buzzer embedded in the old, rotten wood that framed a battered aluminum door.

"Why don't you do the honors," Frost said. "After all, you're the one who found her."

"Finding her and getting her to talk are two entirely different things," Mister Johns said, clarifying the distinction. "You said you know her?"

"*Knew* her," Frost replied, making a distinction of his own. "And it was a long time ago."

"Well," Mister Johns said, pressing the buzzer. "No time better than the present to get reacquainted."

HER EYES WERE A DEEP, DARK BROWN like the color of smoke. And though there was a resilience, a toughness that radiated from her, there was also a sadness in those eyes that offered a window into a world only she would ever know. And as they stood there staring into those sorrowful, sad eyes, they saw in her what he had seen. And it was all they could do not to immediately fall under her spell.

"We'll be sitting in the back," she said, motioning for the men to enter. Frost and Johns passed through the door and entered the house. "All I ask is that you don't touch anything. And there's no need to look for clues."

"Clues?"

"To our relationship, Mister Johns," she replied. "Everything in this house was purchased after we split."

She led them down a long, dimly lit hallway that extended the entire length of the house. "Here we are," she said, motioning to a pair of antique wicker chairs. "So how long has it been anyway, Jack?" There was a pleasant, disarming quality to her voice.

"'77, '78—" Frost replied.

"Oh, that's right, you testified on his behalf, didn't you?" Any pleasant quality previously exhibited had all but evaporated.

"I was booking his gigs, Rhiannon," Frost said coolly. "I had access to all his financial records. It wasn't personal. I was subpoenaed. I'd have been in contempt of court if I hadn't."

"Kind of like how I've been strong-armed into talking today," she replied with equal coolness. "And I go by Ann now, as Mister Johns here has so astutely figured out. Just out of curiosity," she said, turning her attention to Mister Johns, "how in the world did you think to look for me under my maiden name? Most people look for me under one of the myriad of pseudonyms he prescribed to me in his songs."

"You're not a fictional character in a song, Ms. Kazinsky. You're a real person with a real name. Just because you don't go by it anymore, doesn't mean it still isn't yours. I started with that."

"Actually, according to your phone call you started with something else. I understand my name showed up in a ledger." She brought a glass to her lips, took a sip, then placed the glass back on the table.

"That's right," Mister Johns confirmed. "I'm assuming you showed up as well."

"Yes, I was there. He was killed later that night, correct?"

"We're still trying to put together the time line," Mister Johns said, giving nothing away.

"You mean you're trying to see how many times you can put me on that time line."

Apparently, Mister Johns didn't have to give anything away. She knew exactly where the conversation was headed. "So I can assume that *is* your signature in the log, then?"

"Yes, it's my signature." The tone of her voice was toxic. "Why don't you stop talking around the issue and just ask me what you really want to know, Mister Johns. I heard about Minnesota Slim. You think I killed him, too?"

"No one is saying you killed anyone, Rhiannon," Frost said, reinserting himself back into the conversation.

"Ann—" she said disdainfully, "… it's Ann now, Jack, and not yet they aren't." The smoke in her eyes was beginning to smolder. "But that's why you're here isn't it?" she said, dispersing her contempt evenly between the two men. "Neither of you have a clue who did it, and you were hoping if I didn't confess that I might be able to lead you to the person who will."

"Ms. Kazinsky, with all due respect, you yourself have admitted to not only seeing him but actually being with him the night of the murder. We wouldn't be doing our jobs if we didn't speak with you. Now, anything you can offer would be greatly appreciated," Johns said, doing his best to pacify the woman who was clearly on the cusp of tossing them both out on their asses.

"And what exactly *is* your job, Mister Johns?" she snapped back. It seems Mister Johns' conciliatory tone hadn't taken quite the way he'd hoped. "I know what Jack's job is, or should I say—was. But what exactly is *your* job? I mean look at you—dressed in that cheap, Savoy Row knockoff suit, with that pad and pencil, taking notes, writing down every word I say."

"Nervous habit," Mister Johns replied coolly. "And to answer your question—for the second time, I might add—I was brought in by Commissioner Tiresias."

"Ann, I appreciate your agreeing to talk to us," Frost interjected. Clearly, the whole 'good cop, bad cop' thing wasn't working, so Jack Frost decided it was time for him to play the heavy, "But I would appreciate it more if you'd stop jerking us around. You know exactly what Mister Johns' role in this investigation is. You spoke to him on the phone less than an hour ago."

"Oh, I'm sorry, I didn't know I was … what was the term you used … 'jerking you around,' Jack. You see I was under the impression it was the other way around. What with you hunting me down, coming to my house, asking me a bunch of questions about a man I haven't discussed in 35 years. But then again, I guess having the conversation here is better than having it downtown. Interrogation rooms tend to be so cold and impersonal."

"For the last time, Ann, we are not interrogating you," Frost sputtered. "For Christ's sake, *you* invited us into your home. *You're* the one who agreed to talk."

"I agreed to meet you. I never agreed to talk," she corrected.

Mister Johns slid his notebook back into the breast pocket of his jacket. "Come on—" he said, straightening his suit jacket as he stood up, "neither of us needs this shit."

"So you're …"

"Leaving …" Mister Johns confirmed. "I guess I shouldn't have assumed when you agreed to meet with us, you actually had something you wanted to say. Sorry to have wasted your time, Ms. Kazinsky." Mister Johns turned in the direction of Jack Frost, "You coming, Frost?"

"Yeah," Frost said as he rose from the wicker chair, "I'm coming." The 'good cop, bad cop' shtick was back on, and they were sticking it to her pretty good.

They had just about reached the door when she called out to them—

"I was married, soon to be divorced …"

The two men turned. The smoke from her freshly lit cigarette danced like waves before her face. She motioned to the pair of wicker chairs, "You going to stand for this or you gonna sit down?" The two men slid back into the chairs.

It seems they would sit.

FOR A WOMAN WHO WAS AS WELL KNOWN for her disdain for the press, the past and anyone who wanted to talk about the two things she believed had kept her from moving on with her life, Ann Kazinsky wasted very little time turning back the clock.

"At the house in Upstate—" she said, lighting a fresh cigarette, "that's when I met him. His manager's girlfriend and I were friends. The guy—the one I was married to—he was a little older than me. It wasn't going so well and I needed some time to myself. I ended up spending a lot of time at the house that summer. Bob ended up spending a lot of time there, too."

"And you had to keep that quiet? The fact that the two of you were seeing each other?"

"He was dating Hannah at the time," she confirmed.

"You mean the woman from the ..."

"That's right," Frost said, cutting off Mister Johns before he said something both men would regret. As it turns out, Ann Kazinsky's signature wasn't the only unexpected name to appear in Tiny's recording log.

"Hannah and Bob had been an item for a while," she continued, picking up the story. "Bob was the king of the Folk Movement, and she was his queen. They'd been together for about three years. But by '65 it was coming to an end."

"And you didn't want to mess with the perception that their might be trouble in Camelot, so you kept it quiet. Keep the record-buying public happy. What they don't know won't hurt them."

"It was a strategy," she confirmed, a hint of contempt in her response. Apparently, the 'strategy' wasn't one in which she had been completely vested.

"Pretty clever—whose idea was that?"

"Bob's manager at the time—a guy named Judas."

"Yeah, we know the name," Mister Johns said, glancing over at Jack Frost. "Also sounds more than a little manipulative. Frankly, I'm surprised Zeitzman went along with it."

"Everyone went along with Judas back then, especially Bob. He had his hooks in him pretty good."

"That's what we've heard." This time Mister Johns did not glance in Jack Frost's direction. He knew he didn't have to. "But it sounds like he wasn't the only one," Mister Johns raised an eyebrow, hoping to invite further elaboration.

"Yeah, we fell pretty hard for each other," she said, accepting the invitation to delve into the origins of her relationship with Bob Dorian. "He took Hannah with him to England when he went on tour. He never came right out and said it, but I think it was so he could end it."

"You mean break up with her?"

"I mean break her heart. There's a difference. And Bob was *very* aware of the distinction." Judging from the tone of her voice it was clear she had some personal experience with that distinction as well.

"And when he returned from England?"

"We moved to a little walk up on West 4th Street, then ..." she hesitated, taking a deep breath, "... then the Chelsea. Isn't that where you said you found him?"

"That's right—"

"Room 211."

"How did you know?" Mister Johns was genuinely surprised.

"That's the room he and I lived in," she replied. "Those songs he wrote about me—the ones on the '66 album, he wrote those songs at the Chelsea. Whenever he came to town he used to stay up until all hours writing in that room."

"And when was the last time he was in town?"

"I'm sorry?"

"You said he stayed at the Chelsea whenever he came to town."

"It's a saying, Mister Johns. As far as I know, Bob hasn't been back to Elysian Row since he signed our divorce papers."

Mister Johns jotted something in his notebook. "So you didn't go with him on the '65 tour?"

"I never liked the tours. I was never a big fan of the 'let's pack up the family and take this show on the road' mentality. Besides, Judas had hired a documentary crew to get the whole thing on tape. Bob didn't need another person telling him how great he was. He already knew how I felt about him."

"And how did you feel about him?"

"I loved him." There was a short pause, a slight lull in the conversation.

By now Johns had talked to enough people who knew Bob Dorian to know that even the most seemingly forthright answer was filled with ambiguity and uncertainty. And even though Mister Johns was chomping at the bit—'*love* or *loved* him'—he knew that whether or not he clarified that point really didn't matter. *If she just keeps talking, she'll clarify it all by herself.*

"You didn't want to be captured on film for posterity?"

"That is the last thing I wanted, Mister Johns. No, I never wanted a piece of the legend."

"And why's that?"

"Because when the legend fades, or crashes, or burns out, then those people who attached themselves to the legend crash and burn, too. Look around, Mister Johns," she said, motioning to the bay window that looked out like an aquarium over Elysian Row. "This place is littered with the bodies of people whose entire personalities are based on their association with Bob. That wasn't going to happen to me. I didn't need a piece of the legend, Mister Johns. I had something else—I had a piece of Bob. Four beautiful pieces to be exact."

Mister Johns knew she was talking about the children, but he also knew that it was best not to go there. Even a mention of them could spook her. If Ann loved anything more than she had loved Bob Dorian, it was her children. And she didn't want them to have a thing to do with their famous father and the legacy the press had saddled him with. So Johns just nodded amiably, and let her continue.

"Besides, the '65, the '66 tour—those tours nearly killed him. Sure I'd show up from time to time, check in—but I didn't stick around. Couldn't stand to see all those people, those hangers-on. They just drank his blood like wine."

"And did he feel that way? That he was being taken advantage of?"

"He *was* being taken advantage of, Mister Johns," she said, emphasizing the word 'was' so that her point would not be lost. "Bob never

wanted to be viewed as some advertiser trying to con you into thinking you're the one. He hated that. He hated that other people could
define him like that. 'All this talk about equality,' he once told me.
'The only thing any of us have in common is that no one gets out
alive.' Well, the road nearly killed him, that's for sure."

"Are you talking about the fans? Was it his contempt for the fans
that started to get to him?"

"The fans, the label, his manager ... it all started to take a toll. The
road is tough, Mister Johns. Physically and mentally, it's a tough
place. But it's not the excruciating schedule that ends up destroying
you, it's the expectations. As for contempt—I don't think Bob ever
had any contempt for his fans. The only contempt Bob had was for
himself."

"You're going to have to explain that to me," Mister Johns said.
"'Contempt for himself'—I'm not sure I understand."

"Contempt for the fact that he wasn't embracing the songs and
where they could take him. Songs he hadn't written yet, songs that
were trying to find their way out. Those songs, not the fans, were the
things that were tormenting him."

"You know, Bob and I talked about that once," Frost interjected
thoughtfully. Clearly something she had said had stuck a chord in
him. "That the music had started to get away from him. And what
you said about the fans. I never really believed him when he said he
didn't despise them for booing him off the stage night after night on
that '65 tour. But maybe you're right. Maybe it really *was* the songs
that got to him in the end." Frost and the woman he had known all
those years ago as Rhiannon looked at each other like two old lovers.
And while they had never been lovers in a physical sense, at one point
they had both loved the same man. There had been a period in their
lives when they had both pledged their time and undying devotion to
Bob Dorian. And the look that passed between them conveyed that
sentiment in a way no words ever could.

Mister Johns, however, was not moved by the sentimentality of the
moment, "I think it's just wonderful how you can romanticize all this.

I'm all choked up, I mean really I am. But the 'tortured young genius bit' is a little trite, don't you think?" Mister Johns didn't wait for an answer. "Now can we please get back to the reason we're here."

"Frankly, Mister Johns, you've made it very clear why *you* are here, so let me make it clear why I've let you stay."

"All right," Mister Johns said, turning a page in his notebook.

"Earlier, when I told you I have no claim to Bob—well, that wasn't entirely true. You see, for the last 40 years everybody has gone on and on about how I was his muse, his inspiration. But the truth is all I ever wanted to be was a wife to Bob and mother to his children. Everything else is the press trying to turn it into something else."

"Now that's not entirely true, Ann, and you know it." It seems the sentimentality that had brought them together moments ago had lost its grip on Jack Frost. "The last thing I want to do is be an apologist for the press," Frost continued, "but you can't *blame* them for what they did, for the stories they wrote. You may have been an intensely private person …"

"I still am, Jack," she said abruptly.

"And frankly, I'm astonished you agreed to meet with us at all," Frost acknowledged, "but Bob was not a private person. Bob was public. The minute he stepped out on that stage, his life became an open book. That went for you, too."

"They didn't even know me," she snarled.

"Do you think they knew Bob?" Frost asked rhetorically. "Of course they didn't. No one did. Except you. And that's what fascinated them. Who is this woman who's captured the imagination of the most imaginative person on the planet? You had more impact on him than anyone else. You may not recognize it, but you did. I saw it and I wasn't even on the inside yet. And the reason you had that impact was because you had the most presence. You were there."

"And what about Sophia? Hannah? They were there?" she countered. "Sophia was there at the beginning. Hannah, too."

"You may not have been with Bob at the beginning, but you were there during that mayhem that was the late '60s, and you were with him through most of the '70s. You may be uncomfortable with being called a 'muse.' You may think it taints the relationship the two of you had because he was using you. Well, I got news for you, Ann—he used us all."

"Is this supposed to make me feel better?"

"Listen, Ann, I'm not here to reconcile or make excuses for what came between you and Bob. I don't know what came between the two of you. But you need to know that Bob owed you an immense emotional debt for being his anchor for all those years. And the way Bob repaid debts was by writing songs. His debt to you was great—that's what made the songs he wrote about you so great."

"I appreciate that Jack," she said. "I could have used that speech 30 years ago in court when Bob was calling me names, telling everyone he wished he was someone else every time he walked past our house."

"You know as well as I do why I said what I said in court."

"Right," Ann snapped, "you were just doing your job."

"And I'm just trying to do mine," Johns interjected. "So can we please get back on track here?"

"Yes, I think that's a delightful idea," she said, her voice dripping with sarcasm. "Why don't we get 'back on track,' Mister Johns. Now, I've told you just about everything I can about my relationship with Bob. So why don't you tell me what it is that I've left out. What is it you'd like to know, Mister Johns? Because the sooner we get 'back on track,' the sooner you'll be leaving, I assume."

She may have inspired him, she may have been his self-proclaimed muse; but that last comment made it very clear to Mister Johns why Dorian had dispensed with her.

Jesus, this bitch is some ball-buster, Mister Johns thought to himself. *No wonder Zeitzman split.*

But as much as Mister Johns was himself looking forward to splitting, he wasn't going anywhere until he got what he came for. All she had to do was come clean about that night at the studio. Instead, she was being as cagey as the cat that swallowed the canary. She said she had nothing to hide, but Mister Johns and Jack Frost both knew that wasn't true. When it came to Bob Dorian, everyone seemed to be hiding something. Some part of the past, the part they had spent with him, was always obscured and distorted. But if Mister Johns' own past was any indication, he knew the best way to get someone to expose the thing they're hiding is to draw them out into the open. And that's precisely what Mister Johns planned to do. But before he could draw her out, she cut him off right at the knees—

"You know, Mister Johns," she said stridently, "and you can correct me if I'm wrong. But I was under the impression you were here to talk about what happened the other night?"

"That's correct."

"Then why is it you haven't asked me one question about it? Other than determining if I was there or not—which you knew before you even got here—you haven't asked me a single question about that night. All your questions have been about events that took place nearly 30 years ago."

"You'd be surprised how interlinked the past and the present are."

"The only thing that links the past and the present are rumors," she bristled. "Stuff the press pieced together because they never knew the first thing that was going on with Bob. Did you know they still go through Sophia's garbage?" she said contemptuously.

Considering Mister Johns had been accused of doing that very thing less than 24 hours ago, he was quite aware of that fact.

"Why do you think I got rid of everything that connected me to him?" she continued. "Because I was tired of people peering through my windows, taking pictures, making up stories about things that happened—or more to the point *didn't* happen—30 years ago. Rumors, innuendo and outright lies. My whole life with Bob has been meticulously reconstructed by people who weren't even there."

"So there's no truth to any of the things they've written about the two of you?"

"That's why they call them 'rumors,' Mister Johns, if they were true they'd be called 'facts.' I'd imagine a man in your line of work would know the difference by now. And speaking of the 'now,' I'm growing particularly concerned that you are having trouble telling the two apart. So you better ask me everything you want to know right now because after this meeting you and I will not be talking again—certainly not about my former husband." She looked down at her watch, "You have five minutes."

The conversation had taken a nasty turn. Mister Johns was largely to blame for that turn, and he knew it. That little comment about the past and the present being interlinked—he knew the moment that little ditty came out of his mouth it would set her off.

A lot of unsubstantiated facts, a lot of hearsay lurking beneath the surface. A lot of debris down there, Johns silently observed. *You start poking around, you never know what's going to come bubbling up.*

It was, of course, in Mister Johns' nature to poke; and since the conversation had taken this rather acrimonious turn, he decided a good, solid prod might just jar something loose.

"Then let me 'cut to the chase'—to use a phrase from my line of work," Mister Johns said, turning the page of his notebook. "You want to talk about that night at the studio, let's do it. And why don't we start with what time you showed up."

"You know exactly when I showed up," she replied repugnantly. "The ledger's right there at your feet. 7:30—I showed up at 7:30."

"7:30," Mister Johns repeated.

"That's right, 7:30."

"And when you got to the studio, who was there?"

"Bob was playing when I walked in. I entered through the side door; he didn't see me."

"How do you know he didn't see you?"

"The lights were down in the control room and up in the studio. When it's like that the glass partition is like a one-way mirror. You can see into the studio, but the people in the studio can't see into the control room."

"And the band was there?"

"A couple of guys, yeah."

"You recognize them?"

"Dulcimer Don, Middle-Eighth Ed, Lester ..." she said, listing the players who'd shown up for the session.

"So he was in mid-song? In between tracks?"

"He was in the middle of something." It was evident her mind was starting to wander back to that night. "I don't know if it was a song or not. But the minute I walked into the control room whatever it was he was playing he stopped, looked over at the exact place where I was standing and smiled at me."

"I thought you said he couldn't see you?" Mister Johns said, calling attention to the contradiction.

"He couldn't. But it was like he knew the moment I walked in. It was eerie."

"Maybe he just heard someone come in."

"Could be. The door between the control room and studio could have been open. But even if it was, it wouldn't explain how he knew it was me on the other side of that glass."

"Did you say something? Maybe he heard your voice."

"I didn't say a word. And neither did he. He just kept staring at me through the glass, staring *through* me. Then he tapped his foot against the floor and started playing this song."

"What kind of song? An old song, a favorite song of yours?"

"Brand new. Brand new to me, anyway. Apparently brand new to Tiny, too. Said it was the first time he'd ever heard it."

"What kind of song was it?"

"It was a song for me."

"What do you mean, 'a song for you'?"

"Just what I said, Mister Johns." It was evident that she was growing uncomfortable.

A lot of unsubstantiated facts, a lot of hearsay lurking beneath surface, the thought passed through Mister Johns' head a second time. *A lot of debris down there.*

"It was a song about our life together—the summers on the beach when the children were small, the holiday we spent together on the

Algarve Coast when we were first together. Our whole life was in that song."

"And you'd never heard the song before?" Mister Johns inquired.

"No, and judging from the way Lester was staring at Bob's hands, he'd never heard it, either. The chord changes—" she clarified, "when a musician isn't sure where the song is going, the quickest way to figure it out is to look at the hands for the chord progression."

"And where was the song going? You said it was about you?"

"It was as if he was asking me to forgive him. Everything he'd done—all the affairs, the asshole, prima donna behavior, everything he had done to screw up our marriage—it was as if he were asking me to take him back. And when he was done, you could have heard a pin drop—on both sides of the glass. But here's the most amazing part … he did it in one take. All I can say is thank God Tiny had the machine rolling."

"And then what happened?" Mister Johns was genuinely interested.

"Nothing. Nothing happened."

"He didn't get up, walk over, talk to you?"

"Nope. He turned his back to me, and started playing something else—like that moment had never even happened. It was spooky. It was like he'd said, 'All right, I just made the first move—now what are *you* going to do.'"

"So what did you do?"

"I left. Just walked out of the studio. But even if he had said something, I wouldn't have been able to respond. I was completely blown away. It was like I'd been shot."

A moment passed—

"Not really the best choice of words."

"No, probably not," she said, acknowledging the alarmingly ironic phrasing of her reaction to the song Dorian had written for her. "But that's exactly how I felt."

"And this song—" Mister Johns hesitated, "the song he played for you. It was the first time the two of you had seen each other in 30 years?"

This, of course, was the real question toward which Mister Johns had been working.

"He and I talk a few times a year, mostly around the holidays when the kids are shuffling between us," she said. "But reconciliation? Trust me, that went out the window years ago. But that's what the song was about. That's what he was saying. I was floored."

Admittedly, Mister Johns had taken an interest in the song Dorian had performed for her that night in the studio. But whether Ann Kazinsky and Bob Dorian had seen each other in the days leading up to that night was far important than some maudlin curiosity Johns may have taken in an ex-husband's cryptic attempt at reconciliation. As far as Mister Johns was concerned, her answer might just be the key that unlocked the whole investigation.

She, however, had failed to answer Mister Johns' question. Whether her avoidance had been intentional or whether it simply had been an inadvertent omission was uncertain. But rather than press the matter, Mister Johns let it go. He'd get his answer soon enough. Right now he was perfectly content to let her keep digging a hole for herself. That ledger she had so dismissively referred to earlier in the conversation contained a key fact that was going to keep Ann Kazinsky honest.

"And did the song have the same effect on everyone in the studio that night? Was everyone …" Mister Johns paused for a moment as he glanced at his notes for the word she had used, "… 'floored'?" he said, looking up.

"And who exactly would 'everyone' be, Mister Johns?" she said dubiously. "Besides Tiny, Bob, myself and the band, there was no one else there." And there was the answer he'd been looking for …

Ann Kazinsky was lying through her teeth.

"HOW COULD YOU let her get away with that?" Jack Frost sputtered.

"Keep your voice down," Mister Johns chided, banging the heavy, wire mesh fence behind him to mask the fact that he had had to raise his own voice in order to get Jack Frost to lower his. "She's gonna hear you."

"But she's lying!" Frost replied. "She was in that room, same as the rest of them."

"Maybe she was, maybe she wasn't," Mister Johns said coyly. "I suspect the latter is the case."

"Well, there's certainly one way to find out," Frost said as he motioned for Johns to hand him the leather-bound ledger.

"At least wait until we're out of sight," Mister Johns said, looking over his shoulder.

There was a slight wedge of light coming from between where the door and the doorframe should meet. She was watching them ... probably listening, too. The two men exchanged a glance and then, without saying another word, continued down the block.

When they had turned the corner, Mister Johns handed Jack Frost the ledger.

Frost quickly leafed through the first three pages—*Rhiannon, Hannah, Sophia.*

Next to each of the names of the three women was the time they had arrived and the time they had left. All written in tight cursive; all written in their own respective hands.

"Well, I'll be damned," Frost said. "You're right. They came one after the other—7:30, 8:00, 8:30."

"Thirty minute increments," Mister Johns said, flipping through the pages to underscore the point.

"And each of them signed a different page," Frost observed.

"Making it possible that none of them knew the other was there," Johns said, bringing the thought full circle. He closed the ledger and handed it back to Jack Frost.

"But why?" Frost inquired.

"We're talking three exes in the same room—and a very small room at that. In all likelihood it was a tactical decision. Probably the only way to get them all to show up."

It was a perfectly plausible explanation.

But why have them show up at all? Jack Frost thought to himself, *That's the real question here.*

The names of three women had appeared in that ledger. They had already talked with the first two. And if the third woman was anything like Sophia and Ann Kazinsky, the only thing these women despised more than Bob Dorian was each other. Mister Johns was right, Frost realized. The last thing Bob Dorian would have wanted to do was put them all in the same room together. It would have been a bloodbath.

"But," Mister Johns said, voicing the question that would now become a major source of preoccupation for the balance of the investigation, "your question still stands—why put them all in the room in the first place?"

"I could probably come up with a passable answer," Frost replied. "I suspect, however, hearing the woman who showed up after Ann explain it would be much more interesting ..."

CHAPTER 16

▼

HANNAH

She had been blessed with stunning, ravenlike beauty. Her hair, once as jet-black as Arabian oil, now had a few silver, veinlike streaks running through it. But the effects of age did not distract from her resplendence. In fact, they only accented it. And still, after all these years, her face was without imperfection. It was as pristine as a porcelain doll's, and harkened back to a time when she was young, her enthusiasm eternal, and her motives pure. A time when her beauty had made her the envy of every man who had ever laid eyes on her; her voice the envy of anyone who had ever heard her sing. And in the mid-60s, every person on the planet had heard her sing. And though millions had doted on her ceaselessly, there was only one man she had ever loved. And now, for the first time, she was hearing that that man was dead—

"I'm so sorry for your loss."

"I heard you the first time, Jack," she replied, her voice cold and callous.

Perhaps Rhiannon had said it best: if Bob Dorian had been their king, she had been their queen. Two majestic monarchs presiding over a sea of youth awash in hope and optimism. And while she and

Bob had been christened as stalwarts of their generation, it seems the crown they shared had been a thorny one. Judging from the irrepressible contempt in her voice brought on by the news of Dorian's death, evidently she had never gotten used to the prickling sensation that overcame her whenever she heard their names mentioned in the same breath.

She got up from the sofa, walked to the window and lit a cigarette. "What I'd like to know is what you and ..." she motioned her cigarette in the direction of the man in the dour black suit sitting in the corner taking notes.

"Mister Johns," Johns said without looking up.

"... What you and Mister Johns are doing here?"

"Hannah, clearly you're upset. There is no reason for you to get—"

"Defensive?" she said, anticipating Frost's next word.

"Well, 'yes,'" Frost replied. "You and I have known each other a long time, Hannah. I thought it would be nice for me to be the one to tell you."

"You told me," she snapped. "So why are you still here?" Johns looked up from his notebook and in the direction of Frost. It was all he could do not to smile. This woman was good. *Real* good.

"Dammit, Hannah, you know exactly why we're here," Jack Frost replied with equal irritability. "The recording studio, three nights ago, the night Bob was killed. I know you were there."

"So I'm a suspect in a murder?" Neither Frost nor Johns said a word. They both had the distinct feeling Hannah wasn't done talking.

Turns out, they were right.

"That's what I thought," Hannah continued. "So the purpose of this trip *wasn't* just to console a grieving ex on the loss of her former beau. It was to confirm some conspiracy theory that I had something to do with Bobby's death." She took a drag off her cigarette. She was the model of cool, calm and collected. And worries—assuming she had any—she blew those to the sky. "So if I was being a little 'defensive' when you first showed up, Jack, can you blame me? It would appear I have every right to be defensive."

"Hannah, we just want to ask you a few simple questions."

Jack Frost knew the curtness of his earlier comment could have been a fatal misstep. It hadn't, but it could have been. There was a reason Hannah and Bob Dorian had been drawn together all those years ago. They may have been more different than diamonds and rust, but put them together and it made for a hell of a combustible combination. So Jack Frost knew that if he wanted to get anything out of her it was in his best interest not to reignite a spark that judging from her reaction to the news that Bob Dorian was dead had never been completely extinguished.

"Frankly, I've never been accused of murder before," she fired back, "but I have read a few Dashiell Hammett mysteries. Enough to know there's only one question that matters anyway—and that's did I do it. Any other question you came here to ask me is just foreplay to my getting fucked."

"Trust me, ma'am, nobody wants to fuck you," Johns deadpanned.

Frost shot Johns a steely glance.

You are not helping matters, Frost mused to himself. *That 'good cop, bad cop' routine might have worked on Ann. It's not going to work on this one, though.*

"Who the hell *is* this guy, Frost?" Hannah said, confirming Frost's instinct that when the conversation turned, it would turn quickly. "And what the hell are you doing over there anyway?"

Mister Johns held his finger up in the air to signify he needed a few more seconds. Then, he made a quick motion, signed his name to a document he had pulled out of his coat while Frost and Hannah were talking, and lifted his eyes up to her, "Just putting my John Hancock on this search warrant. Frankly, I don't want to waste it on you—just wanted you to know I had it."

Hannah yanked the piece of paper out of Johns' hand. She stared at the piece of paper—long enough to tell it was indeed a court document of some kind, but not long enough to tell exactly what kind it was. The words, 'The Municipality of Elysian Row,' were enough. She took another drag off her cigarette.

Back in the '60s when she was at the height of her powers, raven-like beauty was not the only manner in which she had been described. She had also been heralded as having the voice of a sparrow. It was an understatement. Her voice was far more beautiful than that. But thanks to a steady diet of pills, booze and bad business deals, no one had heard that voice in years. And judging from the fact that she had never tried to stage a 'comeback,' it seems that all those years she had spent slowly sliding into obscurity hadn't weighed too heavily on her. But in that instant something happened. Some part of her that had been suppressed for so long that she had almost forgotten about it, that part completely overcame her. Maybe it was the years of unaddressed anger; maybe it was the rage she had repressed for so long. Or maybe it was just seeing the words, 'Elysian Row,' flashed in her face that forced her to confront all the failure that could have been fame. Whatever it was, it seems Mister Johns' ploy had worked. Hannah brought the cigarette to her mouth, inhaled a second time and then let the smoke curl out from her tightly pursed lips: this bird was about to sing.

"YOU'VE TALKED TO ANN?" she said cautiously.

"That's right," Mister Johns replied.

"When?" Hannah countered, perhaps a bit too quickly.

"I hardly see how that has anything to do with ..." Mister Johns said, continuing to draw her out.

"When did you talk to her, Mister Johns," Hannah persisted.

"Just a few moments ago."

"And what did she say?" It was clear from the urgency that had crept into her voice that if Hannah was going to sing, she wanted to make damn sure she was singing out of the right hymnbook.

"She said Bobby used you to get ahead."

"She said that!?" Hannah sputtered. "She actually said that!?"

"I believe her exact words were—" Johns opened his notebook and began to read, "'The fact he was dating its queen'—oh, she's referring to the Folk Movement here—'the fact he was dating its queen did nothing but *help* his image.'" Mister Johns closed the notebook. "Her words," Mister Johns smiled.

"I'll be the first to admit Bob was attracted to me because I was a star," Hannah conceded. "But by '64 the tables had turned. The tables always turned when you got in bed with Bobby. I'm not saying Bobby was an opportunist, but by the time he left for England in '65, the tide of opportunity had definitely shifted."

"His ship had come in, so to speak."

"And the whole world was watching," Hannah said without missing a beat. "The last thing he wanted was to share the stage with me."

"So he *did* use you?" It was evident that Mister Johns wasn't going to let this point get lost in the mix. "Because if he was using you, and you knew it, that might be a real source of resentment." The insinuation was lost on no one, especially the woman for whom it was intended.

"He got more out of the relationship professionally than I did, 'yes,' that's true," she said dismissively. "So in hindsight, perhaps I did get used a little. But for Ann to leave out the fact that I was very much in love with him—it makes me look like a parasite, like I latched onto him when the tables turned."

"I don't think she ever said *you* were the one who wasn't in love." Mister Johns emphasized the word, 'you'—leaving it out there just long enough for Hannah to grasp the distinction. "Of course, I'd be happy to check my notes."

And while the distinction didn't sit especially well with her, Hannah decided to hold her tongue, "I'd like to tell you to go screw yourself, Mister Johns, but I'd also like to think I'm a better person than that. Ann's a friend of mine—was anyway for a while—so I'm going to write it off as poor transcription on your part. And since you seem adamant about writing down everything I say, why don't you make a note of that as well." Hannah mashed the cigarette in the ashtray and promptly lit another. "So what's with you and that notebook, anyway?"

"It helps me think," Mister Johns replied coolly. "Probably like you and those cigarettes. If my note taking is distracting, however, I'd be happy to put it away."

"I appreciate the offer, Mister Johns. If taking notes helps you to think, you're welcome to take them." She tapped the ash in the ashtray. "But the notes stay here when we're done."

Mister Johns turned the page to a fresh sheet, silently accepting the terms she had set forth. "So you say you didn't kill him?" he said.

"We just went over this, Mister Johns. No, I did not kill him."

"But you were there that night at the studio?" he said undeterred.

"Yes."

"Well, we haven't been over that yet."

"And that's what you want to know about? What happened there that night?"

"In a minute. But first I'd like to know what it was you saw in him that got you to that studio in the first place."

"You're asking me to go back almost 40 years, Mister Johns."

"That's not a problem is it?"

"A problem?"

"You know what they say about the '60s," Mister Johns taunted. "If you can remember them, you weren't there."

"The '60s were a great time. We took the world by storm. And Bob and I were at the eye of that storm." She smiled before continuing, "You know what they say about the eye of the storm, don't you, Mister Johns?" She did not wait for his reply, "It's as clear as glass. Calm, too. So, 'yes,' Mister Johns, I remember. I remember it perfectly." She lit a cigarette. Mister Johns readied his pencil. And when they were both set, she began—

"Bobby and I first met in 1961 at this little folk place down in the Village. Someone told me this new kid had blown into town, had a style, an aura about him, and I ought to check him out. He was still going by Zeitzman then."

"And?"

"And I spent the next eighteen months wondering exactly how dressing up like a rail yard hand was the least bit 'stylish.'"

"So he didn't strike you as special?" Mister Johns said, writing the words, 'rail yard hand,' in his notebook.

"I suppose it would be romantic to say I knew Bobby was the 'one' the moment I laid eyes on him, but it just didn't happen that way." She ran her thin, agile fingers through her long, black hair with a nervous intensity. It was as if she were trying to wipe the image from her mind of the man who had forsaken her all those years ago. "I mean, here's this guy dressed like Jimmie Rodgers, singing songs we've all heard before, and singing them on this huge guitar slung over his shoulder such that you could hardly even see him—so to answer your question, Mister Johns, 'no,' I was not taken by Bobby when I first saw him. Frankly, I just didn't get what all the fuss was about."

"I heard you once referred to him as a 'ragamuffin'?"

Hannah took a drag off her cigarette. She inhaled deeply and kept the smoke in her lungs as if she were holding the smoke against its will. She stared defiantly at Mister Johns, "I thought you and I were done playing games, Mister Johns?"

"I'm sorry?"

"You come into my house, wave some warrant around, coerce me into telling you about Bobby."

"I'm not sure 'coerce' is the right word ..."

"Whatever—the point is that you do all this under the assumption you wanted me to tell you about my relationship with Bobby."

"Right."

"Well, you seem to know plenty already. The fact I used to call him a ragamuffin—" she said, referring to the word that had set her off, "that's a very trivial fact."

"What can I say—the trivial intrigues me."

"It *is* intriguing," she said, carefully studying the lines of his face.

Jack Frost immediately picked up on the elusive nature of Hannah's comment. What he couldn't pick out, however, was exactly what it was she was alluding to. Was she referring to the fact Mister Johns knew such a trivial fact about her life with Bob Dorian, or was she letting Mister Johns know that she thought it highly suspicious he would bring up that fact so early in the conversation. Her statement was both evasive and equivocal—and that's exactly how Jack Frost suspected she had intended it.

"I know only what's been documented," Mister Johns said in his own defense. "And Robert Zeitzman's life has been remarkably well documented. Those four padlocks on your front door are a testament to that. But if you think I'm here to trip you up on facts, you are sorely mistaken. As I told you from the outset, I am more concerned in the less tangible things. I am more interested in your relationship."

"The songs—"

"I'm sorry."

"You asked me what attracted me to Bobby. It was the songs. Now you have to remember, I wasn't but six months older than Bobby. But I thought I was pretty hot shit. I was touring, making records, I was known outside the Village. That's the important part," she said, holding her lit cigarette in midair for emphasis. "I was known *outside* our little community. There's no question I had what Bobby wanted," she said matter-of-factly. "I was established, I could open doors for him, introduce him to people, pave the way for him. But when I heard the songs on Bobby's second record, I thought I'd met my match."

"Had you?"

"It wasn't even close. Bobby was so far ahead of where I was, ahead of the poets he admired, ahead of everyone on the scene."

It was a pretty significant admission, and both men knew it. History may have tagged Bob Dorian as the guy who rallied the faithful with his anthems of angst, anger and injustice, but Hannah was the original sloganeer for the Left. When it came to writing songs that helped to advance the cause of the dejected and downtrodden nobody could touch her. Nobody, that is until Bobby Zeitzman came to Elysian Row. "He was a rocket ready to take off."

"And you launched him—"

"At first it was like a whim, you know. Like an experiment. I used to refer to Bobby as 'my little experiment.' God, he hated that. But that's what he was at first. But somewhere along the way I began to see him as more than that—I began to fall in love with him."

"And this was?"

"1963 … Summer … Fairport. We'd been an item for a while by then, but we stopped hiding behind the façade of professional friendship at Fairport." Hannah paused to light another cigarette. When she looked back across the table at Mister Johns, she could see he was doing the math in his head. And she knew no matter how many times he tried to rearrange it, the dates she'd given him would never add up. "Yeah, he was still with her at the time," she said, connecting the dots. "Sophia—he was still with her then."

"So how'd that work out?"

"You mean announcing to the world that the woman on the cover of his latest album with whom he's blissfully walking arm in arm has just been replaced by the woman who's going to launch his career? Not very well," Hannah deadpanned. "And it certainly didn't help matters when I announced from the stage that the only thing Bobby was protesting was a love affair that had lasted too long."

"It was a rather unsavory moment," Frost chimed in.

"You were there, Frost?"

"Oh yeah. Sophia left in tears. It was terrible."

"I always felt bad about that—" Hannah continued, turning in Frost's direction, "about it being done so publicly like that."

"So who came up with the line, 'The only thing being protested in the song is a love affair that's lasted too long'? Hardly a throwaway line—"

"Come to think if it, Bobby gave me that line. You know I hadn't thought about that until now, but he sure did. He didn't expressly tell me to use it, but he did kind of plant it there in my head. That's so 'Bobby'—" she chuckled. "Always getting people to do his dirty work for him."

"His dirty work?"

"Breaking up with Sophia for him. Problem was that as dirty a trick as it was—getting her to come to the festival and all—in the end, the break wasn't that clean."

"I thought you said he was over her, that he'd 'moved on.'"

"I don't think I ever said that, Mister Johns. You're welcome to check your notes," she said sarcastically, "but I'm pretty sure I wouldn't have said that. And besides—you only got half the equation right."

"And which half is that?"

"There's no question Bobby was ready to move on from Sophia in '63, but he was far from being over her."

"How so?"

"By the time I entered the picture, Bobby and Sophia had been together for almost two years. Now, that may not sound like a long time to you, but for a guy moving as quickly as Bobby two years was an eternity. A lot had happened in those two years. And Sophia had been with Bobby though it all—through thick and thin as the expression goes. Not like what he went through with Ann and the media glare and all that, but they'd been through a lot."

"That's what she said."

"You've talked to Sophia, too," she replied, slowly taking the bait.

"That's right," Mister Johns said. It was now Mister Johns' turn to study the lines of Hannah's face. "We spoke to her yesterday—shortly after learning of Zeitzman's death."

"Is she a suspect, too?"

"There were no suspects per se when we spoke with her."

"But she is now?"

"I think you can assume everyone's a suspect now. You are aware there's been a second murder?" It was evident from her reaction, she was not. "That's right. Minnesota Slim turned up dead last night."

"What? Who would want to kill *him*?" she said incredulously.

"Probably the same person who killed Zeitzman," Mister Johns suggested. "But it's just a theory we're working on."

"I know it may be in my best interest not to defend someone you consider a suspect in this case, but I can tell you with unflinching certainty Sophia did not kill Bobby."

"You're not just certain," Johns said snidely, "but 'unflinchingly' certain? Well then, I suppose we ought to believe you." Mister Johns waited a moment to let the sarcasm set in before continuing—"With all due respect," Mister Johns' smugness was still in full force, "what makes you so sure Sophia didn't kill Zeitzman?"

"She couldn't even kill herself." That wiped the smile clean off Mister Johns' face. And judging from the expression on Jack Frost's mug, the assertion had taken him by surprise, too.

"She tried to off herself?" Johns confirmed.

"That's right."

"Did you know about this?" Mister Johns said, turning to Frost.

"I knew she was upset after Fairport, but 'no' I had no idea how upset."

"Well, I guess that explains why she shied away from talking about the breakup," Mister Johns rationalized. "Sounds like not a whole lot of people knew and she didn't want to start telling them 40 years after the fact."

"There's a little more to it than that, Mister Johns," Hannah said.

Admittedly, Jack Frost did not have as much experience dealing with duplicity as Mister Johns. The years Johns had spent with the relatives of the deceased down on Rue Morgue had given him a little advantage in that department. Jack Frost did know when someone was hedging, however. And it was Jack Frost's experience that whenever someone said, 'there's a little more to it than that,' what they really meant was, 'there's a lot more.' But it wasn't *what* they told you next that was interesting. It was *how* they told it. And so Jack Frost knew if Mister Johns was going to get to the bottom of this new twist, he was going to have to let Hannah start at the top. And that meant letting her finish telling the story.

Considering Mister Johns was sitting there tight-lipped and pen poised, it was evident the two of them were on the same page—

"Like I said earlier, Bobby wasn't over Sophia," Hannah continued. "And even after the embarrassment at Fairport, she wasn't quite over him either. After the suicide attempt—she was living in a flat over on the Lower East Side at this point."

"With the sister?" Mister Johns said impatiently.

Hannah eyed Mister Johns suspiciously, "I thought we'd already been through this once, Mister Johns. You already know the story, you tell me. Save us both a lot of time."

"Sophia told us about the sister when we spoke to her yesterday," Mister Johns said in the interest of full disclosure. "Didn't tell us she moved in with her though. When was this?"

"Summer of '63. Anyway, Bobby goes over there and he gets into it with her—the sister, I'm talking about. I mean he really lets her have it. Calls her petty, a parasite, names I won't even repeat—I mean he really lays into her."

"Doesn't sound like much of a reconciliation?"

"Oh, he wasn't there to reconcile."

"I thought you said they weren't over each other."

"It's because of their attempt at reconciliation that he was there ..." Hannah hadn't come out and said it, but the inflection in her voice at the end of that last sentence had said it for her—there was a little more to it than that. "He was there to talk her into having an abortion."

And there it was.

"Frost—" Mister Johns said without looking.

"Didn't know," Frost replied, his eyes transfixed on Hannah.

"Don't feel bad, Jack. No one knew. Besides Sophia, Bobby, and the sister, that's one of the best-kept secrets of Bobby's long and very winding past."

"So how did you know?"

"She told me."

"She *told* you?" Mister Johns said, not the least bit convinced.

Hannah picked up on Mister Johns' skepticism immediately, "You say that like you don't believe me."

"I just find it hard to believe she would open up and tell you something she'd clearly gone to great lengths to keep from everyone else. I just can't imagine you and Sophia were on the best of terms."

"You obviously don't understand women, Mister Johns."

Hannah reached down, lifted the pack of cigarettes from the table, and shook one out. She took her time as she dragged the match along the side of the matchbox, then carefully brought the flame to the end of her cigarette and inhaled. She knew that last statement had Mister Johns thinking. And that's just what she wanted him to do—think.

"Over the years, Bobby has had a lot of women," Hannah continued. "I'm sure Jack can testify to that—" Frost lifted his chin and smirked as if to say, 'screw you.' "However, there were only three women in Bobby's life. I mean three women who really meant anything to him."

"I'm assuming you're one of them?" Mister Johns said, stating the obvious.

"And it sounds like you've already talked to the other two. Bobby screwed over a lot of people in his life, but there were only three people he ever loved. So I guess you could say the three of us were all in the same boat, Ann, Sophia and me—we were all caught in Bobby's web, only to be cast off once he was done with us."

"That still doesn't …"

"Explain why Sophia told me about the abortion? I'm getting to that. I'm sure you know about the '65 tour?"

"The English tour. The one he asked you to accompany him on?"

"You mean 'tag along on'—because tagging along was all I did on that tour. In hindsight, Bobby had no intention of letting me play. I'd helped him get his foot in the door in '63, only to get the boot two years later."

"Ann told us about that tour—her impression of it, anyway. That Zeitzman had an agenda."

"Oh, he had an agenda all right—get famous and get rid of Hannah. Both of which he did in spectacular fashion. Bobby took off for the stars and I was sent packing back to New York with my tail between my legs. I spent close to a month locked up in my apartment, didn't see anyone, and no one came to see me. Except for one person."

"Let me guess …"

"That's the night she told me about the abortion. I'm not saying that Sophia and I became best of friends—far from it. But there was a bond between us, a tie that bound us together." She mashed the end of her cigarette into the ashtray to emphasize her point. "It was only natural then that I extend that same civility to Ann when Bobby decided to subject her to the same fate."

"So you and Ann *are* friends?"

"Well, I wouldn't say we are friends. Or *were* friends for that matter. We didn't even meet each other until the '75 tour."

"The one to raise funds to spring that boxer?"

"Oh yeah," she said ceremoniously, "Bobby's last feigned attempt to be what he said he never was in the first place—political. Anyway, I know what you're thinking—after everything he had put me through why would I ever agree to go back on tour with him."

"It was a question I had—" Mister Johns deadpanned.

"Judas' idea—'reunited for the first time in 10 years' was the way I think he sold it to the promoters. Pretty successful tour, too, if I recall. Wish I could say the same for Bobby and Ann, however. If they had had a slogan on that tour it would have been—'falling to pieces after 10 years.' They were a mess. Technically, they called it a 'trial separation,' but they weren't kidding anyone, least of all themselves. Divorce was a foregone conclusion. I mean, he'd already put his cards on the table six months earlier when he released the album that basically chronicled every last pent up piece of hatred he felt toward her."

"So what was she doing on the road with him then?"

"If it had been just the two of them, I don't think she would have been there. But they had four kids to think about, and if it was truly over she wanted to know she'd done everything she could to make it work. So anyway—she showed up late in the tour, just blew in completely unannounced."

"And that didn't make him uneasy? To have the two of you in such close proximity? I mean, what did the two of you talk about?"

"Oh, we didn't have to worry about that. Bobby told us exactly what to say. We had lines of dialogue, for Christ's sake."

"You what?"

"Yeah, Bobby and a couple of his buddies thought it would be a hoot to make a film of the tour and have all of us play parts in the movie. I hardly think Ann's arrival on the scene put a damper on Bobby's mood in the least. In fact, I think he loved that we were there."

"And why's that?"

"Bobby cast Ann and me as whores—"

Over the last 48 hours, Jack Frost and Mister Johns had talked to a lot of people. They'd heard a lot of stories. Stories about Bob's insecurities; stories about Bob's deceitful nature; stories about Bob's ability to manipulate, maneuver and mold the people around him into whatever he wanted them to become. But turning his ex-wife and former lover into whores? Telling them what to say and how to act? That took some real skill. That was a story neither of the men had expected to hear.

"And that didn't bother you?" Mister Johns inquired.

"At the time it did, sure. But in the end, the joke was on Bobby. The film was a piece of shit—a real mess. About as messed up as Bobby was at the time. You see, Ann had been with Bobby throughout the amphetamine years."

"The 'amphetamine years'?"

"You don't write three albums—four if you count the '66 album which was a double disc—in less than a year and a half without a little help from your 'friends.' And I'm not talking about the boys in the band."

"I got it," Johns replied, glancing at Jack Frost out of the corner of his eye.

"Ann was with Bobby during all that. You know it's not like today when you can just check yourself into Betty Ford. None of us had that luxury back then. Back then Ann was his rehab. A thankless job I'd wish on no one. Trust me, Bobby was a big enough bastard when he was sober."

"So she wasn't just out on the tour to try and save the marriage," Johns said, filling in the blank.

"No, she could turn on the news and see her worst nightmare was becoming a reality. He was using again. Sure she wanted to save the marriage. But the minute she realized that wasn't going to happen, she stuck around to make sure he didn't go off any deeper than he already had. She probably saved his life. Anyway—" Hannah said, lighting her final cigarette, "despite her strength—and Ann was one of the strongest people I've ever known—she was in a bad way on that tour. As if the fact that he was slowly killing himself wasn't bad enough, Bobby was screwing everything that moved and she knew it. And I could see how hurt Ann was and I knew how she felt. After all, I'd been 'the other woman' myself only a few years earlier."

And as Hannah inhaled on the cigarette, pausing to let the nicotine settle into her system, Jack Frost took a moment to consider what Hannah had told them so far. There was no question she had offered an unwavering glimpse into the private world of a reclusive rock star run amuck. But despite the all-access, no-holds-barred backstage pass her account purported to be, at the end of the day it was just another hackneyed tale of drama and debauchery on the road. The story could have been *anyone's* story. And therein lay the problem. Jack Frost and Mister Johns weren't after anyone's story. They were after Bob Dorian's story. Because anyone can report on what's going on when a thousand flashbulbs are exploding all at once. Anyone can report on the glare. The real story is what's going on behind the shades. The real story is in the shadows, and the things that happen when no one thinks anyone is watching. And it was beginning to dawn on Jack Frost that what he and Mister Johns were after was futile. They had been charged with finding the person who had murdered Bob Dorian; to have gleamed a glimpse into what made the *real* Bob Dorian tick would only have been icing on the cake. Because the truth was that no one really knew what was going on behind those thick, impenetrable shades with the exception perhaps of the man who wore them. And Bob Dorian wasn't going to be offering up any insight any time soon.

Yes, Hannah had told a good story so far. A lot of good stories, in fact. The story of how she had come to meet Bob; the story of how she had fallen in love with him; the story of how he had stabbed her in the back, stole her thorny crown and then humiliated her in front of her fans and friends. But if she stopped talking now, all those stories didn't amount to much more than second-hand hearsay. All they'd have is what Ann had referred to as rumors, innuendo and, potentially, outright lies. Time was running out: Jack Frost didn't need any more anecdotes about the elusive Bob Dorian. Jack Frost needed the *real* story, the story that would provide him with the prism through which all these stories they had been told over the last 48 hours could be evaluated. Jack Frost needed the story that would explain why the three women closest to Bob Dorian had agreed to come to the studio that night. It turns out, Hannah was about to tell that story. Apparently, she'd just wanted to take a puff on that cigarette first—

"So one night after the show, Ann shows up at my dressing room. She wasn't balling or anything. Perfectly lucid, just wanted to talk. So we talked for hours about those days when the 'Roving Renegade'— that was our nickname for Bobby—when the 'Roving Renegade' was two-timing us. And I told Ann I'd never found Bobby to be much at giving gifts, but one time when I was up at the house in Upstate I'd come across this really nice lavender negligee. Bobby saw me in it, knew that I liked it, and told me to keep it. And Ann says, 'So *that's* where that thing went!' We must have laughed for 15 minutes straight. And when we stopped laughing, I told her at least the two of us fared better than Sophia. Ann was probably going to get the house after the divorce; I'll always be remembered as the woman who launched Bobby's career; but all Sophia ever got was some dinky ring that looked like it had been plucked out of a Cracker Jack box."

"A ring?" Mister Johns said, doing everything in his power not to look in the direction of Jack Frost.

"Yeah, real piece of crap. Bobby gave it to her a few months after they had that knock-down, drag-out fight."

And though Johns had given nothing away, obviously he was covering.

Hannah's confirmation that Bob Dorian had given Sophia that ring—something Mister Johns had suspected from the outset—had come from the most unsuspected source. But now that they knew *why* Bob Dorian had given the ring to her, it answered nearly every question surrounding the importance of that 'crackerjack' surprise. In order to prevent some other unexpected surprise from emerging, however, Mister Johns was going to have to treat Hannah's inadvertent admission like some irritating, irrelevant distraction.

"A heartwarming story—" Mister Johns said dismissively, "you and Ann—two spurned lovers—brought together after being jilted by the man they loved. But what does this have to do with Zeitzman's death?"

"You're good with questions, Mister Johns. I'll give you that. But when it comes to actually listening, you might want to take a refresher course."

"Is that so?"

"'What does this have to do with Zeitzman's death?'" she said mockingly. "Think about what I already told you. There were only three women in Bobby's life. I mean three women who really meant anything to him. I would contend that he loved us all equally. I know he loved me."

"After he ruthlessly and systematically deflated your ego, tried to break you down by dragging you across Europe, not even letting you step on stage one time—that was love?"

"That was spite, Mister Johns. But before the spite there was love."

"And you think he loved Sophia?"

"I know he did."

"He made her abort their child!"

"He didn't make her do anything. They made that choice together."

"And Ann?"

"You're really not getting this are you, Mister Johns? He loved us all. And those terrible things he did to us, the way he treated us, his duplicity, his two-faced callousness—he couldn't help it. It was just his nature. That's just who he was."

And who was Bob Dorian? It was a good question. Truth be told, it was *the* question Jack Frost and Mister Johns had been trying to answer from the outset. The problem was that the answer to that question had gone the way of Dorian himself, snuffed out for all eternity when someone put a bullet in his chest.

Or had it?

Both men had bought into the assumption that the only person who knew Bob Dorian was Bob Dorian himself. Maybe that was a faulty assumption. Maybe that was the thing that had kept them running in circles, chasing their tails for a whiff of the truth when the truth was that maybe Bob Dorian *wasn't* the only guy who knew what made himself tick. Hannah was right: Mister Johns hadn't been listening. Dorian wasn't the only person who could offer a window into the dark, disturbing world of Bob Dorian. There were three people who could offer that glimpse. And, it seems, one of them was about to give it a go—

"It was like there were two Bobs," Hannah said, choosing her words carefully, "like two sides to the same coin. The first side was kind and sweet and sensitive. The other side cold, distant and disdainful. The second side would just as soon slit your throat then let you get too close. But that first side—and it wasn't a side he showed to many people—but those who saw it couldn't help but fall for him. Yes, Bobby loved us. I have no question in my mind. The only question—and this is a question I think Bob probably never knew the answer to—in fact, he probably went to his grave not knowing for sure was if any of us ever really loved him. Strike that—he probably went to his grave wondering if *anyone* ever really loved him." And for the first time since she had started to talk, her bravado gave way to an even stronger emotion: regret. And she began to mist up, and a tear formed in her eye—"Bobby was like a lost boy, like a little lost boy. He always bragged of his misery, referred to his being 'misunderstood' like some badge of honor. But the truth is, I don't think he ever truly understood himself. And the thing that was so sad about it was that maybe his dying before his time was, in some strange way, meant to be."

"Like destiny?" Mister Johns said. Hannah considered the thought.

"I don't think so," she said, "Bobby was never into astrology and reading palms and all that kind of stuff. A lot of people in his position—not sure who to trust, no place to turn—they turn to that. Bobby never did. But I do know that as talented as he was, he knew talent can only take you so far. At some point, something else takes over. Now what that 'something' was he never said. Not to me anyway. Destiny—" she said, the thought still rolling like thunder in her head. "You know, everyone always thinks I was the one who plucked Bobby out of obscurity and made him a star."

"But you *did* make him a star," Johns said.

"Don't kid yourself, Mister Johns. Bobby was a star long before I came across him. All I did was place him in my orbit so that he could shine. But if you ask me, *we* were the ones who were destined. Every person who came into contact with Bobby, it was our lives that changed, not his. He changed *us*." The mist began to form in her eyes a second time as the revelation fully sank in. "I haven't seen or heard from him in 40 years, and my life still revolves around him."

Mister Johns reached into his pocket and took out a clean, freshly pressed handkerchief. He placed the handkerchief in Hannah's palm. She gently wiped away the tears, leaving a little hint of mascara. Mister Johns folded the handkerchief to its original configuration and slid it back into his pocket.

Just because Hannah hadn't been on stage in close to 20 years didn't mean she'd forgotten how to work a room. And while she may have been playing to Mister Johns' sense of chivalry, Hannah's insight into Bob Dorian had struck a resounding chord in Jack Frost.

Hannah understood Bob in a way that Frost only wished he had. She hadn't 'figured him out,' but she did understand him. That thing she had said about how Bob was able to flip destiny on its ear—'Every person who came into contact with Bobby, it was our lives that changed, not his'—there was an understanding in those words that had eluded Jack Frost the whole time he had known Bob. Jack Frost had been smart not to ask the questions with this one, and he knew it. He would only have gotten in the way.

Mister Johns, on the other hand, didn't suffer from the problem of letting his emotions get in the way. Mister Johns didn't know Bob Dorian. That meant he could keep emotion out of it, which gave Mister Johns a distinct advantage over Jack Frost when it came to questioning Hannah. By keeping the prescient, impressionable past at bay, Mister Johns could keep the conversation on track.

"Let's talk about the night of the recording session," Mister Johns said with level detachment. "You came alone?"

"Yes. Bobby had requested that."

"You spoke to him directly?"

"With the exception of Jack, I don't think anyone's spoken directly to Bobby in the last 20 years. But to answer your question, 'no,' someone called me."

"Who was it?"

"No idea. Whoever it was didn't leave a name."

"So how'd you know the call wasn't a hoax?"

"I didn't."

"And you went anyway?"

"The address I was given was Tiny Bobbitt's studio. Bobby always liked Tiny, so I thought, 'What would be the harm in checking it out?'"

Yet another good reason to let Mister Johns ask the questions, Frost thought to himself. Because the way it was beginning to sound, Tiny hadn't just presided over the recording session, he had probably been the person who called the killer and told them to show up. Of course, it really didn't matter whether Tiny had unwittingly notified the killer or not. Bob was dead. And Tiny was right there at the scene of the crime. It was Nashville all over again.

Yes, it's definitely best I'm sitting this one out, Frost thought to himself. *I'm too close; I'd get too wrapped up in it to be objective. My emotions would take over, and I'd be no good to anyone.*

Mister Johns seemed to sense the apprehension on the part of Jack Frost, and rather than let him intervene, Mister Johns continued to keep things on course—

"And when you got to the studio who was there?"

"The musicians, Tiny—and Bobby, of course."

"So that was it?"

"That was it, Mister Johns."

"Then what happened?"

"Tiny pressed the speaker button on the console, told Bob I'd arrived."

"And then?"

"You know, Mister Johns, I'm planning on telling you everything that happened. But I could do it a lot faster if you'd stop interrupting me." Mister Johns obediently complied with the request, gesturing for her to continue—"So Bobby knows I'm there. But he doesn't turn around. Instead, he just starts playing. He plays for a few bars, like he's teaching the other guys the song. In hindsight, of course, he *was* teaching them the song. It was clear they'd never heard it before. In fact, I got the distinct feeling *he* hadn't heard it before. It was almost as if the song was coming not *to* him but *through* him. So he plays a few bars. It sounds like G, C, D, G. I think those were the chords, but it was hard for me to tell because he still had his back to me. But the song was definitely in 'A' major—that I know. Anyway the reason I even mention the chords and key is that this was one of the most haunting melodies I'd ever heard. The way the words intertwined—it was frightening."

"So there were words, too? Not just music?"

"Oh, 'yes,' there were words," Hannah said in a foreboding tone that suggested there was more to the story. "So I'm listening to this song, listening to these words, the evocative chord changes, and then it dawns on me: 'This fucking song is about me. It's about us.'"

"He's written songs about you before," Mister Johns said dismissively.

Hannah wasn't going to let the haunting memory of the song be dismissed that easily—

"Do either of you know what the word, 'Gehenna' means?" The manner in which she asked the question elevated it to more of a challenge than an inquiry. "It's a Hebrew word. You see in the Bible there are three words for hell: Hades, Sheol, and Gehenna," she said, quickly ticking them off. "And each of those three words represents the three places through which departed souls pass. The difference between Hades and Sheol, however, is that while these are transitory—meaning you pass through them—you do not pass through Gehenna. Gehenna is eternal. If you end up in Gehenna, you stay in Gehenna." She hesitated for a moment, then continued, "'If the worm never does turn, there is always a body to burn, if the fire is never quenched, then there is always a body to be lynched.'"

"Is that how this place, this Gehenna, is described in the Bible?"

"No, Mister Johns, those were the lyrics to the song."

An eerie silence fell across the room.

"And you thought the song, this ..."

"'Images of Gehenna'—that was the name of the song."

"And you thought it was about you?"

"Of course it was about me," she said undeterred. "It was about how he cast me off into hell and left me there to suffer for all eternity."

"Well, if that's the way you took it I can see how it might frighten you."

"Oh, it didn't frighten me, Mister Johns."

"It didn't?"

"Quite the opposite. It was the most exhilarating thing I'd ever heard."

"And that night at the studio—that's the last time you saw him?"

"Yeah, I left right after that."

"You just left?"

"Yeah. I was so pissed that after 40 years Bobby could still get to me like that. And I didn't want to give him the satisfaction of knowing how much control he still has over me. So I left. But I'll tell you this ... that song, the images of hell and my place in it—it's literally kept me up for the past three nights. He packed so much in there. But ain't that just like Bobby," she considered. "Write a song that I can't get out of my head, then go off and get killed—leave me stranded so I can't ever ask him what the hell it meant?"

"Well, if it's any consolation, I suspect he left quite a few people feeling that way."

Considering Hannah had no idea Bob Dorian had performed for the other women in the studio that night just as he had performed for her, Mister Johns felt confident that his cleverly crafted double entendre would go unnoticed. And while the irony of his response had been undetected, the sarcastic tone had not—

"That may help to assuage three sleepless nights, but it's hardly consolation for a lifetime of trying to get out from behind Bob's shadow, Mister Johns," she said, picking up the pack of cigarettes and shaking them. The pack was empty. "Listen, I hate to be rude," Hannah said, succinctly bringing the conversation to a close. "But it's only a matter of time before this story breaks. Word going around town is that you're planning a concert, Jack," she continued, turning in the direction of Jack Frost. "And when it does they're going to descend on this place—and by 'this place' I mean my house—like locusts. So if you'll excuse me, I'm going to need to buy another padlock for the door."

"Well, I appreciate your time. We both do." Mister Johns started to rise from his chair. "Oh, one last thing—" Mister Johns said, almost as an afterthought.

"Yes."

"You left at what time? The studio—"

"8:00—or maybe it was 7:45. No," she said with certainty. "It was definitely 8:00."

"You were wearing a watch?"

"I remember the clock on the wall."

Mister Johns jotted something in his notebook, then lifted his eyes back up to her, "Again, thanks for your time."

Johns rose from the chair and started for the door.

"Mister Johns—"

"Yes—"

"You weren't going to welsh on our agreement, were you?" Mister Johns looked at Hannah quizzically. "The notebook—" she said, pointing to the left breast pocket of Mister Johns' suit coat.

"Of course," Mister Johns replied. "A deal's a deal." He reached into his coat pocket and retrieved the notebook. He ripped out a single page. He folded the page and handed it to Hannah. She led the men back down the hallway and into the foyer. She unfastened the series of padlocks, opened the front door and watched Jack Frost and Mister Johns descend the landing stairs and make their start for the street.

She closed the door, turned and dropped the page from Mister Johns' notebook into the trash. She had never intended to read, much less keep the pages. She had asked for them partly to keep Mister Johns honest. Mostly, she'd asked for those notes to simply screw with him. But somewhere between her releasing the piece of paper and its landing in the trashcan, the page had opened up. She looked down in the wastebasket and read the words written across the unfolded sheet of paper. It didn't take her long. There were only two—

'You're lying.'

"A *SEARCH* WARRANT?" Frost said, pulling the gate behind him. "You don't have the power to write a search warrant?"

"Hopefully she doesn't know that." It was the closest Mister Johns had come to laughing the entire investigation.

"So what was it that you were waving in her face?"

"A death certificate from the morgue."

"Jesus, Johns."

"It got her to talk, didn't it?"

"Sure, she talked but everything she just told us was taken under false pretenses. None of it can be admissible in court."

"Hopefully she doesn't know that either." It was Jack Frost's turn to laugh. But as soon as the brief moment of levity passed, it was back to business. "Well, it looks like you were right about the ring," Frost conceded.

"It would appear so," Mister Johns replied. "Contrary to what Hannah said, that ring might have been the most meaningful gift Zeitzman ever gave anyone. It certainly seems to have meant a lot to Sophia—for her to have kept it all these years."

"But the question remains—why did she take it off when she spoke to us? She keeps the ring all this time and then takes it off when we show up? And what about her husband? You said the ring has an inscription in it, not to mention Bob's initials. How does she explain that?"

"Maybe she doesn't," Mister Johns replied dismissively.

"No wonder you aren't married any more, Johns. Trust me, that's the kind of thing you would have to explain."

"What I mean is maybe she kept the ring all these years and didn't wear it."

"But you said—"

"I know what I said—she was wearing it when we got there—and she was. But maybe she put the ring on the night she went to the studio, forgets to take it off when she gets home—" Mister Johns paused for a moment to let the logic sink in. "She herself said the husband was out of town for a few days …"

"... Which would explain why she doesn't have to explain anything to him—he never sees her wearing the ring," Frost continued, picking up on the argument.

"Also explains why she didn't want us to see her wearing it," Mister Johns continued. "A ring given to you by the man who's just turned up dead—and who also happens to be your 'ex'—it isn't exactly the thing you want on your finger when you're trying to keep your name out of a murder investigation," Johns said, bringing the logic full circle.

"Okay, that makes sense. But what doesn't make sense is the way she reacted when we told her he's been murdered. I mean, she didn't even flinch."

"Well, I wouldn't go that far, Frost. She reacted."

"Give me a break, Johns. *I* got a bigger reaction when I walked through that door than when we told her Bob was dead."

"People react differently to different scenarios," Johns said, playing out the argument.

"But that's the thing, Johns. Everyone we've told that Bob was dead, their reaction has been the same. Don't you think that's odd? It's like you said earlier ..."

"Like they already knew he was dead?"

"Especially Hannah—" Frost confirmed. "She was accommodating enough, but sometimes I swear it's like that woman has ice water running through her veins."

"Don't worry, Frost, it's just as well she didn't try to explain it all away. I wouldn't have believed her anyway," Mister Johns said, alluding to the words he'd scrawled across the notebook page he'd left behind.

"She seemed pretty credible to me," Frost countered. "In fact, she's probably got Bob pegged the best of anyone we've talked to."

"Except for the fact that she was lying."

"Lying?"

"That's right. When I asked her what time she left the studio she said 8:00."

"According to the log that's exactly when she left—8:00 on the dot."

"Right, except for the fact that she said she knew it was 8:00 because she looked at the clock on the wall."

"Sounds plausible to me."

"Sure it does—except for the fact there's no clock in that studio." Mister Johns paused to let Frost mentally canvass Tiny Bobbitt's domain.

Damn, Frost thought to himself, *I'll be damned if Johns isn't right.*

"So what's your thinking?" Frost said, confirming Johns' observation about the clock.

"My thinking is that if she was lying about the clock, then contrary to your earlier assertion, she, not I, was the one exchanging information under false pretenses."

"So 'everyone lies.' Is that your theory, Johns? That everyone we've talked to has lied to us?"

"Haven't they?"

"We're accusing them of murder!" Frost exclaimed. "Wouldn't you hedge a little, try and shift the facts in your favor a bit if you were accused of killing a man?"

"I don't know, Frost. I've never been accused of murder," Mister Johns deadpanned.

"There's no need to be literal, Johns, I'm trying to make a point."

"Which is—?"

"That our job is not to determine *who* is lying," Frost said discerningly. "Our job is to determine which of the lies we are being told can lead us to the truth."

"Sounds to me like *you're* the one with the theory, Frost," Mister Johns said succinctly.

"Are you kidding me? I'm more uncertain now than when we started."

"Well, I have one—a theory that is—one that might explain why everyone has reacted the way they have."

"Okay."

"You're not going to like it," Mister Johns said.

"And why's that?"

"Because it complicates things a bit. Actually, it complicates things *quite* a bit."

"Let's hear it," Frost prompted.

"People—"

"People?" Jack Frost repeated the word slowly, wringing it out like a damp towel.

"Has it ever occurred to you that we may be looking for more than one person?"

That thought had, of course, occurred to Jack Frost. And the reason it had occurred to him is that in many ways he was one of the people they were looking for. Jack Frost hadn't, of course, literally murdered Bob Dorian. But his desire to get Dorian to return to Elysian Row had set in motion the events that had led to Bob's death. But that wasn't anything new. Mister Johns had already pointed out that little bit of Shakespearean irony in his own amenable way. And Jack Frost knew that's not what Mister Johns was talking about anyway. Mister Johns was talking about finding the man who *had* murdered Bob Dorian. Or—and this was the part of the theory that *was* new—the murderers.

"It only takes one person to pull a trigger," Frost said, hoping this wasn't going to turn into another one of Johns' cockamamie conspiracy theories.

"True enough. But I think you will agree that there are a lot of people who would have been more than happy to help that one person pull that trigger. Now you say you didn't tip anyone off that Zeitzman was returning to Elysian Row."

"That's right—"

"Well, someone did. And I think that person knew far enough in advance that they were able to find someone who hated Zeitzman enough to pull the trigger. We find those people, we've found our killers."

And all of a sudden it all made sense. Suddenly, Jack Frost knew who had ordered the hit on Bob Dorian. Because when Mister Johns had asked Jack Frost if he had told anyone that Bob Dorian was returning to Elysian Row, Jack Frost hadn't been entirely forthcoming. The truth was he *had* told someone—two people, in fact—and he knew exactly where to find them. It was, however, going to require another trip out to Interstate 29 …

CHAPTER 17

▼

TOMMIE THE MAKE &
JULIUS THE SQUEEZE

(Interstate 29 Revisited)

"The promoters?" Mister Johns said, his feet pounding on the pavement, trying to keep up with Frost's hasty gait.

"Yes, the promoters. That pitiless pair of piranhas!" Frost shook his head in disgust. "It all makes sense—"

"Well, considering the fact I'm not clairvoyant it doesn't make a lick of sense to me," Mister Johns replied.

"You were right. What you said about not looking for a single person. We're not looking for one person. We're looking for *two* people. And the people we're looking for are Tommie the Make and Julius the Squeeze."

Frost stopped so Mister Johns could catch his breath. He wanted him to be fully alert when he broke the whole thing wide open—

"About two weeks ago, Bob tells me he wants to come back. Doesn't give a reason, and I didn't press him. Just tells me he wants to come home."

"Back to Elysian Row?"

"Right. Only three people knew Zeitzman was coming to town. Obviously, I was one of them—but I didn't tell a soul. It seems the same can't be said about Tommie the Make and Julius the Squeeze."

"Wait a minute," Mister Johns said, holding up a hand. "Back to the whole 'coming back to Elysian Row' thing—you thought that was a *good* idea because …?"

"Listen, I know there were risks coming back. Of course, I had no idea he'd be risking his life."

"But with risks come rewards, right?"

"And this one would have paid off in spades."

'Go on—" Mister Johns prodded.

What Jack Frost said next was more of a preemptive strike than anything else. He knew the moment he accused Tommie and Julius of double-crossing him on the Dorian deal, the promoters were going to be quick to tell their side of the story. And Jack Frost knew those two sides weren't going to fit together particularly well. Actually, they weren't going to fit together at all. So Jack Frost wanted to make sure that he got his version out there first. And though everything he was about to tell Mister Johns was technically true, there were far more omissions than admissions as to the real reason he had wanted Bob Dorian to return to Elysian Row.

"For the last 10 years, I've been hounded by every label in the country to get Bob to do a tribute show."

"A 'tribute show'?"

"Artists from other labels come and play his songs—the theory being that it would be a fitting tribute to his talent."

"Sounds like a fitting epitaph, if you ask me," Mister Johns observed acerbically.

"Well, that's exactly why he'd been so resistant to the idea. 'It ain't dark yet,' he'd say. 'Let 'em play my songs when I'm dead.'"

"And the irony just keeps on getting better," Mister Johns said drolly. "So how'd you finally convince him to go through with it?"

"I didn't. Like I said, he just came to me one day and said, 'You know that show you've wanted to do all these years? Let's do it.'"

"Just like that?"

"Just like that. Completely out of the blue—but then again nothing was completely out of the blue with Bob. You had his number for sure when you said nothing was a coincidence. The truth is he probably had the whole show played out in his head months before he 'coincidentally' brought it up."

"Okay, so Zeitzman agrees to do this show, you go to Tommie and Julius and set it up—strike while the iron is hot, before Zeitzman changes his mind. I get it."

"The problem is Tommie and Julius *didn't* get it. I told them not to breathe a word of this to anyone until I could iron out the details. That was the deal."

And here was the part of the conversation where Jack Frost was going to need to start wavering a bit if he wanted all the pieces of the story to fit together.

Sure Jack Frost had been bugging Dorian for years to return to Elysian Row. That part was true. Bob Dorian's career wasn't what it used to be. He was still a legend, but he hadn't had a hit in years. And without hits, people stop buying records. And when people stop buying records, it no longer matters how legendary you are: you're no longer relevant. The tribute show would have made Bob relevant again. Sure some of his old buddies would show up, play a few songs, tell a few stories from the 'good old days.' It was only to be expected. After all, most of Bob's buddies were legends themselves. But the real beauty of the show was that a whole new generation of musicians who had been influenced and inspired by Bob were going to come and pay tribute. But what Jack Frost did not tell Mister Johns was that there was more at stake than simply ensuring Bob Dorian's place in the annals of rock history. The concert wasn't just about making sure Bob Dorian would be remembered as a genius. There was more to it than that. There were a million reasons Jack Frost wanted Bob Dorian to do the Elysian Row concert: 40 million reasons, to be exact. Because that was exactly how much money Bob Dorian owed his creditors.

And Bob Dorian didn't have that money. Bob Dorian was broke. Jack Frost had bled him dry. And Bob Dorian didn't have a clue.

The situation Dorian had unwittingly found himself in the months leading up to his return to Elysian Row had actually begun a good year and a half earlier. Bob Dorian's recording contract had come up for review the previous spring. Naturally, as Dorian's manager, it fell upon Jack Frost to handle the negotiations. But instead of asking for more money, Jack Frost did something unheard of: he asked that Bob be *released* from his contract. Jack Frost didn't even let the label make a counteroffer. Instead, Jack Frost decided to reinvest millions—millions of Dorian's money—into remastering his back catalogue so that when the time came to reissue the songs Dorian would get every penny from dollar one. Jack Frost wouldn't fare so badly either. Twenty percent off the top isn't bad when you're playing with other people's money. And therein lay another problem. In addition to the fact the money he was playing with was Dorian's, Jack Frost hadn't told his client what he had done. And while Bob Dorian may have taken chances with his music, he did not take chances with his money. And for that reason, Jack Frost didn't tell Dorian his financial assets were tied up in a deal that had gone horribly wrong. And there was another twist to this little tale. A clause, actually, and it was that clause that had motivated Jack Frost to do the deal in the first place.

As it turns out, the record company contract wasn't the only thing up for renegotiation: Jack Frost's contract was also up for renewal. There were a lot of people circling Bob Dorian, and Jack Frost figured if he could pull this whole thing off Bob would forgive him should he ever find out he'd gone behind his back. But in order for the scheme to work, Bob Dorian needed to return to Elysian Row. That show was going to be the launching pad that made his back catalogue—his newly remastered, wholly owned back catalogue—worth a fortune. The creditors would get their 40 million; Jack Frost would keep his client; Bob Dorian would reclaim his legacy. Win. Win. Win. Of course, nobody had foreseen the fact that someone was going to throw a monkey wrench into the whole plan by putting a bullet in Bob Dorian's chest. Even the promoters had been left in the dark when it came to the real reason the concert was being staged. All Tommie and Julius knew was that they were going to make more money in one night than they had in all the nights that had passed since Bob Dorian skipped town 40 years ago. And that's all they needed to know to get them to pull it together so quickly.

But even if Jack Frost had told Mister Johns why it was so important for Dorian to have agreed to come back to Elysian Row, he still wouldn't have told Johns the whole story. Because there was another piece to this puzzle. Another person was involved. But Jack Frost was keeping that person in his back pocket for the time being.

"So Tommie and Julius jump the gun—" Mister Johns said, referring to the deal Jack Frost had cut with the promoters. "Despite the fact you told them to keep the concert under wraps, they started putting the word out. Is that what you're saying?"

"Not likely. There was too much cash at stake for them to talk," Frost replied. "Someone might come in, try and undercut them— make a better deal. But someone got wind of it."

"Minnesota Slim."

"Right."

"But I thought *you* put Slim in touch with those guys?"

"I did. I told you, I felt sorry for the guy. I wanted to help him out. But I never told him *why* I was putting them together. And I damn sure told Tommie and Julius not to talk to Slim until all the details were ironed out."

Jack Frost was unsure exactly how Slim had learned about the show, but he suspected Tommie and Julius had something to do with it. He had a theory that would explain why they would have told Slim about the show even though he had expressly asked them not to. But Frost would get to that in a minute. Right now he was too busy appreciating the irony: Minnesota Slim had been Tommie and Julius's fall guy when the going got tough. Now Slim was going to take the fall for Jack Frost.

"But Slim found out," Mister Johns surmised.

"Unfortunately, Slim's no better than the rest of the rats around here," Jack Frost continued. "Give him a piece of the pie and he wants a bigger slice. We already know he went to Commissioner Tiresias to play him against Tommie and Julius. But when that backfired—when they found out he was trying to work them—he came to me to bail him out."

"But why come to you?"

"I've helped Slim out of a jam or two in the past." Jack Frost did not elaborate. Mister Johns didn't ask him to. And the reason Mister Johns didn't press the matter was that there was something else on Mister Johns' mind.

The ease by which Jack Frost was able to lay all this at the feet of Tommie and Julius was a bit to convenient for Mister Johns. The fact that he did it so willingly raised more than a red flag. Alarms were blaring. Mister Johns felt like the other shoe was about to drop, and he didn't want to be the guy it landed on when it did.

"And you came up with that whole line of logic from what I said—" Mister Johns asked, a hint of suspicion in his voice. "This link between the promoters, Slim and Dorian's murder—you came up with this whole thing from some throwaway theory I was tossing against the wall?"

"Actually, I have to give Commissioner Tiresias a little credit—something he said when he told me Dorian had been murdered."

"Which was?"

"'A dead rock star is worth more than one who's alive any day.'" Frost paused, then drove the point home—"Nothing sells better than death, Johns. You ought to know that better than anyone. If it weren't for dead people, you wouldn't have a job at all."

"So what are you saying? That Tommie the Make and Julius the Squeeze had Zeitzman killed?"

"And, if my theory is correct," Frost confirmed, "Slim pulled the trigger."

"And how did they get him to do that?"

"That, Johns, is what we are about to find out."

THERE WERE NO DISTINGUISHING MARKINGS—no signs, no placards, no names embossed on a brass plaque—nothing to identify the tenants or the type of business being conducted behind these decrepit stucco walls. In fact, the only thing suggesting there was any life whatsoever lurking behind those walls was a surveillance camera that loomed ominously in the corner of the dark, dingy alcove. The hooded flaps hid the camera's eye, but the men felt its stare pressing down on them like a penetrating, perpetual gaze.

Suddenly, the lock securing the heavy iron gate buzzed loudly. Frost pressed firmly against the metal bars. The door's hinge, badly in need of a fresh oiling, creaked slightly. Frost pressed more forcefully, and the prisonlike gate slowly swung open. The two men stepped into the courtyard.

They paused for a moment to look up at the sky. But all they saw was a hole where God used to be. Nine floors stacked on top of the other like a cracked cement layer cake. It looked like a page ripped right out of Dante's *Inferno*.

"Nice place," Mister Johns deadpanned as he stepped over a couple broken syringes. "Can't wait to meet your partners."

"Actually, this is the first time I've ever been this far out '29.' In the past, Tommie and Julius have always come to me."

"I can see why," Mister Johns said, peering inside a cardboard box containing what looked like forty thousand red and blue shoe-strings—"Look at all this crap," Johns said as he surreptitiously slipped one of the strings into his pocket.

"Stairs or elevator?" Frost inquired.

"Are you kidding me? If the elevator is in half as bad shape as the rest of this place, we might never get out of here."

"I take it's stairs, then."

"Definitely stairs," Johns said, following Frost into the stairwell.

The offices of 'Tommie and Julius, Esqs.' were located on the ninth floor. It therefore took a few minutes to reach the landing.

When they did, they saw an open door at the end of the corridor. The sound of phones ringing off the hook grew louder as they ambled along the concrete terrace. The minute they appeared in the doorway, Tommie and Julius leapt up, stuck out their hands, and motioned for their guests to take a seat.

"So what brings you out to Interstate 29?" Tommie inquired.

"Yes, what brings you out this way?" Julius echoed.

"You could have called us," Tommie continued.

"Phones work just fine," Julius smiled.

"Yeah—" Frost replied, his eyes darting between the two promoters. "Wish the same could be said of Minnesota Slim."

"Yeah, we heard about Slim," Tommie replied.

"Yeah, heard Slim ain't working so good," Julius chuckled.

"No, Slim's dead all right," Frost played along. "Looked a little like a Pez dispenser last time we saw him. But I guess you boys already knew that." Judging from the insinuation in Jack Frost's voice, playtime was over.

"What's that supposed to mean?" Tommie snapped.

"Yeah, what's …"

"I think you know exactly what it means, Tommie," Frost said, raising his hand. "So you can cut the Tweedle Dee, Tweedle Dum shit."

"So who's 'we,'" Tommie said, pointing a sausagelike finger in the direction of Mister Johns.

"This is Johns," Frost said. "He's helping out with the investigation."

"He got a first name?"

"Why you asking me, Tommie?" Frost countered. "He's standing right there."

"You got a first name, Johns?" Julius said. His voice was no longer a high-pitched squeak. His voice was now a low grumble. The Tweedle Dee, Tweedle Dum shtick was long gone.

"Yeah," Johns replied. "I got a first name."

A moment passed—

"You want to tell us what it is?" Tommie said.

"Not especially."

Tommie and Julius exchanged a look that could have killed. There was no question if Frost had not been in the room the men would have definitely made good on that look.

"Well, I hope he's a better dick than discussionist," Tommie chuckled.

"This isn't a social visit, boys, so you can cut the pleasantries," Frost said evenly. "And for your information, 'discussionist' isn't even a word, Tommie."

"So what? *Webster's* is overrated, anyway. You knew what I meant, didn't you?" Tommie the Make smiled. "Now, if this isn't a social visit, then it must be business. So state your business, Frost—what's on your mind? Like Julius said when you walked in, you coulda called."

"I felt we needed to hash this out face-to-face."

"We didn't have nothing to do with Minnesota Slim's murder, Frost," Tommie said. "You want to talk about the concert, we can talk. In fact, we're kind of surprised you hadn't shown up earlier—considering our main attraction isn't going to make the show and all. But you want to talk about Slim, we got nothing to say."

"Is that so?"

"Yes, that's so. Now, last time I checked the three of us had an agreement. And Julius and I are planning on upholding our end of that agreement. What's that old expression: 'The show must go on.' Well, there's gonna be a show. We'll see to that. But if you come down here making accusations and casting suspicion, well that makes us not want to do our jobs."

"Neither of us responds well to insinuation," Julius added menacingly. "That is what you were implying just a moment ago, wasn't it? That Tommie and I killed Minnesota Slim?"

"Actually, I was going to suggest you killed Bob." The two men erupted with laughter.

"Bob!" Tommie exclaimed.

"You think we killed Bob?" Julius guffawed.

"That is choice, Frost!" Tommie was clearly having trouble containing himself.

"It's a cutthroat business—" Frost said. The pun was clearly intended.

"Doesn't mean we're literally chopping heads off! Why in God's name would we kill Bob?"

"Maybe for the same reason you got mixed up in Abramson-Isaac a few years back—" a voice called out.

Tommie the Make and Julius the Squeeze turned in the direction of the voice, which was coming from the corner of the room.

"Minnesota Slim's not the only snitch in town," Mister Johns said smugly. "'Ol Howard runs a pretty good racket as well. And don't give me that 'aw-shucks' look—"

"And what 'look' might that be, Mister Johns?"

"Like the two of you haven't ever engaged in this kind of thing before."

"We're promoters, Mister Johns," Julius said coolly. "What could we possibly gain from having a performer who can't perform?" The truth, of course, was both men had nearly fallen off the floor at the mention of Abramson-Isaac.

Obviously, the fact Mister Johns was accusing Tommie and Julius of cashing in on the death of Bob Dorian didn't sit well with the shifty promoters; but it was Abramson-Isaac—the thing that had given Johns the idea that they were shifty in the first place—that really had them worried.

"And what do you know about Abramson-Isaac?" Tommie said menacingly.

"Apparently enough to know the word on the street just might be true."

"And what word is that?" Tommie pressed.

Yeah, Jack Frost thought to himself. *Exactly what word would that be?*

It seemed the cagey, elusive Mister Johns had returned.

"You can't tie us to Abramson-Isaac," Julius said defiantly.

"Actually, I can—" Mister Johns said, reaching into his overcoat and pulling out the blue and red shoestring he'd slipped in his pocket earlier. The words, 'Abramson-Isaac,' were clearly embossed on it.

"That doesn't prove a damn thing!" Julius sputtered. "We had nothing to do with Abramson-Isaac," he said dismissively.

"You ought to take credit where credit is due," Mister Johns replied with mock reverence. "It was a hell of a fight. I lost a little money on it, but it was almost worth it the fight was so damn good. Then again, you guys really lost your shirts if memory serves. What was it you said earlier Frost?" Mister Johns continued deferentially. "Something like 'nothing sells better than death'? Real shame the ref had to step in and call the fight before Abramson killed Isaac. But I guess that's the risk you take when you forget to give the ref a taste of the fix." An uncomfortable silence fell across the room. It seems Mister Johns' memory had served him pretty well. From the shock on Tommie and Julius's faces, Mister Johns' recollection of the fight the promoters had tried to throw a few years back had knocked the wind right out of them.

"You see, when Frost mentioned he was in business with the two of you I thought I recognized the names. Wasn't until I actually got here that I put it all together."

"We don't have to answer to you," Tommie sneered.

"Of course you don't. The only person you have to answer to is yourself and God. And last time I checked I wasn't either of those. But I am the guy writing the story that's going to be appearing in tomorrow morning's *Dispatch*, which means as long as you're alive and kicking you might want to play ball."

"So you're the law, now?" Tommie said defiantly.

"You got some nerve," Julius said, shaking his head from side to side, "the two of you barging in here like this. One phone call and I could burn you both so fast it'd make your heads spin."

"Oh, we'll be getting to that 'one-phone-call thing' in a minute," Mister Johns said forebodingly, "but first I think Mr. Frost asked you a question."

"Listen, I don't know what kind of goods you think you got on us, Mister Johns, but Abramson-Isaac is yesterday's news. And as for today's catch, we already told you ..."

"You didn't kill Zeitzman," Mister Johns interrupted. "Yeah, we heard you the first time."

Johns' ability to call into question the promoters' dubious business practices was commendable. Considering one of those dubious business dealings had been with Jack Frost, however, letting Mister Johns meet Tommie and Julius face-to-face posed more than a few risks to the man who'd arranged this little get-together. But whatever threat Tommie and Julius posed, it was outweighed by the simple fact that *not* getting the promoters to go on the record as to the extent of their involvement was riskier. There was just too much at stake. Dorian was dead, Minnesota Slim had been garroted, and the two men who had the most to gain from Bob and Slim's untimely demises had holed themselves up out on Interstate 29. And judging from the fact they were stonewalling, they clearly planned on staying out on there until the whole thing blew over.

Sure Jack Frost had taken a risk putting Mister Johns in the same room with Tommie and Julius. The risk, however, seemed to have paid off. Johns knew how to push all the right buttons in order to get all the right answers. How in the world Johns had managed to connect Tommie and Julius to 'Abramson-Isaac' Jack Frost didn't have a clue. But how ever he had done it, it had done the trick. Johns had successfully rattled the cages of the two cagiest characters on Elysian Row. But Jack Frost knew that if you were going to rattle Tommie and Julius's cage, you better slam the door shut and throw away the key. It was time to pin this double murder on someone before it was too late; and the time was now—

"You know even if you didn't pull the trigger it doesn't mean this just goes away," Frost said, reinserting himself back into the conversation. "And this whole Abramson-Isaac thing is really coming up at a bad time, don't you think? I can assure you when Commissioner Tiresias finds out about our conversation here today he's going to want to talk to you boys. You gentlemen weren't the only one who lost a bundle on that fight."

Frost had waited a while to get back into the mix, but now that he had it was go-to time and he knew exactly which of these two lowlifes to go to first. But before he did, he wanted to give Tommie and Julius enough time to savor the full implication of what he was insinuating. And that insinuation included three factors: a fight that had been fixed, a pile of dough that had mysteriously disappeared, and the prospect of spending a little time in jail when Tommie and Julius realized it was the Commissioner's stash they'd stolen. That realization, it seems, hit Tommie a little sooner than Julius—

"Killing Bobby was never our idea," Tommie cracked. "It was Slim's!"

"Jesus Christ, Tommie! These guys don't have shit on us!" Julius screeched.

"We do now." Mister Johns smiled.

"Fuck you, Julius!" Tommie the Make said, turning to Julius. "I'm not taking the rap for some stupid scam that welfare reject dreamed up." Frost and Johns stepped back and watched the two promoters tear into each other like a pair of rabid pit bulls—

"Like you didn't know what he was up to! I knew the minute you cut that little shit in he was going to be trouble!"

"How did I know he was serious about killing Zeitzman?"

"The fact that that's *all* he talked about didn't give it away?"

And there it was. They'd found their man. Minnesota Slim was the shooter. That low-life louse had done it. He'd really done it. Slim had popped Bob Dorian. And for what? A couple of bucks? A bigger slice of the pie? Hadn't Frost said it himself: 'I wouldn't put anything past him.' Well, it seems Slim had proven him right.

But just because Tommie and Julius hadn't personally fired the gun, it didn't mean they were in the clear. After all, Tommie and

Julius weren't that much further up the evolutionary chain than the guy they'd just fingered. Sure they knew how to work the angles a little better, sure they were a little smarter than their coconspirator, Minnesota Slim; but they weren't *that* smart. After all, they'd just implicated themselves in murder.

"So back to that 'one-phone-call thing'—" Mister Johns said with a coolness that brought the heated argument to a standstill. "You want to do that here or down at the station. Personally, I'd do it here," Johns said, peering inside a cardboard box containing a dozen beaten-up old telephones. "Lord knows you got enough of them."

AFTER THEY FIGURED OUT what they had done—that they had effectively sealed their own fate by succumbing to their pent up frustrations—Tommie the Make and Julius the Squeeze went peacefully. Their incarceration was as uneventful and clear-cut as their confession. There was no scuffle, no more name-calling, no last minute attempt to make a run for it. They readily accepted the hand fate had dealt them, and in doing so closed the final chapter in the murder investigation of Bob Dorian. Or so everyone thought ...

"I think there's more to it than Tommie and Julius," Mister Johns said as they stepped out of the police station.

"You do, do you?" Commissioner Tiresias said sarcastically.

"Yes, I do." Mister Johns reached into his pocket. He tossed a breath mint in his mouth.

"If you ask me, Johns," Commissioner Tiresias said, "your breath isn't the thing you need to be worrying about. It's your judgment that stinks." Mister Johns tilted his head back and smiled as if to say, *Fuck you and the horse you rode in on. I'm doing my job, just like you asked me to. What have you been doing all this time?* The look didn't go unnoticed on the part of Commissioner Tiresias.

"Now, you'll pardon me if I seem a bit thick," the Commissioner said disingenuously, "but we already got the killer—the guys behind it anyway. So if you really think there's more to it than Tommie and Julius, perhaps you wouldn't mind enlightening us as to your latest theory. Because by my last count there have been not one, but two murders in less than 48 hours. Suspicious circumstances surrounding them both. For a while we didn't have any suspects, now we do. In fact, we got more than suspects, we got two sworn affidavits saying we got our killers. And here's the kicker, Johns—*you* took them."

"There's more to the story," Mister Johns said, undeterred by the Commissioner's clear attempt at intimidation.

"I'm a cop, Johns," Commissioner Tiresias continued, "and when people say stuff like that—"

"Like what?"

"Like there's more to the story—" Commissioner Tiresias clarified. "It tends to make cops worry. Makes it look like we're not doing our job."

"Don't let the situation mislead you, Commissioner."

"And do me a favor—" Commissioner Tiresias pleaded, "*please* stop talking in riddles. You think there's a loose end that needs tying up? Fine, I'll hear it. But straight up—no more of this talking back and forth in rhymes."

Mister Johns had done some posturing during the case. He'd put up a good bluff or two. But he wasn't bluffing now. He really did believe there was more to this than Tommie and Julius, and he was more than willing to press his case.

"I'm assuming that the murder of Minnesota Slim and Robert Zeitzman are related," Mister Johns said matter-of-factly.

"That note in your pocket—the one left behind at the murder scene—suggests that's more than a fair assumption."

"All right—Slim killed Zeitzman," Mister Johns conceded. Of course, he didn't really believe it, but it wasn't so much a concession as much as it was a way for Mister Johns to make the point he felt had been glossed over in all the congratulatory excitement of closing out the case. "But who killed Slim?"

"Could have been Tommie, could have been Julius ... what the hell does it matter?"

"What if it wasn't either of them?"

"What did I just say about talking in riddles," the Commissioner snapped.

"Listen, Johns," Jack Frost interjected, "I got to be honest with you. I'm leaning to the Commissioner on this."

So much for getting each other's back, Mister Johns thought to himself as he glared contemptuously at Jack Frost.

"Are you familiar with the expression 'the devil is in the details,' Commissioner?"

"Again with the riddles," the Commissioner reiterated with new-found irritation.

Undeterred, Mister Johns turned to Jack Frost—

"Have *you*, Frost?"

"Of course, I've heard the expression, but what does it have to do with anything?"

"It has everything to do with the investigation. In fact, the whole investigation hinges on that detail—the one detail that keeps coming up over and over. A person, actually. We've talked to everyone in this damn town *except* for that person. That, Commissioner, sounds like a loose end that needs tying up."

"This is an open-and-shut case, Johns," Commissioner Tiresias said with bravado. "Tommie and Julius confessed," the Commissioner continued, "said Slim killed Zeitzman and they knew about it. Killer's dead. Accomplices captured. Open-and-shut." Commissioner Tiresias waited for Jack Frost to step in, confirm his appraisal of the situation and put this pestering little patsy in his place once and for all. Jack Frost didn't say a word. It seems Mister Johns' back wasn't the only one Jack Frost had decided to leave exposed.

"Jesus, Frost," Commissioner Tiresias sputtered. "You know who he's talking about, don't you?" Frost knew exactly who Mister Johns was talking about, and it wasn't Jesus—far from it. The man to whom Mister Johns had alluded was not someone with whom either Commissioner Tiresias or Jack Frost wanted to tangle.

They say the best way to beat your demons is to take them on, Jack Frost thought to himself. *Well, it looks like it's time to face mine down once and for all.*

And though the last thing Jack Frost wanted to do was to bring him back into this, it was now painfully obvious he didn't have a choice.

"I'll be the first to admit Mister Johns' theory seems a bit far-fetched," Frost said, considering his words carefully, "but you know if he's right then the clock is ticking."

"Ah, the 'ticking clock,'" Commissioner Tiresias said derisively. "What are we in—a Raymond Chandler novel?"

"Fuck you, Commissioner," Frost said defiantly. Commissioner Tiresias absorbed the verbal jab with a smile that could have charmed the skin off a rattlesnake. "Would you excuse us for a moment, Johns," he said, marshalling up all the civility he could muster.

"Of course," Mister Johns replied.

Commissioner Tiresias wrapped his arm around Jack Frost and led him to the bottom of the stone stairs.

"What did you just say to me," Commissioner Tiresias said calmly.

"You heard what I said," Jack Frost replied undaunted. "This isn't some murder mystery set against a backdrop of broken dreams. This *is* the real thing. Because thanks to the story you solicited Mister Johns here to write, in less than 24 hours the press is going to descend on this place. And if they thought Bob Dorian's return to Elysian Row is a big story, it's not going to hold a candle to the fact that if Johns is right—if the man he suspects is calling the shots really *is* behind this—that doesn't bode well for anyone, especially a cop."

"And your point? Because I kind of tuned out after you told me to fuck myself."

"Johns has had a pretty good track record with hunches so far."

"So you want to get humped over a hunch—that what you're saying, Frost?"

"I'm just saying we should cover all our bases, that's all."

"'Cover our bases,'" Commissioner Tiresias repeated. "That's what you think you're doing?"

"That's right."

"Well, I'm not going to accuse the man who can slit every one of our throats over a 'hunch' just because Johns has a 'nose for news.' Trust me, if he's wrong on this, it's *our* obit he'll be writing." Commissioner Tiresias shook his head back and forth in disgust. "And how does he even know about him, anyway?"

"Like he said, his name keeps coming up."

"So how'd you explain him?"

"I did the best I could," Frost replied.

"Well, obviously your best wasn't very good," the Commissioner countered. "Which if you think back on it was *all* you were supposed to do—explain things to Johns if he got too close to something that might burn us. You weren't supposed to get invested. Clearly, you have."

"How could I not get invested!" Frost said. "Bob Dorian was my friend!"

Commissioner Tiresias waited for the rest of that sentence—the 'but ...' the 'however ...' or some other conjunction that would cancel out the earlier part of that rather prickly proclamation. But when the rest of the sentence didn't come, the Commissioner finally conceded, "You really want to do this?"

"We *need* to do this," Frost replied. "But let me handle him."

"Oh, you're definitely 'handling' him. In fact, this little conversation—" Commissioner Tiresias said, moving his forefinger between the two men, "it never happened."

Of course, the conversation *had* happened. And even though they thought Mister Johns had been out of earshot, he had heard every word they had said.

Bob Dorian had been dead a little over 48 hours, and over the course of that time Jack Frost had been unwavering in his determination to catch the man who had put a bullet in his friend's chest. For the last 48 hours, time had been working in the favor of the killer.

Now, for the first time, Mister Johns got the distinct impression the tide had turned: time was now on the side of Jack Frost. There was just something about the words Jack Frost chose to describe the urgency of the situation; something about the way he spoke those words that let Mister Johns know that Jack Frost *would* catch the man who killed Bob Dorian. But even if Johns was right, even if the patsy, the guy in the dark, dour suit, the guy they brought in to take the fall had figured out who was behind this whole thing, Mister Johns had failed to figure out the most important detail of all: the devil had been Jack Frost's partner all along …

CHAPTER 18

▼

JUDAS

"Back again," he said, feigning surprise at the sight of Jack Frost darkening his doorway for the second time in as many days. "The word on the street is that you got your man—strike that—got your *men*. Frankly, I'm surprised you're not down at the station basking in the adulation. You always were good at taking the credit for other people's hard work weren't you, Jack." The man smiled. It was a soft, inviting smile. So much so, in fact, that all hint of sarcasm was eradicated the moment that broad smile spread across his large, moon-shaped face.

Someone once said he reminded them of a panda bear. With his pallid complexion, gray-streaked hair and black eyebrows brushing out from behind his rose-tinted glasses, he looked anything but dangerous. Of course, looks can be deceiving. Judas was always the most dangerous man in the room.

"Please do me the honor of coming in this time, won't you?" Judas said with mock ceremonialism as he motioned for Frost to enter.

Jack Frost passed underneath an ornate, neo Gothic transom and entered the cramped foyer. A long black coat hung like a sleeping vampire bat just inside the doorway. And while Frost recognized the coat from his earlier visit, it was the coatrack that caught his attention. Frankly, Jack Frost had never seen one quite like it. Gnarled and knotted, it appeared to be constructed out of an old olive tree. And though Frost couldn't discern the exact form those knotted branches had taken, he could have sworn they were in the shape of an inverted cross.

The two men walked the length of the hallway, then turned and entered a formal dining room. Judas motioned for Frost to take a seat at the table. Judas removed his finely tailored English Tweed jacket, and hung it on the back of a Tudor style chair. The jacket, which had hung loosely over his portly frame, had almost made him seem jovial. But Jack Frost knew better than to cozy up to Judas too quickly.

"I thought you might like some tea," he said, placing a porcelain cup in front of Frost.

"Water's fine," Frost said.

Judas shrugged his shoulders dismissively as if to say, 'No skin off my back.' It was an easy, effortless shrug. It really *was* no skin off his back. And besides, he knew he'd be getting what was coming to him in due time. He meticulously arranged two place settings at a long, wooden table that could have easily accommodated a dozen. Quickly taking a silent inventory to ensure the napkin, fork, knife and spoon were all in their proper places, he asked the question Jack Frost did not want to answer—

"So, what brings you back, Jack?" he said, picking up a silver pitcher from the table and slowly angling it over Jack Frost's empty water glass. "You seemed a little rushed last time. We didn't really get a chance to catch up. So many things to catch up on," he said, dropping a few sugar cubes into his cup.

"Your name came up again," Frost said flatly. Judas didn't even flinch.

"The first rule in this business is that you're dead in the water if they stop talking about you." A steady stream of steam slowly rose off the scalding hot tea.

"Your name came up in conjunction with Bob's murder," Frost elaborated.

"A man who cuts straight to the chase. I always liked that about you, Frost." Judas took a sip of his tea then placed the cup back on top of the saucer. Clearly he was waiting for Jack Frost to say something. Frost didn't say a word. "Well ...?" Judas paused dramatically, "You say they're talking about me? What are they saying?"

"You can cut the theatrics. You know exactly why I'm here."

"How's that?" Judas inquired.

And so the dance began—

"Well, as you so perceptively put it when I passed through the door a moment ago, we got our men." Jack Frost appropriated a dramatic pause of his own. "Problem is we didn't get all of them."

"Still one short, are you?" Judas said, pretending to catch on. Jack Frost had caught this two-faced bastard red-handed, and they both knew it. Frost arched his eyebrows. It was his turn to smile.

"So does Johns know you're here with me?"

"Yep. Johns figured it out."

"Jesus Christ!" Judas said. The booming of the drums was about to begin.

"Relax."

"Don't tell me to relax, Frost!" Judas said, his voice reverberating off the walls. "Now how much does Johns know!?"

"He doesn't know about 'us,' if that's what you're asking."

The 'us' to which Jack Frost was referring was his longstanding relationship with the most despised man on Elysian Row. The fact that Judas and Jack Frost had crossed paths over the years was hardly a major revelation. They *had* guided the career of the same man, after all. And if you were going to do business with Bob, at one time or another you had to get into business with Judas.

In hindsight, it shouldn't have come as a shock to Jack Frost that Johns put it together. After all, Judas' name *had* kept coming up. Frankly, that shouldn't have come as such a surprise, either. Judas had been part of the story for the last 40 years. Because it had been 40 years ago that Judas had seen Bob Dorian's future. Truthfully, he'd probably seen it more clearly than Bob himself. And for that, Judas had been compensated handsomely. But any time someone accused Judas of robbing Bob blind, Judas had the best defense of all. He just held up the contract and pointed to Bob's signature. It was all above board and—perhaps most importantly—it was binding. There was no question Judas had made a fortune trading on the bright future of Bob Dorian. But in the process, Judas had seen Bob Dorian sink into the darkest depths of doubt, suspicion and paranoia. And what did Judas do? He just stood there and let it happen.

In retrospect, it had been a brilliant move. Judas had taken a calculated risk watching Bob slowly disappear into a hellish existence filled with pills and booze, cut off from everything and anyone who could have helped him. What started off as a glass or two of burgundy soon turned into the harder stuff. It took a little over a year, but over the course of the next 18 months Bob Dorian became a junkie. And after a while the junk completely debilitated him. Of course the reason Judas had allowed Bob to fall so far was that he had been counting on Bob's genius to pull him through. Judas knew that out of adversity comes art, and Bob was nothing if not an artist.

Judas' gamble paid off. The work Bob created in that dark, desperate year and a half down in Nashville was nothing short of brilliant. Thanks to Judas, Bob Dorian emerged a myth, a legend, an icon forever embedded in the landscape of popular culture. At the age of 26, Bob Dorian was the biggest star in the world. He had reached the pinnacle of fame, ascended to the height of notoriety. But once you've reached the top, there's only one place to go. It took a few years, but he finally came crashing down. It happened right around the time he had his accident in Upstate in the summer of 1966. The former Mrs. Bob Dorian hadn't told them about the motorcycle accident, but the accident turned out to be the perfect cover. The road wasn't the only thing that had sidelined Bob. A gram-a-day heroin addiction had played a fairly large part in Bob's mysterious, rather sudden disappearance.

And while that addiction had sowed the seeds of Bob Dorian's discontent with Judas, it took Bob another 20 years before he was fully able to recognize how badly Judas had betrayed him. Even then, wrestling Bob away from Judas down in Jackson was no easy feat for Jack Frost.

The allegation that Frost had trumped up charges that Judas had his hand in the till so that Bob would turn against the manipulative manager was more folklore than fact. It wasn't true. But it was out there. After all, Mister Johns knew about it. And though Jack Frost might not have set up Judas in order to win Bob's favor, he *had* exploited the situation.

Bob was furious he was the one who had had to bail Tremolo out of that jam. Bob didn't like to expose himself to the media's watchful eye, and coming to the defense of a man charged with sodomy was pretty much telling the press it was open season on Bob Dorian. But it wasn't Tremolo Bob was pissed at. 'Where was Judas?' Bob had fumed. It had gotten hot as hell down there in Jackson, and Bob couldn't believe his manager hadn't taken the heat for him. Bob was fuming. Cooler heads were called for. Enter Jack Frost.

The night after the incident, Jack Frost arrived in Mississippi and promptly removed Bob's name from the bail bondsman's receipt and had his name put on it instead. Bob was clearly grateful, and gratitude was not an emotion that came frequently to Bob Dorian. Jack Frost knew he had Bob's ear, and he used the opportunity to get something off his chest that had been gnawing at him ever since Tiny and Judas had sequestered Bob down in Nashville. It turns out, Bob had been wrestling with a gnawing feeling of his own, and the fact that Judas hadn't come to his assistance when he needed him most only cemented his suspicion that his longtime manager was more concerned about his own well-being than his client's welfare. A client, Bob was well aware, who had made Judas a very wealthy man. Capitalizing on Dorian's newfound mistrust for Judas, Jack Frost took the opportunity to point out just how much Judas had taken advantage of

Bob over the years. Bob didn't like being seen as a chump, and so Bob took Jack Frost's advice: Judas was out and Jack Frost was in.

Looking back on it, Jack Frost often wished he *had* trumped up those charges. Maybe it would have given Commissioner Tiresias the ammunition he needed to put Judas away for good. But in reality Jack Frost had done something far more shameful than lie to Bob. He had taken advantage of the very thing Judas had preyed on all those years—Bob's insecurities. Frost had pulled the ultimate Judas move by whispering in Bob's ear at a time when Bob was at his most vulnerable. And in that moment, Jack Frost didn't 'best' Judas, he *became* Judas.

What had happened down in Mississippi was not, however, what Judas was referring to when he'd asked Jack Frost how much Mister Johns knew about the knotted past that tied the two men together. The 'us' to which he was referring was a *new* partnership—a partnership that had been forged in the weeks following Jack Frost's realization that his plan to regain control of Dorian's back catalogue had backfired. Jack Frost was in desperate need of cash in order to remain solvent while he figured out what to do next. And while cash was a commodity that could be replenished, time was not. And since Jack Frost knew if enough time passed Judas would find out about his misstep anyway, Frost decided better the devil he knew than the devil he didn't. And so, a deal was cut. Frost didn't have to tell Judas about the deal he'd botched; but in order to keep Judas from telling Bob about how he had cajoled Bob into returning to Elysian Row, Jack Frost knew he would have to give Judas a piece of the show. 'It's just like the good old days,' Judas had squealed with mock delight when the deal went down. After 20 years on the sidelines, Judas was back in the game: Judas had his tenterhooks back in Bob Dorian.

Jack Frost had always made a conscious effort not to call attention to his dealings with Judas. Frankly, it pained Frost that he had to get into those past dealings with Mister Johns at all. But Jack Frost most certainly didn't want this new arrangement with Judas ever to see the light of day. There was, however, only so much Jack Frost could do.

At some point, Judas was going to want to reclaim his pound of flesh. And since Bob Dorian was out of the picture, the only person left to carve up was Jack Frost.

"Now answer my question—how much does Johns know?" Judas repeated.

"He knows I'm here. In case I end up like Slim. Someone would need to identify you in a line up."

"Wait a minute. You think *I* killed Slim?"

"That's kind of where I was going, yeah."

"Is this your MO, Frost?" Judas said incredulously. "To go around town and accuse everyone of killing people until someone finally confesses? Because that's kind of where *I* was going," Judas said condescendingly.

"'Don't worry about, Slim. I'll take care of Slim,'" Frost said, recalling Judas' words from their previous meeting. "Those were your exact words, I believe. Sounds like a threat—one that you might just have made good on."

"Insinuation and intimidation is not the same thing, Jack. Especially when your implication is that I killed a man."

"Maybe you did, maybe you didn't," Frost said dismissively. He wasn't so much backing off the allegation as he was moving on to his next point. "Even if you didn't kill Slim, I know for a fact you cut a deal with Tommie and Julius."

"The Zeitzman deal was between you and me, Frost. You and me," Judas said, emphasizing his words by moving his forefinger between them.

"The deal might have been between us, but it seems someone was getting a cut from the names being put on the bill—four 'someones' in fact."

"How apocalyptic—like the Four Horsemen, I'm getting shivers."

"Well, all four have met rather unfortunate fates, wouldn't you say? It seems one of them is in the morgue, two of them are sitting like Buddha in 10-foot cells …"

"And the forth is sitting at the table with you—is that what you're saying, Frost?"

"Looks like I don't have to."

"And Tommie and Julius—they told you this? That we were stacking the bill?"

"They didn't say a word. Just handed over the contracts. Interesting how my signature wasn't on a single one of them—my being his manager and all."

"You'd have done the same thing, Frost," Judas said, not even attempting to deny the allegation that he'd sold Frost out. "An opportunity like that doesn't come around but once in a lifetime."

"I should have known you were behind the whole thing. Frankly, I can't believe it took me this long to put the pieces together."

"Since when did you start getting so paranoid? Bob must really have rubbed off on you."

"Right about the time your name started coming up."

"You and I have known each other for a long time, Frost. And in all those years, we've never talked for more than 10 minutes."

"Our arrangement never required we do a whole lot of talking."

"No, I suspect it didn't. When I handed you Bob, it was a turnkey operation. He was on autopilot. Not a lot you and I needed to talk about. All you had to do was prop him up and get him to the next show."

"Feed the fire, perpetuate the myth—is that what you're saying?"

"You make it sound so dirty, so dishonorable."

"The way you're describing it, it is dishonorable. It's a discredit to his talent."

"It's what we *do*, Frost," Judas said, rationalizing their mutual profession with the same callous frankness Westmoreland probably used to rationalize the slaughter at Mai Lai. "I did it for the first 20 years of his career. You've done it for the last 20. And while it's very noble of you to come to his defense, you and I both know that any talent Bob had was tapped long ago. That is, after all, why the two of us actually broke that 'no talking' rule we had in place all those years a few months ago, isn't it?" Considering that Jack Frost wasn't sure if that last utterance was a threat or a question, he continued to sit there in stone-faced silence. It was just as well. Judas wasn't finished yet. "Now," Judas said, impatiently tapping his fingernail against the edge of his teacup, "what are they saying about me?"

"What?"

"You said you and Johns have talked to a lot of people, and everyone you've talked to has mentioned my name. So what are they saying? I'm curious."

"Does it matter?"

"Doesn't the accused have a right to know what he's being accused of?"

"You're not on trial, Judas. Not yet, anyway."

"This isn't going to trial, Frost, and you know it. A trial would be bad enough. But having your name dragged through the muck would be 10 times worse. So stopped kidding yourself, Frost. This isn't even going to leave this room. You said it yourself, you got your men. It's over. So humor me. What are they saying about me?"

The problem, of course, was that it *wasn't* over. Not by a long shot. The whole thing may have been coming to a head, but it was far from over. Heads were going to roll, and Jack Frost knew if he didn't want his to be one of them, he was going to need to cut Judas out of his life once and for all. That realization did not prevent him, however, from getting a few things off his chest. After all, Judas *had* asked—

"Well, for starters," Jack Frost said, taking full advantage of the opening Judas had provided, "they're saying you were selling his songs to other artists, and not just any other artists—your own clients."

"True. And they were very popular. And because they were popular they were getting Bob's name out there as someone who was a versatile songwriter—someone who understood the changing landscape of popular music and could adapt to it."

"Some would say you were stealing from Peter to pay Paul."

"Very clever, Frost, but you forgot Mary."

"It still doesn't change the way it went down. And you know what the ironic part is?"

"I'm sure you're going to tell me," Judas said drolly.

"As many people as you screwed, you just might have been forgiven if you hadn't screwed him."

"Jeez, not *that* old chestnut again." Judas knew where this was going. "Listen, I'm going to tell you exactly what I used to tell Bob—what I told all my clients. A record company comes to you and offers you an advance—say, $100,000. Lotta money, especially if you get to keep it all. I'm not managing you, so I don't get a cut. But what if I tell you I can get you $250,000? Lotta money, but here's the catch—you don't get to keep it all. I want half. Fifty percent of the net. That's my cut for managing you. But it's your decision."

"But if I decide to go with you," Jack Frost said, playing the devil's advocate, "that decision just made me $25,000."

"You always were a quick study," Judas said, paying Jack Frost a compliment that was as hollow as the man who had given it. "Did Bob and I do well together?" Judas continued. "Sure we did. I'm not saying we didn't make money. Hell, we made more money than most people see in a lifetime. And as for that money we made—I never heard Bob complain. Come to think of it, I never heard you complain either, Jack."

"I worked for every dime Bob and I made together," Frost said resentfully.

"And you think I didn't?" Judas scoffed. "Who do you think got him out of that crappy contract at Columbia? I did. Who do you think refused to let him go on those rinky-dink TV shows? I did. Got him to change his name, taught him the importance of instilling a little mystique into the equation, got him out of that hellhole he was living in over on 4th Street and took him out to the country so he wouldn't be bothered by those sycophants who were feeding his head? I did. I did. I did. I did all those things, so I don't think it's an exaggeration to say that without me there would never have been a Bob

Dorian. Fifty percent was a pittance for what the world got in exchange."

"Wow, to hear you put it that way, it almost sounds as if you liked him."

"What part of this are you not getting, Frost?" Judas said, raising his voice. "I did like him. But I never let my personal feelings cloud my judgment. These people you're talking to, the reason they hate me is that they knew I was grooming Bob for success, and there's a part of them that was jealous I didn't pick *them*. But for each detractor I think you'll find everyone knows that without me, Bob would never have made it. Deep down I think you know that, too. So why don't we just cut the witty repartee and get down to brass tacks?"

"Brass tacks?"

"Yeah, why don't you tell me why you're here. What is it you want? I mean it can't be money. I can't give you want I never got. 'No show, no dough'—you know the drill. And it's not about vindicating Tommie and Julius. I mean, you can pin this whole thing on them and walk away clean as a whistle. Come on, Frost," Judas said, his voice suddenly growing low and seductive, "let's put on a show."

"I told you …"

"That you thought I off'd Slim, yeah, I remember you saying that." The gruffness had returned. That gruffness, however, was nothing compared to the booming of the war drums that would come if Jack Frost didn't get to the point and get there quick. "But we both know I didn't do that, either. So why are you here? You didn't have to haul your ass all the way out here to air a bunch of old dirty laundry, have the same conversation we've had a hundred times before, a conversation that we both know isn't going to change just because we keep talking about it. Everything you've said to me you could have said over the phone. But you came out here instead. And you came for reason. So, I'll ask you again—what is it you want? You've got my attention … speak."

A long, protracted silence fell between them.

"You entered the picture at just the right time," Frost began. "At a time when the Liberals were determined to turn Bob into a mascot, you gave Bob the traction he needed to stand up for himself and not get turned into a lapdog for the Left. I'll be the first to admit, you gave Bob some teeth."

"Then he promptly turned around and bit the hand that fed him," Judas quipped. "And this is exactly the same aforementioned conversation we've had hundred times before."

"There's no question you elevated Bob's profile," Frost continued undeterred. "'Took Bob to the next level.' But in order to do that you isolated Bob, cut him off from everyone who cared about him. Bob once told me, 'People have one great blessing in life—obscurity.'"

"Give me a break, Frost," Judas chided. "He knew what he was giving up."

"I'm not so sure he did. Bob wasn't stupid—far from it. Bob was the most brilliant person I've ever met. But he was just a kid. He was 21 when he agreed to let you take him under his wing. You may have made Bob rich, but you robbed him of his innocence in the process. Sure, Bob was willing to make a deal," Frost conceded, "but he had no idea the toll that deal he cut with you would eventually take on him."

"And you think I did?"

"From the very beginning," Frost said with unwavering certainty. "It's one thing to distance yourself from your fans. It's a defense mechanism. The fans can suck you dry. You're up there on the stage and they think they know you. There's a sense of entitlement that sucks the life out of you. But it's entirely another when you distance yourself from the people who really do care about you. The fact that you challenged Bob, forced him to delve deep into his soul so that he could unearth things that might never have seen the light of day—for that I will forgive you. That you turned him into a junkie down in Nashville in order to do it is a sin. A sin for which I hope you pay for the rest of your life." There, he'd said it. Everything he had ever wanted to say to this man he had said. And it felt good. It felt very good. But it didn't feel nearly as good as the three words Jack Frost would say next—

"It's over, Judas. The deal I cut with you back in '86 to get you to go away, the deal I made with you a few months ago to bring you back in, it's over. You have made your last nickel off Bob Dorian. Even after you turned him over to me, you still managed to find a way to get a piece of him. But now that *he's* gone, *you're* gone." Frost was standing now. His voice had grown large and boisterous—"So why am I here?" Frost asked rhetorically. "Why did I come all the way our here to this hellhole you call a house? Because I wanted to tell you it's over, Judas. And I wanted to tell you to your face."

"It's not a house, Jack—" Judas corrected, "It's a home. My home, Bob's home for a while, too, in case you've forgotten."

"You may have put a price on Bob's soul," Frost said disdainfully. "You won't be putting one on mine."

"Oh, I wouldn't be so sure of that."

Judas' response to Jack Frost's diatribe was as smooth as silk. You would never have known that Judas was preparing to cut Jack Frost to pieces. "In fact, quite the opposite is true," Judas continued, "I *do* plan on putting a price on your soul. But you'll be happy to know that I'm going to let you negotiate your own terms. After all, I want you to be able to live with yourself after the deal goes down." Judas lifted the teacup to his thick, fleshy lips, and took a sip. "Because you see, there is one last thing you and I need to discuss before you make your grand exit."

"I don't have anything else to say to you."

"Then why don't you let me do the talking. And what I'd like to talk about goes back to that part in our discussion earlier when you said I was screwing Bob—that was the term you used wasn't it? 'Screwing,' right?" Frost didn't respond. Frankly, Judas hadn't expected him to. "Because the ironic part is that in the end, *you* were the one who got screwed. And you know what the best part is? You know what the part that's really going to gnaw at you at night is? It's that you screwed yourself. You see, you really have some nerve—criticizing the way I marketed Bob's songs. I mean, that's really the pot calling the kettle black now, isn't it?" Frost had a pretty good idea where this was going. But instead of interrupting, he decided to let the conversation take its course—"Licensing is lucrative," Judas continued. "But I don't have to tell you that now do I, Frost?" Turns out, it went right where Frost thought it would. Judas was right. Frost was about to get screwed—"The word on the street is that you locked Bob into a publishing deal that would have turned you a very nice profit— that is, of course, if someone hadn't put a bullet in his chest." Judas picked the teapot up off the table. "Are you *sure* you don't want any tea?" It was a perfect non sequitur, as seamless as the manner in which Judas was about to slip the knife into Jack Frost's back.

"No, thank you," Frost replied, his voice void of all traces of emotion.

"You sure? Because I can brew some more up in a jiffy?" Judas arched his bushy eyebrows up over his tinted spectacles. "Suit yourself," Judas said as he brought the cup to his lips then placed it back on the table. "You know the old adage, 'Dead men tell no tales,' don't you, Frost?"

"I've heard it."

"Well, it turns out it's not true. I mean, I suppose it's technically true—but Slim wasn't technically dead when I showed up. I will say in his defense, however, he did the best he could—considering he didn't have a tongue and all."

"Get to the point, Judas."

"You mean the point where I'm going to screw you? We'll get there in a minute, but I want you to hear this story. How Slim got that publishing contract, I mean. It's really quite amazing. It seems Slim *was* telling you the truth when he said he found Bob down by the tracks that night. It seems he did help Commissioner Tiresias carry the body to the Chelsea, and it seems in the process," Judas reached into his pocket and pulled out a bloodstained piece of paper. "He found this—"

Judas placed the paper on the table.

Frost gave the paper a cursory once-over, "What's that?" He knew exactly what it was.

"Oh, you're going to go with the 'I've-never-seen-that-gun-in-my-life-before' defense? Appropriate choice since this is the smoking gun that links you, not me, to the murder. But to answer your question," Judas picked up the paper and began to unfold it as he spoke, "this just happens to be the aforementioned publishing contract. Signed by Robert A. Dorian. Oh, and here's another name you might recognize … it's yours, Jack," Judas said, feigning surprise. "And you were all upset that your named didn't appear on any contracts."

"So Bob and I renegotiated his publishing," Frost said disarmingly. "That's not unusual. But your implication that I killed him is ridiculous—it's kind of hard to write songs when you're dead. And in case you haven't noticed, Bob Dorian is very much dead. That contract is worthless."

"Not as worthless as you might think," Judas said auspiciously as he rose from the long wooden table. "You know, as much as Bob complained about the price of fame, if you ask me I think the cost of anonymity is just as high—maybe higher." Judas began to walk the length of the room, "Fame and anonymity—they're really two sides of the same coin. And the only way to escape either of them is to become incognito."

Judas entered the small, well-appointed library, then stopped in front of the ornate oak cabinet. The disc Jack Frost had brought him earlier that night was still on the top of the CD player.

"Why do you think Bob came back?" Judas asked, lobbing the question into the room like a grenade. He didn't really expect Frost to pick it up, and when he didn't, Judas decided he'd try his hand at disarming the question himself—"You, Johns, the Commissioner," Judas continued, "you all seem so determined to find the man who put the bullet in Bob's chest. But have you even stopped for a moment to wonder why he came back in the first place."

Of course I've stopped to wonder why Bob came back, Frost thought to himself. *That damn question is all I've thought about for the last 48 hours.*

It was a question that had preoccupied his every thought since he'd stepped back onto Elysian Row. And the question had filled him with guilt, resentment and an overwhelming sense of self-reproach.

"Like I said," Judas continued after taking a few moments to savor Jack Frost's painful rumination, "we both know Dorian hasn't written a song in 10 years. And I'm not talking about some bullshit single for a soundtrack or some recycled melody—I'm talking about a real song, a song that meant something. For all intents and purposes that contract *was* worthless when he signed it, and frankly it should be worthless now. Sure you've convinced him to release a few greatest hits collections to fill the coffers, but Bob hasn't written a meaningful song, much less a 'hit,' in years. But what if Bob had started writing again?" Judas asked rhetorically. "And what if a few of those songs actually were hits? What if he had a whole album of them?" Judas placed the disc in the CD player and pressed a button. An unmistakable voice, harrowing and evocative, filled the room. "You should never have let me hear those songs, Frost. Got my mind working, just like the old days. Except unlike the old days, I didn't have a client to prosper off of."

"But that's about to change, I imagine," Frost said knowingly.

"Like I said before, this is the part where you're going to get screwed. But before you do, I don't want you to think I'm completely oblivious to the situation. I know Bob cared for you, and judging from the way you've been talking about him, you cared about him, too. It's probably why he renegotiated his publishing with you. He knew he was tapped, and he wanted to take care of you after all the years you spent by his side. It's a beautiful story, really," Judas said, clearly not giving a rat's ass how beautiful the story was. "But in light of the recent events—in light of the fact he recorded what you and I agree might just be some of the best songs he ever wrote; the fact that he signed that contract then was murdered; the fact that those songs are worth God knows how much more now that he'll never lay down another track in his life—well, these are facts that might be best kept under wraps, wouldn't you agree? Makes all that searching for a killer seem like a lot of wasted time since when you stack up the facts you had the most to benefit from Bob's murder—financially speaking, of course. The concert was a red herring, Jack. It was *always* a red herring. Sure, we would have made a lot of money on that show," Judas conceded. "Even after we paid off all those people we had to cut in along the way. But not as much as you now stand to make as a result of renegotiating Bob's publishing. Let's cut to the chase, Jack, we both know the real money has always been in publishing."

"You know I didn't kill Bob," Frost seethed.

"*I* know that, Jack. But there are just so many facts here, and can we really trust the media to get them right?"

"So you're blackmailing me?"

"I look at it more as run-of-the-mill extortion, but whatever makes you comfortable," Judas smiled. "So here's how it works—you're going to sign over a percentage of your royalties to me. In exchange, I'm going to make sure none of these pesky facts get in the way of making either of us a fortune."

"A percentage of my royalties?"

"Right."

"And exactly what 'percentage' would that be?"

"Oh, I don't know," Judas said, stroking his chin. "How about a number you threw out earlier—50 percent. You can live that that, can't you?"

"Fifty percent!"

"Well, if we're going to go back into business together, I can't think of a better way to make sure we both pull our own weight." Judas reached into the desk drawer and took out a gold-tipped Montblanc Meisterstück. He slid the pen across the table. "I sense a little bad blood has been bubbling up between us over the years, Frost. Frankly, I can't think of a better way to kiss and make up." The steam slowly rose from the cup and curled around his face like a serpent.

Judas leaned across the table and whispered seductively into Frost's ear—"Sign it."

Frost wrapped his forefinger and thumb around the pen's black resin barrel and pressed the 18K hand-ground gold nib against the contract. He signed his name in a tight, controlled cursive script, then slowly slid the contract back across the table. At that moment, Frost felt a slight vibration in his left breast pocket. He reached into his jacket and pulled out his cell phone. He did not recognize the number on the screen. He did, however, recognize the voice on the other end of the line. And as Frost listened to what the man was telling him, his face turned ashen.

Bob Dorian was alive …

PART III

▼

The Record Factory

CHAPTER 19

▼

THE TRUTH
REVEALED

Much like the man himself, Dr. Reich's place of business was a mystery wrapped in a riddle. Just one look around this bizarrely decorated office and you knew that getting to the bottom of this guy was a plunge best left untaken. It was a 'Ripley's—Believe it or Not!©' museum come to life. And like the real-life Robert Ripley, Dr. Reich had spent the last 40 years traveling the world collecting the unbelievable, the inexplicable, the one of a kind. And without doubt the most bizarre article on display also doubled as his most prized possession—a stuffed mule's head, which hung hauntingly over the proscenium archway that framed the entrance into this house of waxed horrors.

"You like that?" Dr. Reich said with a grin when he saw Frost had noticed his handiwork.

"It's very ..." Frost searched for the word, "... lifelike."

"Well, thank you," Dr. Reich replied, accepting the highest possible compliment that could be paid to someone who dabbles in the art of animal preservation. "It's just a hobby," Dr. Reich said dismissively. "I've always been very taken by taxidermy." As evidenced by the binoculars dangling from the mule's head, it seems ornithology also tickled the good doctor's fancy. "You like the eyes?" Reich said, clearly fishing for another compliment. "Spent a lot of time on the eyes."

"It's like they're ..." Frost moved from one side to the other, "... following you." Indeed, the eyes did seem to be following him.

"Like the uh ..." Reich snapped his fingers in an attempt to jar his drug-addled memory, "what's the name of that painting ..." the snapping continued, "the one in that big museum in Paris?"

"The *Mona Lisa*?"

"That's the one!" Dr. Reich exclaimed, throwing his hands up in the air as if he'd just won the lottery. "Always felt like she was hiding something. Don't you think so?"

"Never really thought much about it to tell you the truth."

What's up with this guy, Frost thought to himself. *Calls me with his panties all in a knot; now he's giving me a lecture on art appreciation?*

"Oh yeah, that painting's something else," Reich was getting excited. "It was like she knew what salvation was like. You could tell by the way she smiled. It was like she knew something the rest of us didn't."

"Speaking of which—you mentioned something on the phone *I* should know about. Something about Bob?"

"Ah, yes—you seemed a little distracted earlier," Dr. Reich observed. The irony was unintended.

Really? You think so? Frost mused to himself.

It was hardly an unexpected reaction to Reich's acerbic observation, no matter how inadvertent it had been. After all, Jack Frost *had* just signed away half of all his income in perpetuity.

Hell, who am I kidding? the reality of the situation truly sinking in, *I'm not going to see a dime from Bob's catalogue now that Judas is involved.*

It was hardly a secret 50 percent was Judas' calling card. Fifty percent got him in the door. But everyone knew that once you let Judas in, he didn't leave until he'd robbed you blind.

"No, I couldn't really talk," Jack Frost said, underplaying the situation he'd been navigating when Reich had called. "But I'm all ears now. But before we start—exactly how much is this little visit going to cost me?"

"Oh, this one's on the house, Mr. Frost—" Dr. Reich said smugly as he inched his way across the cluttered office. "Now correct me if I'm wrong, but didn't you tell me Zeitzman was on medication?" From his impish albeit determined gait, Reich's destination appeared to be a body atop a granite examination table in the far corner of the room. "That is what you said, isn't it?" Dr. Reich asked. "That Zeitzman was on medication for his heart condition?"

"That's right. Capsofungin."

"Capsofungin, right," Reich said, confirming what he already knew. "Well, after I got back to the morgue I ran some blood tests."

"A bullet in the chest wasn't enough to kill him?" Frost said wryly.

"Sometimes people in Mr. Zeitzman's line of work …" Dr. Reich let the implication of his trailing sentence impregnate the damp, dank air.

"Right, I get it," Frost said.

"Well, I'm pleased to report Mr. Zeitzman was indeed clean."

"I'm happy to hear that," Frost said condescendingly.

"Actually, you might not be as happy as you think," Dr. Reich said with a slight tinge of trepidation. "It seems Mr. Zeitzman was a little *too* clean."

"What do you mean—*too* clean?"

"It means there were no traces of *any* medication in Mr. Zeitzman."

"But that can't be right," Frost said, the realization as to why Dr. Reich had called him rapidly beginning to dawn on him. "I saw him take his pills the morning he was killed. Maybe the fact he was dead for a few days before they found him. Maybe it …"

"Evaporated?" Dr. Reich said sarcastically. "With all due respect, this isn't a fifth grade science project, Mr. Frost. The remnants of a drug as dense as capsofungin would have been present in Mr. Zeitz-man's system for close to a week."

"Well, your tests are wrong," Frost said dismissively. "Run the test again. While I'm here!" he demanded.

"I ran the tests three times before I called you," Dr. Reich said calmly. "I can assure you, this isn't the kind of thing you want to be wrong on. No, Mr. Frost. Three tests, three results, all the same. It's conclusive. There were no traces of capsofungin in this man's system."

"So what are you saying?" Jack Frost knew exactly what Dr. Reich was saying: he just needed to hear it said aloud.

"In my qualified medical opinion, either Mr. Zeitzman wasn't tak-ing his medication or this man—the man they found by the rail yard tracks—*that* man," he said with added emphasis, "isn't Robert Zeitz-man."

"So whose pocket are you in now!?" Frost exploded.

"I'm sorry?"

"Who's paying you! Is it Commissioner Tiresias? Judas? Who is it!"

Frost knew it wasn't beneath Dr. Reich to parlay a bad situation into one that favored him. Hell, Reich made a pretty comfortable liv-ing preying on the fears and insecurities of others. He was a doctor, after all. And while Frost knew there was a chance that Dr. Reich could very easily have lent his 'qualified medical opinion' to the high-est bidder, Jack Frost suspected this wasn't a shakedown. In an odd, perverted way he wished it was; but deep down inside he knew it wasn't.

"Mr. Frost we can run all the tests you want. We can run tests until the cows come home, but it isn't going to change a damned thing." Dr. Reich had thought that Jack Frost would be relieved that his client might still be alive. Apparently, whatever happiness Jack Frost may have derived from knowing his former client might be alive was marred by the complications his resurrection was going to cause. And based on the unwavering gaze Jack Frost had affixed on him, Dr.

Reich feared Jack Frost's next move might actually be to strike him. "Now before anyone does anything they'll regret," Dr. Reich said hastily, "I'm going to ask you a simple question. Would you recognize Mr. Zeitzman if you saw him face-to-face?"

"We've been through all this," Jack Frost bristled. "I've already ID'd the body."

"Well, this time I'd suggest you give him more than a cursory glance. I want you to take a good look. A *very* good look," Dr. Reich said.

"Fine."

Dr. Reich reached down and pulled back the burlap canvas which had been draped unceremoniously over the lifeless body.

Frost moved toward the body and peered down. The pancake makeup that had covered the man's face a few days ago had been wiped off. And though the cadaver bore an uncanny resemblance to the man Jack Frost had known for the better part of a half century, the man was not Robert Zeitzman.

"Five nine, maybe 5'10"—" Dr. Reich said matter-of-factly, ticking off the physical characteristics of the man strewn across the table. "That's about the same height as Mr. Zeitzman. Bone structure also very similar judging from pictures. Other prominent features such as bone structure, weight …"

"The eyes …" Frost said, trying to take it all in. He had finally brought himself to look into the dead man's eyes. "I'll be damned—" Frost said in disbelief as he stared into those pale blue eyes. "He even has the same color eyes. It's like he was …"

"Handpicked," Dr. Reich said, completing Frost's thought. "Yes, there is no question this man was carefully chosen. And it almost worked. If you hadn't mentioned the heart condition in all likelihood I would never have tested him for capsofungin. Truth is we'd have never known."

But rather than rage, rather than fear or panic or a myriad of emotions that could have overcome him, Jack Frost was overwhelmed with a profound sense of liberation.

"You did it," he said aloud, congratulating the corpse as if the dead man were Dorian himself. "You really did it."

"Did what, Mr. Frost?"

"He got out. Got off the ride. Left it all behind."

"Who left it all behind?" Dr. Reich was still a bit thrown by Jack Frost's rather unexpected reaction to learning that the man he had known his entire life wasn't actually dead. "You do understand that the man on the table is *not* Mr. Zeitzman?" Dr. Reich said. "Mr. Zeitzman is alive."

"And if I know Bob, probably a million miles from here. He really did it," Frost repeated, shaking his head back and forth in disbelief. Frost peered down into the eyes of the dead man. And though it was impossible, he felt like he knew him. "Hannah got it right, didn't she?" he said, speaking to the dead man like an old friend—"You *were* like a little lost boy. Spent the first half of your life chasing fame, and the second half trying to evade it. Looks like you finally found a way to do it."

"I didn't know Mr. Zeitzman," Dr. Reich said reverentially, "but to hear you tell it, sounds like he went through hell."

"Gehenna," Frost said distantly as the image of Hannah's ravenlike beauty flashed before him, "the word is 'Gehenna.'"

"You seem to have cared very deeply for Mr. Zeitzman. Did you ever have a chance to tell him how you felt when he was ..." Dr. Reich searched for the words that would complete his thought, "... still with us."

"I didn't know how I felt," Frost replied. Clearly, his answer had taken him by surprise.

"Well, who knows, you may get another chance," Dr. Reich said, reaching down and taking hold of the canvas sheet and pulling it up over the face of the mystery man. "Stranger things have happened. After all, this is Elysian Row." That snapped Jack Frost back to reality.

Dr. Reich was right. Strange things definitely happened in this place. In fact, there had been nothing normal about anything that had happened around here since Jack Frost had stepped into room 211 at the Chelsea a little over 48 hours ago. The realization that Bob Dorian was out there somewhere walking the streets, or better yet riding the rails to some unknown destination thinking about what to do now that he'd broken free of the shackles that had confined him all his life made Jack Frost want to do a soul-searching of his own. The problem was that Elysian Row was a dangerous place when it came to self-examination. You get caught with your guard down here and you get killed. The poor sot lying on that granite slab in front of Jack Frost was proof of that.

"Does anyone else know about this?" Frost asked.

"No, Mr. Frost, you are the only person I called."

"And it needs to stay that way," Frost said, his manager instincts kicking back in. "I'm assuming since it was me you called, I'm your client?"

"Well, 'yes'—" Dr. Reich fumbled as he tried to discern why Frost had referred to himself in such a manner, "but I really don't see how that's …"

"It's important, Reich. There's a little thing called doctor-client privilege. Now I know this place isn't the most ethical, but I assume that principle still holds some credence, even in this wretched place."

"I took an oath."

There was a brief moment when Frost actually thought Dr. Reich might not try and shake him down. The moment was fleeting, however—

"And my allegiance is with the mighty dollar. Currency holds the most credence with me, Mr. Frost. You ought to know that by now." Dr. Reich smiled.

"I thought you said this conversation wasn't going to cost me."

"It wasn't."

"So what changed?"

"You got interested."

Apparently, whatever hesitation Dr. Reich had when it came to fleecing Jack Frost was now gone. And the eyes of the mule hanging on the wall were watching Jack Frost's every move.

"How much, Reich?" Frost said disdainfully.

"I figure you came with at least a couple hundred."

Frost reached into his pocket and took out a roll of cash. He peeled off four crisp one hundred dollar bills. When Dr. Reich failed to lower his clutching, clawlike fist, Frost placed a fifth bill in Reich's sweaty palm. The weight of the last bill seemed to be enough to make the difference.

"My lips are sealed, Mr. Frost," Dr. Reich said, stuffing the bills in his leather cup. "Your secret—excuse me, *our* secret—is safe with me."

"We still have a very big problem," Frost said.

"The identity of the dead man?" Dr. Reich's instincts were dead-on. Depending on who he turned out to be, the identity of the dead man was going to be a problem. There was, however, a larger issue looming.

"The fact remains that someone out there killed this man," Jack Frost said, identifying the paradox that could turn this precarious predicament into the shitstorm Jack Frost so desperately wanted to avoid. "And that someone *thinks* they killed Robert Zeitzman."

"I'm assuming you're going to let them keep thinking that."

"That's the plan. And you are now part of the plan. So if you've got any other questions, you best ask them now."

"Just one."

"I'm listening."

"If this guy isn't Zeitzman ... then who is he?"

"That, my good doctor, is what the murderer is going to tell us ..."

CHAPTER 20

▼

THE CREW ASSEMBLES

They came quickly and they came without asking a single question. They knew any inquiry they made might be construed as an admission of guilt. But they didn't need to worry. As they were about to discover, there was plenty of guilt to go around for everyone. The person who hated Bob Dorian enough to murder him was, in all likelihood, there in the room. And if that person had accomplices, they, too, would be along in relatively short order. And while Jack Frost took comfort in the fact that he knew more than anyone else in that room, there were still a lot of loose ends to tie up before this whole thing could be put to bed. The next fifteen minutes were going to be a real tightrope act, and Frost knew it. All it would take is for someone in that room to expose one of the loose ends, and the whole damn thing would unravel. And if that happened, the weight of the last 20 years of Jack Frost's life would come crashing down on him.

To heck with the next fifteen minutes, Jack Frost thought to himself, *the next sixty seconds are going to feel like an eternity ...*

"I'd like to thank you all for coming on such short notice," Frost said, his cool, calm voice betraying nothing.

"As if we had any choice," Ann said disdainfully.

"You had a choice," Frost replied with a slight, sardonic smile.

"Well, my bed at home's warmer than a cot down at county, and it's getting cold," Hannah said with equal contempt. "So," she said, turning in the direction of Commissioner Tiresias, "can we get on with this?"

"Mr. Frost is running this little gabfest," Commissioner Tiresias replied, disavowing any responsibility for what was shaping up to be a hell of an insurgency.

"And what about that guy with the notebook?" Sophia said, cutting Commissioner Tiresias off.

"Yes, where is Mister Johns?" Ann echoed. The women were still directing their inquiries to the Commissioner, despite his admonishment that he was not running this show.

"I've been told Mister Johns will be along shortly," Commissioner Tiresias said flatly.

"Rounding up the 'usual suspects' is he?" Hannah pressed.

"Something like that," Frost replied tersely.

"Let's just hope they know more than you do."

"They seem to be getting a bit anxious, Frost," Commissioner Tiresias observed. "Perhaps you ought to get started. To tell you the truth, I'm quite interested in what you have to say myself. Hannah's got a point—a warm bed sounds pretty good right now." Ironically, that's just where Commissioner Tiresias had been when he'd received the call—in bed. And it *had* felt good. But the visions that had been dancing through the Commissioner's head weren't visions of sugarplums and fairies. They were far more fanciful than that. Commissioner Tiresias was thinking of all the money he was going to make on this tribute show. But the dream was over. It's just that Commissioner Tiresias didn't know it yet.

Of course, Jack Frost knew it was over the minute he saw that dead man's baby blue eyes staring up at him at Dr. Reich's office. And Jack Frost couldn't help but wonder how it had all come down to this. Twenty years in one of the most cutthroat businesses ever conceived, and Jack Frost was still standing. Jack Frost was a survivor. No question about that. But how had he gotten here? Bob would have loved the irony. After 20 years of doing everything in his power to put this place behind him, Jack Frost was right back at the very place where it had all started. And here was the best part. This was the part Bob would have truly appreciated: the man he thought he'd talked into playing Elysian Row had been playing him all along. And how had it come to this? One deal stacked on top of the next, a proverbial house of cards. It was all an illusion. It was a farce. Sure the tide had turned in Jack Frost's favor more often than not, but one bad break and 20 years of dealmaking and backroom bargaining could be undone in an instant. And what did he have to show for 20 years of hard work and devotion to a man he now realized he never even knew. A couple of lousy deals, that's what he had. The deal he had cut with Commissioner Tiresias: a deal that traded on the legacy of a man that had been entrusted to Jack Frost. And for what? Ten percent at the door. The deal he had cut with Mister Johns: a deal that cemented their partnership on the understanding that they would both wittingly engage in an orchestrated charade, a mock investigation in which they both knew the man who killed Bob Dorian would never be found. And for what? So that one man could bury his past and another could unearth enough dirt to dig his way out of the city morgue? And then there was the deal with Judas: a deal that recently had been renewed, but in reality had been in play for as long as Jack Frost and Judas had known each other. Judas had brought Jack Frost into the fold. Judas had groomed him. And when Judas got greedy, got caught caring more for himself than for his client, it was his protégée, Jack Frost, who became his front. And for what? Sure, Judas had been relegated to Elysian Row for the last 20 years. But Jack Frost had always thought that Judas had gotten the better end of the deal. Now he was sure of it. Elysian Row wasn't purgatory for Judas. It was like throwing Br'er Rabbit in the briar patch. But now Jack Frost was tangled up in that prickly thatch of thorns, too. And to think he'd paid the piper for the privilege. And for what? If only he could have told Bob that he knew what it was like to stand in his shoes. If he only had the chance to tell him he knew what it was like to denigrate your soul so that you could stay in the game one more day. And for what? To be filled with guilt, and remorse and shame? Because that was all Jack Frost felt when he looked back on his 20 years with Bob Dorian. But Jack Frost took solace in the knowledge that he was not unique. Everyone on Elysian Row was willing to make a deal—you had to in order to survive—and looking back on the past 20 years Jack Frost had made plenty. He may not have had the blood of Bob Dorian on his hands, but Jack Frost was just as guilty as the rest of them. Jack Frost was not without sin.

And as he looked out across the faces of the people who had gathered, he took comfort in another thought: he might just pull this off. And while Jack Frost may have been dealt a pretty good hand, he didn't hold all the cards. If 20 years in the game had taught him anything it was that life comes down to a few precious moments. This wasn't just one of those moments, however. This *was* that moment. And sometimes even the guy with the best hand in the room still has to bluff.

"This way—" Frost said, opening a thick, padded door.

One by one, the three women stepped out of the control room and into the recording studio. Once they were inside, Frost pulled the door snuggly behind them, then motioned in the direction of the chairs that had been arranged in a semicircle. Frost waited for each of the women to take a seat. And then he started to lay his cards on the table.

"The reason the three of you are here tonight is largely due to a conversation I had with Bob three weeks ago. You see, it was almost three weeks to the day that Bob came to me with a very interesting proposition. After 40 years of doing everything in his power to put this place behind him, he wanted to return to Elysian Row." Frost's eyes swept across the faces of the women. The faces gave nothing away. "Now, despite the unfortunate outcome of that decision, I wasn't opposed to returning to the Row. Truth is I'd been hounding Bob to come back for years. There was a lot of money to be made on a show like that—" He paused for a moment to let this new piece of information sink in. "Oh, I forgot to mention that, didn't I? Bob was going to play a show when he got here. Sort of a tribute show. You had a great name for it, Commissioner. What was it … 'a million dollar something-or-other—'"

"Bash," Commissioner Tiresias said tentatively. It was at that moment Commissioner Tiresias wished he *was* running this little Q&A. He would definitely have not brought up that little nugget. Not yet anyway.

"That's right, 'A Million Dollar Bash,'" Frost didn't miss a beat. "Shame it didn't work out the way you and I had planned."

"Real shame," Commissioner Tiresias deadpanned.

Jesus, the Commissioner thought to himself, *what the hell is this guy up to? Next thing you know, he's gonna tell these broads I tried to blackmail him.*

"But then again I never did respond too well to blackmail."

Holy shit.

"Funny, I've been with Bob close to 20 years now. He and I have seen a lot of things, been through a lot together. And as unbelievable as this may seem, I actually thought I knew him." Ann muttered something underneath her breath. Hannah and Sophia chuckled at the cryptic reference. Frost didn't need a cipher to figure out what they were chuckling about: they hadn't figured him out, either. "Tell me about it—" Frost said knowingly. "I've spent the last 48 hours talking to just about every person who did know Bob. And trust me, everybody had a theory about him. Turns out, I've got a theory, too," Frost said as if he were snatching the thought right out of the air. "A theory that, if it proves to be correct, isn't going to bode so well for the three of you." The cadence of his walk and tempo of his voice were in perfect sync: slow, deliberate, calculated. For the first time since this whole sordid affair had begun, Jack Frost was in complete control. "So I moved quickly to set it up—the concert I'm talking about. However, in hindsight, it appears Bob moved faster. You see, hindsight is 20-20 and looking back on it now, I don't think a concert was the only reason Bob wanted to come back to Elysian Row. In fact, I'm not even sure if he was ever planning on playing a show in the first place." Frost cocked his head and pretended to ponder the question to which he clearly knew the answer.

"That's ridiculous, Jack. Why else would he have come back?" Sophia asked.

"I think you know the answer to that," Frost said assuredly. "In fact, you *all* know the answer. Except for you, Commissioner." Frost turned in the direction of the one man who thought he knew everything. "You sure sprung into action when you found out Bob was in town, but you didn't know he was coming. Unlike these three, he didn't call ahead to tell you to show up at the recording session."

"Whoa, whoa, whoa," Commissioner Tiresias said, raising a hand. "Recording session?"

"He doesn't know, does he?" Sophia interjected.

Commissioner Tiresias' eyes darted between all the people in the room. Clearly, this *was* the first time Commissioner Tiresias was hearing about a recording session.

"What's she talking about Frost?"

"She's talking about a ledger. Recording logs, actually. Logs in which all of their names appear. Logs that put them in the room with Bob the night he was killed."

"And you knew about this?" Commissioner Tiresias said, turning his attention back to Frost. "You knew Bob was in town for a recording session?"

"I knew he was writing songs. But, no, I didn't know he was recording them."

"Is this some kind of joke?" Commissioner Tiresias was beside himself. He couldn't believe what appeared to be complete incompetence on the part of Jack Frost. And since Jack Frost's lack of knowledge about the situation affected him as well, Commissioner Tiresias decided to let Frost know exactly how he felt. "I mean first your client goes AWOL for three days and you don't seem to notice, then he goes into a recording studio, records some songs—but not just any songs, the first *new* songs he's put down in 10 years—and you don't know about it?"

"I told you—Bob was his own man. He didn't have to clear everything with me," Frost said, standing his ground.

"For Christ's sake, Frost," Commissioner Tiresias said contemptuously. "I could have managed this guy better than you."

"Like you've managed this investigation?" Frost shot back.

"Mister Johns has been running this investigation," Commissioner Tiresias countered. "You got a beef with the way things have been handled take it up with him when he gets here."

The fact that Frost was deviating from an agreement that implicitly stated it was Johns, not the Commissioner, who would take the fall if things started to go off the tracks was more than a little aggravating. But this new development—that there was a recording session the Commissioner didn't even know about—that development had the potential to be a real death nail, and the Commissioner wasn't going to get hammered on a set of books he didn't even know existed—

"But back to these recording logs—" Commissioner Tiresias clamored. "I saw how everyone looked like their tit had just been caught in the ringer when you mentioned them. So would someone please tell me what the hell these recording logs tell us other than Zeitzman was in the studio the night of his murder?"

"They tell us who, in all likelihood, killed him," Frost said.

"This is ludicrous!" Ann exclaimed. "I didn't even know Bob was *in* town until the night of the recording session!"

"Actually, I think you did," Frost corrected. "Let me rephrase that, I know you did. You *all* did." An uneasy tension filled the room. Frost studied the women's faces. Their faces did not betray them so Frost decided to take another tack: he'd get them to betray one another.

"I see you're not wearing your ring, Sophia?"

"Ring? What ring?"

"The one Bob gave you. Gold, some sort of an Egyptian motif with an inscription and date—March of '63, I believe." Sophia remained stone-faced. And for a brief, fleeting moment Frost thought the ring had been a figment of Mister Johns' furtive imagination. It was only when Sophia unconsciously rubbed her left index finger with her thumb that Frost knew he had her. "You knew Bob was in town long before he ever got here. How long before, I don't know. But it was long enough to send your husband away for a few days."

"This is bullshit, Frost!" Hannah exploded. "The only reason you knew about that ring is because I told you! I'm sorry," Hannah said apologetically, turning to Sophia.

"Actually, I know about the ring because Sophia was wearing it just before we arrived to question her," Frost clarified. "I'm sure Mister Johns will be happy to confirm that when he gets here. After all, he was the one who noticed it on the table. So as for the existence of the ring, Hannah, you didn't tell me anything I didn't already know. You did, however, give me a very important piece of information—and that was *why* Bob gave Sophia the ring in the first place."

"You fucking bitch!" Sophia turned and growled at Hannah, her eyes reduced to thin, narrow slits.

"It doesn't matter now, Sophia," Frost said dismissively. "Or should I say, it's not important. But judging from your reaction that ring meant a lot to you, a hell of a lot, otherwise you wouldn't have worn it the night you came to see Bob." Like a bucket of cold water, Frost's comment quelled whatever catfight was about to transpire between Sophia and Hannah. "Now as for you, Ann, you knew Bob was coming to town as well. In fact, you have one up on Sophia and Hannah. I think you actually saw him the night *before* he was murdered."

"What are you talking about?"

"That comment about room 211 at the Chelsea—and how the two of you used to stay there whenever he was in town."

Ann's mind flashed back to her conversation with Jack Frost and Mister Johns. "That doesn't prove anything," she said defiantly

"So you *weren't* at the Chelsea?"

Ann knew Jack Frost wasn't talking about those nights back in '66 when Bob stayed up all night writing songs for her. He was talking about four nights ago. And Ann figured Jack Frost wasn't going to keep asking the question until he got the answer she'd already all but given him.

Dammit, Ann thought to herself. *I knew I shouldn't have told them about the Chelsea.*

"Yes, I was there," Ann conceded. "But you're only half right," she said, holding up a cautionary finger.

"Meaning?"

"Meaning Bob wasn't."

"Care to elaborate?"

"I'd received a call. I went to the room, room 211. But like I said, Bob wasn't there. Just a note. A note saying to come to a recording session." Frankly, Frost didn't know if Ann was telling the truth or not, and it didn't really matter. Ann's attempt to cover her tracks had actually opened her up to a much larger allegation. The fact that she put herself in that studio might just be the thing that put her away for murder. But Frost would get to that when Mister Johns showed up with the motley crew he'd asked Johns to collect.

"And how did *you* find out about the session, Hannah?" Frost said, turning to the third woman.

"I told you how I found out, Frost. I got a call. I showed up at 7:45."

"And when did you leave?"

"Not this shit again. I left at 8:00, Jack."

"That's right. I remember now," Frost said, playing along. "You were very specific with the time. You thought it might have been 7:45, but then you remembered it was actually 8:00."

"That's right."

"Because there was ..."

"Because there was ..." Hannah's voice trailed off, realizing the clock she was about to reference was not on the wall.

"I'd ask you why you lied about the time you left the studio, But we all know why you felt compelled to pinpoint an exact time. You knew what time Bob was going to be murdered and you wanted to make damn sure you were as far away from the studio as you could get when it went down."

"Are you saying I *knew* Bob was going to be killed."

"Not exactly, Hannah. I'm saying that you *all* knew Bob was going to be murdered that night. In fact, the three of you conspired to kill him."

"The three of us?" Sophia said incredulously. "You couldn't even put *one* of us at the scene of the crime, and now you expect us to cop to the fact we were *all* involved?"

"With all due respect, Sophia, you are sitting at the scene of the crime."

The three women exchanged an uneasy glance.

"Just because the three of us were tipped off Bob was coming to town doesn't mean we killed him?" Ann said.

"I didn't say you killed him. I said you *conspired* to kill him."

"Why in the world would we want to kill Bob?

"Conspired, Ann, conspired."

"Jesus, Frost, you're talking in circles," Commissioner Tiresias interjected. "Did *everyone* in this goddamned town conspire to kill Zeitzman? The jailhouse only has three cells—and considering Tommie and Julius are currently occupying two of them, it'd be a little tight."

"Like I said," Frost pressed on, "I've known Bob for close to 20 years."

"Yes, you did say that." It was clear Commissioner Tiresias was growing impatient. "Move along."

"And in all those years, the one word that has come up again and again is 'mystery.' Bob was a mystery. But as much as I cared for him, I never loved him. Not in the way the three of you did."

"Touching, Jack. Very touching. But you have some gall bringing us down here in the middle of the night," Hannah said stridently.

"Accuse us of being conspirators to murder, and then have the nerve to tell us how we felt about Bob. You don't know the first thing about the relationship any of us had with him."

"I know that love, real love, true love has a strange way of strangling you, never letting you go. And though you are each very different people, and each of you fell in love with Bob at very different points in his life, the effect he had on all of you was the same."

"And what effect would that be, Jack," Ann said.

"That you resented him—" Frost's eyes swept across the women's faces. They only gave him a moment's glance, but in that moment he knew he was right. They knew it, too. "Sophia, I think it was you who said it best: 'I gave him my mind and my heart, and all I wanted was a small piece of his soul.' Frankly, I think you all feel that way."

"Fuck you, Jack," Sophia hissed. "I told you that in confidence! And resent him? I loved Bob."

"My point exactly. Love and hate go hand in hand. Put a gun in one of those hands, you never can be sure how it might turn out."

"They're saying they didn't kill him, Frost." Commissioner Tiresias couldn't believe he was actually defending these women. "And frankly, I'm starting to think they might be telling the truth. Now get to the point!"

"The point is that someone wanted Bob dead and that person used each of these women to ensure he would be in this studio between 8:00 and 8:45 the night he was killed."

"What are you saying?" Hannah said, "That I was played?"

"A fitting analogy considering we're in a recording studio, don't you think? Yes, you were played. In fact, you were all played. You all have admitted that you were contacted shortly before Bob came to town and told to show up here that night. The times were staggered, probably on purpose to prohibit any friction from erupting should you bump into one another. Let's face it, you all may have loved Bob, but there was no love lost between any of you." Frost reached down and in a single, fluid motion picked a glass of water up off the table. He took a sip then placed the glass back on the table. "How'm I doing so far?" The fact that every eye in the room was glaring at Frost like they wanted to kill him suggested he was doing just fine. "The person who called you—and it was the same person who called all of you— that person knew you would show. That person knew you would show up not because of how much you loved Bob, but because of how much you hated him. Each of you resented the fact that you'd supported him financially, emotionally; resented that he'd turned your lives together into fodder for his songs. But most of all, you resented yourselves for loving him. And over the years, your resentment for Bob grew like a cancer. Bob had, to borrow a line from someone else with whom we will be speaking tonight, 'taken everything he could steal' from you. And given the chance to get back at him, given an opportunity to cut Bob out of your lives once and for all, you came to the studio to see him one last time." Frost, who had been circling the women as he spoke, suddenly stopped—"You were bait," he said. "Pure and simple. You were used." There was a sense of finality in his voice, and Jack Frost hadn't gotten to the best part yet ... but he was getting close.

"But we didn't kill him," Ann stated plainly. "None of us killed him. We may have been 'used,' 'played' whatever the word is you think it is that describes it, but we didn't kill him."

Suddenly, the door swung open, hitting the wall of the studio with a loud 'smack.' Jack Frost couldn't have planned it any better if he'd choreographed the scene himself.

Standing in the doorway was the cast of characters Mister Johns had been sent to round up and bring to the Record Factory: Tremolo ... Penny ... Lonesome ... Tiny Bobbitt ... Memphis Blues ... Dr. Reich ... Husk the Siberian ... Judas.

"Truer words have never been spoken," Frost said as they filed into the studio one by one. "In fact, nobody killed Bob Dorian. But the person who contacted each of you and told you to show up at the studio that night, the person who ordered the hit on the man they thought was Bob Dorian—that person just walked into the room ..."

CHAPTER 21

▼

THE PENDULUM SWINGS

"Hold the fucking phone," Commissioner Tiresias said in disbelief. "Did you just say, 'the person who ordered the hit on the man they *thought* was Bob Dorian'?"

"That's right."

"So the dead man at the Chelsea wasn't Bob Dorian?"

"That's right."

"But someone *thought* that man was Dorian, and had him killed?"

"That's right."

"And that person just walked into the room?"

"That's right."

Realizing their little tête-à-tête was rapidly turning into a bad vaudeville routine, Commissioner Tiresias turned his attention to the man he had brought in to keep this very scene from happening. "And all along I thought you were the one we were gonna have to keep an eye on," Commissioner Tiresias said, turning to Mister Johns— "Looks like Frost here is the one we shoulda been watching. This guy's more paranoid than John Birch at a Commie convention."

"What's going on here?" Mister Johns said with cautious curiosity.

"I'll tell you what's going on. Not only does Frost here think everyone in town is in on Dorian's murder, now he's telling us Dorian isn't even dead."

"Sorry, Johns," Frost replied. "I needed all these people down here. Figured they'd spook if they knew the real reason they were coming."

"Apparently, that applied to me as well," Johns replied coolly.

"Uh-oh," Commissioner Tiresias said, bringing his hand to his mouth. "Lover's spat," he said in an affected tone.

"Mister Johns and I are on the same page, or should I say we will be when he hears what I have to say," Frost replied.

"Well, we're certainly all listening," Commissioner Tiresias said. "But for those of you who came in late allow me to recap ..."

Commissioner Tiresias moved to the center of the room. What would follow was clearly for the benefit of the characters brought in by Mister Johns, and clearly Commissioner Tiresias was enjoying himself.

"Now let's see if I get this right—" Commissioner Tiresias said circumspectly as he proceeded to take a stab at tying together all the pieces of Jack Frost's theory. "Mr. Frost alleges that someone called each of these women before Bob Dorian came to town, notified them of Dorian's impending arrival. That person then told them that Dorian would be recording at this studio the night in question. The purpose for these women being called out that night was that the person who called them told them that Dorian was to be murdered that night and was trading on the fact that they despised Dorian so much that they'd show up. This, in turn, would ensure that Dorian would also show up." Commissioner Tiresias paused, taking a long, overly dramatic breath before continuing, "That night Mr. Frost also alleges there *was*, in fact, a murder. But here's the twist. A man, but *not* Dorian, was killed. All of which brings us up to the point where all of you walked in, which I also believe is the part where Mr. Frost accused one of you of being behind the whole thing."

Commissioner Tiresias reached for the pitcher of water on the table. He poured the contents into a glass and brought the glass to his lips. He placed the glass back on the table and looked out across a roomful of blank stares—

"Looks like you've got some convincing to do, Frost. I don't think they're buying it. But then again, like I said before—it's some theory."

"It's not a theory," Dr. Reich said, stepping forward. "The man who was brought to the Chelsea Hotel was quite dead. Of that we are all certain. But I can also say with equal certainly that he was not Bob Dorian."

Jesus Christ on a Popsicle stick, Commissioner Tiresias thought to himself, *we bring one guy in to make sure the stiff's dead and another guy in to take the fall. Turns out Reich and Johns both fell down on the job.*

"Well, who was he then?" Commissioner Tiresias said, clearly exasperated at the complete clusterfuck over which he personally presided.

"Don't know?" Frost said, shrugging his shoulders.

"Sounds like you don't care."

"Doesn't matter," Frost said succinctly.

And while Commissioner Tiresias certainly appreciated the brevity of Jack Frost's response, he did not welcome Frost's newfound brazenness, which was severely undermining the Commissioner's credibility. "I think it might matter to Tommie and Julius," Commissioner Tiresias balked. "I think they might be interested in knowing the name of the man they're being held in conjunction with killing."

"Don't you see, Commissioner, we're right back where we started?"

"That's very comforting, Frost. I'll make sure to direct the mayor to you when he asks why we just spent the last three days investigating a murder that's ended up 'right back where we started.'"

"Do you remember what I said to you shortly after you discovered the body, just after Mister Johns was brought in?"

Commissioner Tiresias hesitated. His hesitation, however, wasn't because he didn't remember what he and Frost had discussed. His hesitation stemmed from the fact that he wasn't exactly sure what Frost was going to reveal.

This guy's already accused me of blackmail, Commissioner Tiresias thought to himself. *What's he going to do next—lay it out for everyone?*

It was the first time Jack Frost had seen Commissioner Tiresias squirm since he had come to town, and there was a part of Frost—a rather sizable part to be truthful—that enjoyed it very much. But Frost pressed on. He had a point to make—

"When we first found the body, you will recall I suspected whoever killed Zeitzman had spent a lot of time trying to make it look like he'd been killed the night the body was found."

"Because of the makeup?"

"The foundation, 'yes.' You will also recall that I mentioned to Dr. Reich that Bob suffered from Histoplasmosis."

"I remember some discussion about a medical condition. This Histoplas ..." Commissioner Tiresias struggled for the name of the ailment.

"Histoplasmosis," Frost said.

"I'll take your word for it," Commissioner Tiresias replied.

"Well, Dr. Reich tested him for capsofungin, an antibiotic to counter the viral strands created by Bob's unusual condition. And when he did, he realized that there were no traces of the antibiotic in Bob's system. This, of course, raises two questions. The first is why would someone want us to think the dead man was Dorian? The second question is who was *really* out there by the railroad tracks that night?"

Frost paused for a moment to let everyone catch up. Then like a director cuing up the scene, he motioned to Memphis Blues—

"Memphis, you want to pick it up from here?" Memphis Blues hesitated. "Just tell everyone what you told me on the phone a few minutes ago."

"The voices?" Memphis Blues said tentatively. Apparently this was a scene Memphis wasn't especially keen on playing.

"Yes, the voices."

"Last night, Mr. Frost and Mister Johns came to pay me a visit. Seems they were concerned that that rat fink Minnesota Slim might want to skip town. I told them that I hadn't seen Slim that night, but he had been there a few nights before. But he hadn't shown up alone. There were two other people with him that night."

"But you didn't actually see him, correct?"

"That's right. I heard him," Memphis Blues clarified. "His voice I mean. I heard his voice."

"And his voice," Frost said, "did it sound something like this—" Frost pressed a button on the console in front of him. The familiar, high-pitched voice of Minnesota Slim filled the room.

"Yes," Memphis Blues said. "That's exactly what I heard. Word for word."

"You heard it word for word because what you heard was a recording of Minnesota Slim."

"A recording?" Commissioner Tiresias said, more than a hint of skepticism in his voice.

"Yes, a recording. Minnesota Slim was here the night of the recording session. The man moving around mysteriously in the background wasn't Bello at all—it was Slim. Jump in any time you'd like," Frost called out to Tiny Bobbitt, who was fidgeting nervously in the control room. Unlike Memphis Blues, however, Tiny Bobbitt had not been brought up to speed on this little drama that was unfolding. But Tiny knew enough to know that he'd better get in on the act if he didn't want the curtains to come down on him. Tiny leapt up from the board, passed through the padded door and stepped into the recording studio.

"Yes, Slim was here," he said insolently. "Obviously, he was here. How else would he have gotten the recording log? I'm not an idiot, Frost, don't play me for one."

"Like you tried to play Mister Johns and me?" Frost replied. "Just out of curiosity—why did you give us that phony log? I mean, why give us a log at all?"

"Because I didn't want you to fuck it up, that's why," Tiny said quickly.

"Fuck it up?"

"Let's just say I didn't want another Nashville."

"I didn't have anything to do with what happened to Bob in Nashville, and you know it. Besides, we've already been through all this."

"It was all Judas, right?" Tiny said condescendingly.

The man with the pallid complexion standing in the corner was grinning ear to ear.

Like I've always said, Elysian Row's dark prince smirked, *the first rule in this business is you're dead in the water if they stop talking about you.*

"Please," Tiny scoffed. "Don't give me that old song and dance about how it was all Judas. How he used Bob to get what he wanted—that he didn't so much manage his career as malign it. You and Judas are cut from the same cloth and you know it."

"If I may," Judas said, slowly pushing his rose-colored glasses up the bridge of his plump, puglike nose. "Certainly I enjoy the notoriety as much as the next man, but with regard to my management of Bob, I'm not sure 'maligned' is the word I would use."

"And what word would you use?" Tiny said stridently.

"You know, most people think it's the artist who cuts the deal with the devil. The truth is it's the audience that cuts the deal with the artist. 'Worth,' my diminutive friend, 'worth.' The word I would use to describe what I brought to the picture is, 'worth.' I was the first person to recognize Bob was wasting his time and talent in those coffee shops down on MacDougal. I took him away from all that—got him his fair due. I made Bob 'worth' something."

"And made yourself a millionaire many times over," Commissioner Tiresias chimed in.

"Yes, Commissioner, it's a shame you couldn't get a piece of that deal, too," Judas said knowingly.

Knowing exactly what Judas was saying, Commissioner Tiresias decided not to say another word.

"From what I understand, you screwed a lot of people, Judas," Mister Johns chimed in.

"Was I tough, Mister Johns? You bet your sweet ass I was. But Bob's talent and my tenacity went hand in hand. We were a team. Yet I'm the one who gets the bad rap. Money-grubber, opportunist, traitor, even this name they've saddled me with—'Judas'. I don't particularly like it, but I've learned to live with it."

Jack Frost had heard enough. "We get it, Tiny," Frost said. "Everyone in this room knows Judas' business practices were unorthodox. But ..."

"You're defending him," Tiny sputtered. "Jesus, the two of you really *are* cut from the same cloth."

"Let me finish, Tiny."

"Why don't you let *me* finish, Frost? You talk about how much Bob was your friend, how much you cared for him. Well, everyone in this room knows Bob didn't have friends. He had followers. Each and every one of us followed him. Some of us may have called our devotion to him love, others may have thought of it as friendship, but in the end we were sheep and he was our shepherd. And I'll be the first to admit that I was Bob's biggest disciple. I would have done anything for him. But for God's sake, I would never have killed him!" Tiny was seething. And apparently he was just getting started, "But I'll give you this, Frost—you're spot-on about the tribute show. Bob had no intention of playing a tribute show. He came to town because he had a new batch of songs to record, pure and simple. And the reason I lied to you about the logs was I didn't want you to fuck it up. He told me he'd be coming back the next night. I didn't want you to get in the way."

"So you contacted Hannah, Sophia, Ann—*you* were the one who told them to come to the studio."

"Yes, I was the guy who called them," Tiny confessed. "But you're wrong about why I knew they would come. I knew they would come not out of resentment for Bob. I knew they would come out of love. And you heard the result. It's his best work in the last 20 years— maybe the best of his career."

And right then and there, Jack Frost knew he could rule out Tiny Bobbitt. Tiny might have been many things—a liar, a thief, a para-noid cheat—Tiny Bobbitt, however, was not a murderer. He didn't murder Bob Dorian. But he had played a bigger part in this than he knew.

Bob had contacted Tiny because he was good. Better than good, Tiny was the best producer in the business. But Tiny hadn't just pro-duced the last batch of songs Bob Dorian would ever record, Tiny had inadvertently set in motion the events that would lead to the murder of Bob Dorian ... or, more accurately, the man everyone *thought* was Bob Dorian.

Just as he had always been able to bring together the essential ele-ments that Bob required to make the best music possible, Tiny had brought together the people who would allow his old friend to do something in 'death' he could never do in life: escape. And he'd done it without even knowing it. And for that brief moment, Nashville, and what had happened there all those years ago hardly mattered. Tiny had helped set Bob free, and for that Jack Frost was grateful.

"Okay—" Commissioner Tiresias was growing impatient again. "We got it. Tiny's worked with the best. If he says the tracks are good, I'm sure they are. But what's with all this cloak-and-dagger crap, Frost? This notion Memphis Blues heard a recording that night—it's the most ridiculous thing I've heard in my life!"

"It would be best if you didn't poke holes in this, Commissioner," Frost interjected. "There were three people out by the railroad tracks that night. According to Slim, you were one of them."

"You just said Slim wasn't even there!"

"You really should keep quiet, Commissioner. You're about to be cleared of allegations that you carried a dead man's body to the

Chelsea." Commissioner Tiresias shot Jack Frost a look that could kill. Then he promptly did as Frost suggested. Commissioner Tiresias didn't say another word.

"Memphis Blues saw three people that night by the tracks," Frost continued. "We assumed they all were men. Thanks to a phone call Memphis made a few moments before we all convened here tonight, we now know that's not the case. Turns out one of those people Memphis Blues saw that night wasn't a man at all—it was a woman."

"A woman—" Commissioner Tiresias said incredulously.

"The foundation on the dead man's face, the makeup as you referred to it earlier was just that—makeup. And when Dr. Reich pointed out that the man had been made up to appear to be Bob Dorian, I thought to myself—who is the best makeup artist in town? Or should I say *was* the best until she suddenly disappeared after discovering the body the night of the murder?" Frost was getting pretty good at these rhetorical questions. He paused just long enough to let the name, 'Dela Croix,' be spoken silently by every person in the room. "Dela didn't discover the body at all," Jack Frost said with a dash of bravado. "But she did disguise his identity."

"This is ridiculous!" Commissioner Tiresias protested. "Missing or not missing, anyone could have applied that makeup."

"But they didn't—" a voice called out. The voice belonged to Memphis Blues. "I checked the train manifests 15 minutes ago. Frost's hunch turns out to have been right," Memphis Blues said decisively. "Dela boarded a train for New Orleans the night of the murder. But the train only got as far as Alabama. I know the conductor down there. Called him. Told him what we were looking for. He checked her bags and sure enough there it was. Same makeup used to disguise this fellow the killer wanted us to believe was Dorian."

"So where's Dela Croix now?" Commissioner Tiresias said, still unconvinced.

"Stuck down in Mobile," Memphis Blues replied.

"Bravo," Commissioner Tiresias said as he began to applaud gently. "Really, Frost, my hat's off to you. You did it. You single-handedly implicated every person on Elysian Row in the murder of Bob Dorian."

And while Commissioner Tiresias had found it in himself to make light of the situation, Mister Johns was none too pleased. After all, Frost had just put together the puzzle to which Johns had dug up most of the pieces. And Mister Johns was going to get some of the credit he felt he justly deserved.

"You got *cahunes*, Frost, I'll give you that," Mister Johns said contemptuously. "I do all the work, you take all the credit. I'd ask you to drop your drawers so we could all see those brass balls of yours. But considering the way this has all gone to your head, you'd probably ask me to polish them for you." Mister Johns reached into his breast coat pocket and retrieved his crimson handkerchief. He brought the handkerchief to his face and dabbed a few small beads of sweat from his brow.

"You okay, Johns," Commissioner Tiresias asked.

"I'm fine," Mister Johns said defensively, though it was obvious he was not fine. Unless sweating buckets in an air-conditioned recording studio is fine.

"You sure," Commissioner Tiresias pressed. "You look a little piqued."

"I'm fine, Commissioner," Mister Johns said, bringing the handkerchief to his face again. "Now if you would please let me finish." Mister Johns turned to Frost and continued his diatribe. "You send me out on a wild goose chase, get me to round up everyone we've talked to—everyone who's given us bits and pieces of what now apparently has been meaningless information—while you hold on to the most important piece!"

"You really *don't* have a clue, do you?" Frost retorted contemptuously.

"I got something better than a clue, Frost. I got the facts. And the facts suggest you're about to screw me over."

"We're a team, Johns," Frost said. "We've been a team from the beginning, ever since Commissioner Tiresias put us together. And whether you believe it or not, we never stopped working as a team."

"'The dead man wasn't Dorian?' That's a major piece of the puzzle, don't you think? And you don't tell me until now? Doesn't sound like 'teamwork' to me!"

"I asked you to bring everyone down here, Johns, because one of these people is going to give us the most important piece of information of all."

"And what's that?"

"They're going to tell us why Bob Dorian faked his death in the first place."

Mister Johns was sweating bullets. He clinched his teeth, cleared his throat, gasped for air. But nothing he did seemed to work. Suddenly, Mister Johns clutched his chest. He let out an explosive, electric howl, and then fell on the floor.

Instantly, almost instinctively, Ann rushed to his side. Mister Johns fumbled for his breast pocket. "Here," Ann said, taking the red handkerchief out of his pocket and dabbing it against his forehead. "It's right here," she said, referring to the handkerchief. Johns tried to speak, but words failed him.

"Jesus, Reich, don't just stand there!" Sophia called out. "Help him! And someone call an ambulance!" Dr. Reich motioned to Tiny, who immediately dialed the digits.

By the time they had carried him to the curb, the ambulance had arrived. Under the direction of Dr. Reich, Commissioner Tiresias and Frost hoisted Mister Johns onto the gurney. Once in the back of the ambulance, the tubes from the heart-attack machine were strapped across Johns' chest, the doors closed and the ambulance pulled away from the curb. It was only then that Jack Frost realized the thing Mister Johns had been reaching for wasn't his handkerchief at all.

There in the gutter, mixed in among the used syringes, busted drainpipes and broken penny whistles, was a bottle of pills. The words, 'capsofungin,' were written across the label.

CHAPTER 22

▼

THE DRIFTER
ESCAPES ...

There had been a moment when he had been tempted to tell them. But Jack Frost didn't say a word. He didn't tell them how they had all been carefully chosen; how the plan had been carefully crafted; how they had all played a part in it. Instead, Jack Frost had picked up the bottle of pills, slid them into his pants pocket and did what he wished he had done the moment he saw those pale blue eyes staring up at the ceiling of the Chelsea Hotel three days before: he walked away.

And as he walked back toward the scene where the alleged crime had been committed, there were still a thousand thoughts passing through his head; a thousand questions that needed to be answered. He knew in time the answers would present themselves to him. The answers to the life's best riddles always reveal themselves if you give them enough time. But there was one question Jack Frost wasn't sure he would ever truly know the answer to: 'Why?'

Why had the man to whom he had devoted the last 20 years of his life set this intricate parlor game in motion? Why had he betrayed the people who cared for him most? Why had he left without so much as an explanation? Why had he brought them together in the one place he vowed never to return? He had played each and every one of them with precision and perfection. Certainly, he had played Jack Frost. But he didn't tell them. He didn't breathe a word of it to anyone. He didn't even go to the hospital. He knew he was fine. He knew it was, like everything else in his life, a ruse, a play. He was a rogue, a vagabond, a troubadour, a drifter who had planned, and executed, a perfect escape. But something was missing. He had pieced the whole thing together like an elaborate jigsaw puzzle, moved them around the board like figures on a chessboard. But there was a piece that just didn't fit. Where was the grand finale? Where was the scene in which he explained why he had set this elaborate plot in motion in the first place? Where was the big reveal?

As Jack Frost was about to discover, the answer was just on the other side of the door ...

THE ROOM WAS JUST AS IT HAD BEEN three days ago when he and Commissioner Tiresias had found him lying there draped across the chaise in the darkness. The place was pitch-black, the air deathly still. And all Frost could hear were the heat pipes coughing as an old Hank Williams tune played softly in the background. Hank was going on about no matter how hard we try, we'll never get out of this world alive.

Jesus, Frost thought to himself, *who the hell set the radio to that damn station? Didn't that bastard Hank Williams die in a place just like this?*

When Frost got to the window he tried to pull the curtains apart to let some light in. But when the curtains wouldn't budge, he realized the curtains had been nailed shut again. A provision in his contract, Frost recalled—Dorian had never liked the light. Frost fumbled with the dark muslin curtains, carefully pulling the thumbtacks holding them in place. He had managed to remove most of the tacks along the base of the windowsill and was just about to pull the curtains back when a familiar voice called out—

"Please don't do that ..."

Frost didn't need to see the man in the darkness to know to whom the voice belonged.

"Just out of curiosity," Frost said without turning around, "were you ever planning on telling me?"

"Wasn't planning on it," the voice replied.

Frost cracked the curtains slightly to let some of the evening light in. He wanted to be able to see the man's face when he finally mustered up the courage to turn and look at him. The Hank Williams' song was nearing the end of its fourth and final verse. And no matter how hard Hank struggled and strived, the simple truth was he wouldn't ever be getting out. Bob Dorian, on the other hand, just might have a shot after all.

In the street below, some hood was sucking on a drainpipe reciting the alphabet. Jack Frost watched him for a moment from the window ledge before responding to the voice in the darkness.

"So what changed your mind?"

"Something you said—" the voice replied noncommittally.

"Well, I've said a lot of things over the last few days," Frost said indignantly. "Of course, I thought I was saying them to someone else. But that was the point wasn't it? I mean, that's why you concocted this whole charade, isn't it? To keep everyone off guard, make sure their defenses were down? Find out who your real friends were? Where their allegiances lay?"

Frost turned from the window toward the direction of the voice. He waited, but the voice in the darkness did not answer. Then after a long, pregnant pause, the man behind the voice rose from the chair and stepped into the light. Slowly, he began to remove the pancake makeup from his face with a dingy, old washcloth. And as he did everything about him changed—his voice, his demeanor, his whole persona. And Mister Johns became Bob Dorian before Jack Frost's very eyes.

Standing before him was a man he had known for close to 40 years. He had been standing next to this man for the last 72 hours, and not once did the thought cross his mind that he was anyone other than Mister Johns, the patsy brought in to take the fall. And as he stepped out from behind the long black veil of secrecy in which he had shrouded himself for the last 40 years, it wasn't the words of the great poet and prophet that rang in Jack Frost's ears. Instead, Jack Frost heard the words of the man who had been a thorn in both of their sides from the very beginning: 'Most people think it's the artist who cuts the deal with the devil. The truth is it's the audience that cuts the deal with the artist.' The words that rang in Jack Frost's ears belonged to Judas. And though he didn't ask, he couldn't help but wonder if Bob heard those words, too.

"Have I ever told you about where I grew up?" Bob Dorian said as he meticulously folded the washcloth into halves, then quarters, then placed the washcloth on the wooden table.

It's so obvious now, Frost thought to himself, *that's exactly the way he folded my handkerchief after he wiped it across the dead man's face. It's all so obvious now.*

And the more Jack Frost thought about it, the more obvious it became. Bob Dorian had been giving him clues. He'd been giving them *all* clues. Jack Frost knew there was something eerily familiar about this man, this 'Mister Johns,' the minute he had stepped into that room. But Frost hadn't trusted his instincts.

But that's how he got away with it, isn't it? Frost realized. *Bob always taught us to question everything. And then when he's standing right there in front of us we don't question him for a moment. That's exactly how he got away with it.*

"Frost," Dorian called out, lifting his chin slightly in an attempt to get Jack Frost's attention. "Have I ever told you where I grew up as a kid?" Frost wasn't sure if he was about to be led down memory lane or taken down the path to eternal damnation. "The North Country—" Dorian continued, his voice warm and reflective. "It was a little North Dakota town, as close to the border as you can get. Population 642— well, that's what it was when I left. Winters, cold as hell. Sometimes the snow, it'd be on the ground as late as May. But when the spring came, the spring was something else. Honeysuckle blooming, Aberdeen waters flowing."

"Sounds nice," Frost said pensively, still unsure where the conversation was headed.

"It was paradise," Dorian said fondly, his memory taking him back. "Used to be an Indian trading post back in the 1700s. Sioux, Chippewa, Assiniboine—good people, I'm told. Course the only Indians live up there now work in the Motor Coach factory making buses for Greyhound." Dorian paused, then added thoughtfully, "Did you know there was a time when Greyhound carried more people from one end of this country to the other? More than railroads, even more than airplanes?"

What the hell is he talking about? Frost thought to himself, uneasy about the non-sequiturous turn the conversation had taken. *What could a bunch of underemployed Native Americans and an antiquated mode of transportation possibly have to do with each other?*

"Yes, sir, old Greyhound had Amtrak beat there for a while—Boeing, too. And you know what the irony is?" Dorian paused again. And it was in that instant Jack Frost realized Dorian's digression wasn't a digression at all. He was making a point, and that point was about to be brought full circle—"I bet of all the people who lived up there when I left, every single one of them is right where I left 'em."

Jack Frost had been feeding Bob Dorian's insatiable ego for the last 20 years; he saw no reason to stop now, "But not you, huh, Bob?"

"No, sir, Jack, not me," he replied assuredly. "But from the moment I was born I wanted to be someone else, be somewhere else. Sure I was born at the right time." It seems the only person Bob Dorian was planning on conversing with at this point was himself. "But I never saw it that way. There's no question I left a part of myself there when I headed out for the city. Now, if you'd ask me about it back then …" Dorian said reflectively, his mind drifting off again.

"They did ask you about it back then," Frost said, reminding Dorian of the interview he'd done to promote his arrival on the scene back in 1961.

"I told them I was an orphan, that I'd been born to the wrong parents. Yeah, I remember. Well, shit, Jack, I felt like an orphan. Felt like I didn't belong. Like I was out of time, out of place. Left home when I was nineteen. Wanted to get as far away from home as possible. But as the years went by, I realized the thing I was searching for *was* home. The problem was that I'd been gone so long, I didn't know how to get back. It's like I'd lost my bearings. I just didn't know the direction home."

Dorian reached into his pocket and pulled out a short, snub-nosed cigar. He brought the cigar to his mouth and lit it. The cigar came to life.

"You never told me any of this," Frost said. "I've known you 40 years, and you've never told me anything about where you came from."

"It's one of the great ironies of fame, I suppose," Dorian said, considering the paradox. "You dedicate your whole life trying to snatch it, and once you do you spend the rest of your life trying to run away from it." Dorian exhaled and the smoke he been holding in his lungs curled out from the corner of his thin, pursed lips. "Eh, don't beat yourself up," he consoled. "There's no way you could have known."

Jack Frost appreciated Dorian's generosity in letting him off easy, but he wasn't so sure.

If I'd just paid attention, if I'd just trusted my instincts, if I'd just been more like you, Frost thought to himself. *What kind of man spends his life with someone and doesn't recognize him when he's standing right there next to him the whole time?*

"Look around you, Jack. Look around this place. Look at the people we've been talking to. They're not real. You *couldn't* have known."

"You're telling me none of this exists? Because in case you've forgotten, I used to live here, Bob. You did, too."

"No. They do exist. Just not in the way you and I define the term. Think about it." Jack Frost *was* thinking about it, and frankly he didn't have a clue what Bob Dorian was talking about.

"All the people we've been talking to—" Dorian continued, "every one of them represents a part of my life, a part of yours, too. We've been together a long time, Jack. Been through a lot of shit together, you and I. But over the years I've abandoned my past. Friends, business associates, family—I abandoned them all. And for what? To achieve success? To gain fame and notoriety? Well, I've been successful and God knows I've been famous. Fame was mine before I even knew what fame was. And let me tell you, it's a horrible existence—a three-ring circus. Sure everyone shows up, but they're not coming to see you perform. They're paying to see the freak. It's a Faustian bargain disguised as some divine comedy."

"Elysian Row is the biggest freak show on earth, Bob. If you wanted to escape your past why would you ever come back here?"

"That's exactly why I came back," Dorian said as if it should have been crystal clear. "I came back *because* this is where my past was. I was tired of running. Tired of pretending to be someone I wasn't. It was time to face the demons. Time to face down all the parts of myself I thought I could relegate to the ash heap of my life. To see where I stood."

Jack Frost wasn't buying it for a minute.

'That's exactly why I came back ...' 'It was time to face my demons ...' 'To see where I stood ...' Dorian's words were as hallow and empty now as they had always been.

Does he really expect me to believe this crap? Jack Frost thought to himself. *These aren't explanations, they're excuses. His whole life has been one big fucking excuse.*

And for the first time in his life, Jack Frost wasn't going to let Bob get away with selling him the same bill of goods he'd been selling everyone else for the last 40 years.

"That's very eloquent, Bob, but it's bullshit and you know it. You say you were tired of pretending to be someone you weren't, yet you literally became someone else. You didn't just hide behind a mask, you wore a mask for Christ's sake."

"Why don't you let me explain."

"Explain or offer up another excuse?" Jack Frost said tersely. "Because frankly, Bob, I'm getting tired of the excuses, the protracted justifications and pleas for exoneration. You're right, we *have* been together a long time. And I think it's time for the truth. Why did you *really* come back to Elysian Row?"

The moment of truth had indeed come, and Bob Dorian was going to do his best to be true to it. He took another pull on the snub-nosed cigar, then began to tell his side of the story—

"All my life, everybody's always thought I had all the answers. The fans, the press, the people who surrounded me. They all thought I knew the secret. Shit, the only thing in my life I have ever known—I mean really known for sure—is that I am an artist. And artists create. And my creations have always been my songs." There was a brief moment when Jack Frost could tell Bob was tempted to step back into the darkness, but Dorian fought the urge and continued to stand firmly in the light. "I haven't written a song—a meaningful song—in years. And I knew I'd never write another unless I came back here. I was stuck somewhere between my idyllic childhood home and hell. I was in limbo. I felt like a prisoner in a world of mystery."

"That doesn't justify what you did," Frost sputtered.

"What I did?"

"You killed a man! Stole his identity! Misled Sophia, Hannah, Ann. Misled the people who loved you into believing you were dead? You misled me, you shit!"

"Is that what you think?" Dorian replied, genuinely bewildered at Jack Frost's impassioned outburst. "That I'm a murderer? That I could kill a man? That I killed Johns?"

"Didn't you?"

"Of course, I didn't. And I most certainly didn't steal his identity. After all, you can't take what never belonged to someone in the first place."

"What are you talking about!" Frost said, standing his ground. "The Commissioner pegged you to a tee. All you do is talk in rhymes—stop talking in rhymes, Bob!"

"You remember that heart scare a while back?"

"What the hell does this have to do with Johns?"

"Just answer the question, Jack," Dorian said calmly, the tenor of his voice was relaxed and disarming.

He always could defuse a bomb with that voice, Frost thought to himself.

And, of course, Frost was right. That voice, or a version of that voice anyway, had certainly helped Dorian avoid a few major potholes over the last three days.

"Of course I remember it," Frost said almost apologetically. "I thought we'd lost you. We all thought we'd lost you. I got to confess, I was scared."

"You weren't the only one."

"You didn't seem too shaken up at the time."

"Well, I was. I might not have shown it, but I was. The nights I had to sleep out on the street when I was getting started, the motorcycle accident in '66, all I sacrificed to get to the top, the friends I lost along the way—none of that even held a candle to the sheer terror I felt after the doctor said I might not make it."

"What about it was so frightening?"

"I wasn't ready," Dorian said flatly. "There I was sitting on that gurney my heart about to fly out of my chest and all I could think of was that I'd spent my entire life trying to get to heaven before they closed the door. And there I was knocking on that door and I wasn't fucking ready." Dorian brought the cigar to his lips and inhaled. Again, the cigar came to life. And as the light from the cigar illuminated his face, Jack Frost noticed for the first time how frail his old friend had become.

"Three years ago, right after the heart scare, I came back to Elysian Row," Dorian continued. "There was a guy, worked the obits desk at the *Dispatch*. Name was Johns. I paid him a little money, told him to take a vacation."

"And nobody realized this guy had disappeared? Nobody realized you'd taken his place?"

"Johns was the kind of guy nobody took the time to get to know. He was exactly as Commissioner Tiresias described him—a patsy and a poser. Didn't have a clue."

"So nobody would miss him when he was gone," Frost said.

"And here's the best part. I never actually had to take Johns' place. All I had to do was write an obit from time to time."

"I bet you got some good stories," Frost said, realizing how truly perfect the plan had been.

There may have been a lot of things Jack Frost didn't know about Bob Dorian, but one thing he knew for sure was the guy had a mind like a steel trap: if there were stories, he'd remember every one of them

"Pretty much an entire album. You'd be amazed what people will tell you about their so-called 'friends' if they think they're dead." The irony of Dorian's acerbic observation, not to mention what had transpired over the past few days, was not lost on Jack Frost. "And all that time you didn't think I was writing," Dorian said smugly.

Jack Frost hadn't actually heard all the songs Dorian had recorded that night at Tiny's, but he knew Bob Dorian had always been his toughest critic. If he thought he had something, he probably had it in spades. Jack Frost was pretty sure of something else, too. He figured it was a pretty safe bet that Mister Johns—the *real* Mister Johns that is—never came back. It only stood to reason. Someone gives you a little cash, stamps your passport brown and sends you on your way—who in their right mind *would* ever come back to Elysian Row? And while there was a moment when Jack Frost was tempted to ask Dorian if he'd ever heard from Johns again, he let it go. There was another question he was more interested in knowing the answer to—

"So who was the dead man?" Dorian said, anticipating the question. "Wish I knew—"

"He was exactly your height, same color eyes, his hair was the same, everything. Nearly a perfect match."

"Got lucky, I guess."

"Got lucky?"

"Sometimes life just comes down to a simple twist of fate." Dorian shrugged. "Mister Johns may have been carefully selected. I wish I could tell you the guy they found by the railroad tracks was hand-picked, that I'd been following him, that I'd been watching him for weeks. Be a good story. Trouble is the truth isn't nearly as exciting."

"And what is the truth?"

"He was a junkie. OD'd. I found out about him when the call came into the morgue. I called Dela—the part about Dela Croix being the best makeup artist in town—you got that right. Dela helps me out, then skips town. Who'd have known she'd get stuck down in Mobile. Like I said, simple twist of fate."

"So you create a mystery no one could possibly solve by becoming the man we were all looking for," Frost said, finally getting it.

"And whenever you started to go in the wrong direction, I put you back on track," Dorian confirmed.

"But why? Why go to all that trouble?"

"I already told you—to see where I stood. To draw everyone from my past out so I could sort through this mess I'd left behind when I skipped town all those years ago. But when I came back something magical happened. Something I couldn't have imagined in my wildest dreams—" A thin smile crept across his face, "I started creating again. The songs came back to me. Songs that had been building up inside me, but hadn't found their way out."

"Until that night with Tiny."

"You should have been there, Frost," Dorian said with all the pride of a father showing off his newborn son for the first time. "The words just flowed through me. Suddenly all these people we've been talking about, all the people in my life that I was running from—I was able to rearrange their faces, give them all another name. And I gave myself a new lease on life."

"But why did you need me?"

"Why did I need you? Are you kidding me? You were the most important part, Jack. The most important piece. The past is one thing, the present is something else entirely. And the future—well none of us, myself included—has been there yet. I came back to Elysian Row to see where I stood with you."

"So this was a test? You were testing me?" And then it hit him—

He knows. He knows I went behind his back; put everything we had built together over the last 20 years at risk. I'll be damned, Frost paused to consider the thought. *He's known the whole time.*

"We all make mistakes, Jack. God knows I've made more than my share," Dorian said, acknowledging that he had indeed known about Jack Frost's back catalogue scheme going south all along. "So, 'yes,' I was testing you at first. But then, right around the time Slim turned up dead, I realized *you* were testing *me.*"

"I was testing you?"

"Just after Slim was murdered, you asked me why I was doing this—or should I say why Mister Johns was doing this—looking for the man who murdered Robert Zeitzman. And do you remember what you said after I told you I thought Zeitzman was like a conundrum, a puzzle I wanted to figure out."

Jack Frost might not have been endowed with the same steel-trap mind as Bob Dorian. He did remember, however, what he'd said— "'Robert Zeitzman was many things to many people, but to me he was always a friend,'"—and he had meant every word of it. "But how does my telling you that you were a friend test you?"

"Because *I* had to trust *you*," Dorian said matter-of-factly. "I've never trusted anyone in my life, Jack. I had to trust you. You've been a good friend. A true friend. And over the course of our friendship you taught me how to trust. Took me 20 years, but I think I got there."

"Well, if it's any consolation you've taught me a few things, too."

"Really?" Bob Dorian was genuinely surprised.

"You know for someone as perceptive as you, I'm surprised I have to tell you." Considering the silence that had fallen between them, apparently Jack Frost was going to have to do just that. "That bit about being a mystery, a conundrum, a puzzle everyone wants to piece together? What you said to me after we found Slim. You *are* a mystery, Bob. To your fans, your friends, even to me. Trust me, I've spent the last 40 years trying to figure you out. But in the last few days, I've learned more about you than I've learned in all that time."

"I'm listening—"

"Maybe being an anomaly isn't such a bad thing after all, Bob. Maybe sometimes the people closest to us are the biggest mysteries of all. That's what makes them interesting. We care enough to try to figure them out, and in the process they become our friends."

"So, I'm not the only one who likes conundrums?" Dorian replied dryly.

"It appears you're not the only one who likes conundrums," Frost repeated good-humoredly.

"Well here's one for you," Dorian replied. "Actually, it's not so much a conundrum as a quotation I've been thinking about for the last couple of days. Do you remember when you asked me if I knew my way around the Bible?"

"That was a rhetorical question, if ever there was one," Frost replied with a newfound appreciation of the exchange. If anyone knew his way around the Bible it was Bob Dorian.

"But that question got me thinking: 'For what shall it profit a man, if he shall gain the whole world and lose his own soul?'"

"Mark 8:36," Frost replied, identifying the Gospel to which the quote was attributed.

"For years, I justified what I did in the name of my art. I was an 'artist' I told myself. And those who understood my art would understand why I had turned into the person I had become. The problem is that after a while, even *I* didn't know who I'd become. I couldn't even recognize myself."

"You lost your soul," Jack Frost said, linking the scripture to Dorian's admission that he had lost a piece of himself somewhere along the way.

"So I became someone else with the hope that I could find that kid who dreamed of nothing but riding the rails, just being free and unfettered and alive."

The two men shared a smile. And there was something about the moment that let them both know this would probably be the last time they shared anything this close to pure, unconditional friendship for a long time. Certainly, it was the last time they'd ever share it with each other.

"So, where do we go from here?" Jack Frost said, finally breaking the silence.

"I don't know about you, but I think I'm going to disappear for a while. Maybe I'll take a crack at being that kid again."

"So where you going to go?"

"Not sure. Somewhere where they won't recognize me. Being noticed can be a burden."

"And to think—all along we thought you were so oblivious to what was going on. Turns out we were the ones who didn't have a clue."

"Hey, don't give me that gruff. If you think about it—this is all your fault."

"And how do you figure that?" Frost said playfully.

"You should have never let me come back to Elysian Row."

"Well, it looks like I'm going to need to get into a new line of work."

Frost's wry observation caused the two men to laugh comfortably.

Dorian inhaled deeply on the cigar one last time. And then the man to whom Jack Frost had given the last 20 years of his life turned and walked toward the door and into the darkness.

"Just out of curiosity—" Frost called out. "Did you find what you were looking for? Was it worth coming back?"

Dorian stopped and turned—

"The truth?" he asked earnestly.

"If you can stand it," Frost chided.

"I caught a glimpse. Thanks to you, I caught a glimpse. And just so you know," Dorian said, tying up the last loose end of his long and carefully crafted charade. "Husk didn't kill Minnesota Slim." Dorian remained in the light just a moment longer. He wanted to make sure he saw Jack Frost's reaction to what he was going to say next—"Our old friend, Judas killed him. He killed him just after you told him about the tapes. He was looking for them, the masters, that is. Of course, he didn't find them because you have them." Dorian hesitated. "You *do* have them, don't you?" he said after the brief pause.

"Actually, you do. Look inside your coat."

Dorian touched the outside of his suit jacket and felt something pressing against his chest. He reached into the inside breast pocket of his coat and pulled out a box the size of a matchbook. It was a DAT tape, the masters from the session with Tiny Bobbitt.

"Put them in there just after they strapped you to the heart-attack machine," Frost said, smiling at the fact that after 20 years he had finally pulled one over on the all-knowing, infinitely perceptible Bob Dorian.

"You're giving me the masters?" Dorian asked suspiciously. "You could have made a fortune."

"But then I would have been no better than Judas. I would have had to betray you. But trust me, it's not totally out of the kindness of my heart. No masters, no more money for Judas. Do with them what you want. But this way he's out of both of our lives."

"Now that we've laid all our cards on the table, why don't we get out of here and not come back—what d'ya say?"

"What d'ya say I walk you downstairs," Frost replied. "Just let me grab my bag."

Frost stepped into the hallway and turned the doorknob to his room, but the doorknob didn't catch. He turned it again. Still, it stubbornly refused. He leaned against the door, but that didn't work either. He jiggled the knob slightly. Finally, the broken doorknob caught. Jack Frost stepped into his room and picked up his bag. He turned and stepped back into the hallway. Bob Dorian was nowhere to be seen.

Jack Frost shrugged his shoulders, slung the bag over his arm and descended the stairs. He walked through the lobby of the Chelsea, passed through the front doors and stepped out into the street. He reached into his pocket and took out the empty bottle of pills. He stared at the bottle for a very long time, then dropped it into the gutter. No sooner had the bottle hit the ground than a street sweeper pushed it into her pan.

"You okay, Mister," the girl said.

"Yeah, I'm fine," Frost said. "Why do you ask?"

"Cause you actually look happy."

"I am," Frost replied, a smile crossing his face. "I am happy … happy for a friend."

"You don't live around here do you?"

"Used to—but that was a long time ago."

"You look like you're headed somewhere," the girl observed.

"I'm leaving, actually."

"You're one step ahead of me then, mister. You want to stay happy, get out while you can. And don't come back to Elysian Row."

"Yeah, somebody just told me that very thing."

"Was it that guy who just left?"

"You saw him?" Frost said, perking up.

"Yeah, I saw him. And here's the weird thing—felt like I knew him."

Frost chuckled. "Yeah, he gets that a lot. But trust me, the first person who says they got his number—that's the guy who's lying through his teeth," Frost said, remembering the conversation in which he had befriended a man who had no friends.

"Well, whoever he is, he's a smart guy—the advice he gave you, I mean. I'd listen to him if I were you."

"I will …" Jack Frost's voice trailed off awkwardly.

"… Cindy," the girl replied comfortably. "Name's Cindy. It's short for something else. Mom always thought I was a princess—named me after one anyway."

"Thanks, Cindy."

"Sure, Mister."

Frost turned and walked down the Row one last time. And as he did, he realized that the ambulance sirens had been replaced by the sound of someone playing electric violin—that and the sound of Cinderella sweeping up on Elysian Row ...

THE BEGINNING

Acknowledgements

I imagine no endeavor worth doing is ever done alone. Certainly, this was the case with this book. Over the last two and a half years, I have called on family, friends, colleagues, acquaintances—even a few unsuspecting strangers—relying on them in ways they will probably never know. And while I am indebted to many, I am beholden to one. Thanks, Bob. If not for you ...

978-0-595-69984-1
0-595-69984-7

Printed in the United States
97392LV00004B/1-3/A